•THE SEVENTH DEMON•

Someone, featureless in the gloom, was standing at the end of her bed. Indigo forced herself to speak.

"Who are you?" The figure did not answer, but moved a step closer. Indigo's heart lurched painfully.

A voice said clearly, "Anghara."

It hit her like a hammer blow. Sweet Mother, he had come back! He wasn't dead, he was here, he was—

The memory vanished like smoke, and a strange, agonized cry bubbled in Indigo's throat. She flung herself upright in the bed, flailing at the blankets as they took on a life of their own and tried to impede her.

The candle flared suddenly with a last surge. Indigo tried to cry out, tried to move, but her mind and body were frozen. . . .

AISLING

LOUISE·COOPER

TOR
fantasy

A TOM DOHERTY ASSOCIATES BOOK
NEW YORK

This is a work of fiction. All the characters and events portrayed in this book are fictitious, and any resemblance to real people or events is purely coincidental.

AISLING

Copyright © 1994 by Louise Cooper

Cover art by Gary Ruddell

A Tor Book
Published by Tom Doherty Associates, Inc.
175 Fifth Avenue
New York, N.Y. 10010

Tor® is a registered trademark of Tom Doherty Associates, Inc.

ISBN: 0-812-50808-4

First edition: May 1994

Printed in the United States of America

0 9 8 7 6 5 4 3 2 1

"Things and actions are what they are, and the consequences of them will be what they will be: why, then, should we desire to be deceived?"

—Bishop Joseph Butler (1692-1752)

For Sophie Mounier
Who has brought my characters to life in portraiture
as I have tried to do in words.

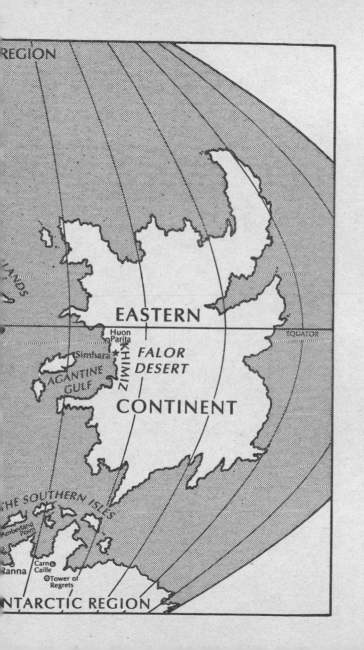

REGION

LANDS

EASTERN

Huon
Parita
Simhara

KHIMIZ

*FALOR
DESERT*

AGANTINE
GULF

CONTINENT

EQUATOR

THE SOUTHERN ISLES

Amor-land
Point

Ranna

Carn
Caille

Tower of
Regrets

NTARCTIC REGION

•PROLOGUE•

The great cargo ships of the Eastern Continent have rightly earned their reputation as monarchs of the seas. Captained by the best masters, who may take their pick of crew from the cream of the world's mariners, they ply their trade from north and south to east and west, and their reputation at all the ports large enough to accommodate their huge bulk is second to none.

The *Good Hope* is the doyenne of these fine ships and well known in Ranna, first sea harbor of the Southern Isles. But on this latest of her voyages to the Isles, the *Good Hope,* unwitting, carries an unusual newcomer among her crew, and one to whom the ship's destination is of vital and desperate importance.

For fifty years she has roamed the world, unchanging, unaging, immortal. When first she left her homeland she had another and kinder name, but now she is known only as Indigo, a word that, in the land of her birth, is the color of mourning.

Indigo has known much grief and much mourning in her long sojourn across the world. But in her wanderings she has also undergone many experiences and learned many lessons that have transformed her life. She has known love and hatred, friendship and enmity, happiness and sorrow; and in knowing them, she has encountered and reconciled many aspects of her own self.

Indigo has conquered six demons. Demons from within her soul, each of which has had its reflection in the lands and the people she has known. But now she is putting the memories of those lands behind her. For the one hope that has driven her onward, inspiring every quest and every ordeal, is finally within her reach. For fifty years she has clung to the knowledge that her own love, Fenran, still lives ... and at long last she knows where she will find him.

Indigo is going home. Home to the land from which she was exiled, her father's own kingdom. Another king's line rules now at the royal seat of Carn Caille, and there are none left who remember the young and reckless princess who brought such tragedy upon her home. Or almost none ... For in these isles, on the barren tundra between lush green pastures and the icy vastness of the polar waste, Indigo knows that Fenran is waiting. Waiting for her to release him from half a century of limbo, to live again, to begin again, to love again. This is the final journey, and it is carrying her to her heart's desire.

Indigo has conquered six demons ... but the number of her demons is seven. One still remains. And in her eagerness, in her joy at the reunion ahead, perhaps she has forgotten that what she may find outside herself, she must also search for within. . . .

•CHAPTER•I•

"So, you see it now." The big Scorvan sailor made a sweeping gesture that encompassed the entire eastern sky, and his pleasant, weather-browned face creased in a grin. "High cloud streaking out, like horses' tails, with them big rolling kind of clouds—what you say you call them in your language?"

The woman who stood beside him at the ship's rail grinned in return. "Cumulus."

"Cumulus. Ya. One of these days I get to remember it." He delivered a friendly hand-jab to her shoulder that made her rock backward. "Well anyway, you see it. Horses' tails above, cumulus below, and all moving against the wind. That means we in for it. Big storm, gale, rain, everything." His smile widened as though he actively relished the prospect. "I take a bet with you, eh? How long before the skipper come rolling down deck and yelling for us to batten hatches and look to the sheets to get storm-rigged? I put twenty karn on it. Eh? You take my money?"

She looked out at the sea. Idyllic sailing conditions: a running tide, a good but steady following wind chasing them south-eastward to their destination now only a day away. To a landsman the picture would have been unambiguously simple, but seafarers knew from bitter experience that such conditions rarely lasted and recognized the signs of brewing trouble. In past years—long past, though that was something she never spoke of to any other living soul save one—she herself would have known those signs by instinct, just as her companion did. But time had eroded the memories and the old training. Too much had happened, too much had intervened, and she could only trust to the Scorvan's wisdom.

A shadow clouded her eyes, but too briefly for him to notice before she laughed. "I've lost more than enough karn to you on this voyage already, Vinar. I'll take your word for it." Then her brow creased. "Will we reach harbor safely?"

Vinar had been a sailor since he turned ten years old. An eternal freebooter, he was nonetheless born to the sea and of that rare breed prized by all ship's masters to whom he gave his temporary but wholehearted allegiance. He'd seen the best and the worst with which the sea tested her servants, and to make light of her was a concept alien to his nature.

"I don't know," he said. "There'll be trouble, that's for sure. Maybe we'll have to put in at some small bay, not Ranna port like is planned, or maybe we'll outrun it and get in safe before the worst comes. If we clear Amberland Point before it hits, no problem. If not . . ." He shrugged. "Then we be in the hands of the Sea Mother, and She judge our fitness to see it through. At least this voyage we got a ship big enough to weather most storms."

That was true. The *Good Hope*, with her sister ships *Good Cheer*, *Good Will*, and *Good Spirit*, was one of the largest cargo vessels to ply the trade routes of the Earth's oceans. Her home port was Huon Parita, on the shores of the Eastern Continent, but there could be few deep-water harbors in the world that hadn't at some time played host to her. With her massive, bull-nosed hull and four towering masts supporting plain brown sails she was functional rather than beautiful—a far cry from the elegant passenger vessels of Khimiz or Davakos—and grimy from stem to stern from her years of carrying every imaginable cargo from livestock to timber to iron ore. But, as her name suggested, she was a *good* ship, rugged, steady, and looked on with affection by her crew.

Vinar was leaning on the rail again, watching the slowly forming cloud bank and thinking his own thoughts. Glancing obliquely at his face the woman felt a worm of discomfort move in her. She knew that look, knew what it meant. He was plucking up his courage again, trying to find a way to ask the question that he had tried to ask, and she had evaded, on so many previous occasions.

Suddenly he sucked in a deep breath. "Indigo, listen, huh? I got something to say. Something about me and you."

"Vinar, I don't think—"

He didn't allow her to finish. "No. I *do* think, and I'm going to say. We less than a day out from the Southern Isles now, and when we put in to Ranna you going to be home, for the first time in—how many years?"

"Enough." She wouldn't meet his gaze.

"All right; maybe you forgotten or maybe you don't want to tell me. Doesn't matter. So—you get home, first thing you want to do is see your family. You got family there, I know that."

"Yes." She'd told the lie so many times that it came easily to her tongue now.

"Right. Then I don't know who's top of your family, father, granfer, brother, whatever, but I want to meet him. And when I do, I tell him that I want to marry you, and see what he say." He turned a triumphant stare on her. "There. What you think of that?"

"Oh, Vinar . . ." She'd tried so often to make him understand without having to utter the cruel words, but she should have known better. They'd been shipmates for three months; long enough on even a vessel the size of the *Good Hope* to get to know each other well. They were friends, firm friends. But for Vinar it had turned into more than that. For all his rough looks and brash Scorvan manner he was an idealist, even a romantic. He didn't chase the dockside harlots who flaunted their charms on the quays at every port of call; for most of his thirty-five years the only women in his life had been his mother and two sisters, and until his parents died and his sisters married and moved away to their husbands' districts he'd been content to stay single. All this he had told her in small episodes, his first shyness gradually fading, when they were on the same night watch and he was able to get her away from the other crew members who wanted her to sing or play her harp for them. Now that he knew her better—or believed he did—and had confided his secrets to her, Vinar was in love. Deeply in love. And the worst of it all was that Indigo had no doubt his feelings were genuine.

She had tried, kindly, to dissuade him. But as well as being an idealist and a romantic, Vinar was also a very determined and optimistic man. He accepted her gentle rebuffs and made no attempts to coerce her, but her words rolled from his shoulders like a wave rolling over the ship's deck; a temporary discomfort to be shrugged off. One day she would change her mind. He believed that as firmly and as simply as he believed in the Great Earth Mother, and by his reckoning all that was needed to win Indigo over was a store of patience.

· To any other woman in Indigo's apparent situation, what Vinar had to offer would have been hard to reject. He was warm, honorable, intelligent, loyal, and—a further bonus—even handsome, with his big frame, powerful build, and shock of blond hair. As a freebooting seaman he earned far more than any ordinary sailor; his name and reputation were well known, and wise captains paid well over the odds to secure him for their voyages. He had his own house on Scorva, with enough land to farm comfortably when he retired from the sea. As a husband, provider, and potential father of children he had no flaws.

And he wanted the one eligible woman who would not, *could* not, respond to all he had to give.

"Listen." Vinar's lively imagination was gaining a hold now, and he warmed to his theme. "I going to do it all properly, like we do in Scorva. Nothing under the table, not with me! I speak with your father, granfer, whatever, ask permission." He grinned down at her. "*Then* you give me your answer, huh?"

Was that what he believed, that she had refused him because she hadn't yet gained the leave of her family's ruling man? Despite her discomfiture, Indigo smiled.

"Vinar, it isn't like that, not in the Southern Isles. Perhaps Scorva is different, but—in my homeland a woman makes her own choice once she's of age. Or at least . . ." Then she bit the words off as an inward shock went through her. She had been about to say, *Or at least that's how it was.* But she couldn't reveal that secret. Perhaps things *had* changed in the Southern Isles. Vinar would know better than she did, for he had visited her homeland many times since he took to the sea, whereas she herself had not set foot on that dearly remembered ground for more than fifty years. . . .

Vinar hadn't noticed her sudden chagrin, and anyway he was undaunted. "Don't matter," he said. "I'm Scorvan; I do things the Scorvan way. Only right and proper. Get approval from your head man, get him to like me." Again he gave her his infectious, ingenuous smile. "I can do that. Then you'll like me too, more than you do now. And then . . ." He snapped his fingers and chuckled with laughter. "You'll change your mind. I don't give up easy—I'll wait, and one day not too long off you'll change your mind!"

A harsh metallic clamor from the direction of the stern startled them both while Indigo was floundering for a reply to that. Vinar's head came up sharply, and his light blue eyes enlivened. "Hey, that the galley gong!" He reached out and grasped her arm. "Come on. All the gannets and goony birds be flocking any minute; let's get first and get the best pickings!"

The day-crew were already starting to converge on the galley hatchway, from which an appetizing smell wafted in competition with the smells of tar and canvas and seasoned wood and salt water. They looked a motley bunch; fair and aquiline easterners, small, swaggering Davakotian men and women with cropped hair and gemstone-studded cheeks, dark Jewel Islanders, some Scorvans and Southern Islers, and even a scattering of recruits from the depths of the Western Continent. And among them as they gathered, wriggling lithely between legs to gain the head of the line, a brindle-gray furred body and an eagerly wagging tail were just visible in the crush.

"Hey, Grimya!" Vinar's voice could cut through solid stone when he chose to raise it, and heads turned. "Save some for us human slaves, huh?"

There was laughter, and the gray animal squirmed

around and smiled a lupine greeting, her tongue lolling. In her head Indigo heard an enthusiastic message:

Meat! We all have meat! Only a day from land, so the last salt-barrel has been broached and the cook has made a stew!

Grimya the she-wolf, her dearest friend and companion of half a century, was as ardent as a young cub on its first hunt as she bounded to Indigo, jumping up to reinforce her telepathic words. *It will be so good to eat meat again! How long has it been, Indigo? Five days? More? It feels like more, and I'm very tired of fish!*

Indigo laughed and ruffled the wolf's fur while Vinar reached down to pat her fondly.

"Grimya's sense of smell beat us," he said. "I get it now and it's stew. *Real* stew. We make sure she gets second helpings, ya?"

Indigo nodded. Vinar didn't know Grimya's secret, didn't realize that she was a mutant who could understand and speak human tongues. And the telepathic link that Indigo and the wolf shared was something that, perhaps, would have been beyond his comprehension. However, Vinar and Grimya had become great friends during this voyage, and now Grimya made a path for the Scorvan through the press of hungry crew to the hatch, where the Davakotian galley-girl was handing out wooden bowls steaming with the midday meal and yelling stridently for everyone to "Wait your turns, Sea Mother blast and rot the lot of you, wait your *turns!*"

Vinar came back to where Indigo waited, incredibly managing to juggle three laden bowls between his two hands, and further hampered by Grimya, who was drooling and pressing against his legs. The firstcomers were spreading out across the deck, and the three of them found space with their backs against the mizzenmast to sit down and enjoy their food.

"All praise the Great Mother for a good cook on this ship!" Vinar raised his first spoonful of rich, spicy stew skyward in homage before shoveling it gratefully into his mouth. "Worth more than an armful of gold and gems; you believe it, because I know!" He swallowed, smacked his lips, then looked intently at Indigo. "You know how to cook, or not? Never mind; if you don't know, I do it!" And his laughter rang vibrantly out across the deck. "One day, one day. You'll change your mind. Just wait and see!"

When the meal was over, Captain Brek, with a good seaman's prudence, let it be known that from now onward all watches would be doubled until the *Good Hope* was safely in port. Yes, he knew it would mean more work and less rest for all, but if the weather boiled up to anything like the storm he anticipated in his bones they'd all thank him for his foresight. In these latitudes the spring gales were savage and could strike with barely a few minutes' warning: the more crew awake and alert at any one time and ready to cope at a moment's notice with whatever the elements threw at them, the better.

There was some hasty adjustment to the duty roster, and Indigo found herself posted to the evening and dawn watches while Vinar was on the midnight turn—dubbed, along with several more vulgar epithets, the Corpse-Revel. Ordered to rest while they could, she and the others in her shift climbed down the companionway to the communal sleeping quarters, where three tiers of hammocks were slung between iron stanchions on one of the lower decks. Indigo chose a hammock on the lowest tier and settled herself, with Grimya curled up on a folded blanket beneath her. The sleeping-cabin had no ports and was lit only by a single, smoking lantern that swung with the ship's gentle roll and cast soporific shadows. Most of the sailors were soundly asleep within minutes; for a while Grimya lay silent, watching the shadows' patterns, then a little warily she looked up and one ear pricked.

You are not asleep. It wasn't a question but a statement, and her mental tone was reproachful.

Indigo sighed and shifted in the hammock above her. *No. I'm not asleep,* she projected back.

You should be. The next watch will be tiring with only a short break, and you need to rest.

I know, love, I know. But . . .

Grimya interrupted. *It's Vinar, isn't it? He has put you in turmoil again, and you still don't know what to do about him.*

Yes. There was no point in denying it, even though she had been making a determined effort to think about anything but Vinar in the past few minutes. *It's becoming so difficult, Grimya. He's a kind man, a good man, and I know he loves me.* She paused. *When we reach port, I'll be faced with a choice. Either I must look him in the face and tell him that I loathe and despise him, scorn his advances, and never want to set eyes on him again—*

Which, Grimya interrupted again, gently, *would be a lie.*

Yes. Yes, it would. I am fond of Vinar, though not in the way he hopes, and I don't want to hurt him unless I must. But my only other option would be to tell him the truth— and if I did, he'd refuse to believe it.

Grimya uttered a soft whining sound from the back of her throat. She understood. Vinar, like any reasonable man, would find it impossible to accept that Indigo was not what she appeared to be; not a woman in the prime of her youth, but an outcast who for more than half a century had carried the burden of immortality on her shoulders. Never aging, never changing, unable to die since the day far and far in the past when she had opened a forbidden door and uncovered a long-forgotten secret. . . .

He wants to meet my family, Indigo communicated bit-

terly. How can I tell him that I have no family, that they have all been dead for fifty years and that I killed them?

You did not— Grimya began to protest, but Indigo silenced her.

I did, love, and there's no point denying it. Directly or indirectly, I was responsible for their deaths. Time had healed many of the wounds and dimmed Indigo's memory, but although her father, mother, and brother were now no more than faintly remembered shadows she sometimes still felt her guilt like a deep, physical pain within her. When this voyage had begun she had formed a hope that, in returning to her homeland to face those ghosts after fifty years of exile, she might find a way to exorcise them and make her peace with the past. But as the ship sailed closer and yet closer to the Southern Isles, hope had failed and dread had taken its place. She would have lost her nerve; she would have jumped ship in any of the dozen harbors at which they'd called in their long voyage from the north, and fled, over land, over sea, anywhere to put an unbridgeable distance between herself and her one-time home . . . but for one thing. She knew—no; she *believed*, though, in this, belief could not be separated from knowledge—that of all those she had known and loved so long ago, one was not lost. Not lost, not dead, but alive, unchanged, and waiting for her. To release him from the limbo in which he had been held for fifty years, Indigo was prepared to face any and every ordeal. And that was the truth that Vinar could never understand, the reason why she could never love him. She had another love, and she was going home to find him.

I should have told him a distortion of the truth, she said to the wolf. *It would have been so easy to say, "I am betrothed to another, Vinar, and when we reach harbor he will be standing on the dock to welcome me home." He would have accepted that. But instead I invented an elab-*

orate lie about kinfolk and a farm steading. I thought to avoid making him overly curious or suspicious, but all I've achieved is a tangled web from which I can't escape without hurting him.

That is true, Grimya agreed, *but how were you to know? At first Vinar wanted only to be your friend. How could you have guessed that it would become so much more for him?*

I couldn't. But I should have been more careful, and now it's too late. She shifted again in the hammock, restless and unhappy. *I'll have to do it, Grimya. However cruel it may be, I'll have to turn on him and spurn him. There's no other way—and in time he'll forget me, even if he never forgives.*

Grimya was less sure. She had an ability to see a little more deeply into the minds of others than her human friend could do, and she had seen the true extent of Vinar's dedication to Indigo. Perhaps he would forget . . . but she suspected not. And though nothing would have induced her to say so, she believed that it would take more than mere words, however harsh and final, to persuade the Scorvan that he had no place in Indigo's life.

She uttered her soft little whine again and laid her muzzle on her outstretched front paws. *Perhaps it will not be as hard as you fear,* she said hopefully. *Perhaps we shall find a way to do what must be done without hurt to anyone. But whatever the truth, I do not think it will help you to dwell on it now. Vinar and Captain Brek are right; the weather is changing. I can smell it, and I don't like the feeling that it gives me in my bones. Try to sleep, Indigo. Please try, while you can.* Her nose twitched uneasily. *It may be your last chance before we meet trouble.*

Indigo did sleep, though shallowly and fitfully, until the clamor of the watch-bell jolted her awake. As she scrambled blearily from the hammock she thought for a wild moment that the lower deck was on fire, for the sleeping-cabin was a chaos of jagged brightness and shadow, and figures milled about her in apparent confusion. But then as her vision cleared she realized that the thrown spears of light were created by the lantern swinging wildly on its mooring, and that the jumping shapes were only her crewmates, awake and piling toward the corridor and the companion steps beyond. Under her feet the deck was lurching drunkenly as the *Good Hope* pitched in rough seas, and she realized that the "trouble" Grimya had predicted was beginning.

Most of the roused sailors were out of the cabin and pounding toward the top deck; one straggler, a wizened little Scorvan with whom Indigo shared no common language, paused at the door to look back at her, grin, and pantomime violent seasickness before he disappeared in the others' wake. Indigo looked for Grimya and saw her still under the hammock, on her feet but hesitant.

"Stay here, love," she said. "There's nothing you can do to help on watch, and you'll be more comfortable below decks."

The wolf dipped her head in relief. She was a good sailor by her own lights but had never taken kindly to really rough weather. *Take care,* she projected. *I will wait for you.*

Indigo gave her a reassuring smile and ran toward the companion steps.

Dusk was falling, she saw when she reached the open air, an early, murky dusk made all the more ominous by the cloud bank that now blotted out the sky. The wind was as yet no more than a bluster and it hadn't begun to rain, but the sea was giving the *Good Hope*'s crew fair warning of what was to come. A huge tide was running, beating at a perilous angle against the starboard quarter, and Captain

Brek had ordered hands to the ropes, trimming the towering banks of sails to hold the ship on course for as long as
he could until the danger of her turning broadside onto the
heaving swell became too great. Indigo added her own
weight and skill to the team on the mainsail halyard, aware
in the failing light of the wheelman calm but alert at his
post as the ship plowed resolutely onward. All had been
brought firmly under control and as yet there was no danger, but tension was palpable among the crew.

Captain Brek stalked through their ranks, saying little
but constantly watchful. He was a Davakotian and typical
of the breed; his crew were handpicked and he trusted
them implicitly, but the ultimate responsibility was his
alone and nothing would induce him to relax his vigilance
for a moment. Small, swarthy, and fearsomely efficient,
with close-cropped hair and two rubies glittering like a
second pair of feral eyes in his sharp cheekbones, he gave
an order here, a word of encouragement there, and gradually the new watch began to settle into a confident rhythm.
The sea was fierce, Brek said, but it would be a while yet
before the storm struck and the real work began.

Bolstered by his reassurance tension relented, and before long the familiar demands for song and entertainment
to while away the hours went up. In principle the captain
pretended to frown on such frivolity, but in practice he enjoyed the fun as much as anyone and had a good baritone
voice to help swell out the shanties. As dusk became darkness and then blackness, the crew roared out old favorites
such as "High Seas Rolling" and "The Girls of North and
South," and, as often before, Indigo was prevailed on to
tell a tale in the bardic way that held her listeners rapt.
The *Good Hope* sailed on, her sails beating and booming
and defying the coming storm, and at last the watch-bell
clanged out again and she returned below decks to find
Grimya and seek a few more precious hours in her ham-

mock before the dawn watch, while Vinar and others went up, with much good-natured teasing, to take the Corpse-Revel.

This time Indigo was weary and spent enough to fall soundly asleep with barely more than a fleeting thought for her own troubles. She neither dreamed nor stirred a muscle—until, several hours before the dawn watch was due to begin, three wet, disheveled, and wild-eyed men rushed into the sleeping-cabin.

"Wake up!" Even through a haze of semi-consciousness Indigo recognized Vinar's stentorian bellow as she was wrenched from oblivion into reality. "Stir your bones, all of you—*all of you!*"

There was real alarm in the Scorvan's powerful voice, and the sleeping crewmen and -women woke and jolted upright. The cabin was pitching madly; even as startled eyes opened and limbs instinctively moved to obey the order, a huge lurch flung them all sideways, and several crashed from their hammocks to hit the floor in a tangle of flailing limbs. Through the confusion Vinar's voice cut again like a double-handed sword:

"Gale's hit, and it's far worse than anyone reckoned! Rudder's gone; we can't hold her on course, and we're being driven onto Amberland Point! Up, you numskulls, up—*ALL HANDS ON DECK!!*"

•CHAPTER•II•

It was only one small watch station among many ranged along the coasts of the Southern Isles mainland, but the sentinels who manned the cliff-top beacons at Amberland Point knew from long and bitter experience that they, more than any others, were likely to be called to their posts during the great spring or autumn storms.

The dutymen had been closely observing the sky since dawn of the previous day, and as the first great wing of night swept in from the east and the wind rose and the sea began to roar and moan, the men of the watch-house went out, leaning into the strengthening northwester, to ignite the fires that would warn approaching ships of danger.

The night was already murky, tattered clouds scudding across the sky and obscuring the moon, and in the squat stone beacon-towers the wind howled like a banshee through every crack and cranny, rattling the glass prisms that shielded the warning fires and magnified their light.

By the time full dark came the three beacons, a mile apart, were blazing, tended by two men apiece, while in the watch-houses between the beacons others kept a shivering vigil with spyglasses and alarm wailers. With the sea lanes open barely a month, following a particularly harsh winter, a great many ships were heading for Ranna and the lesser ports along the coast; cargo vessels were due in any day from Scorva, the Horselands, and the Agantine Gulf, and any ship caught among the outer islands when the storm blew up was likely to try to run for mainland harbor ahead of the gale. In such circumstances all the islanders could do was pray that the worst wouldn't happen while ensuring that, if their prayers went unanswered, they would be ready.

Night deepened and the gale grew to a frenzy. Huge squalls of rain drove torrentially in from the sea, and the noise of the rising tide was thunderous as huge waves pounded the coast. People in the villages and fishing settlements made their homes fast against the elements and prayed fervently for the Sea Mother's protecting hand to bring all sailors safely to shore, while beyond their bolted shutters the wind shrieked and yelled and rocked the houses to their foundations, and rain and sea together scoured the harbors in a battering onslaught.

No one knew what hour it was when the first flare was sighted off the Amberland cliffs. A tiny, frail pinpoint of light in blackness, it soared skyward and was flung away, lasting only a brief second or two before the gale extinguished it. In the larger watch-house the lookout sprang to his feet with an oath, alerting his two companions. Fastening their hide coats more closely they threw their combined weight against the door, forced it open, and struggled outside into the maelstrom. Hair streaming, water lashing their faces as they leaned hard into the wind, they strained their eyes seaward.

"*There! Another!*" The lookout's bellow was inaudible above the roar of the storm, but they had all seen the second signal hurtling into space, blazing momentarily and desperately before it winked out.

The three men wasted no time. They turned; one, lurching and stumbling, pelted away toward the eerie glare of the nearest beacon, a quarter of a mile distant, while the second set off along the inland track that wound down to the nearest village. The third man hurried to the lee of the watch-house where the stone wall gave some shelter from the violence of wind and rain and struggled with a leather bag strapped to his belt. From it he pulled a hollow tube of wood, some two hands-lengths from end to end and perforated with holes. A sturdy chain was attached to the tube and the man began to swing the chain, first from side to side and then, as momentum grew, in a widening circle above his head. The wind, beating round the wall from the far side, tore and tugged at the chain but he held on, swinging harder, harder, and suddenly the racket of the storm was eclipsed by an unearthly shriek like the howl of a soul in torment as the wailer gave voice. It was an incredible sound, rising even above the din of gale and sea and, to anyone who knew its dire siren song, unmistakable. Minutes later a second wailer answered from the nearest beacon-tower, then in the distance a third lament went up as the alarm was passed along, following a path that would carry it from beacon to steading and finally to the village. The man behind the watch-house let his wailer drop and thrust it into his bag once more before turning and hunkering down by the wall, his shoulders hunched against the rain and his eyes intent on the inland path. Soon—within minutes, if all went well—he'd see the first flicker of hurricane lanterns as the men of the fishing village came with ropes and harnesses in answer to the summons. Until then, all he could do was wait—and pray that when the distressed ship struck the Amberland reefs, as she surely would, they could save the lives of her crew before they were lost to the raging tide.

The men onshore had their first sight of the *Good Hope* only minutes before she struck the rocks off Amberland Point. Like a monstrous phantom she loomed out of the roaring murk, her main- and mizzenmasts broken and the tatters of her sails flying madly in the gale. There were no lights aboard, but in the glare from the beacons, blazing out their silent warning on the cliff tops high above the bay, the watchers glimpsed human figures moving like frantic ants on the deck as the towering hull bore down. Some still struggled valiantly with halyards in a last, hopeless effort to bring the ship round and stand off from the coast, but many of their comrades had given up all hope of their vessel's survival and were striving to lower her dinghies.

She hit the reef broadside, with a slow, grinding crash made all the more ghastly by the competing storm noise. The two remaining masts swayed wildly, then one snapped clean in two and the top half smashed down onto the deck, bringing sails and rigging and crosstrees with it. One of the dinghies was caught by the falling debris and hurled overboard, sweeping some half-dozen crew in its path; the shore party saw them flailing in the surf but were powerless to help. In this sea even the strongest and most courageous swimmers wouldn't risk the reefs; until and unless the tide swept the struggling crewmen closer to shore, they must take their chances.

In the short time they'd had between their perilous climb down the cliff path to the beach in the teeth of the gale and the distressed ship's appearance, the villagers had done all they could to prepare for rescue. Four young men, stripped of boots and coats and tied to lifelines, shivered under blankets as they waited to plunge into the sea at the first sight of an incoming body. Behind them each lifeline was manned by a dozen pairs of strong arms, ready to haul in the swimmers against the tide's huge undertow, while others fought to assemble ropes and tackle, hoping for a miracle that would enable them to rig a breeches buoy to the foundering *Good Hope* before the rocks broke her back.

Then, thin in the scream of the gale and the thunder of the sea, a lone voice went up.

"She's going over!"

Even as the warning was yelled, there was a second thunderous smashing sound and the *Good Hope* began to heel. Her remaining masts tipped terrifyingly toward the beach like felled trees, and then with a great rending crash the ship keeled right over onto her side. The villagers heard the shattering of her hull on the reef, and geysers of spray roared skyward as masts and sails smashed down into the sea, creating a colossal, inrushing wave that drove the would-be rescuers back. The crew had no chance; the huge impact catapulted them from the ship like helpless rag dolls and flung them into the boiling tide. Spars and barrels and the wreckage of the dinghies rained down on them, and a second enormous wave swept wreckage and bodies shoreward. As the wave surged in, the young men on the lifelines raced to meet it, hurling themselves into the surf and swimming with all their strength to reach the struggling mariners. One man was washed directly onto the shore and dropped, apparently lifeless, facedown on the beach; men ran to drag him clear before the next wave thundered over him, then ran into the sea, hands reaching out as a second body came tumbling amid a mass of foam and flotsam. Suddenly it seemed the wrecked sailors were coming in on every wave; the four young swimmers were hauled back to shore with limp and sodden burdens only to return to the surf as more and yet more of the *Good Hope*'s crew were glimpsed thrashing in the wild water, and those who weren't manning the lifelines waded into the surf to do what they could, or, safe from the tide in the lee of the cliffs, began the urgent task of trying to revive those already dragged from the sea. Many, though, would never reach the beach at all but had been swept away in the currents and cross-tides. The rescuers had seen a dog among these unfortunates; the animal was alive and conscious and swimming valiantly in an effort to get to the shore, but it too had been carried away. Most of the bodies would be washed up along the coast during the days to come, but for the time being the men onshore had no time to grieve for the dead. All that mattered was succor for the living.

Some, though, were beyond help. Three Davakotians, two men and one woman; several Easterners, a gnarled old Scorvan, and a sad toll of others, some drowned, some battered to death on the rocks before they were carried to the shore. Of the survivors three were badly injured, including a woman whose bedraggled mane of auburn hair covered the weal of a fearsome blow to her skull, but the rest had taken a lesser battering, and by the time the last man was hauled from the water one or two were showing signs of regaining consciousness.

The gale was at last beginning to abate. Its scream had dropped to a hollow whistling that mingled with the tide's roar to sing painfully in the ears, and it was almost possible now to stay upright without leaning into the wind. On the eastern horizon a thin and vicious dagger of cold white light cutting through a break in the clouds showed that dawn was breaking, and as the light grew stronger the extent of the wreckage was revealed. The *Good Hope* lay on the reefs, her hull broken in two and her smashed masts reaching toward the beach like fingers clawing desperately for a hold. The beach was littered with wreckage; not only spars and timbers from the ship herself but the remains of her cargo—barrels and bales and crates—and great lengths of iron flung up by the sea as carelessly as though they were matchwood. Among the jetsam and the piles of seaweed littering the beach were a dozen or more small groups of men, each group working doggedly to revive a survivor from the wreck. The tide had turned and was starting to ebb, though the waves still boiled and raged; and the terror and tumult of the rescue was ebbing too, giving way to the weary aftermath of fatigue. As dawn turned to day another party arrived from the village, among them women with blankets and flasks of herbal restoratives. The exhausted swimmers were warmly wrapped and shepherded away back up the cliff path to home and food and rest, and makeshift stretchers were put together to carry the wreck victims to the village. Two—a Davakotian and a big, bearlike Scorvan—were fully conscious and able to walk with some help, and little by little rescuers and rescued alike started to straggle from the beach. Within an hour the last stretcher was maneuvered onto the cliff path, less hazardous now that the gale had weakened. Not a man or woman among the rescue party looked back at the ruined hulk on the reefs that had been the *Good Hope*, and the beach was left at last to the scouring wind and the receding, thundering tide and the scavenging gulls.

"Ya, I know; I know what you say, and I understand!" Vinar waved his hands agitatedly as though by doing so he could get his plea across with even greater emphasis. "But I want to know will she be all right. I want to *know*!"

"Vinar, leave it!" Captain Brek laid a restraining hand on the big seaman's arm. "The healer's doing all he can for Indigo, we know that. It's been less than a day; you can't expect her necessarily to wake yet."

"Better for her if she doesn't regain consciousness for a while anyway," the healer, a middle-aged, brown-haired man, said. "The best answer to a blow like that is sleep." He glanced at Vinar, then at Brek, whose eyes betrayed his utter weariness. "You should both go back to your lodgings and to your own beds. I'll send word to you the moment there's anything to tell, but until then you can't help her or the others by waiting here."

Brek's grip on Vinar's arm strengthened a little. "Come on, man. Healer's right; we're only in the way. Come with me and we'll have a drink or two together, huh? Then we'll both take this good man's advice and get some sleep."

Despite the fact that he was twice Brek's size, Vinar yielded to his captain's authority. His blue gaze flickered one last time to the closed door behind which Indigo lay, then he sighed.

"All right, I come." A pause. "But if she should die . . ."

The healer smiled. "I'm sure you needn't fear that. The blow was serious, but her skull isn't broken and there's no sign that blood might have gathered under the wound. I think all she needs is rest now, and care and caution when she wakes."

Vinar wasn't content, but he allowed Brek to lead him away to the house where they were both billeted. The people of the fishing village had rallied quickly and generously to the survivors' aid, and nearly every cottage was now temporarily home to one or more of the *Good Hope*'s crew. One house had been turned into an infirmary, and here the three badly injured mariners, together with several more suffering from shock and exposure, were in the care of two local healers. The gale had finally blown itself out around noon, and in the extraordinary stillness that so often followed such tempests the village men had gone down to the bay to salvage what they could from the wreckage on the beach. Now darkness had fallen again, with a clear sky and a full moon; the salvagers had returned, the healers had done their best for the injured, and all that remained was to wait and hope that they would make a complete recovery in good time.

Captain Brek estimated that more than half of his crew had survived. That was, as he had said to the healer, little short of a miracle, and though he grieved deeply for the lost ones, he also gave fervent thanks to the Sea Mother that so many had been saved. A messenger had been dispatched to Ranna port to bring word of the disaster and the tally of survivors, and there would be free berths on other ships for all who wanted them once they were fit to set sail for their own homelands. Some, Brek knew, would scorn the idea and simply take work with other masters; he himself intended to return to Huon Parita, where he could be sure that a new commission would be offered to him. No wise ship owner blamed a captain—especially a Davakotian captain, and one as experienced as Brek—for a vessel's loss; it was a hazard of the sea and a risk that must be borne. Brek would be neither disparaged nor disgraced for the fact that his efforts to save the *Good Hope* had been in vain. But he would have his memories, and they would always haunt him.

Oddly, and perhaps a little perversely, one of his greatest sadnesses was the loss of Grimya. He and all the crew had grown very fond of the wolf during the voyage, and he was also well aware of the bond between her and Indigo. Breaking the news to Indigo would be an unhappy task; she'd take it very hard. But there could be little doubt that Grimya was drowned, for if the strongest men had been helpless in that fearsome sea, what chance could an animal have stood?

Brek and Vinar reached the house where they were billeted and went inside. The wife of their host was there, having just put her children to bed; she gave them bowls of hot broth with strong oat-bread, then fussed them away to the room they shared under the eaves, answering Vinar's agitated pleas with a promise that she would wake him the moment news came from the healer of his woman. Brek fell immediately into a heavy, unhappy sleep, but for a while Vinar sat at the small window, staring out at the quiet night while worry gnawed at him. Finally, though, even he couldn't resist the pull of exhaustion. His head drooped on his folded arms, and he slid into uneasy oblivion.

The moon was setting when Indigo woke. As she stirred, murmuring and turning in her pallet bed, the girl set to keep night vigil rose quickly to her feet and crossed the room to peer at her by the light of a shielded candle. What she saw made her hurry from the room to rouse the healer.

As she returned to consciousness the first thing Indigo became aware of was a dull, throbbing pain in her skull. Had she drunk *so* much? she wondered vaguely. No—no drinking, she recalled no drinking. Something else. She'd been roused out of sleep; someone had come crashing into her room—no, not her room, not that—but they'd come, shouting, and . . . and . . .

"Indigo?" A man's voice spoke softly close by. "It is Indigo, isn't it?"

She didn't understand what he meant. Her mind was muzzy, her head hurt. And it was dark. Then she realized that her eyes were still closed and, with an effort, she forced them to open.

The light that met her gaze seemed intolerably bright,

but the man beside her said something and the source of the brilliance moved a little farther away. Indigo could make out the blurred contours of a room, but her sight was as yet too clouded to discern any detail and judge whether or not this place was familiar. Then a shadow fell across her; she moved her head slightly, wincing as the throbbing became a brief, agonizing stab, and managed at last to focus on the face bending over her.

She didn't know him, but he looked kind and calm and that reassured her.

"My name is Olender," he said gently. "I'm a healer. You're safe here now, Indigo, and all's well. No"—putting out a restraining hand—"don't try to raise your head. You've taken a bad blow to your skull and it's better that you lie still. Jilia is bringing a draught that will help to stop the pain." He paused. "Now, this may seem a strange request, but please indulge me. Can you see my hand?" He held it up before her and she nodded fractionally. "Good. How many fingers am I holding up?"

Somewhere in her memory a snippet of knowledge stirred; she knew this test. "Th ... three," she whispered.

"And now?" The hand vanished, reappeared.

"Two."

"Very good." Olender turned to someone behind him. "The concussion's mild, I think."

His companion said something in which she caught the word "Vinar," but it meant nothing to her.

"Yes, I promised to send word. Ask Jilia to go when she's prepared the draught." Olender turned back to the bed. "Now, Indigo, do you recall what happened to you? What's the last thing you remember?"

Remember ... there had been a ship, surely? Hadn't she been onboard a ship? And ... and ...

"Wreck . . ." The word came out so faintly that Olender could barely hear it. "Storm . . . there was a storm. . . ."

Olender nodded to the other man. "Yes, she recalls it, if not in detail. We'll say nothing more about it for now, until she's more fully recovered."

"But . . ." Indigo said.

The healer turned back. "Yes?"

"What did . . . what did you call me . . . ?"

Olender frowned. "Your name *is* Indigo, isn't it? I was told—"

She uttered a strange, frightened sound that cut him off in midsentence, and before he could stop her she tried to sit up.

"Lie back!" He pressed her down again, anxiety in his voice.

Her hand came up and clutched at his wrist. "Say it again! The word, the name!"

"Indigo?"

Fear hit her and caught light in her eyes as they suddenly opened very wide. She was reaching desperately into her mind, searching, hunting, but the knowledge she sought wasn't there. Who she was, where she came from, where she had been—it had vanished, and in its place there was only a void, a great, yawning emptiness of nothing.

"I don't know my name!" Fear swelled into panic. *Indigo, Indigo* . . . she was repeating it silently, over and over, but it was only a word without any meaning to her. "It's gone, it's *all* gone, I can't find it!" Her voice rose to a shrill pitch of terror. *"I don't know who I am!"*

"We can only wait and hope." Olender looked sidelong at the big Scorvan sitting dejectedly opposite him and sighed sympathetically. "I know that's little comfort to you,

Vinar, but I'm afraid it's the best I or anyone else can offer. Physically she'll make a full recovery, thanks be to the
Mother; but whether she'll regain her memory is something we simply can't predict." He waited, and when Vinar
didn't reply added in an effort to cheer him. "I've encountered this more than once before; it's known to happen on
occasion after a blow to the head. More often than not the
memory *does* return. . . ."

Vinar looked up. "But not always, huh?"

Olender couldn't bring himself to lie. "No. Not always."

There was a long silence. The healer didn't know it, but
Vinar was wrestling inwardly with himself, as he had done
since the news of Indigo's amnesia had been broken to
him. Olender knew that he and Indigo had been good
friends, and he had tried to ask questions that could help
the villagers to trace her kinfolk, or at least someone on
the Southern Isles who might know her. Vinar had managed to evade the questions thus far, but now he knew he
must give an answer—and in doing so, must either quell
or yield to his conscience in the making of a very important decision.

Olender said gently, "I'm sorry to have to press you
when you've more worrying concerns, but if there's anything you *can* tell me about her family—"

"Ya." Vinar interrupted him, his voice abruptly emphatic. He had decided. It might be wrong, it might be
wicked, but he was only human, with human failings.
And, he told himself desperately, it would bring no
harm to Indigo. In fact, it would bring her nothing
but good, for he was sure, he was *sure*, that he was only
anticipating the decision Indigo herself would finally
have made.

"Ya," he said again. "I can help. She got family in the
Isles, she told me that, though I don't know whereabouts.
But I'll find them, no doubt of it. You see, she was going

to take me to them, to see her father." A slow smile spread across his face. "She and I, see, we're going to be married. I asked her on ship, she said yes. So I can take care of her now, and as soon as she's better we'll leave here together, find her people, and then everything will be all right for us both!"

•CHAPTER•III•

In the aftermath of a great storm there were always gleanings to be had along the coast around Amberland, and in the days following the gale many people went down to the beaches and coves at low tide to comb along the strand for anything that might be salvaged. No one sought to profit from others' misfortune, but for the villagers of the district, brought up on the principles of thrift and frugality, the jetsam of a wreck provided much that was valuable, from timber for winter fuel, to lengths of rope, scraps of sailcloth, and, often, the remnants of perishable cargoes useless to their owners now but a welcome find for a poor household.

Most of the beachcombing was done by the children and by those too old or infirm for regular work, and for two days after the gale, as the sea gradually calmed, individuals and groups patrolled the shorelines, explored caves, and scrambled among rocks searching for whatever the last high tide had offered. Aware that the easiest sites would already have been picked clean, some of the most agile harvesters tried their luck and risked their necks at the less accessible coves farther afield, and it was at one such cove, on a bright but chilly morning when the tide was at its lowest ebb, that two young brothers saw something moving among a pile of seaweed on the beach.

Esk, who at ten was the younger of the two, ignored his elder brother Retty's warning to be cautious, ran forward at once, then slithered to a halt a few yards from the pile of weed.

"It's a seal," he shouted back, then: "No, it isn't. It's . . ." His voice trailed off and he looked over his shoulder, his eyes wide. "It's a *dog*!"

"Don't touch it!" Retty warned. "If it's hurt it may savage you. Stay where you are—I'll come and look."

His canvas sack bouncing on his back he hurried to join the younger boy, pausing on the way to snatch up a spar of driftwood, which would serve to keep the dog at bay if it proved vicious. But as he caught up with Esk and together the two slowly approached the animal, they realized that it was in no condition to attack them. Matted and bedraggled, its soaked fur plastered to its body and giving it a skeletal look, the creature lay among the weed, moving its head and one forepaw feebly but too exhausted to do more. Its eyes were half shut, its tongue lolling and its breathing stertorous and painful; moving closer the boys could hear a faint whimper coming from its throat.

"It isn't a dog," Retty said suddenly. "It's a wolf."

"A *wolf*?" Esk was incredulous. "How did a wolf get into the sea?"

A shrug. "I don't know. Maybe it fell off the cliff or something."

"Wolves don't fall off cliffs."

"Maybe the gale blew it off, then. But it *is* a wolf; look

at the shape of its head, and its thin legs. And that tail. That's a wolf."

"What are we going to do?" There was compassion in Esk's voice. "We can't leave it here or it'll drown when the tide comes in again. Could we get it on its feet, d'you think?"

His brother shook his head. "I think its back legs might be broken. Look—they're bent all wrong, see how they turn? It can't walk, and I wouldn't like to try carrying it in case we hurt it more."

"It might bite, too," the younger said pragmatically.

They stood staring down at the pathetic bundle of fur. If the wolf was aware of them it showed no sign; the whimpering had stopped now, the animal's eyes were shut and it was impossible to tell whether or not it was still breathing.

After a few seconds Esk looked up uneasily. "Has it died?"

"I don't know." His brother was about to crouch down and reach out a hand to touch the wolf when a voice hailed them from somewhere above.

"Retty—Esk—all well with you two down there?"

The boys looked up and saw a figure, silhouetted against the bright sky, waving to them from the cliff top.

"It's Granfer!" Esk shouted eagerly. "He'll know what to do!"

"Granfer doesn't know anything about wolves!" Retty protested, but already Esk was running up the beach toward the cliff, waving his arms energetically. "Granfer, Granfer, come down! We've found a wolf, it's hurt! Come down!"

From the cliff top their grandfather couldn't hear what Esk was shouting, but the urgent summons was clear enough and he moved to the edge and began to climb carefully down. Retty clenched his teeth and winced, dreading his mother's wrath if the old man—who Ma said was far too old to go scrambling and cavorting on rock faces and "don't you children *dare* encourage him"— should fall and injure himself. But Granfer reached the foot of the cliff safely and, with Esk tugging at his hand, came to see the discovery for himself.

"Well, now," he said, wonder in his voice, "that's a big animal. Larger than most of the wolves we get in this district; it's more like a tundra-born animal than one of our forest breed."

"Is it dead, Granfer?" Esk asked.

The old man bent to touch the wolf and feel under the salty, drying ruff. "No-o, I don't think it is. But it's badly hurt."

"Its back legs are broken," Retty told him somberly. "It can't walk; if it stays here it'll be drowned when the tide comes in."

The boys' grandfather straightened and considered the injured wolf's plight. Killing animals for meat was one thing; meat was a necessity of life, and he'd always enjoyed hunting game as well as the next man or woman. But no right-thinking Southern Islander would kill an animal for any other reason, or see it suffer needlessly. Animals and humans alike were all the Earth Mother's children, and the islanders respected wolves in particular, not as competitors but as fellow hunters in their own right. Perhaps, he thought, this wolf was beyond salvation, but he couldn't be sure. It deserved a chance—and anyway, he didn't think he could find it in himself to dispatch it, even for the sake of mercy. Besides, it was market day today, wasn't it? That might make all the difference. . . .

"Retty," he said, indicating the cliff, "you climb back up, then run as fast as you can to the village and find two men to come back here. Tell them to bring some rope, and a stout piece of wickerwork for a stretcher. Then, when you've done that, I want you to go to Ingan."

"Ingan?" Retty was baffled. Ingan was the nearest large town, five miles inland. He'd been to Ingan barely two dozen times in his life. "What for, Granfer?"

"It's market day," his grandfather told him. "There's a good chance Niahrin will be there. If she is, I want you to ask her—politely, mind!—if she'll come and see what she can do for the wolf."

Esk, who was listening intently, screwed up his face in a grimace. "Niahrin? *Uggh!* She's a horrible old witch—she's *hideous*!"

The old man rounded on him. "That's enough, boy! Niahrin can't help the way she looks, and you know as well as I do that the forest witches are good, wise women, so I'll have no insults paid to her!" As Esk blushed shamefacedly Granfer turned back to Retty. "Tell your ma you've my permission to go, and that you may borrow a pony from the farrier; say I'll settle up with him later. Now, get on your way, and hurry. Tide's turned already and we haven't got long."

Buoyed by pride in the responsibility his grandfather was setting on him, and also by the thought that the wolf might be saved, Retty nodded. "Yes, Granfer. I'll run all the way!"

The old man and the younger boy watched him climb the cliff and disappear over the top with a quick wave of farewell. Then they turned their attention back to the wolf. The creature seemed to be conscious again but was too weak and dazed even to attempt to move. Its filmy amber eyes watched them helplessly; the tip of its tongue lapped at its jaws but with no coordination. The old man considered trying to straighten the damaged hind legs, but decided against it for fear that his well-meaning but unskilled hands would only make matters worse. Better to

wait for the wise-woman; though if she hadn't gone to Ingan market today the Mother alone knew what they'd do
then. The village had its own healer, of course, but
Niahrin's way with animals was a legend in the district.
The gossips said that, once, she'd even brought a horse
back from the dead. . . .

A small hand suddenly insinuated itself into his and he
saw Esk gazing earnestly up at him.

"*Will* Niahrin be able to save the wolf, Granfer?" It was
Esk's roundabout way of apologizing for what he'd said a
few minutes earlier, and the old man smiled to let him
know he was forgiven.

"We'll have to wait and see, boy. But if anyone can, she
will."

In the early afternoon Retty returned from Ingan on the
borrowed pony, with the witch Niahrin riding pillion
behind him.

Everyone in the district knew Niahrin, but long acquaintance hadn't diminished the stares, a blend of curiosity and sympathy, that the villagers gave her even as they
called out their greetings. Niahrin was probably no more
than forty years old, and from behind, with her trim,
slightly buxom figure and jet black hair wound round her
head in two braids, she looked like any village wife, even
if her clothes were old and a little odd and their colors
sometimes clashed. When she turned and revealed her
face, however, that illusion fled.

Niahrin's right eye was a clear, warm brown, her right
cheek had a healthy glow under the wind tan, and the right
side of her mouth was full and almost pretty. But her left
eye was covered by a colored patch, made from a piece of
old tapestry, and the skin beneath it was puckered by old,
gray-white scars that ran down to her jawbone like the

marks of an animal's claws, dragging the left corner of her mouth down and giving a terrible twist to her smile.

No one knew what mishap had caused such ruin, and Niahrin would not speak of it. But one persistent rumor claimed that her disfigurement was the result of a curse put on her by her grandmother when Niahrin was barely more than a child. No one remembered the old beldam now, or even recalled her name, but it was agreed that a woman who could visit such a cruelty on her own flesh and blood must have been a creature of pure and unrelenting evil. A few feared that Niahrin might have inherited some of her grandmother's traits, but deeds spoke louder than words: Niahrin was a skilled herbalist and used the old magics only for good, and the great majority both respected and liked her.

As she had already told him, Retty had been lucky to find Niahrin at market today. Like many of the Southern Isles witches, Niahrin preferred a solitary life in the forest to the more social atmosphere of a town or village. Her home was in the great woodland tract between the Amberland coast and the king's stronghold at Carn Caille; she grew her own vegetables and herbs and was well supplied with meat by the foresters, so her visits to Ingan were few and far between. Indeed she'd almost not troubled to come today, and only an intuition that she would find something of particular interest had persuaded her to walk in to the town. Perhaps, she said to Retty, tapping the side of her nose and giving him a conspiratorial wink with her one good eye, the wolf had called to her for help, in the way animals could sometimes do to humans who understood their ways.

Retty couldn't help but like Niahrin, despite her unnerving appearance. On the ride back from Ingan she had entertained him with stories of the woodlands, of hunting parties and animals and foresters, and of the one occasion when the king himself had ridden by with the queen and all his court in attendance, and on passing had made a bow to her just as though she were a high-born noblewoman. The queen was very young and beautiful, Niahrin said, but looked frail and low in spirit, though the witch added that it was probably nothing a bottle of her own herbal tonic wouldn't have put to rights if she'd had the courage to offer it.

They reached Retty's home near the harbor at last, and at the sound of the pony's hooves the boys' mother and grandfather emerged. Courtesies were exchanged, and Niahrin was taken through to the scullery at the back of the house, where the injured wolf lay on a pile of sacks. The family crowded into the small room behind her, even Esk bold enough now in the witch's presence to peer round his mother's skirts.

"The boy says he thinks the poor creature's hind legs are broken." Niahrin crouched beside the sacks and ran a firm but light hand over the wolf's spine and down the flanks. A reflexive spasm made the animal's body twitch and the witch nodded. "Hmm ... well, I'm not so sure. There may be a break but if so it's a clean one, and she still has feeling in her back. The damage isn't incurable."

"It's a female?" Granfer peered over her shoulder, surprised. "Looks too big. And those scars on the muzzle—I thought it was only the males that get into fights."

Niahrin chuckled softly. "Oh, you'd be surprised. Wolves aren't so different from us humans—the women can always give the men a run for their money when it comes to a good scrap. Now," she reached to a small satchel slung over her shoulder. "First, I'll give her some of my special cordial. She's in pain, see, so a few drops will help ease that. She's got some wounds, too; I'll need some boiling water to mix a poultice, then I'll splint up and bind the legs, just enough to get her back to my house without further harm."

"To your house?" Retty was dismayed. "Oh, but I thought *we* could keep her."

His mother made a shocked noise and Niahrin shook her head. "No, my dear, that wouldn't be right, and it wouldn't be the best thing for her. She needs the proper care and the proper healing—no disrespect, goodwife, but I'm sure you've got more than enough on your hands without looking after a sick animal into the bargain." She smiled over her shoulder at the boys' mother. "If you've some strips of linen or sailcloth and a couple of short lengths of wood to spare, that's all I'll ask of you."

"Of course." The woman, with Esk at her heels, hurried away to fetch them and, seeing Retty's crestfallen face, Niahrin smiled at him.

"Don't fret. I'll send word to tell you how she's progressing, and if your ma and granfer allow it, you can come and visit her for yourself in a while. Sometime after next new moon; she should be well enough for visitors by then."

"Can I, Granfer?" Retty looked up hopefully.

"Yes, yes, if your ma agrees."

Niahrin was examining the wolf again. "Well, there's no milk in her, so we've no motherless cubs to worry about." She paused. "You found her on the beach, you say? Washed up by the tide?"

"That's the way it looks," Granfer told her. "Though how she came to be in the sea, let alone stray so far from the forest, the Mother alone knows."

"Ye-es. They do wander, of course, but they usually go south to the tundra rather than north. In fact I doubt she's one of our local wolves at all. I don't recall ever seeing her before, and with those scars and the brindling she's not one I'd be likely to forget." As she spoke Niahrin had been moving one hand over the wolf's muzzle while the other traced small, quick sigils in the air above the creature's brow, then abruptly she paused and peered closer.

"She's waking."

The wolf whimpered and stirred. Retty tried to look but his grandfather drew him back two paces. "Let her have space, boy. Too many strange faces all at once will frighten her."

Niahrin was crooning softly over the wolf now, words whose meaning the man and the boys didn't understand. Slowly the creature's amber eyes opened. They were filmy and unfocused; she seemed to be struggling to breathe. Then, so feebly that only the witch could hear, a weak but distinct voice issued from her throat.

"Wh . . . where is Indigo? I w . . . I w-ant Indigo. . . ."

Niahrin drew in a sharp, shocked breath. Great Mother, the creature *spoke!*

"Is anything amiss?" Granfer was moving forward, and Niahrin's intuition sounded a swift warning in her mind.

"No," she said sharply. "No, nothing amiss." The wolf's jaws began to part again and she laid a hand on the brindled muzzle. She didn't want the old man or the boys to know what she had seen and heard—there was something uncanny here that she couldn't yet fathom, and until she did fathom it, it would be wiser to keep the knowledge to herself.

"There, look." She wrenched her tone back to normal and gently prized the wolf's lips apart, inserting the neck of her cordial bottle between the long teeth. "She can swallow the cordial, and that will send her back to sleep and stop her from feeling the pain." She watched carefully as a good dose went down the wolf's throat. "Now, is the water ready? Best to get her patched up quickly as possible, and then I can be away and home with her before dark."

* * *

They offered her a pony and cart to carry her and her patient back to the forest, but Niahrin refused. She wasn't used to handling horses, she said; riding pillion was one thing, but if left to her own devices she'd get all in a tangle, and besides she had nowhere to stable a pony overnight. Thanking them kindly, she would prefer to borrow a wheelbarrow that could be returned at a later date; the wolf would be comfortable enough in that, and the walk was nothing to her. Before leaving she prescribed draughts for one neighbor's cough and another's teething child, gave the boys' mother a parcel of cooking herbs, and graciously accepted four salted fish, a heavy-cake, and a basket of new-laid eggs in return for her services. She also promised again that Retty might visit the wolf when she was recovered, which lifted a little of his glumness as he watched her trundle the barrow away up the hill and out of sight along the Ingan road.

The villagers had offered her an escort, but Niahrin had been determined that no one should accompany her on her journey home. For one thing she wanted to keep the secret she had discovered to herself, at least for the present; for another, the solitary walk would give her time to ponder the mystery without any distractions.

The wolf lay in the barrow, as comfortable as it was possible to make her in a bed of sacks and straw. She was in a deep, trancelike sleep—Niahrin had given her more of the cordial than was strictly advisable, but she had her reasons—and as the witch settled into her long, sturdy stride, the barrow rattling and bumping before her on the uneven track, she went over in her mind the little she did know.

A wolf that spoke in human tongues. Had she ever heard of such a thing before? She thought back over the tales her mother had told her, then further back to her

grandmother's schooling and lore, and decided she had
not. And the creature had been washed up from the
sea. As a rule wolves didn't venture anywhere near the
sea; they seemed to have an instinctive fear or dislike of
it, and to her certain knowledge none lived within a mile
or more of the coast. Could there, she wondered suddenly, be any connection with the ship wrecked off
Amberland Point in yesterday's gale? News traveled fast
in this district, and the wreck had been the talk of Ingan
market. There were many survivors, so she'd heard (and
thank the Mother for that), who were now recovering in
one of the Amberland villages farther down the coast.
Perhaps she might send word there, with one of the foresters' lads, to inquire if a wolf had been onboard the
ship. It was unlikely, but Niahrin had learned long ago
that it was unwise to dismiss even the wildest speculations.

Then there was the matter of what the wolf had said.
Something about wanting Indigo. What, she wondered,
was Indigo? A person? A place? An object? Or had she
misheard altogether, and had the poor creature been trying
to say "Wanting to go" or some such? Wanting to go;
wanting to die, perhaps, because of her pain? Yes, that
would make sense. But Niahrin's bones told her that she
had not misheard.

She looked speculatively at the sad bundle of gray fur,
dry now, but still bedraggled, lying in the barrow. First
things first: Comfort and healing were what mattered
above all, and those she would provide in full measure.
But when she had done all she could . . . well, then there
would be time for deeper investigation.

Niahrin reached the forest an hour before sunset, which
pleased her. The days were growing rapidly longer as
spring stretched toward summer; already many of the trees
were showing the vivid color of new, young leaves like a

green haze, and the grass in the broadleaf clearings was surging lush and vigorous. She'd have a good picking of scallions from her vegetable patch any day now, and it was almost time to sow beans and summer roots. A growing time, and a good time for healing. And, she thought with an odd, rueful, and very private little smile, a good time to reawaken an old magic, and one she'd not used for a few years now. The thought of it gave her a frisson that wasn't pleasant, for in a deeper part of her mind she still feared it as she had always done, and it brought back memories that she would have preferred to leave alone. But then a gift was there to be used. And the gift her grandmother had given her, twenty-five years ago, might be her only means of solving this conundrum. . . .

Her house lay a half hour's walk from the forest's edge, in a clearing among oaks and ashes and birches, which in high summer formed a pleasant, dappled canopy. Like others hereabouts it was built of wood with a turfed roof, and it stood sturdy and foursquare in its own wicker-fenced plot. It had only one story and two rooms, but that had always been ample for Niahrin's needs.

She pushed the door open—there was no lock; no Isler would ever dream of entering a witch's house uninvited—and lit two of her candles before drawing the barrow up to the threshold and lifting the wolf inside. The animal was heavy, and despite her fitness and strength Niahrin was thankful that it wasn't awake to suffer the awkward maneuvering. At last, though, the creature was laid on a hay-stuffed pallet by the hearth, and Niahrin set light to the fire she'd left ready that morning. She would put her meal on to simmer first, for no one worked well on an empty stomach, and while the pot was steaming there would be time to make a proper job of the wolf's splints and bandaging and add a spell or two, which she hadn't been able to perform under the villagers' gaze, to give the healing power.

By the time she was finished, a rich smell was wafting from her cooking pot on its trivet and the room was warm and bright with firelight, defying the night outside. As she ladled her rabbit stew generously into a bowl and cut a piece of heavy-cake to follow, Niahrin sang a soft song in a minor key, partly to soothe the sleeping wolf and partly to create the still, soporific atmosphere that would allow her mind to make the transition from one reality to another. She ate slowly, almost ritually, then poured a mug of water from a pitcher, drank it, and moved to sit cross-legged on the side of the hearth opposite from where the wolf lay. For perhaps a minute there was silence; then from somewhere in the depths of the forest an owl uttered its lonely, mournful cry and Niahrin knew that the moment was right.

She raised a hand to the patch over her left eye, and lifted it away. Since she was sixteen, since the thing had been done to her, she had possessed no looking glass, but she remembered well enough the horror on the faces of others to whom she had revealed herself, the recoiling, the revulsion, the pity for a woman condemned to spinsterhood by her grandmother's gift.

She was special, that was what her grandmother had said. Niahrin bore no grudge, for she had known even then that the old dame was right and she had accepted the gift willingly, even loved Granmer the more for it. What did it matter if no man would ever look at her except in repugnance? She was wed to her craft, and that was something that those who pitied her could never understand.

Niahrin's left eye was the eye of a monstrosity. Lashless, the skin puckered tightly around it, its color was drained to a ghastly, deathly gray, the iris seeming to fade into the white and become one with it. And its gaze was fixed and unmoving, slanting sideways in a dreadful, wall-eyed stare; a look of sheer madness.

But Niahrin was far from mad. And this eye, this gift, grotesque and ugly though it might be, gave her something that was uniquely her own.

Softly Niahrin began to sing again. Her terrible walleye blinked, once, and on the image of the firelit room new landscapes began to impinge, fading in slowly but surely, other realities blending with her own comfortable world. Past, present, and future, drawing together like threads on a weaver's loom. What was; what might have been; what might come to be. And in her mind, like rustling ghosts, the voices of *might* and *could* and *if* began to speak to her. . . .

•CHAPTER•IV•

Niahrin sat up far into the night, pondering what she had learned—or, perhaps more saliently, what she had *not* learned—from her journey into the worlds of possibility.

She sat by the smaller of the cottage's two windows, watching the changing patterns of the moon's light dappling through the trees around the clearing while images continued to haunt her. Now and then she would turn her head and look at the wolf's recumbent form, hard to discern now in the fading firelight, and in those moments it seemed to her that the images drew closer, reaching out from the shadows to become almost a tangible presence in the room. An old woman, her back rheumatically bent, her eyes wild and filled with silent, raging bitterness. A handsome young couple, carefree and laughing. A man in fine clothes lying facedown in a bed with his blood staining the linen sheets. An elderly sage, white-haired, gentle of face, who played a harp that mourned and cried. And one other.

One whose face she knew she had seen before at some time in her life but to whom her memory couldn't give a name or identity. That was the strangest mystery of all.

Perhaps it was the exhausting effort of her scrying or perhaps it was simply the fire's soporific effect that had lulled her and made her lose concentration, but she woke suddenly and with a start, in time to hear the echoes of a familiar sound dying away in the forest. Rubbing at her right eye to clear it—the patch was back in place now—Niahrin peered through the window's thick pane, cupping her hand against the glass to see better. The moon must have set, for the clearing was in darkness. But somewhere out there, quiet as the night itself, *they* were awake and aware. She wouldn't see them, not unless they chose to show themselves, but she felt their presence surely and strongly. The forest wolves were old friends and she had no fear of them. Doubtless they sensed the new presence in their midst, in her cottage, and were curious. Or something more . . .

Behind her there was a stirring and a faint whimper. The witch looked round and saw that the wolf was twitching in her drugged sleep. Her tongue lapped at the air, one foreleg clenched, and her tail tried weakly to beat against her pallet bed.

"Hush, now." Niahrin raised one hand and traced a sign in the air. "Hush, little one; sleep. No dreams, no pain."

The injured wolf uttered a humanlike sigh and relaxed once more. Niahrin watched her for a few moments longer, then quietly rose and went to the door. The night air breathed cool on her face and bare arms as she stepped outside; she waited until her eye had adjusted to the darkness then walked to her garden gate.

"Don't fret for her," she called softly. "She is in my care, and I will do all within my power to help her. She'll return to you soon, you have my promise."

The wolves, if they were listening, made no answer. There was only the faint rustling of the woodland and the murmur of a light breeze dancing through the garden's vegetation. Niahrin sighed and returned to the cottage. Tonight, she had done everything she could. All she wanted now was to sleep.

Grimya, too, had heard the wolves call from the forest, but the sound came to her through a fog of semiconscious confusion. Somewhere in her numbed mind she was aware that she hurt, though the pain was removed from reality; she knew it was there but she could not feel it. She thought she had been asleep for a long time, and she had dreamed a great deal—strange and bewildering dreams in which she tried to run after Indigo but found that her hind legs wouldn't obey her and she was unable to move. The sound of the wolves calling made her unhappy and afraid, but there had been another voice, one she didn't know, which had crooned to her and driven the fears away. When she was thirsty, hands held water for her to drink, and the water had a strange sweetness that soothed her back into sleep. On another level she sensed periods of light and darkness, and then at last there was a feeling of emerging, of struggling upward through gray clouds toward brightness as true consciousness slowly returned. She felt the pain then; a searing, throbbing agony that shot through her in a red-hot shaft, and she uttered an involuntary and uncontrollable bubbling yelp. Instantly there was movement behind her, then a shadow blocked the light from the cottage window as a woman bent over her.

"You're awake?" One hand came down lightly to touch the top of Grimya's head. "Ah, yes, I see you are. And in pain. Wait now, wait a moment, and I will ease it." She moved away; Grimya heard small sounds, then the woman returned with a dish of what looked but did not smell like water.

"Can you lap? Try, see if you can drink. I will help you." Gently she assisted Grimya to raise her head a little, and the wolf managed to lick at the dish's contents. The liquid tasted strange but not unpleasant, and almost immediately there was a lessening of the pain.

Niahrin held the dish steady until she had finished, then withdrew it. "There: all done. Don't move. Stay still." She stroked Grimya's fur reassuringly, but her gaze was alert as she watched the wolf's face with covert interest. Did the creature understand what she was saying? It was so hard to be sure; her scrying had been inconclusive, and in the three days that had since passed Niahrin had begun to wonder if she'd been wrong from the beginning and had mistaken the animal's cries of pain for human speech. But though the wolf's amber eyes were still dazed, there was tension and wariness in their look—not simply the wariness that would have been natural in any animal, but something more . . . *intelligent*. Well, Niahrin thought, there was only one way to be sure, and that was to challenge the creature directly. If the attempt failed she would do nothing worse than make a fool of herself, and as there was no one here to laugh at her, what did that matter?

A lidded pot was keeping warm on the hearthstone; she fetched a wooden dish from an alcove and ladled some of the pot's contents into it. "I've food here for you. It's gruel, and though you may not like it overmuch it has herbs and barley in it and it will do you good. When you're stronger you shall have rabbit and perhaps some venison if I can get it, but for now you must eat this." Yes, it seemed likely that the creature *did* understand, for she made a submissive sound as though offering obedience. Niahrin set the bowl down before her, then stepped back.

"And when you have eaten," she said, "perhaps we might talk together."

The wolf looked at her in astonishment and chagrin, and instantly Niahrin's doubts fled. She smiled, dropping to a crouch so that they were almost on a level. "My name," she added softly, "is Niahrin. But I don't know yours, or even if you have a name at all. Will you tell me, my dear? Because I believe you can, if you should choose to."

Grimya stared back, her mind racing. She didn't know what to do, and with uncertainty came fear. How did this woman know her secret? Had she simply guessed, or had she some power that enabled her to divine the truth? Throughout her years with Indigo, Grimya had revealed her ability only to a very few strangers and then only when desperate circumstances had given her no other choice. She knew nothing about Niahrin and couldn't guess what the witch might do if she capitulated. To many people an animal with the power of human speech would be a prize to be exploited, and Grimya feared that this woman might want only to imprison her and either show her in a cage or sell her to someone else who would. A talking wolf could bring its captor a good deal of money, and the woman was clearly poor and thus might be easily tempted.

Niahrin was watching her carefully, and now she spoke again. "There's no need to be afraid of me, my dear. I mean you no harm." She started to hold out a hand but Grimya showed her teeth suddenly and the hand withdrew. "Please," the witch said. "Please. I've no wish to hurt you in any way."

Grimya wanted to believe it. After all, the woman had taken her in, fed her, cared for her, even taken away the pain in her back and legs. She still couldn't move her legs and had wondered for a brief, apprehensive moment if that had been the woman's doing, a way of imprisoning her and making her helpless. But as her mind cleared, memory of the shipwreck came back and with it an ugly recollection of being hurled into the sea, fighting to reach shore but being unable to swim against the huge current that swept her away from the bay, away from the crew and their rescuers, and had finally driven her helplessly onto rocks that battered her before she was flung upon a deserted shore like a spar of driftwood. There had been pain then, terrible pain that made her howl, and when she tried to struggle upright her legs had failed her and she lost consciousness. From that moment her memories were no more than disjointed fragments in a miasma of red agony. There had been children's voices, jolting movement, muttering and dimness and someone trying to dry her fur, then nothing until the moment when she had woken to find herself here. No, this woman hadn't harmed her but was doing her best to help her. Grimya *wanted* to trust, but . . .

Suddenly there was noise outside the cottage, a heavy thumping sound and a voice shouting. Niahrin started as she heard her name being yelled.

"Niahrin! Witch, are you in there? Come out, woman; stir yourself, damn it, and help me drive them off!"

Niahrin swore under her breath. She sprang to her feet and ran to the door, pulling it open and hurrying outside. Why *now*, of all the moments to choose . . . ?

"Perd! Perd, is that you making such a commotion outside my house?" Mouth tense with anger she ran toward the garden gate, and as she approached it the bushes at the edge of the clearing rustled and a man emerged. He was tall, unstooped, and wirily vigorous, though his seamed face and lank, thinning white hair marked him as well into his seventies. He wore an assortment of ill-matched and ill-fitting clothes that had once been of good quality but were now sorely in need of washing and mending, and as he stamped toward the gate he waved a gnarled blackthorn staff angrily in the air.

"Woman, you're neglecting your duty!" His voice was a petulant screech. "Idling indoors with no guard to keep the wolves away and everything going to wrack and ruin! Do you want them to come and tear your throat out? Do you? Do you?"

Niahrin's anger became fury. "Perd Nordenson, what are you doing here? What do you want? I am busy—unless you have business with me, go away and leave me in peace!"

The old man sneered. "Business? You may count yourself lucky that I've business with you, woman, for if I hadn't, then like as not you'd have been found in your own bed with your throat torn out by morning! But I saw them. I saw them, and I drove them away!"

Niahrin sighed as she understood. Perd and the wolves. Always with Perd it was the wolves. Why he loathed them so much neither she nor anyone else who knew him could fathom, but even to utter the word *wolf* in Perd's hearing was to invite a tirade of passionate execration. And Perd had a powerful ability to hate.

She walked more sedately to the end of the garden and, keeping the barrier of the gate between them, tried to judge the old man's state of mind. It seemed likely that this was one of his better days, for he was at least coherent and hadn't yet spat at her or hurled his stick at her head, both of which she'd known him to do on more than one occasion. Hoping she was right, she said soothingly, "Well Perd, you must know, for I've told you often enough, that the—the creatures don't trouble me and I've nothing to fear from them. But I thank you for your concern."

She had touched the right chord, for the flame died down in Perd's manic eyes and he looked away. His hands twisted and twisted on his blackthorn stick.

"There." Suddenly he pointed an accusing finger at a spot by Niahrin's fence. "They were there, right *there*, bold as you please! Two of them, sitting, staring at your door! They were going to—"

"No, Perd, they were *not* going to tear my throat out!" Dear Goddess but his obsession was unswerving, and iron crept back into the witch's voice. It was vital to be firm with Perd and not let him take the upper hand even for a moment. At the same time, though, her mind registered and puzzled over what he'd said. Two wolves, simply sitting . . . that was out of the ordinary; not like them at all.

"Sitting," Perd repeated with savage emphasis, as though a corner of his twisted mind had picked up her thoughts. "Sitting. *Waiting!* To tear—"

"Perd, enough!" Niahrin snapped back to earth. His face creased at her tone and she repeated less vehemently, "Enough." She hissed in a breath, let it out again. "I'm grateful for your concern, as I told you, but I don't want to hear any more. Now: You said you have business with me. What is it I can do?"

He stared down at his feet, shook his head. Knowing this of old, the witch sighed. "Come, my dear, say what it is. You know I'll not tell anyone else; you know you can trust me."

Silence again for a few moments, then abruptly he shuffled forward until they were only inches apart, though with the gate still between them. Niahrin caught a familiar smell on his breath—the harsh spirit distilled by some of the less reputable foresters and sold to anyone fool enough to rot themselves for the sake of a few hours' oblivion. Well, in Perd's case the stuff seemed to do more good than harm; at least it kept his delusions at bay and put him on an even keel for a while. He had dropped the blackthorn staff now and thrust one arm toward her, pushing up the sleeve of his filthy coat as he did so. Niahrin stared at the long gash running from elbow to wrist. It wasn't deep but it was caked with dried blood and there were signs of festering under the general grime of his skin.

She looked at his face. "How did you do that?"

Perd didn't answer, which was enough to tell her the truth. "With that knife of yours? Yes?" A nod, and she clucked her tongue. "How many times have I warned you about that wicked thing? You're not fit to be trusted with such a blade; if you're not menacing shadows with it then you're menacing yourself."

"I need it," Perd mumbled. "I *need* it. Or they'll tear—"

She interrupted briskly before he could begin that tack again. "You'll lose the use of your arm, or worse, if it isn't cleaned and dressed."

"I cleaned it. Washed it."

"Licked it with your own tongue, more like. Now, come you into—" Then she remembered the wolf in the cottage and swiftly changed what she had been about to say. Perd mustn't see the creature, or she'd be unable to control him. "Come you into the garden and sit down on the bench, and I'll fetch what I need." The gate-latch clicked; he came in and sank down on the wooden form she indicated. "Wait for me here, and don't move. Don't go away."

He was still there when she came out, and he'd begun to cry, the tears making pale rivulets down his dirty face. Niahrin was used to this and said nothing; she didn't know the reason why he wept, or even if there was a reason at all, but to ask him was futile, for he could—or would—give no sensible answer. She brought warm water and a cloth and one of her own herbal preparations with a clean bandage, and Perd sat passive as a small child while she cleansed and treated and finally bound the knife wound. Niahrin wondered what had caused him to strike out at himself this time. Perd was followed wherever he went by ghosts and devils, and during his bad times he often tried to exorcise the horrors that possessed him in his imagination, letting his own blood in a desperate attempt to pull out and destroy his illusory tormentors. Though she couldn't claim to like Perd—indeed, she doubted if there was a living soul in the land who could *like* such a man— the witch pitied him deeply and had often wished that her nostrums had the power to cure insanity.

Now, though, she concerned herself only with the old man's physical well-being. Soon the bandage was on and tied in place, and she repeated three times a stern instruction that he was *not* to tear it off but to return to her in two days, or at least as soon as he remembered, so that she might see how the healing progressed.

"And where is your knife now?" she asked.

He looked at her obliquely, slyly. "Somewhere. Somewhere safe."

So he wasn't rid of it. Niahrin sighed. "Very well. But you must *remember*, Perd. The blade is sharp, and it does harm. Try not to touch it. Will you promise me that?"

"I . . ." For just one moment an extraordinary clarity came to the old man's eyes, and with it terrible misery. "I'll try. . . ."

"Good." She patted his uninjured arm, helping him to his feet and steering him toward the gate. "Well, then; be away home with you, and I'll see you again in two days."

He shuffled out of the garden, then suddenly stopped and looked down at himself. "Sweet Goddess . . ." he said in a thin, broken voice. "Sweet Goddess, the *filth* . . ." Abruptly he turned and looked pleadingly at her. "I want to be clean! Dear Mother of all life, what's *happened* to me? How did I *become* like this?" He grabbed at her arm. "Can I wash? Can I?"

This, too, Niahrin had seen before; a brief but violent return to complete lucidity, and disgust at himself. "Yes, my dear," she said, "you can wash and bathe; it won't hurt the bandage to get wet. But don't take it off. Remember that."

"Yes." He turned his face away from her as though ashamed to meet her gaze. "I'll remember this time. I know I forget so often, but I'll remember. Th ... thank you. You're always so kind, aren't you? I don't know why."

Niahrin watched him go, watched the dappled light-and-shadow patterns of the forest conceal him as he walked away. He'd left his blackthorn staff behind and she picked it up and propped it by the gate. He might remember and return for it, or he might simply cut himself another with that terrible knife of his. Shaking her head, sad for him yet despairing of him, Niahrin turned back to the cottage.

She entered—and on the threshold had a shock. The injured wolf had twisted herself about and was half lying, half sitting with forelegs braced and hackles up, her fangs bared and her eyes glinting red. Saliva trickled in a thin rope from her jaws, and as Niahrin's shadow darkened the doorway she snarled menacingly.

Niahrin stopped still, astonished and alarmed. She started to say, "What is—" but before she could utter another word the wolf said, gutturally but with dramatic clarity, *"Send it away! Send the evil away!"*

Prickles of hot and cold sweat broke out on the witch's body. "You spoke—"

"Yess. I spoke. Send it away! *Please!*" Then, as though with a terrible revelation, "Oh, I hurt ... I hhh ... *hurt!*"

Grimya hadn't meant to do it. She'd been too uncertain still, too afraid to trust the witch despite what instinct and evidence had told her, and she'd been thankful for the interruption that had saved her from being forced into making a decision. But as she listened to the voices outside the cottage, another instinct had awoken within her. Whoever was out there and whatever they were saying, Grimya was afraid. No, more than that: she was terrified. And she felt a surge of bitter hatred such as she had never felt in her life before, even when as a cub she'd been turned on and attacked and driven out of her pack for being different. The man out there, he was different too, but instead of sympathy she felt only intense horror and revulsion, and with it a dreadful sense of vulnerability. She'd managed to cling to her self-control when Niahrin returned briefly for the water and herbs and bandage, but when the witch went out again the suffocating fear began to build and build until Grimya could no longer constrain it. There was *evil* outside, a dreadful threat, and in panic she had fought the pain to prepare herself to meet its attack. Now though, there was no attack and the pain had overcome her, and she hadn't the strength left to combat it or to hide her distress. She couldn't even care that she had given herself away, for the agony she felt eclipsed every other thought.

Niahrin's response was swift and efficient. She gave Grimya a strong sedative that eclipsed her pain in the relief of sleep, and by the time the wolf woke again her splints had been reset, her bandaging renewed, and she lay in a comfortable position by the fire once more. The witch was sitting cross-legged on the floor on the other side of the hearth, watching her, and as soon as she saw that Grimya was awake she said, "Has the pain gone?"

Grimya blinked, then remembered that her secret was out and there was no point pretending not to comprehend.

"Yess," she said hoarsely, then after a pause added abashedly, "thank you. . . ."

Niahrin proceeded to deliver a short, kindly but stern lecture on her foolishness. Did she not realize how badly injured she was? A bone in her right hind leg was broken and her hindquarters had suffered some crushing. She bore

sores and cuts too numerous to count, she had suffered
shock and exposure, and it was only thanks to a small miracle from the Sea Mother that she hadn't drowned altogether. So, please and thank you, she would *not* undo all
Niahrin's good work, which was intended solely for her
benefit, by behaving like a foolish cub and trying to get to
her feet when she was fit only to lie *quite* still until bidden
otherwise. Grimya accepted the scolding in silence and
with drooping ears; in truth she hadn't realized the extent
of her injuries and wasn't sure even now what a broken
leg meant and how long it would take to heal. But when
the lecture was done the witch's expression and manner
changed abruptly.

"Well now," she said, "I think we may let it go at that
for now, provided I have your promise that you will obey
me."

She had little choice, Grimya thought uneasily. She
licked her muzzle. "Yess. I prromise."

"Good! Now—I think you and I have a good deal else
to say to each other, haven't we?" Niahrin gave her
twisted smile and the brow above her undamaged eye rose
quirkishly. "A wolf who speaks with a human voice.
D'you know, my dear, I believed at first that I must have
been deluded." She hesitated. "That is, if you truly *are* a
wolf, and not some chimera?"

"I am a wolf. Nothing more." And, aware that she
couldn't evade the truth, or at least a good part of it,
Grimya told Niahrin of the mutation with which she had
been born and which had made her an outcast from her
own kind. The witch listened with sympathy, and it
seemed that she had no difficulty in accepting the story,
strange and fantastic though it was. Grimya couldn't quite
trust in her apparent acceptance and at last she paused and
said uncertainly, "You . . . *believe* me?"

"Believe you?" Niahrin looked surprised. "Why, of

course. Why should I not? Only a fool believes that the Great Mother's creation has any limits—and besides, I have the evidence of my own ears and eyes, and there's nothing convinces me better than that." Her odd smile suddenly became a grin. "Unless you're not a living creature at all but some mischievous sprite come to play a joke on me!"

"I am not—" Grimya began in distress.

"Hush, my dear, hush! It was my joke, just my joke. I know what you are, I've no doubts at all. But it puzzles me that I've not encountered you before. I like to think I know my wolves, and I'm sure I should have noticed an outcast. Are you not from this part of the forest?"

"No," Grimya admitted. "I . . . I am not from this country at all."

"Not from the Isles? Ah!" Niahrin clasped her hands together. "Then it's as I suspected—you were aboard the ship; the ship that was wrecked on the Amberland reefs!"

Grimya couldn't weep, couldn't shed tears as a human would, but suddenly there was such a depth of misery in her amber eyes that Niahrin leaned forward with a little cry of sorrow. "My dear, what have I said? What has upset you?" Then she remembered the incident at the village house, and the word the wolf had uttered in her delirium. *Indigo.* Not a place, Niahrin thought, and not an object. She was beginning to understand.

"Grimya." She hoped she had the wolf's name right. "Who is Indigo?"

Grimya stiffened. "You . . . *know* about her?"

Her . . . Well, so she'd been right; and now she knew a snippet more. "No," the witch said, "but you spoke her name in your sleep, you called out to her." She reached to touch Grimya's head with great gentleness, stroking, soothing, reassuring. "Who is she, my dear? Trust me, and tell me all."

Grimya did trust her. Her mind was clearer now, and she sensed with her sure instincts that this woman would not betray her or use her or seek to profit from her in any way. Her earlier fears were unfounded; and it would be a relief, such a relief, to unburden herself to a kindly soul, and one who might have the power to help her.

She told Niahrin of Indigo. Not all the truth, for caution still remained and it was an old rule that neither she nor Indigo would ever reveal the whole of their secret to another living soul. Indigo was her dear and long-cherished friend, she said, and since their first chance encounter in the forests of the Horselands, her own birthplace, they had traveled together for . . . well, for a long time now. They had seen much of the world, but at last they had tired of roaming and had planned to return to the Southern Isles, Indigo's homeland. Indigo had taken work on the crew of the *Good Hope* . . . and the rest, Grimya said, Niahrin already knew.

"Dear Goddess." The witch's voice was filled with compassion. "Such a sad ending to what should have been a happy tale . . . That you should survive, yet your friend is . . . is gone."

Grimya's eyes glittered. "No. She is not gone."

Niahrin looked at her sadly. "Oh, my dear. I don't wish to dash your hopes, but—"

"*No,*" the wolf said again, more emphatically. "Indigo is *not* dead." She couldn't explain, for she hadn't told Niahrin that Indigo was immortal and could not die; that was part of the greater secret that couldn't be revealed. Her eyes looked up appealingly. "You hh-ave to believe that I *know* this. I *know.*"

Niahrin groped for understanding. A telepathic link, the wolf had said. Perhaps that was it; perhaps she was still linked to the mind of her friend.

"Do you—*sense* her?" she asked cautiously. "Sense her presence—her existence?"

Unwittingly she had given Grimya the help she needed. The wolf's eyes lit up and she said eagerly, "Yess! I sense her. That is hh-ow I know Indigo is alive."

This was a strange and wonderful thing, Niahrin thought to herself. She knew a little about telepathy though she wasn't gifted with the talent, but never before had she imagined that such an extraordinarily powerful link could exist, and she began to wonder just what manner of person the mysterious Indigo might be.

Her expression intense, she asked, "Do you know where she is, Grimya? Can you find her—or she you?"

The light faded from the wolf's eyes. "No." She had told Niahrin a lie, for she had already tried to reach out and make contact with Indigo and her efforts had met with no response. Either Indigo was not awake to hear her, or the distance between them was too great. "I do not know where she is," she added. "But I know she is alive. I *know*."

"Yes, yes. Quiet, now; I believe you." Niahrin pondered for a few moments then added: "Indigo. It's a strange name for a Southern Isler to have. Do you know that indigo is the color of mourning in our country? Surely that can't be her birth name!"

Grimya dissembled uneasily. "I . . . do not know."

"Do her family live? Do you know her clan name?"

"They are dead, and I . . . do not know their names."

Maybe that explained it, Niahrin thought. Maybe Indigo had adopted a new name as an expression of her grief; maybe that was why she had left the islands and ventured abroad for so long, hoping to forget some great personal tragedy. But although that theory seemed plausible enough, Niahrin felt in her bones that something was awry with it. It was simply her intuition at work, but something didn't fit.

And then there were her visions, and that brought another unexplained matter to mind. . . .

She looked at Grimya again. "My dear," she said, "if your Indigo is alive—and yes, I believe you when you say she is—then I will find her for you." That should be no hardship, she thought. It would be a simple enough matter to send word to the villages along the coast inquiring after the survivors of the wreck, and a woman with the strange name of Indigo would be noted and recalled by the islanders. Chances were she would be in Ranna, or at least have set foot there. And knowledge of her whereabouts would be a better medicine for Grimya than any wise-woman's nostrums.

"I'll send a message with one of the foresters," she promised. "They often have business with the homesteads and villages hereabouts, and they'll spread the word quickly. We'll find your Indigo, have no fear."

Grimya's eyes glowed warmly. "You are very k . . . kind."

"Kind?" Niahrin gave an odd little laugh. "Nonsense. No one would do less; why should they? Now, if you're not famished I know that I am, so we'll eat now and then you shall sleep. Sleep is the best healer of all." She got to her feet a little stiffly. "Ah! Must be getting past my prime, I've not the suppleness I used to have. Oh . . ." She hesitated. "One thing." Abruptly her good eye focused hard on Grimya's face. "What was it you were so afraid of that made you hurt yourself anew?"

Grimya was caught unawares, which was precisely what Niahrin had intended. Her lips drew back a little, showing the tips of her fangs, and she made a peculiar noise deep in her throat. "I . . . I was . . ." The words trailed off.

"It was only an old man. A mad old man, but he can't

help his madness any more than you and I can help our own afflictions. He has a fear of wolves, but he isn't truly evil, Grimya." Her brows knitted tightly together. "Or wasn't it Perd at all who frightened you? Was it the wolves—was that it? Did you know they were there, and did you fear them because of what your own pack did to you so long ago?"

Grimya couldn't answer her, for she didn't know the truth herself. All she could recall was sensing something so dark, so threatening, so ugly, that it had swamped her mind and brought terror to her heart. Perhaps it was the wolves; perhaps that. Certainly she did fear her own kind, and with good reason. Yet instinct told her there had been more to it, *much* more, though she was desperately reluctant to ask herself what it might have been.

Niahrin saw her distress and relented. "No, my dear, don't think about it if it troubles you so much. It doesn't matter, and we've more important things to concern ourselves with now." She picked up a wooden spoon and waved it. "Food first, then sleep!"

And I hope, she thought as Grimya began to relax, *that neither Perd nor the wolves return too soon. At least not until I've begun to fathom some of the depths of this strange mystery.*

•CHAPTER•V•

Perd Nordenson didn't return to the cottage during the next two days, and if the wolves were about and watching, Niahrin was unaware of their presence and Grimya untroubled by it.

Niahrin was both surprised and gratified by her patient's rapid progress. Grimya had taken the witch's lecture to heart and conscientiously obeyed her every instruction, and Niahrin's promise that she would do all she could to find Indigo had lifted her spirits enormously. Her greatest enemy now was boredom and—a little to Niahrin's surprise, for she'd never thought she had such a frivolous streak—Niahrin found herself shamefully neglecting her cottage and garden in order to keep the wolf entertained.

Grimya loved music and Niahrin loved to sing; her voice was a little gruff but true and pleasant, and she knew many of the songs that the wolf had learned from Indigo in their years together. Delighted to hear them again,

Grimya was eager to teach Niahrin new songs in return; tunes from the Western Continent, from Khimiz, from Davakos. Niahrin had a wooden pipe that she hadn't played for several years but with which, after a little practice, she was soon fluent again, and though Grimya couldn't sing she was able to voice most of the notes closely enough for Niahrin to find and play the melody. So the time passed pleasantly enough, though Grimya was dismayed to discover that she must wait some time before her broken bones would be mended and she could walk again.

"Don't fret," Niahrin urged her kindly, seeing her distress. "You can start to try out three of your legs before too long—not overmuch, mind, but a little exercise will help bring back your strength—and then it'll seem but a short while until you're whole again. And meanwhile the search for your friend Indigo will be continuing. There's every chance she'll be found and will come here to you before you're ready to go to her!"

On the fourth morning after her encounter with Perd, the witch had another and more welcome visitor. She was tending her garden, giving water to a row of young cress plants that needed extra moisture if they were to get off to a sturdy start, when she heard her name called and looked up to see Cadic Haymanson, one of the foresters, approaching the gate.

"Cadic—good day to you." Niahrin straightened from her work, smiling. Cadic was a man of around her own age or a little younger, who kept a lodge a mile or so distant where, like their ancestors before them, he and his wife coppiced and tended the trees and ran their small herd of pigs in the commonwood. He had the forester's look about him: lightly but strongly built, skin brown as bark, good homespun clothes in muted, earthy shades.

"Your crops are coming along." Cadic leaned on the gate and nodded approvingly at the vegetable patch.

"I'm well pleased with the season so far," she agreed. "I'll have some scallions and fresh herbs for you in a few days, and I'll be needing a bundle of kindling and another two baskets of logs when you're next passing this way." She dug a knuckled fist into the small of her back to ease a twinge. "Milla's well, I hope? And the children?"

"All thriving. Milla says to tell you that the syrup you sent her worked a treat on Landie and she's sleeping soundly every night now."

"I'm glad to hear it." Niahrin glanced over her shoulder toward the cottage, then added, "And glad to see you, Cadic, for another reason. I need a favor from you, and from anyone else who may be able to help."

"Ask it. Anything I can do."

"I want to find someone," Niahrin told him. "Someone who I believe was aboard the ship wrecked on Amberland Point in the last gale."

Cadic frowned. "That's been the talk of the district. She was a cargo vessel from the east, by all accounts—some of the crew were rescued and they've been taken to one of the villages along the coast, but I don't know which one, or how many survivors there were." He paused. "You knew someone on the ship?"

Niahrin smiled an enigmatic little smile. "At one remove, you might say. We share a mutual friend."

"Well, if you can give me his name, I'll put the word about."

"Not he, she. A young woman, an Isler by birth. I don't know who her kin are but I'm told her name is Indigo."

"Indigo?" Cadic looked at her incredulously.

"I know; it's hard to believe that any Isler would give his child such an ill-omened name, and I've little doubt that she must have changed it for some reason of her own. But it's how she's known now."

"If nothing else it should make her easy enough to find," Cadic said. "No one's likely to overlook a name like that, or forget its owner in a hurry."

"My thoughts exactly. So if you'll put the word out, Cadic, I'll be in your debt. If anyone succeeds in finding her, I'd also ask them to give her a message. Tell her I have Grimya safe, and tell her where and how to find me."

"Grimya? Who is Grimya?"

"Our mutual friend. And don't look at me in that hopeful way, Cadic Haymanson, for I've no intention of revealing any more than I've already said."

Cadic knew the tone and knew Niahrin well enough to realize that he wouldn't persuade any more out of her. "All right," he said good-humoredly, "if you want to keep your secrets, keep them. But I'd lay any wager that there *is* a story here."

"Maybe there is, and maybe one day I'll tell it to you. But for now I just want to find a woman called Indigo."

He nodded. "I'll put word out, then. It might be worth sending a message to Ranna next time the timber wagons go in. There's a good chance some of the poor devils from the wreck may find their way there."

"Thank you." Niahrin bent and plucked several sprigs of pale, feathery green from among her herbs. "Here—there's enough leaf on the Lad's Love to make a picking. Wear these in your hat; they'll keep fresh enough. When you get home, tell Milla to put them in her oak chest, and the moths won't make a meal of your best linen."

Cadic took the bunch, sniffing their clean, pungent scent appreciatively. "That's kind, Niahrin, and I thank you. I'll remember your logs—two sacks, wasn't it, and a bundle of kindling? Expect them tomorrow or the next day." He made to wave farewell and move on, then halted. "Damn me, I almost forgot what brought me by this way in the first place! I'm trying to solve a small mystery of my own, and you may be able to help. It's about Perd Nordenson. Have you set eyes on him lately?"

"Perd? Why yes, he came to see me . . . what—four, five days ago." Niahrin frowned. "He had a bad gash on his arm; from what I was able to get out of him he'd inflicted it on himself with that wicked knife of his. I cleaned and bound the wound and told him to come back in two days for me to look at it again."

"And he didn't come?"

"No, he didn't. Mind, that's nothing unusual with him. He forgets things the moment after he hears them, more often than not. . . ." She looked keenly at the forester. "Why, Cadic? Is something wrong?"

"In all truth, I don't know. But no one's seen him for a good few days now. He hasn't been to any of his usual haunts—hasn't even shown his face at Ilior's tavern, and you know how often he makes a nuisance of himself there. We began to think some harm must have come to him, so last night a few of us went to his hut. He wasn't there, either, and from the look of it most of his possessions have gone, too."

"Possessions?" Niahrin echoed wryly.

"I know, he's got little enough; but the less there is to begin with, the easier it is to be sure that certain things are missing. His knife, for instance. And his cooking pot, and those old boots the charcoal-burners gave him winter before last. And his cloak."

"He had a cloak?" Niahrin was surprised. "I've never seen him wear it."

"Nor has anyone. He keeps it—kept it—hung on a nail by his pallet. It's a filthy, moth-eaten thing, probably nearly as old as he is, and so far as I know he never put it to use. But it's gone along with the rest."

"So," Niahrin said, her voice troubled, "you think Perd has simply taken it into his head to leave?"

"Either that, or he was visited by thieves who took his goods, killed him, and hid his corpse elsewhere. But that hardly seems likely. He had nothing worth stealing; even the worst kind of bandit wouldn't trouble with him. No: You were the one person who might have been able to shed light on this conundrum, but if you've not seen Perd either then it seems certain he's simply gathered up what he wanted and left. He's probably made a habit of it all his life—it's how he arrived here a few years ago, after all; suddenly and out of the blue. Though the Mother alone knows where he might have gone this time."

"Or why," the witch added. Then, thoughtfully: "He was in better straits than usual when he came to me. He ranted about the wolves, of course, but besides that his mind seemed quite stable." Her frown deepened. "There was one moment when I think he saw himself very clearly. Perhaps *too* clearly. If that mood lasted more than an hour or two, it might have had some lasting effect on him."

"And caused him to take flight?" Cadic sucked air between two teeth. "It's possible. But where would he go? Where *could* he go? He has no living kin as far as anyone can tell; I doubt if he can even claim to have a true friend anywhere in the Isles."

Niahrin nodded soberly. "That's true. But who can fathom the mind of a man like Perd?" She smiled wryly. "The Mother knows, enough of us have tried and failed. Well, I'm sorry to hear this news, Cadic. I can't claim to feel affection for Perd, any more than you do, but it's a sad thing to think of him lost and roaming and alone. I don't doubt he had his own reasons for going, and whether he was searching or fleeing is a question that will probably never be answered. I'll look for him in my own ways, as

you'll look for him in yours, and if I discover anything
you'll be the first to hear of it."

"I'd be grateful." Cadic returned her smile. "Now I'd
best be away. Thank you, Niahrin—and I shan't forget to
put the word out for your lost friend."

When the forester had vanished into the wood, Niahrin
finished watering her young plants and returned to her cottage. Grimya was sleeping—no bad thing—and the witch
stood gazing at her for a minute or two while she mulled
over what Cadic had told her and wondered how it fitted
with the fragmented and elusive picture she had begun to
piece together over the past few days. Grimya, the mutant
with the power of human speech. Her own wolf-friends,
curious, coming to sit silently outside the cottage as
though keeping vigil. Perd Nordenson, with his strange ha-
treds and obsessions, who now had disappeared. Logically
there was no connection, but Niahrin had learned long ago
that logic was a rare player in the game of life and that the
unlikeliest threads were more often than not connected.
Besides, her visions did not lie. And Perd had had a part
in those visions; a part she didn't yet understand.

She turned her head at last and looked at the narrow
door, covered by a woolen curtain, that separated the cottage's living space from the second and smaller room.
How long was it since she had ventured in there? Two
years? Three? More? Probably more, for she couldn't even
recall what had prompted her last foray or on whose behalf
it had been. Since then the door had remained barred, the
curtain undisturbed. Niahrin didn't want to change that, for
there was always a price to be paid in that room and the
price was high. But instinct told her that where other talents failed or produced at best clouded and ambiguous answers, this might be her only sure resort.

She glanced at Grimya again, saw that the wolf was still
sleeping soundly, and moved toward the inner door. The

curtain was dusty; as she pulled it back a spider scurried from the folds, ran down the wall, and vanished into a crevice. Murmuring an apology to the little creature for the disturbance, Niahrin unbarred the door, lifted the latch, and stepped through to the room beyond.

The spider's kin had woven a pattern of cobwebs over the small, square window, so that the light filtering in had an opaque, dreamlike cast. Other than that though, and under the dust that lay like a soft blanket over everything, it was exactly as she remembered; as she had left it when she last stumbled drained and heart weary from the punishing travail of mind, body, and soul that this room imposed.

The spinning wheel stood in its corner, a low chair set beside it. The silver spindles, empty, gleamed amid the patina of disuse; a draft skittered in at the door and the wheel shifted a fraction, creaking in its mounting with a sound Niahrin remembered well. But dominating the room, dark and angular and just a little sinister, was the weaving loom. Neglected and untouched and with no bright patterns of warp and weft to enliven it, it lay dormant, as it had lain for years—dormant, but not dead. Niahrin felt the touch of it, the pull of it, as her grandmother and great-great-grandmother had done before her. Another piece of her legacy; a powerful servant and a demanding mistress together.

She stared at the loom and the wheel for a very long time, and then, calmly, she made her decision. Beyond the woodland borders, on the rough moors that separated the forest from the southern tundra, they would have started shearing the hardy little sheep. Shearing their fine wool to be carded and dyed and then sold to the spinners and weavers, who would gather in Ingan next market day to buy the first and best of the spring gleaning. Very well then, very well. She would go to Ingan, she would buy and she would let intuition and the Mother choose her colors, and then she would awaken the old powers again and see what was to be seen. Surer than visions, surer than mind alone. If the questions she had were to be answered, this was the only way.

Niahrin withdrew from the room and barred the door once more, leaving the wheel and the loom and the spiders to their secret silence.

Cadic Haymanson was a reliable man, and within two days word began to spread in the coastal villages that the witch Niahrin was seeking news of a woman named Indigo, thought to have been aboard the *Good Hope*. At first the search was fruitless, producing only shaken heads and expressions of surprise and curiosity that any Isler should have such an unfortunate name. But at last, as the inquiries spread wider and farther, they met with success.

"Indigo?" One of the beacon watchmen, on the way home from his turn of duty, had encountered a pack-trader from Ingan where the coast and inland roads intersected. "Yes, I've heard it. There was someone of that name—a woman—brought off the wreck last full moon." The watchman grimaced. "Peculiar name for an Isler to have; unlucky, I'd have thought. But she survived the wreck, so luck must have been on her side that night at least."

In answer to further questions he said that yes, the ship-wrecked crew had been taken to his village and he thought one or two might still be there. But he couldn't say who had gone and who remained; best ask Olender the healer for that information. The pack-trader thanked him, promised to call at his cottage later to show his wife some newly tanned hides, then their talk broadened to more general gossip and the latest news from Ingan as they walked down into the village together.

The trader had no cause to dwell on the question of Indigo and no reason to go to any trouble in making further inquiries. This was simply one small message among many that he was asked to spread in the course of his travels, and of no especial importance to him. However, as he planned to stay overnight in the village and thus had a little time to spare, he asked directions to Olender's house when his business was completed. The healer was at home, and the pack-trader discovered that his inquiry had come just a day too late. Indigo had been here—for some days in fact, Olender said, recovering from a head wound—but yesterday morning she had left for Ranna, along with the *Good Hope*'s captain and several other crew. He'd advised her to wait a while longer, the healer added. She'd suffered a nasty blow that had resulted in loss of much of her memory, and if she was to get it back she'd be better off resting than traveling before she was fully fit. But Vinar had insisted she'd be safe enough in his hands and had said that perhaps a visit to Ranna would help her to recall what she'd lost. Vinar? A Scorvan; big man, like a bear, with blond hair. He and Indigo were betrothed.

The trader thanked Olender, bought a pot of saxifrage salve for a troublesome whitlow on his finger, and bade the healer good day. He'd put the news about on his return to Ingan; Ranna was well beyond his domain, but several carters made regular journeys there and would pass the word along.

It took a further five days for the search to reach Ranna, this time by way of a young man who rode in on a passenger-cart in the hope of taking up a trade at sea. Ranna was the largest port in the Southern Isles, a bustling, noisy, cheerful, and confusing sprawl of a place. But even for a stranger it was easy enough to find the quays and taverns where captains gathered to sign on new crews, and it was in one of these taverns that the young man encountered the Davakotian, Brek.

Brek was wary, almost suspicious, when the *Good Hope* was mentioned, but on hearing Indigo's name his attitude changed.

"Someone's looking for her?" He leaned forward, his eyes suddenly intent. "Who?"

The young man knew only that the message he carried had come by roundabout ways from the foresters in the woods near Amberland and said so. Brek nibbled at his lower lip. "The foresters . . . I wonder, could someone among the foresters be her kinsman?"

"Don't know about that, sir," the young man said. "But there was a message, so I was told. To say that someone's got her friend Grimya safe, and the foresters can tell her where."

Brek started. "*Grimya?* She's *alive*?"

"Alive and well, they said."

"Sweet Sea Mother! That's good news—no, more than good, it's astonishing! I thought Grimya was lost, I thought she'd had no chance!"

The young man ventured to ask, "Was Grimya another one of the crew, sir?"

"What? No—no, she wasn't, not in that sense. Grimya's not a person, she's a wolf. A tame wolf; she was Indigo's pet." Brek whistled through his teeth. "I was certain she'd drowned!"

Eager to ingratiate himself and earn the favor of a potential employer, the young man said, "If she—Indigo, that is—if she's here in Ranna, sir, I'll gladly take word to her. I'm sure she'll be happy to hear the tidings."

"You might have done that, boy, if you'd come to me a few days ago, but it's too late. She's already gone."

Dismay filled the youth's expression and he glanced involuntarily to the open frontage of the tavern and the view of the harbor beyond. "Back to sea?"

"No, no; inland, with her man. She lost her memory, you see; can't recall who her family are or where they live. So she and Vinar have gone to search for them." For the first time Brek's face relaxed a little. "Vinar asked for her hand onboard and she accepted him, but he won't hold with marrying her until he's got her father's permission. Still, that's a Scorvan for you. Stolid and stubborn." His eyes glinted suddenly with humor as he wondered belatedly if he'd delivered the lad an insult. "You're not a Scorvan, are you, boy?"

He returned the look with a hesitant smile. "No, sir. Isler, born and bred."

"Looking for work?"

A nod.

"Well, now. Maybe I can help. Not immediately, for I've no ship to command at present." Brek's mouth quirked, not bitterly but at a hard angle as cruel memories were renewed. "But there are two Davakotian hunter-escorts waiting in port for a commission to the Eastern Continent, and I've signed on to crew with them to Huon Parita." Brek paused. "D'you know what hunter-escorts are?"

"Yes, sir," the other said immediately and eagerly. "Small ships but fast, with a ram below the waterline and a deck-mounted ballista. They guard the valuable cargoes and protect them from piracy."

Brek nodded, satisfied. If the boy had taken the trouble to learn a little about vessel classes and duties then he was obviously keen enough to be promising material. He said, "Chances are the escorts will be assigned to a Bear class that's due in in seven or ten days. The convoy will be putting out from Ranna in about a month, and one of the escorts still needs a sweat-boy. In exchange for an errand for me, I'll see you get the place if you want it."

The young man's eyes lit with excitement. "Yes, sir! Anything you want of me, only say and I'll do it—thank you, sir!"

Brek smiled dryly. "You may not be so keen to thank me when you've had a month jumping to a Davakotian skipper's orders. Sweat-boy's the lowest and the worst job on any ship, and life on a hunter-escort's more arduous than most. You'll be doing all the dirty work—and I *mean* dirty—that no one else would touch with a ten-foot pole; you'll be at everyone's beck and call at all hours, and if there's trouble you've a better chance than most of getting yourself killed."

The eager light didn't diminish. "That's no more than I'd expect, Captain. I want to be a seaman, and everyone knows you can't learn better than on a Davakotian. It'd be a privilege, sir. A real chance and privilege, and I won't let you down!"

No, Brek thought, he probably wouldn't. "Well, then," he said, "what I want you to do is follow the road that Indigo and Vinar took, catch up with them, and give them the message you brought here to me. You'd best make sure it's Vinar you speak to, for there's no way of knowing whether Indigo's recovered her memory yet."

"I'll do it, sir," the boy promised. "Only, how will I know them?"

"Indigo's a handsome woman with chestnut-colored hair, and Vinar—" Brek chuckled, and the sound of his own laughter surprised him for it seemed a long time since he'd heard it. "Well, you'll not mistake Vinar; I doubt if anyone could. *That* high," pointing to the rafters above their head, "and *that* wide," extending both arms to full stretch, "with a mane of yellow hair and a seaman's pale blue eyes, and though he speaks the Southern Isles tongue passably enough he's got an accent you could cut with a blunt knife. For sure, the Mother didn't make two of *him*. Find him, like I say, give him the message, then come back here to Ranna. You've got a month before we sail."

"That'll be time enough, sir." The youth rose smartly to his feet and gave Brek a salute, which, while it wouldn't have passed muster with a real stickler of a captain, was a fair effort for a beginner. "And thank you again, sir. *Thank* you!"

Maybe it was because he saw echoes of himself at a similar age, or maybe it was simply a reaction to the news of Grimya's survival, but Brek felt oddly contented, and that awoke a genial impulse.

"Here." He dipped into his belt-pouch and drew out a generous handful of coins. "You'll need board and lodging on your journey, and I wouldn't mind betting you're down to your last crust by now." He saw the lad's mouth open to protest and waved him to silence. "Call it a loan if it makes you happier, though it's no more than I'd pay for any courier. Go on, now; sooner you leave, sooner you'll be back and ready for some real work. A month, mind. No longer."

Brek shut his ears to the boy's further thanks, embarrassed by their profuseness, and watched him hurry out of the tavern, his step quick and his head high. Yes, he was promising material. Should have asked his name; that was something he'd forgotten. Never mind. He'd be back soon enough with his mission successfully completed, and Brek was pleased to feel that he'd done a favor for two friends. Altogether, it hadn't been so bad a day.

·CHAPTER·VI·

It was a rough-and-ready entertainment, improvised on the spur of the moment, but all the same a good-sized crowd gathered to enjoy the fun. The day had been warm—certainly the warmest day of the season thus far and promising to set fair for a while—and so with work completed, the sun westering, and the air filled with the scents of thorn-blossom and new grass, the town square quickly began to fill with people. The sheep pens had been cleared away to create dancing space, and a wagon had been hauled from the communal barn on one side of the square to act as a makeshift stage for the musicians. The audience contrived to sit wherever they could: some on bales of last year's hay from the barn, some on benches brought from Rogan Kendarson's tavern opposite, others simply settling themselves on the ground, which was dry enough if you took care to pick your place. Friends and neighbors from the town and outlying farms greeted one another and chattered in voices that carried on the balmy air, children's shrieks and laughter echoed, and as the sky darkened torches and lanterns were lit, turning the square to a bright, warm oasis.

As occupants of two of the lodging rooms in Rogan's tavern, Indigo and Vinar had privileged places on a bench outside, where they could lean comfortably against the stone wall and enjoy a good view of the proceedings. Vinar had ordered a jug of apple wine and a tray of mutton pasties, which he cheerfully and liberally shared with anyone in reach. He was eagerly anticipating the evening's entertainment, not least because he hoped that music might succeed where other strategies had failed and reopen the locked doors of Indigo's memory. She sat beside him, happy enough on the surface, smiling and animated as she talked with their neighbors and Rogan's wife, Jansa, but Vinar knew that the mask she wore was shallow. Beneath the surface Indigo was in torment. He'd watched her carefully in recent days, and often when she thought his attention was elsewhere he'd seen her eyes darken with confusion and her face grow tight and tense as she strove fruitlessly to remember something, *anything* that might turn the key. Glancing at her now, Vinar felt a sharp pang as he recalled the small, secret joy he'd felt during the first days after the shipwreck, when he had realized what Indigo's memory loss might mean for him. Not that he was *glad* it had happened, not in any way at all . . . but if it had to be, then the temptation to grasp such an undreamed of chance to fulfill his dearest hopes was one that Vinar had been unable to resist.

The pleasure hadn't lasted, though. His conscience had seen to that, for Vinar was essentially too honest to go on deceiving Indigo, who knew no better than to trust him. He was aware that her own feelings troubled her; she believed she had once loved him and was distressed to have no memory of that love and feel no spark of it within her. Vinar couldn't live with the lie—yet neither could he summon the courage to confess the truth, at least not yet. To admit what he'd done would be to risk losing her forever, and that prospect was too terrible. There was, he had finally decided, only one course he could honorably follow. He must do all within his power to bring Indigo's lost memory back—for then, and only then, could he win her fairly. And he *would* win her. However long it might take, however hard he must strive, he *would*. Then, when she loved him as he loved her, he could tell her the truth without fear of the consequences.

So, buoyed by his resolve, Vinar had persuaded Indigo to set out with him on a journey of discovery. Somewhere in the Southern Isles, he believed, her kinfolk must be waiting to welcome her back among them, and it couldn't be beyond the wit of a resourceful man to find them. They could afford to travel, for the *Good Hope*'s surviving crew had received their due pay from the harbormaster at Ranna who kept account with the ship's owners in Huon Parita. They could live for three, possibly four, months, which would surely be enough; and as they searched, the subconscious tug of her homeland's familiarity might be enough to turn the vital key in Indigo's mind.

They had been traveling for eighteen days now and the Isles hadn't yet worked their hoped-for magic. But tonight's events, Vinar thought, could change that. Indigo loved music and had often played her harp for the *Good Hope*'s crew during their voyage south, and though he couldn't claim to be any manner of expert, Vinar believed that she had a rare and unusual talent. Her harp was lost, but the talent must still remain. And tonight, so Rogan Kendarson had told him, a local harpist was to be among the musicians at the festivities. . . .

A shout from across the square and a sputter of applause

turned heads suddenly, and Vinar looked along with the rest in the direction of the barn. A thin, vigorous-looking man had climbed up onto the wagon and was calling for quiet; one or two good-natured catcalls greeted him, then a cheer went up as he announced the first dance. A fiddler, two pipers, and a girl with a borran-drum scrambled up beside him, and couples moved into the cleared arena to form up for "Sweethearts A-Courting."

As the music began Vinar laid a hand over Indigo's and grinned. "You want to dance?"

She returned his smile, but warily and with the uncertainty that had become all too familiar. "I don't know the steps."

"No more do I know them! But we get by, ya?"

"Well ..." Then her blue-violet gaze slid aside. "Not this one, Vinar. Perhaps later."

"All right, whatever you want." He hid his disappointment. "Better to listen to the music for a while, eh? See if these players are any good."

She nodded, seemingly relieved to feel that he wasn't going to press her, and Vinar refilled their cups as they settled back to watch. The dance was simple and strenuous, the musicians certainly lively and competent if nothing exceptional, and when the first set was over there were cries for long-standing favorites. The impromptu band obligingly swung into "The Cuckold's Secret," "Plowing the Furrow," and several others whose names Vinar couldn't catch; then the crowd yelled for "Pigs in the Orchard," a wild jig in which every measure ended with two lines of dancers dropping to all fours, grunting and snorting and squealing as they pretended to snuffle up windfallen apples. Vinar, who had never seen this dance before, was almost helpless with laughter, and with another cup of apple wine inside her, Indigo too shook with mirth. When the hilarity finally ended to a storm of cheering and renewed pig noises from the audience, Vinar got to his feet and grabbed Indigo's hands.

"This is no good," he declared firmly. "I can't sit and watch—I got to dance, and you with me!"

From atop the wagon the thin caller was announcing "The Handsome Maid's Fancy," in which the women chose and changed their partners and no man dared argue the choice. As Indigo began a little reluctantly to rise, a girl with black hair and enticing eyes, who had been watching Vinar for some while, glided to their table and held out her arms.

"I choose you!" She gave Indigo a mischievous grin to show that there was no malice in the demand. Vinar hesitated, but Indigo was already smiling back at the girl and retaking her seat, leaving him with little choice. The girl towed him away into the melee of dancers, and as the music began Indigo watched the two of them. They were an ill-matched pair, Vinar towering over the girl's small, slight frame, and he certainly wasn't the most accomplished of dancers. But on an occasion like this no one cared for elegance or accuracy of step; sheer fun was all that mattered. The music was lively and Indigo's foot tapped in time, the fingers of one hand unconsciously drumming an accompanying rhythm on her knee. She shouldn't have dampened Vinar's spirits by her reluctance to dance, she thought; it was unkind and unfair when all he wanted was to make her happy. When this dance was over she'd make it up to him, join in with a will and dance all night if that was what he wanted. He was such a good man, so loving and solicitous, and for the hundredth time she wished anguishedly that she could reawaken the feelings she believed she had had for him.

She liked him, respected him, was fond of him . . . but her emotions were like those she might have for a brother, not a lover and future husband. Vinar understood, he said, and he had promised her that things would change in time. But Indigo wasn't yet convinced. If only she could remember *something*. . . .

And then, for an instant, she did.

The tune of the dance had no words, but suddenly words were in her mind, slipping so easily into the music's pattern and rhythm that she almost sang them aloud before she could stop herself.

Everyone, everyone, play and sing: Join with us in the merry ring!

No, she thought, no, it wasn't quite accurate. The tune was wrong, and the words—not *everyone* but a name, someone's name. Fe . . . but it wouldn't come. Fen . . .

"Ahh!" Indigo started violently as for one fleeting moment the name came, flashed through her mind, vanished. Her elbow knocked her tankard and apple wine flooded across the table, splashing her and spilling over an old man on the bench beside her.

"I'm sorry . . . Oh, I'm so sorry. Your clothes—" Shocked and shaken, Indigo stumbled over her words as she tried to apologize.

"That's nothing that won't dry off," the old man assured her, then gave her a shrewd, curious look. "You all right, lass?"

"Yes. Yes, thank you, I . . . something must have made me jump. . . ."

"Horsefly, like as not," another granfer on the bench opined sagely. "Proper nuisance at this season. I've been bit more times than I can count, and some in places I wouldn't care to show even to my old woman!" He grinned, displaying three yellow teeth in shriveled gums.

There was general laughter and Indigo's further efforts to apologize were waved good-naturedly away. Jansa came out with a cloth to mop up the worst of the spilled wine, and Indigo asked for a fresh jug to be brought and shared

out. The accident had diffused her shock, for which she
was thankful, but it had also driven the momentary
glimpse of memory back into hiding and try as she might
she couldn't recall the name that had so nearly come to
her. Unnerved and feeling a little queasy, she pushed away
her thoughts and forced herself to concentrate on more immediate matters. "The Handsome Maid's Fancy" was
coming to an end; Vinar bowed to his partner, then turned
and cleaved determinedly through the crowd toward the
bench as the band struck up "Green the Willows Green."
Hands on hips he planted himself squarely in front of Indigo and grinned.

"Come on," he said. "I don't want no other girls. I'm
going to dance with my Indigo, or not with anyone!" -

Indigo stood up. Dear Vinar. She could learn to love
him. She *could*.

She gave him the most radiant smile she'd ever be-
stowed on him as she let him lead her out to join the
dancers.

It was nearly midnight by the time the last diehards finally
admitted defeat and allowed the weary musicians to rest.
But the night's revels were by no means over. Everyone in
the square, it seemed, had brought bags or baskets of food,
and soon bread, cheese, fruit, pies, pasties, and heavy-cake
were being shared about while Rogan Kendarson and his
elder son rolled out a new barrel of beer and announced
that all could help themselves. When the impromptu feast
had been eaten, a few revelers left and a few more fell
asleep where they sat, but the rest, fortified and in no
mood for bed yet, called for more music and for songs to
sing. This was what Vinar had been waiting for, and his
pulse quickened as he saw several new musicians moving
toward the stage-wagon, among them a young man with a
small lap-harp under his arm.

"Hey, Indigo." He nudged her. "Look. Rogan told me they got a harp player. I'll bet he's not half so good as you."

Mellow in the wake of so much dancing and food, Indigo peered through half-closed eyes, then smiled. "I wouldn't dream of taking your money!" Time and again he'd told her how she had played for the crew onboard ship, but his praise was so fulsome that she was certain he must be exaggerating. All the same she flexed her fingers, as though plucking at invisible strings. *Was* there an instinct in her hands, a skill that hadn't vanished along with all the other memories? Her fingers had old calluses, suggesting that she'd played often, but her harp was lost and—as with so much else—she had only Vinar's word that she had ever been a competent, let alone talented, player.

Nonetheless she leaned forward, watching intently as the harpist and a reed-pipe player took places together on the wagon. There was a brief burst of applause, then the pair swung into a lively, lilting air. The harpist was good, Indigo thought; at least he seemed so to her, though now she knew no standard by which to judge. Better, anyway, than the pipe player, who produced more than one sour note and fumbled a little, though no one seemed to notice or mind. When the air was done the duo played a song that the townsfolk seemed to know, and the sound of their massed voice rising on the quiet night air was oddly moving. Vinar, stealing a covert glance at Indigo, saw a telltale shimmer in her eyes. Whether it was simply the singing that touched her or whether the song itself was tugging at something forgotten, he didn't know, but it saddened him while at the same time it gave him hope. The song ended, and as the crowd called for more Vinar leaned toward the end of the bench, where Jansa stood in the tavern doorway.

"Indigo plays the harp, too," he confided in a whisper. "And she sings. Got a lovely voice."

Jansa knew Indigo's story, knew what she and Vinar were searching for, and understood the big Scorvan's motive at once. She leaned down to put her face on a level with his and murmured, "Then why don't we persuade her to play? New talent's always welcomed at these gatherings, and who knows what mightn't come of it? It could help to remind her. Or there could even be someone in the crowd who'll recognize a face and a voice."

Vinar gave her a grateful look. "That's just what I been thinking."

She nodded. "Leave it to me, then. I'll have a word in the right ear and we'll surprise her; Kess won't mind lending his harp." She paused. "But if I were you I'd see she has another tankard or two first, or you won't get her to agree."

Vinar took that sound advice, and Indigo was too engrossed in the music and singing to notice when he filled her cup twice more. She was relaxing in a way she'd not done since the shipwreck, worry and confusion and unhappiness fading away under the soothing influence of the wine, and her mind was becoming pleasantly fuddled. So much so, in fact, that when she found Jansa standing before her and asking her if she'd oblige the company with a song, she only stared at the woman in blank incomprehension.

"A song . . . ?"

"That's right. Vinar tells us you're a fine harpist and splendid singer." Jansa carefully ignored Vinar's eagerly prompting nod as she added the white lie, "And it's tradition here that no one with a musical skill is allowed to stay silent at one of our gatherings."

"But I can't play!" Indigo protested in dismay. "Or if I

could, I've forgotten how and forgotten all the songs I ever knew!"

"No you haven't," Vinar put in. "I taught you two, these last days since we left Ranna." He grinned at Jansa. "We been singing them on the road, her and me together."

Jansa grinned back. "Well then, there's no excuse! Come on, Indigo; you'll not be allowed to disappoint us."

Indigo began to realize that she was trapped and she made one last desperate effort. "But if I can't play, if I've forgotten—"

Jansa swept this aside before she could finish. "You're afraid to make a fool of yourself? Oh, nonsense! Who'd know or care even if you did?" She reached out and caught at Indigo's hand, pulling her to her feet. "Come along, and no more argument!"

She wouldn't be allowed to escape, Indigo realized, and she turned to Vinar in appeal. "You'll have to sing with me!"

"All right, I do that. Both of us together, eh?" His smile grew broader still. "Both of us together."

As she walked beside Vinar to the wagon, with the crowd's curious eyes following their progress, Indigo couldn't shake off the feeling that the whole scene about her was unreal. The harp player, Kess, was waiting and handed over his instrument with an encouraging grin as she climbed up. Settling herself on the wagon's bench Indigo let her hands run lightly over the wood of the harp. Was it well made, properly tuned? She didn't know. But she felt a sense of familiarity, and when she sat down on the wagon bench the harp seemed to settle into her lap of its own accord. She touched a string; it resonated and it was the note she had expected. So far, so good.

Below in the audience someone cleared his throat noisily, and looking down from her vantage point Indigo realized that people were growing tired of waiting. Hastily she nodded to Vinar and, seeing that they were about to begin, the audience gave them a ripple of polite applause.

Indigo touched the harp strings and, a little to her own surprise, began to play.

"It was charming, quite charming!" Jansa beamed as she placed two brimming tankards on the table. "You both have splendid voices; they weave together so well. And Indigo, Vinar was right—you're a very fine harpist indeed!"

The night's celebration was finally over, and the crowd, drunk with beer and wine and happy tiredness, had woven their unsteady ways home from the silent square. Officially the tavern had closed its doors an hour ago, but Vinar and Indigo had insisted on helping their hosts to clear away and wash the piles of mugs and plates left from the revel, and in return Jansa had insisted they should all have a last drink together before seeking their respective beds. The fire in the big ingle was banked down, and with only two lamps to light the taproom the atmosphere was pleasantly soporific.

"I've not heard that first song before," Rogan said as he emerged from behind the counter and joined the others at their table. "Is it a Scorvan ballad, Vinar?"

"Ya," Vinar said. "Scorvan sailors' song. My pa taught it to me and now I teach it to Indigo."

There was an odd edge to Vinar's mood, but no one seemed to have noticed it. Rogan continued, "We all knew the second one, mind. I reckon the singing nearly lifted up the sky when everyone joined in the choruses."

"Ya, well, I teach Indigo that one, too. It was one she used to sing on ship, till . . . well, till what happened." Vinar took a long pull from his tankard, then stared into it as though looking for something that wasn't there.

Indigo touched his arm lightly. "Is something wrong, Vinar?"

"Huh? No, no; nothing wrong. It's been a good night, a *good* night."

She wasn't entirely convinced but she was also too tired to press him. "Well," she said, rising, "if you'll all excuse me, I'm for bed." She glanced toward the window. "The moon's long gone. It must be nearly dawn."

"Another hour or two yet." Jansa smiled at her. "But don't worry, we'll see you're not disturbed until you choose to wake. Good night, Indigo. And thank you again."

There was silence for a few minutes after she had gone. Rogan was beginning to nod sleepily and Jansa stifled a yawn. Then, unexpectedly, Vinar said, "She used to be better than that. Much better."

Rogan started at the sound of the voice, raising his head, and Jansa looked at Vinar curiously. "Better?"

"Ya. At the harp."

"But her playing was—"

"Was good, I know. Good enough to please anyone, maybe even good enough for kings' halls. But before the wreck, before she hit her head, she was *better*. Like"— Vinar fumbled for the right word in a language with which he still wasn't at ease, his hands making gestures in the air—"like there was—*magic* in her fingers." He snorted, suddenly self-conscious, and his blue gaze shifted quickly between his two companions. "You think I'm some kind of mad numskull, saying things like that—"

"No," Jansa told him. "No, we don't." A smile tugged at one side of her mouth. "Or if you are, then so are we and everyone else in the Southern Isles. We believe in magic, Vinar, surely enough. And there can be magic in music, though it's a rare thing. Some of the old bards had the gift; some maybe still have. So we don't disbelieve you, Vinar." She sighed. "If only something had come of her playing tonight. If someone had recognized her face, or her voice . . ."

"They'd have known her playing before," Vinar said unequivocally. "They'd not have forgotten. No one could."

Rogan and Jansa exchanged a glance. Even making allowances for his obvious bias, Vinar could well be right, and if he was, that made the conundrum of Indigo's past stranger still. A woman whose name was the color of mourning, who had the witch-talent, the bard-gift . . . such a one would surely be known and remembered in the Southern Isles. And if she had changed her name through grief at some great tragedy, what might that tragedy have been? There had been no plagues, no epidemics, for many years; and even had the sorrow been a lesser thing, involving only one clan or family, then the pack-traders and balladeers and other itinerants who traveled the roads for their living would have carried and spread the tale as they did the smallest snippets of news and gossip. Yet they'd known nothing at Amberland, nothing in Ranna, nothing in any of the towns and villages and settlements through which Indigo and Vinar had passed in eighteen days of searching. It was uncanny, Jansa thought.

She said, speaking softly as though afraid that Indigo might hear from her room on the upper floor, "Have you thought to consult the forest witches, Vinar?"

"Witches?" Vinar looked blank.

"Yes. They have ways—their own ways—of seeking what is lost. Even if they haven't the power to restore Indigo's memory, they might have means of helping you to find her kinfolk."

Vinar frowned. "Is a good idea, perhaps. But how to find them? I don't know where to begin."

She smiled softly. "That needn't trouble you. We can set you on the right path; and anyway, if Indigo has the gift you believe her to have, there's every chance that the witches will be seeking you even as you seek them. They know and care for their own." She stood up, gathering their four mugs with a clink that seemed loud in the quiet of the taproom. "For now, though, I think we're all too tired to think or talk further. Let's go to our beds and consider what's best again in the morning."

She pulled Rogan to his feet and they stood together, arms about each other in a warm, affectionate way that made Vinar ache wordlessly inside. He nodded. "Ya. Ya, you're right. Think again in the morning." He made a bow, the jerky, stiltedly courteous bow peculiar to Scorva. "You're both very kind; I thank you. And it was a good revel!"

Climbing to his small room in the tavern's eaves, Vinar paused on the landing outside Indigo's door. There was no sound from within, and the ache came back as he tried not to picture her asleep in her solitary bed. He thought, as he had thought for several nights past, that if he had gone to her she would not have refused him; that she would have welcomed him, cleaved to him gladly, a friend and a lover to take away loneliness and give comfort and security. But Vinar couldn't do it, for it simply wasn't his way. Only when all was proper and as it should be, only when he had her unstinting love and they both had been granted her kinsmen's blessing, could he let himself be to her what he so yearned to be. Until then—and the day *would* come—he would care for her and protect her and champion her and be her friend. But nothing more. For her sake, and for his own.

Rogan and Jansa were talking softly below as they prepared to follow him up the creaking wooden ladder, their voices like the faint hum of bees in a clover field. Vinar touched his fingers to his lips and blew a kiss, silent but heartfelt, toward the room where his love slept and tiptoed away.

A short way from the edge of the village square, on the farmland side where there were no houses but only fields, a young man who had made good time on the long walk from Ranna was trying to find a place to sleep in the hedgerow that followed the winding course of the rough road. He'd entered the square to find it unlit and deserted, even the tavern shuttered, and though he had money in his pocket he wasn't arrogant enough to hammer on the door and brave the wrath of the landlord at such an uncivilized hour. Fool he was to have tried to cover the distance between this town and the last in the space of an evening, fool and optimist; anyone with a grain of sense would have realized that he'd arrive too late to be housed anywhere. Still, dawn wasn't far away, and from the look of the sky the weather was set fair, so he retraced his steps along the road and the hedgerow until he found a likely elder tree under which the grass grew thick and lush and promised some comfort. Giving thanks to the Earth Mother that the night was warm, he unrolled his one thin blanket and crawled, yawning, into a makeshift bed, content to snatch what sleep he could before the sun roused him.

And as he fell asleep, the young would-be sailor who carried Captain Brek's message began to dream an unusual and peculiarly vivid dream.

·CHAPTER·VII·

Niahrin had seen to it that Grimya was sleeping and was thankful she'd taken the precaution, for in her present condition she couldn't have faced the prospect of trying to explain to the wolf the thing she had done and why it had reduced her to such a state of shivering, enfeebled wretchedness.

She had stopped being sick but only just, though there was nothing left in her stomach and the last five minutes had been a torment of dry, fruitless retching until at last she was able to bring the spasms under control. Rising from her knees proved difficult; her body resisted her efforts to move and she wanted only to lie down in the grass where she was and go to sleep. But training and habit made her resist the weariness and climb painfully to her feet. She had expected this and had prepared for it; there was a restorative brew waiting for her that would soon set her to rights. And her work wasn't finished yet.

She limped painfully back into the cottage, shutting the door behind her, shutting out the night. Grimya was a dark, immobile shape in the dim light of the banked down fire. She was snoring gently.

The restorative stood in a small, lidded cup beside the fire and was still warm. Niahrin drank it, then crouched down by the hearth, rubbing her upper arms vigorously and shivering as the embers' heat started to warm skin chilled by the night air. For a while she avoided turning her head to look at the curtain that hid the barred inner door, but at length, knowing that she must face it one more time before all could be completed, she straightened and moved reluctantly but purposefully toward it. She'd left another candle ready; lighting this she pushed aside the curtain, lifted the bar, and stepped quietly into the room beyond.

Shadows danced at her from the corners, skittering across the bare walls. The room felt unnaturally cold and Niahrin fancied she could hear a faint half-singing half-buzzing sound, like insects swarming a long way off. The weaving loom was still and silent, a darker shape in darkness; but where before there had been only its bare skeleton, now a dim confusion of colors showed on the frame.

Niahrin took a deep breath to steady her quavering heart and, holding the candle high, stepped forward. For a moment as she looked down terrible memories attacked her; shuttles flying, the loom creaking and rocking as though it were a cage in which some fearsome animal thrashed and fought to escape, her own hands pulling and twining and working, her feet a blur on the treadles as her maimed eye stared madly at nothing and the images came rushing and crowding and screaming at her. And all the while praying, crying aloud to the Earth Mother to protect her from the enormity of the power she'd summoned, to grant her understanding, and, above all, to preserve her sanity.

It had been over very suddenly. She didn't know what she'd created; she never did, was never able to look until later when the awful aftermath had passed and her mind and body were back under her own control. The room seemed to whirl about her, all coordination had fled, and she felt the first upheaval in her stomach as she flailed blindly away from the weaving-stool and stumbled through the door, through the other room, out into the garden just in time.

Now the sickness was gone and it was time to look at her handiwork. She was astonished, and more than a little unnerved, to see how much she had woven. The tapestry was more than an arm's length from top to bottom and spanned the entire width of the loom. . . . How much time had passed, and for how long had she been in the grip of the magic? The moon had set and she had only her instinct to guide her; an instinct that, wrongly it seemed, told her that there were still several hours to go before dawn. Unless the power had been far greater than she'd thought possible, and her hands had worked at a speed beyond imagining. . . .

She moved closer, pushing the stool aside, and peered more closely at what she had made. The candlelight was dim, muting and dulling the colors, and the unsteady flame gave the tiny pictures an uncanny semblance of life, so that they seemed to move of their own accord. Niahrin shook her head and squeezed her eyes shut briefly before looking again.

The scene in the tapestry was dominated by a great, sprawling bulk of stone, with the full moon hanging directly above its central tower. A crimson sun with an angry and bitter face at its heart was setting in the west, while in the east another sun rose, pale and spectral. It, too, had a face, but a cloud obscured the mouth and it was impossible to judge whether its expression was happy or sorrowful, for its eyes were blank and blind. Minute figures, stylized and strange but finely detailed, paraded across this eerie landscape, some on horseback, others walking. They went one by one and two by two toward the gates of the great stone fortress, and the gates themselves were fashioned in the form of a great harp, its strings parting to admit the vanguard of the procession. In the vanguard was a man mounted on a chestnut horse, and from the one glimpse she had had of him in the woods Niahrin recognized the dark brown hair and beard of Ryen Cathalson Ryenson, King of the Southern Isles. He was holding up a hand as though in rejection, while behind him the figure of a weeping woman went in chains between two hooded guards. One look at the woman and Niahrin felt her spine prickle, for this tiny figure, too, was familiar—Brythere, King Ryen's consort and queen. And behind Brythere came others. An old man leaning heavily on a staff, his face muffled from sight. A younger man, big and fair and cheerful, who looked as though he were singing. A child with silver hair, running hand in hand with a forest sprite who seemed to be a curious blend of human and tree. And ... again Niahrin felt the prickling sensation, for the next two figures were that of a big, brindle-gray dog—or wolf—and a woman with a patch over one eye.

So, then; the message that the magic had brought her was clear enough. Niahrin had never seen Carn Caille, the royal stronghold, but she had heard enough travelers' tales to have a clear picture of it in her mind's eyes, and this image in the tapestry could be no other place. She knew what she must do. But as to what the deed would lead to, what it portended ... Niahrin twitched with a cold, eerie shudder, for she knew certain other things now, things she should not have known, and in revealing them to her the magic had laid a burden on her shoulders that she was reluctant to accept. She didn't understand its significance, but she was afraid of it. The magic was leading her toward doors that had been barred and bolted for too long to be opened again in safety now; not doors in her own life but in the lives of others. To meddle was unwise, possibly dangerous. She hadn't the *right*—

A voice said softly: *You are wrong, granddaughter. You have not merely the right but the duty. The magic has told you that. Will you dare to turn away?*

"Granmer—?" Niahrin started like a hare surprised by hounds and spun round as though expecting to see a figure in the shadows of the doorway behind her, eyes cold and bright, mouth smiling without the smallest hint of laughter. But her grandmother was not there. The woman she had loved and feared and whose powers she had inherited, the kind and the cruel together, was only a ghost in her mind. Niahrin often heard Granmer speaking to her across the years, though whether her voice was truly a visitation from beyond death or only the echoes of memory, she didn't know. But Granmer's voice and the magic's compulsion said the same: She couldn't escape her responsibility. She couldn't deny the power and what it told her to do.

The candle guttered as she exhaled a long sigh, and her breath almost extinguished the flame. Niahrin lowered the candle and quietly withdrew from the room, barring the door once more and letting the curtain fall back into place. Tomorrow she would take the tapestry from the loom and fold it away, for it had told her all it had to tell. Now though she had just one more small magic to perform, and that an easy and gentle magic, then she could sleep.

She sat down by the hearth and put a fresh log from her basket on the fire. Then she reached to a second, smaller basket, and from it carefully selected a handful of twigs. Apple first; always there must be apple to bring blessing and goodwill for her work. Then holly, to give strength to the spell, and lastly rowan and willow and sweetbriar, creators and deliverers of dreams. She formed the twigs into a little star, which she dusted with a fine aromatic powder. Then as the new log began to sizzle she laid the star in the fire's heart.

Blue-green flames flickered from the star and a sweet, heady scent wafted into the room. Niahrin smiled and closed her good eye. Hands clasped, she began to rock gently back and forth, and as she rocked she sang a song without words, its notes like the sound of water flowing. There was no pain in this magic, no harshness and no sacrifice of strength; indeed, it would buoy her and calm her and ready her for peaceful rest. And somewhere, if all was well, someone would dream an important dream tonight.

Grimya said reproachfully, "You drugged me. You gave me something to make me sleep." She blinked up at Niahrin uncertainly. "Why did you do that? Don't you trr-ust me?"

"Oh, my dear." Niahrin dropped to her knees beside the wolf's bed and stroked her drooping ears. "Of course I trust you, there's no question of it. But I didn't want to involve you in what I was doing. It wouldn't have been fair."

"I knew that s ... omething had happened." Grimya rose cautiously to her feet; the splint was off now and she was able to take short, unsteady walks about the room, though Niahrin had sternly forbidden her to put her injured leg to the floor. "I smelled it as soon as I woke, like smoke in the air."

"I thought you might." Grimya's talents, Niahrin suspected, ran to more than simply the ability to speak human languages. She paused, then went on. "Grimya, I have learned certain things that mean that you and I must change our plans. Instead of waiting for your friend Indigo to come here to us, we must go in search of her."

Grimya's eyes lit eagerly—then her ears drooped once more. "But I c-cannot walk properly yet!"

"You shan't need to." The means of transport she had in mind would make the journey slow and cumbersome, Niahrin thought, but there was no help for it. The magic had told her what must be done and the journey couldn't wait. "A forester friend of mine has the very thing, and I can repay him in kind so there'll be no trouble over the borrowing of it. I'll spend today preparing what we need, then visit him tomorrow, and we may start the day after."

Grimya's plumed tail began to wag. "Then," she said, "you know where Indigo is? You know where we will *f . . . ind* her?"

"I know where she will go." Where she *must* go, the witch added silently to herself, for even without her message to act as a goad Indigo would be drawn there; the magic had made that clear. "We will find her at Carn Caille."

The wolf froze. "Carn Caille . . . ?"

"Yes. Why, my dear, what's the matter? I know it's the king's own citadel, but there's nothing to fear from it."

But there was, Grimya thought, there *was*. Once, Carn Caille had been Indigo's home. It was a place of ghosts— and perhaps of something far worse.

She looked at the witch and licked her own jaws nervously. "I hh-ave never been to Carn Caille," she said slowly. "I . . . do not know if I want to go there now."

Niahrin, to the wolf's relief, mistook the reason for her unease. "It isn't so forbidding a place as you fear, Grimya; indeed, from what I hear, the king makes his subjects welcome and holds public court for several days in each month." She smiled reassuringly. "I've never been there either, so it will be an adventure for us both, won't it?"

Grimya didn't argue, but as Niahrin turned away and
began to prepare breakfast for them both she moved a few
awkward steps then lay down again, her mind troubled.
Carn Caille. Indigo had told her so many stories of it, but
the tales, and Indigo's memories, were far in the past now.
What did she hope to find there, and—this question was
far more disturbing—what dark echoes from the past
might be uncovered? Niahrin knew only a small part of
the truth about Indigo, and Grimya dared tell her no more.
But the wolf felt a growing sense of dread deep within her.
She was more afraid of Carn Caille than of anything she
and Indigo had encountered in their long years together.
For in Carn Caille, she believed, the last of seven demons
was waiting.

And this last demon would be the worst of all.

When she opened the tavern's front door to a persistent
knocking halfway through the morning, Jansa found a
stranger standing on the threshold. He was a young man,
not a beggar but not well-to-do either; he carried a small
pack on his back and looked as though he'd emerged only
minutes ago from the depths of a hedge or hayrick. There
were green and brown stains on his clothes, grass and
leaves in his hair, and his eyes were heavy-lidded. But he
made a good try at a courteous bow and said, "Morning to
you, ma'am. I wonder if—"

Jansa thought she had his measure and interrupted,
though pleasantly. "If you're selling wares, peddler, I'd
best warn you now that I'm not buying this month. But
come you in anyway. I'll at least give you a piece of bread
and a mug of beer, for you look as if you've had no breakfast." Her mouth twitched in a smile. "If you don't mind
my saying so, you also look as though you slept with the
foxes and weasels last night."

He returned her grin ruefully. "I did, ma'am! I arrived

too late to seek a room anywhere, so I made the best I could of it in the hedgerow just outside of the village, along the road there." He paused. "But I'm not a peddler, ma'am. I'm a messenger, come from Captain Brek at Ranna Port." He waited as though hoping for a reaction, but Jansa looked blank. Ah, well; no reason why he should be luckier here than anywhere else.

"Who's your message for?" Jansa asked, leading the way into the taproom. She indicated for him to sit down and went behind the counter to draw a mug of beer. "Someone here in the village?"

"Well . . . that I don't rightly know. Captain Brek says they were traveling this way, but I can't tell where they might be by now. Two people together, a man and a woman; betrothed they are, the captain says, and good friends of his. He's my master, you see; and if I find the ones he's seeking, he's promised me work on the crew of a—"

"A betrothed couple?" Jansa had stopped and was staring at him as she suddenly realized the significance of Brek's rank, if not his name.

"Yes, ma'am. A big, yellow-haired man from Scorva, and a woman with the name of Indigo."

Jansa's expression changed as though the sun had suddenly lit up the room. "Vinar and Indigo!"

The young man's face lit eagerly, too. "You know of them, ma'am? They've been here?"

"Better than that." Jansa grinned broadly. "They're asleep in their rooms upstairs this very minute!" With quick energy she finished filling the mug, skimmed round the counter, and set it down on the table before him. "Drink up, lad, with the tavern's compliments. I'll go and wake them this minute, and you can see them for yourself!"

* * *

"Grimya's *alive*?" Vinar's eyes widened with a blend of astonishment and delight.

"Alive and well, sir, so Captain Brek told me to say—though he's not seen the creature for himself, you understand."

"Indigo, you hear that?" Vinar turned delightedly to the woman at his side, who so far had sat smiling but saying little. "Grimya's alive!" Then he saw her expression, the puzzlement in her look, and his shoulders sagged. "Ya, well, like the captain told you, she can't remember."

"I'm sorry," Indigo said. "It means nothing to me, Vinar. It means nothing at all."

The youth watched her a little furtively, saddened and also embarrassed by her affliction. He felt uncomfortable in her presence; partly, he knew, because of her name, which to an Isler was like a dark aura hovering about her, but also for a less definable reason that he didn't want to probe.

Vinar patted Indigo's hand, soothingly but a little awkwardly. "Well then, it's not to worry about for now. Maybe this will be what you need, seeing Grimya. Maybe she'll bring the memory back where I can't—after all, you known her longer than you known me!" He grinned ruefully, easing the tension in the taproom a little, then looked at the young man again. "So, where is Grimya? Where we have to go to find her?"

"She's waiting for you, so the captain told me, at—" There was a hesitation, so brief that neither Indigo nor Vinar noticed it, then the young man finished, "At Carn Caille."

"Carn Caille?" Vinar was stunned. "But—" He rummaged in his mind, convinced that what he thought he knew of the Southern Isles must somehow be awry. "But I thought that was—"

"It's the king's own citadel." Jansa, who was sweeping the floor and had overheard much of the conversation, stopped with her broom in midair and stared curiously at the messenger. "Are you sure that's right, lad? Are you *sure* it's what your captain said?"

For a brief moment the boy's certainty wavered and he almost, but not quite, seemed to recall that Captain Brek had given him another instruction entirely. But then the suspicion fled. Carn Caille, the captain had told him, there was no doubt of it. And the dream he'd had last night, the dream Niahrin had sent to all who were seeking Indigo, stayed safely hidden in the unconscious depths of his mind.

"It was Carn Caille right enough," he said confidently. "The word came from one of the forest wise-women in that part, and they're never wrong."

"That's true." Jansa's voice carried a note of awe. "But in the king's own household . . . it's astonishing!"

Vinar suddenly laughed aloud, startling them all. "Trust Grimya to land on all her four feet!" he said, then abruptly his expression changed to a frown. "But one thing don't fit. How do they know it *is* Grimya? Lot of wolves in the Southern Isles, same as in Scorva, and most of 'em look alike."

The young man shrugged. He was beginning to feel out of his depth with all this talk of wisecraft and the king. "Maybe the witches just know," he said.

"They would," Jansa put in. "You needn't fear they're wrong, Vinar; it's quite within their powers to have found out where your pet wolf came from and that she belongs to a human owner. What truly astonishes me is how she fetched up so far from Amberland. There's more of a tale here than any of us knows as yet; I'd take a wager on that."

"Ya. Ya, I think you're right." Vinar nodded soberly.

His eyes grew thoughtful and a cautiously eager light began to appear in them. "And that might mean something else, eh? That might mean someone at this Carn Caille knows about Indigo's kin. Maybe even someone there *is* Indigo's kin." He looked up quickly, hopefully at Jansa. "You think that's possible?"

"It could be, Vinar. Yes, I believe it could."

During this exchange Indigo had said nothing more, but now she reached out and laid a hand over Vinar's. "I'm almost afraid, Vinar," she said quietly. "Afraid to raise my hopes, in case . . ."

"I know. I understand." He moved as though to touch his lips to hers, then hesitated and withdrew, as he always did. Since her memory loss, Indigo thought, he had never once kissed her; though before, surely, it must have been different. And now he told her she had had a pet, a tame wolf, whom she'd loved almost as dearly as she'd loved him. Though he couldn't comprehend it, that knowledge hurt her even more than did the gulf between herself and the man to whom she was betrothed.

"I want to go there," she said suddenly. "I want to go to Carn Caille. Maybe there *will* be someone there who can help me. And maybe if I see this wolf, this—Grimya?—I might remember her. It's a slender chance, I know, but—oh, Vinar, if it *should* work—"

Vinar's fingers gripped hers tightly, but he was looking down at the table, not meeting her gaze. He'd counted on a little more time. Time in which her emotions might stir and awaken, and in which he might come to feel more sure of her. But he couldn't deny her this. He didn't want to deny her; he wanted above all else to make her happy, for that was a part of his love and perhaps the most precious part of all.

"Ya," he said, and with a small effort threw off the

doubt and the fear, turning at last to smile warmly at her. "Ya, we go. In fact we leave today, soon as we can be ready, eh?" He saw her face light up and it rewarded him. "We go and find Grimya, and while we're about it we see the king and tell him our travelers' tales! Who knows— maybe we catch two fish on one hook?"

•CHAPTER•VIII•

Everyone who slept within earshot of the round tower in the northern wing of Carn Caille was woken by the screams from the queen's bedchamber, and King Ryen emerged from his own apartments to find servants already hastening toward the tower's topmost floor. Ryen strode to the staircase, calling the agitated attendants back in a sharp, angry tone, and with only one man-at-arms behind him ran up the steps to his wife's door.

As he approached it, the door opened and a tall, sallow woman wearing a night shift with a woolen shawl over it came out. Ketrin, who was the queen's personal servant, saw Ryen and made a stiff bow.

"There's no alarm, sir." Her voice had the lilting coastal accent, but with a hard edge. "The queen has had a bad dream, nothing more."

"Again?" Though he tried to quell it Ryen felt the old

irritation and resentment rising, and it showed in his tone. "Is anyone with her? You haven't left her alone?"

"Her Grace is there, sir. She came straight away and said she would see for the queen herself."

Ryen muttered something under his breath and pushed past her into the room.

One candle glowed in the round chamber, illuminating the pale figure of Queen Brythere sitting bolt upright in the great, curtained bed. At the sound of his footsteps she looked up distractedly, and the Dowager Queen Moragh, Ryen's mother, turned where she sat on the bed's edge and gave her son a disapproving frown.

"Quietly, Ryen; there's no call to come stampeding into the room like a bull."

Ryen ignored the reprimand. "Ketrin says she's had another nightmare."

"So she has, but you won't make matters any better by addressing me in that tone, or by not addressing Brythere at all." Moragh's blue-gray gaze raked him as she spoke then slid expressively toward the young woman in the bed, and Ryen's anger withered.

"I'm sorry. I'm sorry—it was the surprise of being woken, the fear that—" He swallowed the rest of what he'd been about to say and approached the bed, reaching out both hands toward his wife. Brythere looked at him, her face tear-blotched and her expression warily uncertain, and he said tiredly, "Forgive me, my heart, I didn't mean any unkindness." He sat down on the bed as Moragh moved to make room for him. "What was it? The same?"

Brythere nodded. "He was here." Her voice quavered. "He was *here*. Standing over me. He had a *knife*, and ... ." The words choked off in a sob.

"It seems he wasn't alone this time," Moragh said in an undertone. "When I came in she was babbling about an old woman standing at the bed-foot and goading him on."

Ryen looked keenly at her. "She used to dream about an old woman some years ago. When we were first wed, and Father was alive . . . but I thought that nightmare was a thing of the past."

"So did we all, but it appears we were wrong." Moragh nodded to Ketrin, who had followed the king back into the room, and the servant crossed soft-footedly to a side table, where she began to mix a draught. "She used to see the hag-figure by daylight, too; in the corridors sometimes—do you remember?—and once she went into hysterics because she swore the beldam was among the diners in the great hall. I hope and pray *that* isn't going to begin again."

Before Ryen could answer, Ketrin appeared at the bedside with a brimming cup in her hands. Moragh took it with a nod of thanks, then waved the servant away and turned to Brythere.

"Here, child. Drink this, drink it all. It's soothing and calming and will help you back to sleep."

Brythere's eyes widened. "I don't want it! If he should come back—"

"He shan't come back, for he was only a dream. He's long gone from Carn Caille, probably dead now and good riddance to him. He isn't here, and he can't possibly hurt you. Now." With the air of one used to being obeyed Moragh took a grip on her daughter-elect's arm, forcing her to be still. "Do as I tell you, and drink. I'll stay with you until morning and see that all is well, so you've nothing more to fear."

Cowed as she always was by the dowager's authority, Brythere reluctantly took the cup and began to sip at it. Ryen watched in silence for a few moments, then gave a sigh and rose to his feet.

"If there's nothing I can do . . ."

"A moment, Ryen." Moragh's eyes were still on

Brythere but she made a gesture that halted him. "I want to speak with you in private. It won't take long." She raised her voice. "Ketrin, watch over the queen and see she takes all the draught. I'll be but a minute or two."

Brythere seemed unwilling to look up as the two left the room, and she had no parting word for Ryen. Outside, the man-at-arms hovered; Moragh dismissed him and then, her aquiline face and severe pile of graying fair hair sharply shadowed in the light of a torch burning in its wall-bracket, turned to her son.

"Ryen, this can't go on. Something must be done, and done soon, or these dreams and obsessions of Brythere's are going to wreck both her own life and yours!"

Ryen turned his head away. "Mother, what *can* I do? I've tried every tack I can think of, but I'm as powerless as you are; probably more so, in fact, for I can't even get through to her anymore. You saw her just now—what influence could I possibly have on her?"

"A good deal more than you seem willing to exert," Moragh retorted acerbically. Then the quick flare of anger vanished and she sighed. "Oh, perhaps I do you an injustice, my son. Perhaps we were at fault, your father and I, for choosing her as a bride for you. Perhaps we should have allowed you to wait, as you wanted, and not pressed you to an early marriage. But there were so many other considerations, and Brythere seemed an ideal choice—"

"She was," Ryen interrupted helplessly. "She was everything I could have asked for in a wife. And I do love her, Mother. I *do*."

Moragh was tempted to say, "Do you?" but held her tongue. It was an old sore and one that she and her son had wrangled over on many unhappy occasions, but she was certain now that Ryen was as incapable as she was of comprehending why his marriage had gone so disastrously wrong. As for Brythere herself . . . Well, Moragh was honest enough to admit that she and her daughter-elect had nothing in common other than their ties to Ryen, but that didn't prejudice her judgment. She liked the girl well enough and made allowances for what she saw as frailties in her nature, and in the early days after the marriage they had been making progress, albeit slow and cautious, toward a kind of friendship. Until, that was, Brythere's strange fancies had begun and everything had started to go wrong.

Ryen clasped his own forearms and stared at the darkened stairwell. "It's this place," he said moodily. "Carn Caille. Even in the beginning Brythere was never happy here, and now she can hardly bear to be within its walls." He turned to stare at his mother almost challengingly. "She believes Carn Caille is haunted."

"Ryen. I've told you before—" Moragh started to say.

"No. No, Mother, I know what you've told me and I know what you think. But Brythere's fears are no different from the ones I used to have when I was a child. You remember as well as I do the nights you or old Lalty were obliged to sit up with me, trying to persuade me to go back to sleep in the face of the Goddess alone knows what terrors."

"But you were a *child*, and you grew out of your terrors as children do. Brythere isn't a babe anymore." Moragh paused, then: "Ryen, listen to me. You may not like what I'm about to say but I want you to take it to heart nonetheless. This must be stopped before it gets completely out of hand. Brythere must be made to understand what her folly is doing to herself and to you—and if she refuses to pull herself together of her own accord, she must be compelled."

"Compelled?" Ryen almost but not quite laughed, then his voice grew suddenly savage. "How should we do that, Mother? Are we to lock her in her bedchamber and have

Ketrin beat sense into her? Or perhaps I should have her put away in one sense or another and take a new and more compliant wife."

"Don't be ridiculous, Ryen; you know perfectly well I'm not suggesting anything of the sort. I mean, quite simply, that Brythere has created a web of fears and phantasms around herself and has become enmeshed in it to the exclusion of all else. She no longer attends the evening gatherings, no longer rides with you or takes her place at public audiences; she pleads to be excused from almost all of her duties, and because we are concerned for her well-being we have indulged her. Well, that must change. Our concern has gone too far and is doing more harm than good. As your consort Brythere has responsibilities; she should be obliged to meet those responsibilities instead of being allowed to languish in hiding like an invalid. She is *not* an invalid, she is a perfectly healthy young woman, and the way to make her realize that is to see that she spends more time in the real world and less in her private world of apparitions!"

Ryen sighed. Moragh was all but impossible to argue with under any circumstances, and in this he knew she was right. But it was hard, so hard. His mother might dismiss Brythere's terrors as nonsense, but they were real enough to Brythere. And there was something else, something that Ryen was reluctant to think about, let alone discuss with anyone else. One night, in the early days of their marriage when they had still shared one bed, Brythere had awoken screaming in the middle of the night. It had been only the second or third time such a thing had occurred, and as Ryen, bleary-eyed and shocked and by no means fully awake, had tried to comfort his sobbing wife, he saw—or thought he saw, for the image vanished in the next instant—a figure dimly outlined beside the bedpost. Cronelike, its sex indeterminable and its face hidden by the cowl of a long cloak, it held a withered hand before it in a menacing gesture, and clutched in that hand was a long-bladed knife.

Pushing the memory away as he always did, Ryen said heavily, "I don't know, Mother. Perhaps you're right. But things are so unsettled between us that I don't know if Brythere will even listen to me."

"She'll listen to me," Moragh replied in a tone that suggested Brythere would have no choice, then added before he could protest, "and of course I won't be cruel to her. Just firm. That's what she needs. In truth I think that's what you both need."

He looked away. "Must we go over that again?"

"I've no intention of dwelling on it, for there's nothing to be gained and we both need some sleep tonight." She began to move back toward Brythere's door. "But I may as well say this as think it. If you and Brythere were to have a child it would do more to heal your ills than anything I can hope to achieve. Yet until and unless some changes are made, there seems to be little hope of that ever coming to be."

A flush came to Ryen's face. "The wish for separate apartments was Brythere's, not mine."

"But you did nothing to dissuade her."

"Damn it, what *could* I have done? She was adamant! I would have been content to do my duty—"

"Your *duty*?" Moragh repeated, incredulous. "Is that all it would have been to you? For if that's so then there's little wonder Brythere chose as she did!" She put a hand to her face, pinching the bridge of her nose hard as though trying to ease a headache.

"Mother," Ryen said, "it isn't as simple as that. You know it isn't."

"Yes." Moragh nodded. "Yes, my son, I know." She let her hand fall to her side again. "But somehow an answer *must* be found, Ryen. You've been wed eight years now, and Brythere is already twenty-six. You don't have all the time in the world." She turned then, reached out to the doorlatch. "I think there's nothing more we can say to each other. Best go back to bed and sleep. You're to hold public court in the morning and you need to be fresh for that."

Ryen watched as she lifted the latch, then suddenly said, "Mother . . ."

Moragh looked back at him.

"Mother, I love Brythere. Maybe not so dearly as you loved Father, and he you, and I know that's been a disappointment to you. But I *do* love her, and I truly believe that the failing in our marriage isn't due to my want of trying!"

"Hush! Lower your voice or Brythere will hear."

"Oh, what does it matter? I'm saying nothing she doesn't already know as well as any of us!" But he did drop his voice almost to a whisper. "I *have* tried, Mother. I've tried to understand and I've tried to be patient. But there comes a point beyond which there's nothing more I can do, and when that point is reached I start to ask myself if it's worth trying any further."

Moragh stared at him. "Ryen, that is a terrible thing to say."

"Sweet Goddess, do you think I don't *know* that? But I can't work miracles! Brythere seems resolved to turn her face and her mind away and refuse to let me reach her. Well, so be it—if she doesn't want anything to do with me, then perhaps I should have nothing more to do with her!"

The dowager didn't answer him for a few moments but stood motionless, her brow creased in an unhappy frown. At last she looked up again. "Very well." Her voice was resigned and had a bitter edge. "If that is how you feel, then there *is* no more to say. I, too, have done my best, but it seems that's not enough for anyone. I'll wish you good night, Ryen."

She opened the door to Brythere's room. Candlelight spilled out, and in its glow Ryen glimpsed the figure of Ketrin by the queen's bed. The servant's expression was inscrutable. Then Moragh went in, and the light and the scene were cut off as the door closed behind her.

Ryen's man-at-arms was waiting at the foot of the spiral staircase, a discreet position where he would overhear nothing of the conversation above yet would be on hand in case of need. The king glanced once at him.

"Go to bed."

The man opened his mouth to wish his master a good night, but the salute was stillborn when he saw Ryen's expression. He bowed and walked quickly away. For a moment Ryen looked back at the tower's dark stairwell, and anger racked him as he thought of Brythere safe in his mother's well-intentioned but stern care. *He* should be at her side now, not Moragh, and in the old days, the early days, it would have been so. But that was before Brythere's terrors had begun, before fear had turned her laughter to shadows. He knew why she had rejected him. Not because he could not defend her from her dreams— though that was true enough—but because he was the king and she, as his queen, was bound to live with him at Carn Caille and so was trapped within the very walls that had given birth to her nightmares.

There was no sound from Brythere's tower now. Ryen waited a few moments, listening to the silence. Then he turned and moved slowly away in the direction of his own bedchamber. His face was as hard and blank as marble.

The gates of Carn Caille had been open since the early hours of the morning, but by midafternoon the great courtyard was still crowded while the greensward outside the fortress accommodated a further throng of people who had completed their business or who had come along only to see the fun and hope for a glimpse of the king.

Firstly from Jansa and later from other travelers encountered on the road, Vinar had learned that these public courts, held three or four days each month, were vastly popular with the people of the Southern Isles. The practice had been inaugurated by the old king, Cathal, and greatly expanded by Ryen, who had also done away with most of the formality usually associated with royal occasions. All his subjects, high or low, wealthy or poor, were welcomed and given the opportunity to petition the king on any matter, and the public courts were also a forum for the announcement of important news and any new edicts or laws.

Southern Islers needed little encouragement to turn any occasion into a fair, and King Ryen's innovations had brought a ready response. Along its last mile the road leading to the fortress was lined with peddlers selling everything from food and drink to children's toys, and the greensward was a chaotic carnival of vendors, hucksters, and entertainers, each with his own booth or wagon or small patch of ground. Business was very lively; to attend the public courts was a great fashion for rich and poor alike, and a pot-mender with whom Vinar had fallen into conversation on the road estimated that at least three-quarters of the crowd around Carn Caille had come today simply for the diversions to be had. With the long winter behind them and summer on the way, the pot-mender added cheerfully, the springtime court days were always the best.

Vinar's enjoyment of the spectacle was lessened, however, by a niggling worry about Indigo. She seemed cheerful enough now, laughing at a buffooner capering by with his beribboned stick, or pointing out a booth where a whole ox was succulently roasting, but two miles back on the road it had been a different story. As the gray stones of Carn Caille came in sight on the horizon, Indigo had stopped walking as suddenly and unexpectedly as though she'd slammed into an invisible wall. Perplexed, Vinar had looked at her and saw that her face was rigidly immobile, eyes staring fixedly at the distant gray towers, mouth open but motionless. Then, in a voice that seemed on the verge of cracking into hysteria, Indigo had said: "I don't ... I don't want ..." and cut the rest of the sentence off with an audible snap of her teeth.

Vinar was at a loss. He tried to persuade her to tell him what she had left unsaid, but she either couldn't or wouldn't answer him; she only continued to stare ahead as though hypnotized. Then—and this to his mind was stranger still—she abruptly blinked, shook her head as if to clear something obscuring her vision, and continued to walk along the road without a further word. Vinar was taken completely by surprise and she was already a good way ahead of him by the time he ran to catch up. As he recovered his wits his mind filled with questions, but one look at her face stilled his tongue. She didn't recall what she had said; she didn't even remember her lapse. The incident had been wiped from her mind as though it had never taken place, and she was walking on toward Carn Caille without a qualm.

Since then Vinar had been watching her closely, constantly alert for another such episode, but there had been nothing, and he didn't know whether to feel relieved or disappointed. For a moment it had seemed that something had reached through the blockage in Indigo's mind, stirring up a recollection from her past, yet it had fled before either she or he could grasp hold of it. *I don't want ...* Don't want what? Vinar asked himself, but the question was fruitless. Only Indigo could answer it, and the barriers had risen again, shutting out memory and understanding.

He gazed now at the towering bulk of the fortress, a stark and almost ugly contrast with the colorful activity flowing like a tide around its walls. Though he had no evidence to support the feeling, he was firmly convinced that Indigo had some deep-buried knowledge of Carn Caille, though where that knowledge might stem from was a question he couldn't begin to answer. Could she have lived within its walls, the child, perhaps, of a royal retainer? Or had she simply visited the fortress at some time in her life, perhaps to attend a gathering like today's? The possibilities filled Vinar with a discomfiting blend of hope and fear: hope that Indigo's face might be known and remembered at Carn Caille, yet fear of whatever secret or tragedy might have driven her away to seek another life altogether.

They were in the thick of the crowd by this time and the road had petered out save for a faintly marked track leading to the open fortress gates. Through the gates Vinar could see a dense press of people, and a line of sorts seemed to be waiting before a set of double doors that, presumably, led to Carn Caille's great hall and the king's presence. Indigo had veered aside to examine a stall selling hides and leather goods; a fat woman behind the display was trying to interest her in an ornate belt and some soft shoes. Vinar went after her and touched her shoulder.

"Indigo. There's a lot of people waiting to see the king. We better not delay if we want to have our chance."

She turned, smiling, but not, he thought, overly interested. "I'll not be long. I just want to look at these."

Vinar felt a flutter of disquiet. It was as though she didn't *want* to see this thing through.

And she had said: "I don't want . . ."

"Indigo." He touched her shoulder again. "Stay here,

wait here a minute or two, ya? I go and see what's to do, then I come back to you here."

"Of course, yes." She immediately turned back to the stall and he didn't think she'd really taken his words in. For a moment Vinar stared doubtfully at her back, then he strode off toward Carn Caille's gates.

The gates were guarded, but it seemed the men-at-arms were there only for appearances' sake, for people were passing back and forth without challenge. Vinar slowed his steps as he approached, looking for someone who might tell him what the form was for anyone wishing to approach the public court, and he was still staring uncertainly about him when a voice at his elbow made him start.

"Prinkum-prankum!" Something hit him a light blow on the arm and he spun round to see the buffooner dancing on the spot a pace away. The joker shook his ribbon-stick and grinned. "And a merry day to you, good sir!" Then he dropped the comical facade. "You look like a lost soul, if you'll pardon my saying so. Can I be of assistance?"

Vinar relaxed and returned the smile. "Well . . . maybe you can, I think. I want to get to see the king, but I don't know how I do it."

The buffooner raised a painted eyebrow. "You're not alone in that." A pause. "You're Scorvan, aren't you?"

Vinar laughed. "That obvious, uh? I thought I done well passing as an Isler."

"Not with that accent, I assure you! But seriously, it's not just the voice. I've a talent for placing people's origins—it's useful in my proper work, and we get visitors from all parts of the world here."

Vinar noted the words *we* and *here*, and his interest quickened. "You live at Carn Caille?"

"I do indeed." With a sweeping, self-mocking gesture the buffooner indicated his riotous clothing. "Don't be deceived by the costume, my friend; I don't go about playing prinkum-prankum on people for a living. It's simply a piece of fun when I'm not on duty for the public days, and as I have a small talent for clowning I enjoy adding my own contribution to the general merriment." He held out a hand, palm upward. "I'm Jes Ragnarson, bard by proper calling, and in service to King Ryen."

Vinar laid his own hand over the proffered palm, dwarfing it; Jes Ragnarson was slightly built. "Vinar Shillan. Seaman twenty-five years, expert ticket." His smile grew a little harder. "I was with Captain Brek from Scorva, on the *Good Hope*."

"The recent wreck at Amberland?" Jes's interest quickened. "We had word that a good many had survived that, thanks be to the Mother. A report came in from Ranna only a few days since, and it said—"

"Ya, ya." Vinar didn't want to appear dismissive but neither did he want to dwell on the loss of the *Good Hope*. Realizing it, Jes changed his tack. "So you want to present a petition? You've come a little late in the day; the great hall's already awash with people and there are still more waiting in the courtyard, as you can see. However, if it's a matter of great importance—"

"It is," Vinar stated flatly. "To me, it is."

The bard studied him carefully for a few moments. He had noticed the Scorvan stranger some minutes ago, and noticed something else, too, something that had both startled him and aroused his curiosity. He nibbled at his lower lip. "Well . . . it's *possible* that I may be able to help you." Then he added in a tone that, had Vinar's perception been more subtle, would have sounded just a little too casual, "But I thought you had a companion. Didn't I see a young lady at your side?"

"Ya." Vinar nodded confirmation and gestured toward the hide-seller's booth. "She's over there; I said I come and see what's what, then go back for her. It's for her we're here."

"Ah." Jes followed the direction of Vinar's gesture until his gaze lit on Indigo. His eyes were thoughtful. "She's your wife?"

"Not yet." Vinar grinned proudly. "But she will be soon, I reckon. That's why we've come; to find her kinfolk, get their blessing."

Was that the entire truth? Jes wondered. Or was there some other question at stake here? His mind's harp strings, to coin a phrase of his old bardic master's, were vibrating. . . .

Aloud, he said, "Well, well. A very handsome lady—I congratulate you both. May I ask her name?"

"She's called Indigo."

Jes's head came round sharply. "Indigo? That's an . . . unusual name. Not one I'd have thought any Isler would choose to give his child." Vinar, who was used to this reaction by now, shrugged but didn't comment, and the bard added quickly, "Not that it's my concern, of course, and what's in a name, after all? Well, maybe I *can* help. To join the petitioners you need to be on the steward's list."

"But if it's full—"

Jes made a negating gesture. "There may still be room for you. I can't promise, but I'll see what I can do."

Vinar hesitated, wondering why a complete stranger should be so ready to grant him a favor. "I don't want to take your trouble—" he began.

"It's no trouble at all." Jes smiled again, quickly, ingenuously, and sidestepped any need to explain his motive by adding, "Fetch your lady and bring her to the courtyard. I'll return in a few minutes and meet you both here."

The bard's expression was meditative as he watched Vinar head away toward the booth. For the space of perhaps five or six breaths he stood motionless, absorbed by his thoughts. Then, abruptly, he turned and hurried toward the press of people in the courtyard.

If Ryen had despaired of Brythere, the Dowager Queen Moragh had not, and when she chose to exert her will there were few people within the walls of Carn Caille capable of opposing her. Brythere had neither the strength nor the resolution even to try, and so under the dowager's firm supervision she had risen in the morning, eaten a fortifying breakfast that she didn't want, and prepared herself to appear at the public court. She sat now at Ryen's side in the great hall, upright in her chair on the high dais and dressed in formal court clothes with a small silver coronet set on her immaculately groomed hair.

A little to her own surprise, and despite the tiredness that always followed herb-induced as opposed to natural sleep, she was enjoying the day. The warm welcome from petitioners in the hall when she made her appearance was very gratifying, and when word had reached them that the queen was present the crowd outside had cheered her. Ryen was pleased both by the display of affection for his wife and by her response. She had even agreed, albeit cautiously, to his suggestion that later they should go out to the courtyard together to greet the throng, and he gave silent but heartfelt thanks to his mother for her resolve.

The afternoon was wearing on now, the sun slanting in at the tall windows and casting a bright halo around Brythere's hair. The hall was hot and a little stuffy despite the open doors, and seeing Brythere stifle a yawn behind her hand Ryen leaned across to her and whispered, "The list of petitions is nearly done. Just a little longer, then we'll step outside to make our greetings." She nodded and he turned to the steward who stood beside his chair. "How many more to come?"

The man consulted his list. "Another five or six, my

lord, and none of them complicated matters. Mostly applications for leave to run stock or cut wood in the game forests, and two farmers in dispute over sheep-grazing rights."

"Good, good." These were simple enough and would require Ryen only to give a brief audience, where he would hear the bones of each argument and, if he judged it reasonable, grant the petitioner a hearing before the Bench of King's Justicers who would see that all was resolved fairly.

"Oh, but there is one other, my lord," the steward said suddenly. "A latecomer—too late, strictly speaking, to be included, but Jes Ragnarson has especially asked that he might come before you."

"Jes has asked it?" Ryen was surprised. "Who is it? A kinsman of his?"

"No, sir. I understand the petitioner is a Scorvan, but betrothed to an Isler. In fact she—his betrothed—is the subject of the petition. It seems she has lost her memory, and they're trying to trace her family. They hope that you, my lord, might be able to help them."

This was a change from the usual gamut of appeals that came before him, and Ryen was intrigued. "How did Jes come to be involved in this?" he asked.

"I don't know, my lord. But he asks that you might grant him the favor of allowing the couple to come before you."

The king raised his head and cast a brief glance around the crowded hall. The remaining petitioners on the steward's list were waiting patiently, while those who had already had their turn stood by to hear the rest of the proceedings. Though no one would dream to question this delay while Ryen and the steward consulted, people were restless and a little puzzled; there was a low-pitched murmur of voices in the hall, some shuffling, a cough or two.

Ryen could hardly blame them for their impatience; he, too, had no wish to prolong the court any more than was necessary. But if Jes had made an especial request . . .

"Yes," he said to the steward. "Have them come in. I'll be glad to help them if I can."

The man bowed and hurried out, and Ryen turned his attention to the next case. Both it and the two that followed were as simple as he had anticipated, and the fourth and penultimate petitioner was just bowing before him when there was movement near the doors as a section of the crowd pressed back to allow some newcomers to enter. On the edge of his vision the king glimpsed Jes Ragnarson in his gaudy buffooner's costume, and at his side a blond man head and shoulders taller than most of the gathering. He had a woman with him; Ryen had time to note that she was auburn-haired but saw little else before he was obliged to return his attention to the matter at hand. He heard the petition and the one that followed, gave courteous and considered replies to both, then signaled that the two newcomers should step forward. As the throng made way for them he glanced at Brythere and saw that she was frowning. He leaned a little toward her, lowering his voice almost to a whisper.

"Is something wrong, my heart?"

"That woman." Brythere had had an opportunity to study the newcomers, albeit at a distance. "I'm sure I've seen her somewhere before." She looked directly at her husband. "The steward said she has lost her memory?"

"Yes, and is trying to find her kinfolk." Ryen's interest quickened. "Do you think you know her?"

"I can't be sure. But . . ." And abruptly Brythere stopped speaking as Vinar and Indigo emerged from the press of people and they both saw Indigo clearly for the first time.

"*Ryen . . .*" Brythere's hand clamped hard over her husband's where it rested on the carved chair arm. *"Remember the painting in the old apartments. . . ."*

"Sweet Earth—" He bit the expostulation back, staring in astonishment at the young woman approaching the dais with her paramour. Blue-violet eyes, auburn hair—she wore it braided, but it was easy to imagine it loosed and falling like a curtain over her face. And that face was shockingly familiar.

"The princess," Brythere whispered, and her voice was beginning to shake. *"The princess Anghara, King Kalig's daughter!"*

Ryen was too stunned to answer her. In the south wing of Carn Caille was a suite of rooms that, once, had been the royal family's private sanctum. And in one of those rooms hung a portrait. It depicted Kalig, King of the Southern Isles, his queen, Imogen, and their son and daughter. Ryen's grandfather had decreed that the portrait should hang framed by a swath of indigo velvet as a symbol of mourning and a token of respect; for his own elevation to the throne had come about because Kalig and his entire family had died in the terrible plague that swept the Isles half a century ago. Ryen knew the painting well, had absorbed every detail of the images depicted in its pigments. And now, incredibly, he was seeing the perfect mirror of one of those images in the face and form of a complete stranger. Anghara Kaligsdaughter, dead for more than fifty years, had come back to life. . . .

"Ryen . . ." Brythere's hand clenched hard on his, her nails digging painfully into his skin. "Ryen, she can't— I'm not— Oh, Ryen, is she a . . . a ghost . . . ?"

Her face had turned dead white and she was visibly shaking. The steward, back in his place beside the chair, saw the sudden change and looked at his lord in alarm.

"No!" Ryen pulled his hand free and grasped Brythere by the arm as she seemed about to lurch to her feet. *"No!*

She's not a ghost. Princess Anghara is dead, and this woman is flesh and blood. She isn't Anghara. It's a coincidence, nothing more. An incredible coincidence."

Brythere subsided, though he could feel through her sleeve that she was still trembling with the shock. The two strangers were approaching the dais now, and as he squeezed his wife's arm, trying silently to reassure her, Ryen began to see the small but vital differences between this woman and the long-dead princess, differences that he'd overlooked in his first astonishment. The Scorvan's betrothed had the same eyes and hair and cast of feature as Anghara Kaligsdaughter, but she must surely be older, for her face had the lines of experience and there were streaks of gray at her brow. And her skin had the tan of a life spent outdoors in sun and wind and rain, and her hands were work-roughened as no princess's hand could ever be. . . .

The pair reached the dais, stopped. The big blond man had seen Brythere's extraordinary reaction and was clearly discomforted by it and by the fact that Brythere was now rigid in her chair, staring at Indigo with wide, fearful eyes.

The king cleared his throat.

"I . . . I apologize to one and all." His voice wasn't quite steady. "The queen felt a little faint momentarily . . . the heat, I think. The hall is very airless." He didn't release Brythere's arm but managed a smile as he addressed Indigo and Vinar. "You are welcome to Carn Caille. I understand. . . ." He cleared his throat again. "I understand that you are seeking a family of the Southern Isles and that you have come to ask this court's assistance?"

Indigo didn't utter a word. She was looking at the king and queen much in the way that Brythere had looked at her. There was a small frown on her face, and it seemed that she was struggling to call something back to mind.

Vinar, disconcerted by her silence, made a hasty and inexpert bow in the direction of the dais.

"I—uh—I don't know how to say the proper things in your language, Lord King, but I—we—thank you for your"—he struggled to find a better word but couldn't—"for being so kind to us. And to the dear and beautiful queen, I say—"

He got no further, for there was a sudden and unexpected disturbance behind him. Outside in the corridor someone started shouting, ranting by the sound of it; other voices quickly joined in and the open doors shook as those nearest them were pushed roughly back by what appeared to be several brawling men. A woman shrieked, in indignation rather than fear, then abruptly the knot of fighters barreled into the hall. The brawl seemed to be a chaotic affair between two stewards and, extraordinarily, Jes Ragnarson on one side, and on the other a solitary man dressed in a grimy, cowled coat, who was flailing about him with a blackthorn stick.

Outraged, King Ryen sprang to his feet and roared, "What by all that's civilized is this? Guards, restrain those men—knock them senseless if you have to, but put a stop to this at *once*!"

Ryen had a powerful voice when he needed to exert it, and at the sound of his bellowed command the fighting men broke apart. Seeing his chance the cowled figure swung the blackthorn staff and caught one of the stewards a cracking blow on the shoulder; as the man howled with pain and spun away to collide with the onlookers the miscreant made a staggering rush toward the dais.

"She is here! I know she is here!" To the astonishment of everyone, his screech was that of an old man, and the realization momentarily confused the four men-at-arms who were running to intercept and restrain him. On the dais, Brythere's face turned haggard and she clapped both hands over her mouth as though to stifle a scream.

"Show her to me!" the old man yelled. "Show her! I want her, I have come for her—*ahh*!" as the guards, recovering their wits, pounced on him and wrested the stave from his grasp. "*No*, carrion, don't *dare* to touch me! I have come for her, and *I will have her*!"

He had the strength of madness, but against four trained warriors that wasn't enough. The guards pinioned his arms and threw him to the floor. As he fell, still kicking and struggling, the cowl of his cloak flopped back, leaving his head bare.

And Queen Brythere uttered a shriek of abject and uncontrollable terror as she looked on the twisted face and crazed eyes of Perd Nordenson.

•CHAPTER•IX•

The Dowager Moragh had had enough of public courts during her husband's lifetime to have no interest in them now, and as the weather was fine she had chosen to spend the day riding with some favored friends of her personal retinue. Her party returned to Carn Caille an hour before sunset. On the surrounding sward all was well; a sizable crowd still remained to enjoy the day's pleasures to the last and the dowager was cheered loudly as she passed. But once inside the gates, Moragh found Carn Caille in a ferment.

It took her only a few minutes to discover that Brythere was at the center of it all. The queen, she was told, had had an "unfortunate experience," though no one seemed either able or willing to recount the details, and was now in the private anteroom behind the great hall, attended by the king and her own servant. Tight-lipped with irritation at what she felt must be yet another outburst of foolish hysteria from her daughter-elect, Moragh went to see for herself what was amiss this time.

In the anteroom she was surprised to find not only Ryen and the sallow-faced Ketrin in attendance on Brythere, but also Carn Caille's senior healer and, strangest of all, Jes Ragnarson. Brythere was a pitiful figure in the midst of all the attention, her face spectrally white, her hands moving helplessly and tears streaming down her face. Moragh took one look at her and opened her mouth to demand an explanation, but before she could utter a word Ryen took three quick strides across the room toward her, one hand held up in a warning gesture.

"Mother." He glanced back over his shoulder to be sure that his wife wouldn't overhear him. "Please, say nothing. This isn't another of Brythere's episodes. This time there's good reason for it." His face was tense with a mixture of worry and anger as he added, "Perd Nordenson has come back."

"Perd . . ." Moragh's expression changed and she stared at him. "Good Goddess! After all this time— I'd thought he must be long dead!" She drew Ryen a little farther away. "Tell me what happened."

Ryen recounted the events that had taken place in the great hall: the sudden brawl, the old man's savage strength that had allowed him almost to reach the dais before he was overpowered, and the threats and demands he had shouted.

"It was Brythere he wanted, there's no doubt of it," the king finished grimly. "When the men-at-arms finally got him out of the hall he was found to be carrying a knife. I shudder to think what might have happened if he'd had the chance to use it."

Moragh looked back at the small tableau of Brythere and her attendants. The young queen had stopped trembling now and her eyes were closed; doubtless the healer had given her something stronger than a mere simple to put her so soundly to sleep.

"All this again . . ." the dowager murmured and added a fearsome imprecation under her breath. "What have you done with Perd Nordenson now?"

"I had him driven out and told a party of men to follow him until he was at least seven miles along the west road."

"Driven *out*?" Moragh was scandalized. "Is that *all*? Why, by all that's sane, didn't you execute him?"

The king's mouth set stubbornly. "I don't believe in execution except in the greatest extremity. You know that."

"And what was this if it wasn't the greatest extremity?" Moragh demanded. "The man was a menace in your father's time, and he's a menace now! Have you forgotten what he tried to do in the past? The attempts he made on your father's life and later on yours—the poisoned mead, the figure in your bedchamber at the dead of night, the 'accidental' bowshot that nearly killed you in the forest—"

"There was no proof that any of those acts was committed by Perd."

"*Proof!*" The dowager snorted her contempt. "We may not have incontrovertible *proof*, but we've always known the truth! Perd Nordenson is a madman with an obsession, and as the years pass they both grow worse!" She clasped her hands together as though ferociously wringing the life out of some invisible object. "Your father should *never* have been so lenient with him. He should have tried him for treason decades ago and done away with him for good and all!"

Ryen remembered the arguments between his parents on the subject of Perd Nordenson, which had been a regular occurrence during his childhood; and he also remembered what his father had said to him during a private moment.

"Perd is an old man, and life has not treated him kindly," Cathal had told his son. "His mind is injured, much as a leg or arm might be broken, and during his bad times he can't help the things he does. But he's been in our family's service for a long time, and he was your grandfather's friend, so we must make allowances and treat him with kindness and patience."

Though he couldn't bring himself to like Perd Nordenson, Ryen had taken those words to heart. But then he had married Brythere and a year later King Cathal died, and after that the problem of Perd had grown worse. Brythere was terrified of the old retainer and Perd knew it. With what seemed cruel deliberation he had begun to terrorize the queen. Nothing too flagrant and nothing that could reasonably lead to accusations, but wherever Brythere went Perd seemed to be there, too, silently following, constantly watching, until Brythere's nerves were close to breaking point.

During that time her nightmares had begun and with them the first signs of real estrangement from Ryen, and Moragh declared—though Ryen disagreed—that Perd was delighted by the rift and saw it as a personal triumph. Then had come two further attempts on Ryen's life, and though there was no evidence to suggest that either was Perd's doing, Moragh had finally put her foot down. Only the king himself had the authority to order Perd's death, she acknowledged, but if Ryen refused to take action, then he would wake one morning to find that the old madman had been dispatched during the night by an unknown hand. Moragh had enough loyal friends and servants in Carn Caille to ensure that the task would be carried out willingly and efficiently, and—unless he was prepared to try his own mother for conspiracy to murder and cite this conversation as evidence—the culprit would never be found.

Ryen had given way. In truth he knew Moragh was right; Perd Nordenson's continuing presence in Carn Caille could not be tolerated. But still he had refused to order the old man's death and instead had banished him, with a good horse and enough money to enable him to settle into a new and comfortable life elsewhere. Moragh had been mollified if not entirely content, Brythere shudderingly thankful, and Ryen himself relieved to be rid of the old man without too great a cost to his conscience. What Perd had thought, nobody knew, for he had taken what was offered him and ridden away from Carn Caille without a word to anyone. And that, they had thought, was the end of it. Until today.

Moragh's first anger had cooled a little by now and she said to her son, "Brythere's sleeping now. Leave her in Ketrin's care and come with me to my sitting room. I think we should discuss this further."

The king nodded. He started to follow her out of the room, but Jes Ragnarson saw them departing and hurried to intercept them.

"Forgive me, Your Grace." The bard bowed low to Moragh then turned to Ryen. "My lord, what should we do about the—ah—" His gaze flickered, a little furtively Moragh thought, to her and then back to the king. "The guests . . . ?"

"Good grief, in all the rumpus I'd entirely forgotten! Where are they now, Jes?"

"In another anteroom, sir, awaiting your pleasure."

"Guests?" Moragh demanded. "What guests, Ryen? Don't tell me we have important visitors and you've left them unattended without so much as a cup of beer to sustain them!"

"Your Grace," Jes turned hastily to her and made another bow. "These aren't guests in the usual sense, but two strangers who came to the public court. Their plea is an odd one, and though they arrived too late for the lists, His Majesty was kind enough to make an especial allowance for them." Briefly he sketched out the story that Vinar had told him, and as she listened Moragh's shrewd senses judged that there was more to this circumstance than met the eye. Jes seemed flustered, almost nervous, and wouldn't look directly at her or at Ryen as he spoke. And as for Ryen . . . Yes, the dowager thought, there was something afoot here.

By the time the bard finished his explanation she had made up her mind. "Jes," she said pleasantly, "take us to the anteroom, if you please. If these good people have been kept waiting through all this furor, I think the least we can do is convey our apologies personally."

"Yes, Your Grace." Was that relief she saw on the bard's face? Hard to be sure, but he looked as though he anticipated the relinquishing of an unwanted responsibility. Ryen said nothing, and Jes led them back through the great hall and along the passage to a closed door. Bowing again, he opened it and announced King Ryen and the Dowager Queen Moragh.

The two strangers were sitting on a cushioned bench under the window of the small but pleasant room. They sprang to their feet in consternation as the visitors were announced, and Moragh, entering first, smiled reassuringly.

"Please, we are not great ones for formality at Carn Caille, and besides, the fault is ours for . . ." The words trailed off as she saw and registered Indigo's face. She was suddenly very still, and her expression changed. Now she understood the cause of Ryen and Jes's discomfort.

Vinar made a deep bow. "Madam Queen," he said, hoping that was the correct way to address this formidable-looking lady. "We don't want to make any nuisance of ourselves, but when Jes said to wait here—"

Moragh interrupted him. Her composure had returned, and she was too experienced a diplomat for anyone, with the possible exception of Ryen, to have noticed her lapse.

"No, no," she said. "It is *we* who have made nuisances of ourselves, by leaving you unattended and doubtless quite bewildered. We have had a small upset, as I think you know, and it has taken a little longer than anticipated to put it to rights. Now, though, all's well and we must make amends to you." She turned to the bard. "Jes, go and find my personal steward and tell him that I will be dining in my own apartments, with three companions. And send word to Mitha that Carn Caille will accommodate two guests tonight." Smiling, she looked at her son. "Come along, Ryen; you and I will entertain these good people and see how we may be able to help them. Under the circumstances"—a glint in her eyes hinted at deeper meaning in that—"I think it's the very least we can do."

By the time the meal served in the dowager's apartments drew to a close, Vinar was half convinced that he must be dreaming. For upward of two hours he and Indigo had been treated as though they were royalty in their own right. They sat in deep-cushioned chairs while deferential servants served them with fine food and drink in quantities that defeated even a Scorvan sailor's appetite, and a king and queen conversed with them as though they were their own kin.

At first Vinar had been so overawed that he could barely say a word, but their hosts, Moragh in particular, were so kindly and affable that before long his nervousness began to abate, and soon he was gleefully imagining what Captain Brek and his crewmates from the *Good Hope* would say if they could see him now.

Indigo, on the other hand, had seemed quite at ease from the start. She had little to say, but her smile was unaffected and her manner relaxed if somewhat distracted; watching her, Vinar could easily have believed that she had been born and bred to such exalted company, for it seemed to hold no terrors for her.

When the dishes of meats and fruits and fresh young vegetables had been carried away, and the cakes had been eaten, and a great bowl of almonds preserved in honey and carried to the Isles from the Eastern Continent had been placed on the table with flagons of sweet mead, the conversation turned at last to the quest that had brought Vinar and Indigo to Carn Caille. Moragh was an adept questioner and it took her only a short time to draw the entire story of the wreck and its aftermath from Vinar, and to learn of the strange message they had received through Captain Brek at Ranna.

"And your captain clearly said that the wolf would be brought here?" There was surprise and curiosity in the dowager's voice. "There's no mistake?"

Vinar was eyeing the honeyed almonds with great interest, but he didn't dare take one until his hosts did so and showed him how they should be eaten. "No mistake, Your Grace, that we can tell," he said. "And if Captain Brek trusted the boy he sent to get the word right, well ... I reckon to trust him, too."

"This is very strange." Moragh glanced at her son. "We've had no word from any of the witches here, have we, Ryen?"

"No, indeed," the king agreed. "I can only suppose that you have traveled faster than any message to us and have taken us by surprise." He smiled to show that he implied no fault on anyone's part.

"I reckon," Vinar said a little diffidently, "that these witches—if they are what everyone say, and I got no reason to disbelieve it—know a thing or two more than they've told yet."

Moragh's eyes glinted with quickened interest. "What do you mean by that, Vinar?"

"Well, ma'am . . . maybe that they think there's something or someone here that can help Indigo in ways we don't know. Like with her kinfolk; someone here maybe who know something about who they are and where we find them. I think maybe that's why their message said to come here."

"Yes. Yes, I see." The dowager exchanged an unfathomable look with her son. "Perhaps you're right; it would certainly be in keeping with the way our wise-women tend to work. . . . Well, we will do all we can to help you in your search, and I think we might begin by sending word out through the Isles to find Indigo's family. That should be simple enough, Ryen."

"Yes," Ryen said. He was still looking at Indigo. "Yes . . ."

"But for now," the dowager shifted in her chair then rose to her feet. Hastily Vinar did the same and, a little belatedly, Indigo followed his example. Moragh smiled at them. "No, no, Vinar, there's no need for formality. But the hour's late and from the look of her I think Indigo is exhausted. We should all retire, I think; a good night's sleep will refresh us all. Your rooms have been made ready. I'll summon the servants and they can show you the way."

She crossed the room to where an embroidered bell-rope hung, and as she did so she made a small gesture that Ryen alone saw and that clearly indicated that she wished him to stay. Two stewards answered the bell's summons; good nights were exchanged at the door and, as had become the custom between them, Indigo touched her lips lightly to Vinar's in an affectionate but chaste salute before one servant escorted her away. Vinar bowed deeply to the dowager, then followed the other steward away down the corridor.

The door closed behind them, and Moragh waited until

she judged they were out of earshot before turning back to the table. Ryen was sitting down again, staring at the litter of empty dishes but apparently oblivious to them. The dowager poured more wine for them both and set his refilled cup before him.

"There's something wrong with her, Ryen. Something more than mere loss of memory."

Ryen looked up quickly. His mother's tone had changed from the light affability of the past few hours; there was a new energy in her voice, and a distinct edge.

"Yes," he said. "I know."

Moragh sat down. "Tell me exactly what happened when they arrived in the great hall. I've heard only garbled accounts so far and I want the whole story."

Ryen recounted the tale of Jes Ragnarson's request that he should hear a last-minute petition, and of his own shock, and Brythere's more extreme reaction, when they had seen Indigo's face for the first time. Moragh listened thoughtfully, then pursed her lips.

"So Jes must also think that there's more to this than meets the eye, or he wouldn't have taken such trouble over their petition."

"He saw the resemblance."

"Yes, yes, of course; but knowing our bard I'd wager that wasn't his sole motive." She looked about her at the table. "Did you notice how she ate?"

"No." Ryen was puzzled.

"Well, I did. She's no ordinary seafarer; she has manners that wouldn't be out of place at the Khimizi court, let alone at ours. And she was selective about the wine. Vinar was happy to drink anything we put in front of him—and I don't mean to slight him; he's a very decent and personable man. But Indigo knew what she was chosing and knew what she liked. I suspect that whether she knows it or not, her background is about as far from his own as it's possible to be."

"Not far enough to prevent her from becoming betrothed to him," Ryen pôinted out.

"Um. Well, as to that . . ." But Moragh decided against voicing her thoughts on the subject. "She lost her memory in the wreck, Vinar said, as the result of a blow to the skull. Presumably she was treated by the village healers at Amberland, but though I don't doubt they're adequate enough with fevers and broken bones, I imagine a case like this would be beyond their scope."

"You think our own physicians might succeed where they failed?"

"I wasn't thinking of our physicians," Moragh said, "but rather of the forest witches."

"Oh. Oh, yes . . . I begin to understand. The pet wolf . . ."

"Exactly. The pet wolf, and the fact that one of the witches is apparently very anxious that the creature should be reunited with its mistress here at Carn Caille. Now, Ryen, doesn't that strike you as a little peculiar?"

The king frowned into his cup. "You're saying that the witches might have some . . . ulterior motive." Then he looked up, met her gaze. "Or that they might know something that hasn't yet been revealed to us?"

"We both know their ways, even if we can't fathom them," Moragh said. "If there *is* some deeper mystery involved, the witches will be the first to discover it. And that's why I think that this wise-woman, whoever she may be, has a reason for wishing to bring Indigo here."

There was silence for a few moments. Then, softly, Ryen said:

"And perhaps we shouldn't overlook another of the witches' functions. . . ."

"What?" Moragh had been absorbed in her own speculations and hadn't heard him clearly. Ryen glanced at her again, his eyes uneasy, then rose and paced across the room to the window. He lifted the curtain, looked out. The courtyard was deserted and the towers beyond were a vague, dark mass, outlined by a faint afterglow far to the south. The sky overhead was sprinkled with stars. When the king spoke again his voice was indistinct.

"Mother . . . is it possible that any of Kalig's kin might have survived the plague?"

Moragh stared at him. "*Survived* it? Ryen, that's *impossible*! The records—"

"The proper records weren't made; we know that. The epidemic struck too quickly and too violently—people were dying like leaves falling from a tree in autumn. In such a dire emergency there was no *time* to keep records, so the only accounts we have are those that were pieced together after the worst of the plague was over."

The dowager continued to stare at his back. "Ryen," she said quietly, "what are you getting at?"

He drew breath, held it pent for a few moments, then let the curtain fall and turned to face her.

"Don't you see, Mother? With the Isles in such turmoil as they were at that time, it *is* possible that Kalig's line survived. No one in the immediate family; but perhaps a cousin, or even some by-blow of Kalig's or his son's. We don't *know*. We can't be *sure*."

Moragh began to understand. "But they searched. The bards, the wise-women . . ."

"Yes, and they found no living kinsman or -woman. So they were compelled to elect a successor to take the throne and begin a new dynasty, and that is how we came to Carn Caille. But our family has no blood tie with Kalig's. My grandfather was simply chosen. By the bards . . . and by the witches."

"The bards, and the witches." Moragh repeated his words very softly. "Oh . . ."

"Yes. That was what I meant, Mother, when I said we shouldn't overlook the fact that the witches sometimes carry out other duties. When Kalig and his family died they searched the Isles for a survivor from his bloodline but failed to find one. However, if one such survivor had fled from the epidemic, left the Isles altogether—perhaps with children, who in turn came to have children of their own—"

Moragh dew in a sharp, unsteady breath. "It could be," she said. "It could be. Even her name: the color of mourning. It could have been chosen in remembrance."

"The witches have already sensed something afoot," Ryen said. "And the resemblance is too close, too uncanny. If we're right, Mother, then—" He hesitated, had to steel himself to say it. "If we're right, then it's very probable that Indigo is the rightful queen of the Southern Isles."

However hard she tried, Indigo couldn't shake off the feeling that the events of the past few hours had happened to someone else and not to her. Even when the steward had departed, and the servant-girl assigned to her had brought washing-water and turned down the bed and made a deferential exit, finally leaving her alone, she couldn't assimilate all that had taken place.

Her bedroom was one of Carn Caille's best guest chambers, spacious and pleasantly and plentifully furnished. There were thick rugs on the floor, heavy curtains at the window and over the door, chairs and tables, and an oak chest, and the bed had posts about which a canopy was hung, with draperies that she could draw together if she felt the cold. Indigo washed herself in the warm water—a rare luxury—then for a long time sat on the bed, listening to the distant, intermittent sounds of footsteps and soft voices and closing doors as the stronghold composed itself for sleep. She couldn't sleep; though her body felt heavy with weariness she was finding it impossible to settle into these strange surroundings. And without knowing why, she felt uneasy. It wasn't discomfort at the company into which she had so suddenly been elevated; King Ryen and his mother were the kindest of hosts, and for some reason she didn't seem to share Vinar's sense of awe. No, it wasn't the people within Carn Caille; it was Carn Caille itself. Something about the noble old building disturbed her, like a nagging ache in a tooth. Something was *wrong* here, and she couldn't pinpoint it.

She climbed into bed at last and sat for a while longer, arms wrapped around hunched knees, wondering where Vinar's room was and if he was asleep yet. She wished he would come to her, if only to say a more private good night, for she felt isolated and a little vulnerable and longed for the presence of a familiar face and voice. Then immediately on the heels of the wish came the old dilemma that had beset her since the shipwreck and her convalescence: the paradox of her feelings for the man to whom she was supposedly betrothed. Still the emotions she looked for stubbornly refused to stir within her, and still she didn't understand why. Vinar was her dear friend, her close companion, and as a man he was more than attractive. She felt affection for him, and sometimes—as now—she felt desire for him, a secret longing to take him to her bed and to give herself as, she knew, he would give to her. But even as it rose in her the desire became cold ashes, for she knew that though there might be pleasure there would not be love, at least not for her. It was as though—she struggled to grasp at a glimmer of understanding—as though someone else stood between them, a ghost of her forgotten past that held her back and either could not or would not be exorcised. And since setting foot in Carn Caille, she had felt its presence more strongly than ever before.

The fire had died to almost nothing and the room was growing chilly. Indigo slid down beneath the blankets but was still reluctant to extinguish the candle at her bedside. If Vinar *did* come to her tonight, would she . . . ? But no. Speculation was pointless, for he wouldn't come, he wouldn't try, as he saw it, to take advantage of her. Perhaps, she thought recklessly, it would be better if he did, for that would take matters out of her control once and for all and relieve her of a responsibility she didn't want. But Vinar wouldn't take such a step. It was as if he, too, sensed the unspoken barrier and refused to cross it.

The corridors outside her room were quiet now, and the only sounds to break the silence were an occasional sluggish hiss from a dying fire and the soft moan of a rising wind beyond Carn Caille's walls. The wind's voice seemed to stir echoes in Indigo's marrow, like the half-recalled voice of an old friend . . . or an old enemy . . . and she turned restlessly in her bed.

The candle guttered in a draft that the curtains couldn't entirely exclude; shadows flickered on the wall and across the floor, distorting and looming . . . and she must have drifted briefly into the troubled shallows of sleep, for she was unaware of the presence in her room until a sound in her mind, like a sharp musical resonance, snapped her back to consciousness.

The fire had gone out and the candle had burned down to a dim blue pinpoint. And someone, featureless in the gloom, was standing at the end of her bed. Indigo tensed instantly as on a subliminal level she realized that the silhouetted figure was too tall to be Moragh or the servant and too slender to be Vinar. Her lips were suddenly dry; she forced them to part, forced herself to speak.

"*Who are you?*" It wasn't the clear challenge she had intended but a mere whisper. The figure didn't answer but moved a step closer, and Indigo's heart lurched painfully. She started to rise, one hand instinctively groping under her pillow for something—*what? A weapon? She didn't know*—

A voice said clearly, "*Anghara.*"

It hit her like a hammer blow. *Sweet Mother, he had come back! He wasn't dead, he was here, he was*—

The memory vanished like smoke, and a strange, agonized cry bubbled in Indigo's throat. She flung herself upright in the bed, flailing at the blankets as they took on a life of their own and tried to impede her. The figure took a darting pace backward, and suddenly where there had been one there were two. An old woman—Indigo couldn't see her face, but somehow knew what she was—and she was holding something, holding it out to the first shadow, pressing it into his hands.

"*Anghara . . .*" The name was uttered again, hoarsely, urgently, and though she couldn't tell which of the two shadows had uttered it, it sent a second violent shudder through Indigo's soul. Then she saw what the crone was pressing on her companion. A knife . . .

"*Do it now, my love.*" Still she didn't know which figure had spoken, but the voice had a terrible timber: bitter and harsh and desperate. "*Do it, and all will be well. Do it, and we shall have what is rightfully ours.*"

The candle flared suddenly with a last surge. In that instant Indigo saw the knife blade gleam—and she saw the two faces that loomed avidly, hungrily, behind the upraised weapon. She tried to cry out, tried to move, but her mind and body were frozen. The two faces swam toward her, and now they were smiling.

And one of the faces was her own.

With a muffled yelp she woke among a tangle of blankets. Reflex flung her from the bed, and she only just stopped herself from falling heavily to the floor as her scattered wits came back in the wake of shock.

It had been a dream, just a dream. The bedside candle was still burning brightly, augmented by banked-down firelight, and she was alone in the room. No voices, no shadowy intruders. Indigo let out a pent breath and shakily uttered an oath she'd learned from Vinar. The imprecation brought her crudely but comfortingly back to earth, and she set about rearranging the disordered bed. She was overwhelmed by a desire to leave Carn Caille. There was something wrong here, something *evil*, if dreams such as that could ooze out of the walls to attack the unprepared sleeper, and she wanted no more of it. In the morning she would speak privately with Vinar, explain, ask him if he'd agree to—

The thought broke off in mid-sentence as, cutting into her mind and echoing her fears as though by some dreadful telepathic link, a woman's shrill, frantic voice started to scream from a distant part of Carn Caille.

•CHAPTER•X•

In the villages and farmsteads through which they passed, the sight of Niahrin trundling her little borrowed handcart along the road, with Grimya ensconced inside, attracted a good deal of attention. People came to their doors, smiling and pointing and laughing, but the laughter was good-natured on the whole and those who at first shrank from the witch's disfigured face were soon reassured by her jovial manner. Niahrin herself was hugely amused by the interest she aroused, and as a bonus the people she encountered proved eager customers for the simples and remedies packed into the cart with Grimya.

"It's a pity I didn't think of this trick before," she told the wolf cheerfully as, with coins jingling in her pocket, she waved farewell to the family of yet another homestead. "Wheeling an animal about the countryside like a showman's turn—I'd have been a rich woman by now!"

"But also a very tired woman," Grimya replied, and her

tongue lolled to show that she shared the joke. She had grown very fond of Niahrin during their time together; the two of them had struck up a strong rapport, and despite her anxiety to reach Carn Caille and Indigo the wolf would be sad when the time came to part from her new friend.

They had been traveling for two days and by Niahrin's calculations would probably reach the gates of Carn Caille by the evening of their third day on the road. They could have made much better time by cutting across country, but with Grimya still unable to walk properly and thus obliged to be a reluctant passenger, Niahrin thought it wiser to keep to the roads, where the going would be easier. Cadic Haymanson, the forester, had been happy to lend his handcart, knowing that Niahrin would scrupulously repay him either in herbal remedies when needed or in produce from her garden. He had also cut and fashioned her a sturdy wooden club and, despite her indignant protestations that she was perfectly capable of looking after herself without resorting to violence, insisted that she should carry it with her.

"You never know what manner of vagabond you might meet on the road," he'd told her firmly. "And I'd never forgive myself if any harm were to come to you, so you'll kindly take it and allow me to sleep easy in my bed!"

Thus far at least, Cadic's fears had been unfounded, and Niahrin was thoroughly enjoying her adventure. Grimya, however, was less certain. She made a show of sharing the witch's pleasure, but beneath the pretense the sense of dread at what might lie ahead of them still haunted her. She constantly reminded herself that Carn Caille was nothing more than stone and mortar and in itself could pose no threat. But the knowledge did little to reassure her, for she also knew that beyond Carn Caille lay something else. Out on the tundra, solitary and ancient, the Tower of Regrets was waiting. And though Indigo believed that behind the rotting walls of that tower lay her ultimate goal and her ultimate joy, Grimya feared her belief was wrong.

To add to Grimya's unease, she and Niahrin had unexpected company on their journey. The wild wolves took great care not to be seen, but both Grimya and the witch were aware of their presence. When the roadside was wooded they kept pace alongside, silent as shadows; when the country opened out and there was no cover to be had they fell back and followed at a carefully judged distance. And on the first night, when they made camp at the roadside, the wolves gathered just beyond the range of their fire's light, for all the world, Niahrin said, like vigilants at a wake. The witch thought there were perhaps two or three of them, certainly no more than four, and not necessarily always the same individuals. And though she could find no rational motive for it, she had the unshakable conviction that the wolves were guarding them.

"It's you they want to protect," she told Grimya during that first night, when they were settled close to the fire. "I don't know what it is they know that I don't, but I sense that there's a purpose in this as surely as I've ever sensed anything." Her brow creased, making her face more grotesque. "I wish you would communicate with them, Grimya. I wish you would ask them what the purpose is."

Grimya didn't reply. She refused to speak aloud when she knew the wild wolves were in earshot, for the old terror from the days of her cubhood, the terror of being *different*, of being hated and reviled by her own kind, gripped her like a strangling hand. She couldn't explain it to Niahrin. She didn't even know if after fifty years she was still capable of communicating in the way of wolves; the skills she should have perfected had been abandoned when her mother turned on her and drove her out, and now she feared she might have lost them altogether. Furthermore, though she knew no more than the witch did about the wolves' purpose, she didn't share Niahrin's conviction that it was entirely benevolent.

Grimya had barely slept through that first night and had been thankful when morning came and they could be on the move again. Now though, with the sun declining and the steading and its friendly occupants lost to sight behind the brow of a hill, the prospect of another uneasy night loomed, for they were unlikely to reach the next village before dark. Lying among her blankets in the cart, comfortable in body but troubled in mind, Grimya nervously watched the surrounding landscape and tried not to think about the hours ahead.

They made camp just before the last daylight faded from the sky, on the edge of a small copse of trees set a little way back from the road. Niahrin helped Grimya out of the cart and onto the grass, where she could sprawl more comfortably and exercise a little. Then she made a fire, whistling through her teeth as she worked, and set her iron cooking-pot over the flames to prepare a hot brew. Pouring water into the pot she paused suddenly, listening, then looked over her shoulder at Grimya and said, "No wolves tonight."

Grimya looked back at her, startled. She had been so sure that the wild wolves would be there, following them still, that it hadn't once occurred to her to seek about her for any sign of their presence. Now, as her physical and psychic senses attuned to her surroundings, she realized that the witch was right. Their silent, stealthy attendants had gone.

"That's rum." Niahrin straightened and looked around as though she expected the wolves' gray shapes to materialize from the trees. "Two days, or the best part of it, on our trail, and suddenly they vanish without warning and without any apparent reason."

"Per-haps," Grimya ventured, "this is not their territory." She blinked uneasily. "In which case, others may come."

Niahrin was less sure of that but she could think of no better explanation for the strange departure. She shrugged. "Well, I don't doubt they have their own reasons, though I can't begin to fathom them. Anyway, it will make little difference to us. The brew's nearly hot. I'll pour you a dish, and some cold meat and bread to go with it."

She bent to the cooking-pot and was reaching for her ladle when abruptly Grimya's hackles rose. *"Niahrin!"* The she-wolf's voice was a hiss, a warning.

The witch spun. "What?"

"Hush!" Grimya's eyes gleamed ferally in the firelight; she had scrambled to her feet, fangs bared and body tense with instinct and apprehension. She was staring back toward the road. "Ss . . . omeone is coming."

Niahrin strained to see into the darkness with her good eye, but the flames' glow had impaired her night vision and all she saw was a dim gray haze.

She took a sidelong step toward the wolf and crouched down. "Are you sure?" she whispered. "I see nothing."

"I am certain. A shape in the dark. And a scent. Human scent."

Niahrin glanced edgily at the fire, but it was too late to consider smothering the flames. Their camp must already be clearly visible to whoever approached.

"It's probably just a peddler looking for some friendly company to keep the night at bay. Or a forester wanting to know what we're about." She smiled but at the same time reached to the cart, groping for the wooden club Cadic had given her. Under normal circumstances she didn't fear attack, but she had a sudden feeling of creeping and none too pleasant intuition. Probably it was simply a reaction to Grimya's disquiet and there was nothing to worry about, but there seemed no point in taking chances.

Her fingers closed round the club and she drew it out.
Then, signing to the wolf to be silent, she withdrew to the
fire again and resumed her whistling, making a pretense of
stirring up the brew.

Something rustled a few paces off, and a shadow moved
unnaturally. Quickly the witch straightened, and her voice
rang out.

"Who's there?" She peered hard into the gloom again.
"Share my fire and welcome if you've a mind to, but if
you've anything else in mind I'd strongly advise you to
leave while you can."

The shadow halted. No reply came, but Niahrin heard
the sound of uneven breathing. Her skin crawled.

"I don't take kindly to games," she called sharply.
"Make yourself known, or—"

She was interrupted by a savage snarl. Grimya's ears
were flat to her head and her hackles stood out like a wild,
stiff mane. The wolf's eyes glittered crimson with rage
and fear together, and from her throat a single savage word
ripped—

"EVIL!"

An ululating screech echoed shockingly through the
night, and a dark figure came flying from the trees at
them. Niahrin had one fleeting glimpse of a cloak, a nimbus of ragged hair, the glint of metal; then dull steel turned
to flaring brilliance in the firelight as the assailant's knife
sheared down toward Grimya's skull.

Niahrin let out a yell and leaped forward. She had no
chance to think; she swung the wooden club wildly, felt it
connect, saw the shadow-figure go spinning backward to
crash into the undergrowth. Grimya, moving rapidly despite her handicap, had backed out of range, snarling and
barking. The shadow-shape was trying to flail upright,
hampered by his cloak; though she hadn't glimpsed his

face Niahrin knew the truth, *knew* it, and the knowledge roused her to blind fury.

"Touch her again and I'll kill you!" She sprang like a cat, placing herself between Grimya and the man on the ground. He froze, and she sensed his eyes, invisible in his black silhouette, staring at her. Her rage towered, almost beyond control.

"Get up!" she spat. "Don't come crawling like an assassin from a rat-hole—get up and *face* me!" She hefted the club and had the icy satisfaction of seeing him flinch back. Behind her she could hear Grimya's breath rasping, exertion and emotion combined, and renewed growling threats rumbled at the back of the wolf's throat.

Slowly their would-be attacker started to move. He'd dropped his knife when Niahrin's cudgel struck him, and the blade now lay glinting dimly a few inches from his left hand. Niahrin saw his fingers begin to scrabble toward it, and snapped, "Don't touch that!" She darted forward, kicking the weapon out of his reach as he cringed away from her foot. Then the silhouetted head turned back toward her, and he spoke for the first time. As soon as she heard his voice, any doubts Niahrin might have harbored about his identity vanished.

"But I m ... must," the man pleaded in a cajoling whine. "I must, don't you see, Niahrin? Don't you see? It'll kill me—and it'll kill you, too, if you let it get near—"

"By all that's sanctified ..." Niahrin muttered under her breath, then gave a weary sigh. "Get up, Perd, for the sake of the good Mother. Grimya is my friend and she won't harm you. Get up, now, have a cup of hot brew with me by the fire, and tell me what in the name of all creation brings you here. For I'm sure of one thing—this is no coincidence."

* * *

"So you see, I *must* go back." Perd Nordenson's thin fingers worked at the empty tin cup he held as though he were trying to mold it into a new and bizarre shape. "I *must*, Niahrin. I must see her. I must speak to her. I must *tell* her—"

"Wait, Perd, wait." Niahrin interrupted, forestalling yet another outpouring of senseless words. Despite the abortive attack he'd tried to launch, Perd was in a more lucid state of mind than normal, and with time and effort she had been able to coax him into something approaching calm coherence. But for all her pains the nub of his rambling explanations still eluded her. And Grimya's reaction didn't help. It had been hard enough persuading Perd, against all the instincts of his twisted mind, that the she-wolf was a friend and a companion, not to be attacked, not to be hated, and that he could sit by the fire in her company without putting his life at risk; but while Perd was eventually mollified, Grimya was not. Niahrin didn't know what lay at the root of the trouble, for Grimya refused to speak in Perd's presence. But she lay on the far side of the campfire, her ears low and her hackles high, watching the old man in mute and fearful distrust, and occasionally a soft snarl competed with the crackle of the flames. Niahrin, interposed between them and feeling uncomfortably like a choice bone over which two dogs were squabbling, was resolved to ignore Grimya's hostile show. Perd alone was quite enough for her to cope with; for the time being at least, Grimya must look to her own salvation.

"Perd." She took the cup from him and refilled it, though only halfway to the rim because he'd spilled a good part of his first drink and it seemed senseless to waste more. "Perd, listen to me and *try* to pay heed this time. I understand some of what you are saying. I know you want to go back to Carn Caille—though what you were doing there in the first place is a question quite beyond me—"

"For *her*—" Perd began.

"Yes, for *her*, I know. But who is she?" She dropped her ladle back in the pot; the clatter made Perd jump visibly. "That's what you haven't told me." That and a good deal else, she thought, but didn't say so. "Just tell me that, Perd. Tell me who *she* is."

His hands were still working feverishly together; Niahrin prized his fingers apart and pushed the steaming cup into his grasp. He stared down at it for a few moments as though he had never seen such a thing before, then his tongue touched his lower lip, like a child deep in thought.

"Perd," Niahrin prompted again when he didn't speak. "Just tell me who you mean."

Perd smiled. He raised his gaze to her face and his faded eyes had a strange, faraway look.

"Why, the queen, of course. Who else?"

"The *queen*?" Niahrin was shocked. What possible connection could Perd Nordenson have with Queen Brythere?

"I don't understand," she said. "Are you trying to tell me you *know* the queen?"

"Oh, yes. Oh, yes. I know her. And I . . . and I . . . love her." Perd's face crumpled and tears welled in his eyes. "I've always loved her, *always*. But she—when they— she—" And suddenly he began to cry, a deep, pain-racked weeping that shook his entire frame. Niahrin was at a loss; his extraordinary revelation had thrown her completely off balance and she didn't know what to think or do. Awkwardly she reached out and laid a hand on his shoulder, trying to offer what small, wordless comfort she could; but as she touched him his misery changed abruptly and violently to rage. He threw her off, striking out with clawed fingernails, and his voice rose in a petulant shout.

"They put me out! All those years, so many *years*, and

they put me *out*, as though I was a worn garment to be discarded!" He flung his cup at her; Niahrin dodged and the cup rebounded with an echoing clang from a nearby tree trunk and bounced into the undergrowth. Grimya snarled and Niahrin shouted, "Grimya, *stop* that! He doesn't mean it!" Clenching her teeth and breathing hard to calm herself she turned to the old man again. "Losing your temper with me won't profit either of us, Perd. Whatever injustice may have been done to you, I wasn't responsible for it! Now, try again. Tell me what happened to you at Carn Caille."

But Perd was crying once more and this time he either wouldn't or couldn't stop. Niahrin listened to the sobbing, aware that she was helpless in the face of this. Old grievances and griefs had been stirred up from the murky depths of Perd Nordenson's damaged mind, and they were powerful enough to have driven him to seek redress at the king's court. Piecing together what little he'd told her, Niahrin could picture the scene at Carn Caille only too well. Small wonder that they'd driven him away, and if he'd tried to beleaguer the queen herself with some crazed declaration of love he was lucky to have escaped as lightly as he had.

Yet for all his senseless jumble—Perd's obsession with Queen Brythere and all the folderol about some past injustice—Niahrin's intuition was at work, warning her not to dismiss the entire tale as a madman's ravings. Perd *was* mad, no doubt of it, but she felt instinctively that what he had told her was at least an approximation of the truth. And the revelations of the tapestry she had woven, which now lay carefully folded and wrapped in the handcart, were a surer proof than any speculation. The power that guided her hands upon the loom had shown her that Perd Nordenson had a part to play in this strange affair, and that power could not lie.

A rasping sound brought her suddenly and sharply back to earth. Perd had slumped forward, head resting on his knees, and he was snoring. Torn between pity, relief, and faintly amused pique that he hadn't even had the wherewithal to bid her good night, Niahrin rose stiffly. She couldn't leave him sitting as he was or like as not he'd tip forward into the fire; she caught him under the arms and drew him back into a supine position, then wrapped his cloak more closely around him so that he wouldn't take a chill. Perd didn't stir, and she judged that he'd sleep soundly now until morning. When he was as comfortable as she could make him, Niahrin moved quietly round the fire and crouched down beside Grimya.

"He's sound asleep," she said. "You can speak without fear that he'll hear you."

The she-wolf looked at her with unhappy eyes. "I do not ll . . . *like* this man," she said hoarsely. "I have trried to be calm but it is very hard. There is something *evil* in him." She paused. "He is the one who came to your house. The one I was afraid of."

"Yes, he is." Niahrin stroked the wolf's head gently, soothingly. "But he isn't evil, Grimya, as I've tried to explain to you before. Damaged, yes; and he has a fear and hatred of your kind that I've never been able to understand. But not evil." Her stroking hand increased its pressure slightly. "Trust me, my dear, please. Perd won't harm you, for I won't allow him to and I know how to divert him at his worst times. But I do want to help him if I can."

Grimya was silent for a few moments. Then: "Do you mean that you want him to come with us?"

"Yes, I want him to come with us. It isn't only for his sake; it's for mine as well, though that's something I don't think I properly understand yet. And perhaps . . . well, I can't be sure, but perhaps it's even for your sake, too."

The wolf dipped her head. "I d-do not understand, Niahrin. I don't want him to come. I am afraid of him."

"Oh, Grimya." Niahrin ached inwardly with the impossibility of explaining to anyone, let alone to this kindly friend with her clear and direct reasoning, the nature of the power that had guided her hands on the loom and was guiding her mind now. It had placed a responsibility on her shoulders, and she couldn't escape it. Whatever lay ahead, she must see it through.

"My dear"—her voice was soft—"please be patient with your friend Niahrin. I think that in this I'm as helpless as you are. But one thing I know: Perd must come with us, for to deny him that would be to deny him hope. And that's something I will do to no living creature."

Gray clouds were massing to the northwest and Niahrin judged that the rain would be on them within an hour. She was thankful to see the bulk of Carn Caille ahead, and doubly thankful—though it was accompanied by a stab of guilt—that Perd had not, after all, accompanied them on the last stage of their journey. The old man had vanished sometime during the night while she and Grimya were asleep, taking half their food rations and leaving no clue to the direction in which he had gone.

Niahrin fervently hoped that he wasn't on his way back to Carn Caille. However, the fact that he had made no further attempt to attack either Grimya or herself before leaving the camp suggested that he was still in a relatively lucid state of mind, so with luck he might have the sense to give the place a wide berth, at least for the time being. Grimya made no secret of the fact that she was glad to be rid of him, and so they had set out in a mood of relief.

But though Perd might be absent, he wasn't forgotten. Throughout the day as she wheeled the handcart along the road Niahrin had mulled over the conundrum of the old man's disjointed revelation. It made no more sense in the light than it had in the darkness, and Grimya's attitude was a further puzzle. It was understandable that the wolf should have taken strongly against Perd in the light of his declared hatred of her kind, but this went further than mere enmity and Niahrin couldn't put her finger on the cause. Grimya was unforthcoming; she simply refused to discuss the matter at all, and at length Niahrin had given up her musings to concentrate on the road.

Carn Caille loomed nearer, and now the witch could smell the change in the air and the freshening in the wind that heralded the rain. She quickened her pace, apologizing to Grimya for the jolting discomfort, but the wolf didn't reply. She was staring at the fortress and she looked as though she were trying to crouch lower in the cart, as if to hide from what lay ahead.

They were barely a hundred paces from the open main gates when there was a flicker of movement within and a woman on horseback emerged. Grimya uttered an odd little cry, her ears pricking eagerly, then sank back again as she saw that the rider was a stranger. Niahrin, however, recognized her immediately.

"It's the queen!" Surprise and pleasure suffused her voice, and as the horse came toward them she drew to the side of the track and made a bow.

Queen Brythere was dressed for hard riding, in a divided woolen skirt and leather boots with a hide coat, its collar fastened high at her slim throat. Her head was uncovered and her red-gold hair caught back in a severe coil. As she approached, Niahrin saw the expression on her face—an extraordinary mixture of misery, fear, and determination—and unanswerable questions piled into the witch's mind. The queen looked ill, ill and distraught. Her skin had no color and her eyes were heavily shadowed, and her hands on the reins were as pale and thin as a ghost's.

The horse—a handsome gray—slowed as it drew level, and Brythere looked down. She frowned a little at the peculiar sight of the one-eyed woman and the wolf in the cart, but Niahrin had the distinct impression that their presence registered only on a peripheral level and that the queen's thoughts were inflexibly fixed elsewhere. The witch made another respectful bow and, collecting herself, Brythere smiled a distracted, meaningless little smile in acknowledgment, then spurred her horse away, wheeling it toward the south and the open lands bordering the tundra.

"No escort, white as an invalid, and a look in her eyes as though she'd just been told the day of her own death. . . ." Niahrin didn't realize she'd spoken the words aloud until Grimya turned to look uncertainly at her.

"She is not a hh—happy woman," the wolf said. Then: "Where do you think she might be going?"

"The good Mother alone knows." Niahrin glanced at the threatening sky. "But if she's any intention of riding far she'll enjoy little more than a soaking. Still, that's her concern; it isn't my place to question what the queen chooses to do." She wheeled the handcart back onto the road and walked on toward the fortress gates.

To her surprise, and to Grimya's great relief, they were expected. As soon as the witch began to tell her story the guard at the gate swept her explanations aside and waved her through. King Ryen, it appeared, had given word that his sentries were to watch for the arrival of someone from the forests with a tame wolf. And yes, the seafarer by the name of Indigo was here, along with her betrothed. At this Grimya made a strangled sound but quickly controlled it, afraid she might give her secret away. The guard asked Niahrin to wait while he fetched someone to escort them, and as soon as he was out of earshot the wolf's head swung round to Niahrin.

"H-he said . . . *betrothed*." There was fear and confusion in her voice. "Indigo is not betrothed! She is not betrothed to anyone! She *cannot* be, she *would* not—"

"Hush!" Niahrin warned. "Hush, or someone might hear you!" She laid a calming hand on Grimya's head. "Listen, my dear, I think there's a good deal we don't yet know, and it's likely as not that the guard made a mistake. Be patient a little longer and we'll find out what's what."

The first drops of rain started to fall as the sentry returned. With him was a young, brown-haired man whom Niahrin recognized instantly as a bard.

"Madam." The young man hesitated briefly, but if the witch's marred face disconcerted him he was quick-witted enough to disguise his reaction. He bowed, and Niahrin saw his swift appraisal of her on more than simply the physical level. "You are welcome to Carn Caille. I am Jes Ragnarson, bard to King Ryen."

"I am Niahrin," the witch told him.

"Yes. Yes, I've heard of you." He smiled. "Your name and reputation are highly respected by my peers as well as your own."

That did surprise Niahrin and she gave a throaty laugh. "Well, I won't pretend I'm not flattered, Jes Ragnarson." She indicated the handcart. "And this—as I gather you already know—is Grimya."

The bard gazed down at the wolf for a few moments, then nodded. "There are two people here who'll be very glad indeed to see her." He turned to the witch again and treated her to a second long, hard look. "And a few more who may also be glad to see you." Then, before Niahrin could query this peculiar statement, his manner changed again and he glanced up at the leaden square of the sky above Carn Caille's walls. "The rain's getting heavier;

your arrival was timely! Come, let's get under cover before the downpour starts. Your friends are waiting for you."

They hurried from the meager shelter of the gate arch and across the courtyard to a door on the fortress's west side. Niahrin saw faces at windows, watching them with interest, then they had ducked through the door and were in a spacious and surprisingly warm entrance hall with curving roof beams and wide passages leading away to either side. Servants paused to glance curiously at them; one or two, seeing the handcart and the wolf, smiled. Jes Ragnarson led them down the left-hand passage, through a big, echoingly empty chamber that Niahrin guessed must be a council hall or some such, and finally to the door of an anteroom. Here he knocked; for a moment there was silence, then the door was opened.

Niahrin could see directly into the room, and for a startling moment she thought that an entire reception committee awaited them. Six people—there must have been six, if not more: a big, blond man, an auburn-haired woman, a child with silver hair and strange eyes, a tall, imposing figure with hair like willow leaves, an ancient woman, a—

Then suddenly and shockingly the vision flicked out of existence and only two people remained. The witch shook her head dazedly, staring at them and wondering whatever could have come over her, but before she could gather her wits the burly blond man was rushing forward.

"Grimya!" His heavily accented voice boomed in the room's small confines. "Grimya, it is you, it *is*! You're not drowned!"

Niahrin was still too shaken to warn him to have a care for the wolf's injured leg. Vinar dropped down beside the handcart and began to rub Grimya vigorously between the ears. Grimya whimpered with delight, writhing, but her gaze was fixed on the woman standing behind Vinar, who thus far hadn't moved to greet her but was staring at her with disquieted eyes, and with her mental voice she cried out ecstatically to her.

Indigo! You are safe, you are here! I've been so afraid for you!

But Indigo didn't reply. Her expression didn't alter, she didn't speak, and there was no answering surge of emotion from her mind.

Indigo, what's wrong? the wolf asked, distressed. *Why don't you greet me?*

Still Indigo only continued to stare at her, and the wolf's distress turned abruptly to dread. Frantically her psychic senses reached out again, but still there was no response from her friend. In fact . . . in fact, Grimya realized, there was *nothing*. The mental link between them had vanished as though it had never existed.

Indigo! Grimya flung all the power she could muster into the silent shout. *Indigo, please, PLEASE—*

"I'm sorry." Indigo's voice cut across her desperate mental call, and she turned away. "I'm sorry, Vinar. I don't remember. If this is Grimya, and if she ever belonged to me, I simply don't remember anything about her."

Panic snapped all semblance of caution in Grimya's mind, and her voice—her physical voice—broke from her throat in a cry that was half speech and half howl.

"Indigo, why don't you know me? *Why don't you know me?*"

Vinar jumped back as though a whiplash had cracked across his face. He lost his balance and sat heavily on the floor, jaw dropping open as he stared at the wolf in disbelief and fright. Indigo froze where she stood, her face a mask of shock, mouth half open, as from nowhere a succession of disjointed images stabbed violently into her mind. *Wolf—forests and firelight—journeys that seemed to have no end—and a burden, a terrible, inescapable burden—*

"Animals can't speak. . . ." She took a pace backward, raising both hands palms outward as though to ward off something too dreadful to face. *"They can't speak!"* Her head jerked up and she gave Niahrin a wild, terrible look. "This is a trick, some game you're playing with me!"

"No!" Niahrin protested. "Lady, I assure you—"

"I don't believe you!" Shrill with panic, Indigo's voice cut her off in midsentence. Then, before anyone could stop her, she pushed past the handcart, past the witch, and with a cry of what sounded like despair fled the room.

•CHAPTER•XI•

"She never told me. That's what I don't understand. All that time at sea, and she never *told* me!" Vinar paced the room like a caged cat, to the window, to his chair, to the door, back to the window again. Then he stopped and looked at Niahrin in mute appeal. "*Why* didn't she tell me? You can't answer that and no more can't I; it don't make no sense!"

The witch was crouched beside the handcart, one hand stroking Grimya's head with a steady, gentle movement as she tried to offer the wolf mute comfort. Grimya had sunk into abject silence, refusing to speak after her one outburst and refusing now to meet the gaze of either human. Realizing that her efforts were having no effect, Niahrin sighed and rose stiffly to her feet.

"You're right," she said ruefully. "I can't answer the question, and in all honesty I don't think it's my place to try." She glanced at the wolf. "Grimya may want to tell you more in good time; I don't know. But for now, all we can do is wait."

For a moment she thought Vinar would argue, but after a few seconds' pause he shrugged in helpless acquiescence. "Ya. Ya, I suppose so." He returned to the window, restless. "Can't see the courtyard from here. Damn it, where has she *gone*?"

Niahrin wished she knew. Indigo's precipitate flight had shocked them all, but what had followed had been an even greater surprise, at least to her. Vinar, recovering his wits, had rushed from the room in Indigo's wake, but she had already vanished and he collided instead with Ryen as the king emerged unexpectedly from a side passage. Niahrin was stunned when the two men returned to the room together, but her incoherent attempts to make obeisance fell away as Ryen told them briskly to remain where they were. He knew Carn Caille's corridors far better than they; he personally would find Indigo and persuade her to return.

Niahrin couldn't pretend to understand what lay behind the king's obvious concern with Vinar and Indigo's affairs, and Vinar was too agitated to answer the myriad questions she wanted to ask—indeed, he had questions of his own. How was it that Grimya could speak? How was it possible? How long had she had the power? Had Indigo known? How long had she known? Above all, why hadn't either of them trusted him enough to tell him about such a momentous thing? Throughout his tirade as he veered turbulently between anger and pleading, Grimya refused to utter a further word, and though she struggled valiantly to explain what little she could, in truth Niahrin's knowledge was as flimsy as Vinar's.

"One thing I'm sure of," Vinar said suddenly, turning round again. "Something's going on here. Something I don't know; maybe nobody knows. But whatever it is, Indigo's at the middle of it."

Niahrin glanced at Grimya. The wolf looked quickly away, and the witch knew instantly that her suspicion was right. Grimya could explain a great deal of this mystery if she chose to, and Niahrin felt a premonitory shiver run through her as she recalled the spell-tapestry she had woven and what she had glimpsed within it. She was tempted to speak her mind to Vinar but caution prevailed. She didn't know him, and though her intuition told her he was a good man she was reluctant to reveal her thoughts to a stranger.

Avoiding a direct answer, she said, "It may be so. But I can't pretend to know enough yet to make any sense of it." *So many unanswered questions,* she thought again and added, "Indigo's memory, for instance. Amid all these shenanigans I gathered enough to realize what's happened to her. I had no idea, and neither did Grimya." She indicated the wolf, who still refused to look up. "That's why she's so upset, I think, and why she won't talk now. I understand that she and Indigo were very close companions."

"Ya, they were." Vinar's mouth twitched humorlessly. "But I didn't know *how* close, did I?" He moved past Niahrin to the handcart and looked down at Grimya. "Hey, Grimya, why won't you talk to me, eh? I know about you now, so no reason to be secretive. Aren't we friends, too?"

He held out his hand as he spoke, making it impossible for the wolf to ignore him. To his consternation, Grimya bared her teeth menacingly.

"Grimya!" Vinar's voice was bewildered, and Niahrin cut in quickly.

"Grimya, what is it, my dear? What's wrong?" Doubt flared suddenly. "This man *is* Vinar . . . ?"

"Yess." The reply came so abruptly, so unexpectedly, that it took her aback, as did the venom in Grimya's tone.

The wolf looked at her at last. "Yess, this is Vinar. But he is not my friend anymore!" Her head swung and she glared accusingly at the Scorvan. "You have told lies! You have told the people here that you are betrothed to Indigo, but I know you are not!"

Vinar was shocked to the core. He backed away, one hand upraised in protest. "Grimya, it isn't how you're saying," he tried to protest. "I don't tell lies, not the way you mean. Indigo and me—"

"*No!*" Grimya interrupted furiously. "*Not* Indigo and you! She has not said she will marry you. She *will* not say it, she c-*cannot* say it! I know that—I know it!"

Niahrin had forgotten the small incident with the gate sentry, but at this outburst it came back clearly to mind. The man had mentioned Indigo's betrothal quite casually, as though it were common knowledge at Carn Caille, and Grimya had been horrified. What had she said? "*She is not betrothed to anyone; she cannot be.*" Almost the same words she now used to Vinar, and underlying them an air of desperation—almost terror—that set alarm bells ringing in Niahrin's psyche. *Cannot,* she thought. Why *cannot*? What was the secret Grimya still hid from her?

Vinar was again trying to protest and explain himself at one and the same time, and she interrupted him. "Wait," she said. "Wait, both of you. I don't pretend to know what this is about, but we'll gain nothing by wrangling, now or. at any other time." She was a little surprised to hear the authoritative edge in her voice—more like Granmer than her own self—but shook the frisson off. "We must talk," she declared. "*All* of us," this with a firm look in Grimya's direction, daring her to object. "But this is not the place and certainly not the moment. When His Majesty finds Indigo—"

"No!" Grimya and Vinar spoke together, urgently. Niahrin hesitated.

"Please, lady," Vinar entreated. "Don't tell Indigo what Grimya said. At least, not to begin—not till I can explain."

The wolf growled softly. "He is rrr-*ight*." She sounded reluctant to admit it, reluctant to agree with Vinar on anything. "It would not help her, not as she is now. And do not tell anyone else about me. You must not. Not yet."

Outnumbered, Niahrin sighed and made an acquiescent gesture. "Very well. But I think the three of us should—"

Someone knocked on the door, and they all turned.

Jes Ragnarson, the young bard, came in. He smiled a cordial but distracted greeting at them all. "Please forgive the sudden intrusion, but I've a message from the king. Indigo's gone. She took a horse from the stables and rode out of Carn Caille—there's a little more to the story, but that can wait. His Majesty's going after her; he knows the direction she took and he'll catch up with her soon enough. He asked me to bring word to you."

Vinar started toward the door. "I go too! Indigo might be in danger—"

The bard caught his arm. "No, Vinar, best not. I wouldn't mind wagering you're no horseman, so you'd only be in the way. She'll come to no harm; the king and his own men will bring her back safe and sound."

Vinar saw the sense in that and subsided, and Niahrin said, "That's kind of you, Jes Ragnarson, to carry the king's message to us. We'll wait here for further news."

Jes was a true bard and he glimpsed the fact that there was a good deal more in Niahrin's mind than she was prepared to reveal, at least to him. He made a bow. "Thank you, lady. With the Mother's goodwill, the wait shouldn't be overlong."

"I'm sorry, my lord, but I simply didn't think to ask if she had leave to take the horse." Carn Caille's head groom buckled the chestnut gelding's bridle and began to back the animal out of its stall, his gaze shifting briefly, uneasily, to Ryen's face. "In truth, I . . . well, I didn't like to question her command. It was the—the *manner* she had about her, sir. She seemed to know the stables as well as if they were her own, and as I didn't know who she might be I thought it wasn't my place to make any objections. Then when she rode off southward, in the same direction that madam the queen took earlier—"

"Yes, yes; I understand." Ryen moved aside to allow the horse to pass him, trying to keep his worry, if not his impatience, from showing in his voice. The four men he'd deputized to ride with him were already mounted and he was anxious to be away without any further delays; too much time had already been wasted searching Carn Caille for Indigo. "There's no blame to you, Parrick," he added tersely. "My only regret is that no one thought to tell me the queen had also taken it into her head to go riding unaccompanied." Then he checked himself as he realized his tone was becoming unguardedly angry. His troubles with Brythere were no fault and no concern of Parrick's. Less brusquely, he asked, "Which horses did they take?"

"Her Majesty took her own favorite, the white mare, and the other lady asked for the iron-gray gelding." Parrick frowned. "In fact, my lord, she insisted on the iron-gray, wouldn't have any other. That was another reason why I thought she must have had permission, sir."

Ryen grunted; he wasn't interested in the reason behind either woman's choice of horse, only in which animals the search party should look out for. They were out in the courtyard by now, and despite the increasingly heavy rain the chestnut was dancing, eager to be off. Ryen quieted it with a pat then swung himself into the saddle. As he gathered the reins he heard quick footfalls and a familiar voice calling his name.

"Ryen? What's amiss?" The dowager Moragh, cloaked

and with a hood pulled over her hair against the rain, was hurrying toward them. Parrick withdrew tactfully into the stable, the mounted men saluted and stared into the middle distance, and Moragh stopped beside the horse, looking up at her son.

Ryen told the tale in a few short sentences, and Moragh's mouth pursed. "I see. I thought Brythere had been resting these past two hours—clearly someone has been careless." She sighed with annoyance. "If you're going after her you'd best be on your way. As for Indigo . . ."

"We'll bring her back, too, if we can," Ryen said. "If we can find her. But Brythere is more important."

"Yes, yes, of course. But do you know which direction she took?"

"Parrick saw her turn south."

"Well, that's something; at least she's not foolish enough to make for the forest, with that wretched madman still at large." The dowager stepped back from the horse, then as though as an afterthought said, "Where is Vinar?"

"In the west anteroom behind the great hall. The witch has arrived, with Indigo's pet wolf—it was something about that reunion that triggered the trouble, I think, though I haven't had time to discover exactly what went awry."

"How strange. I'll instruct Jes to give them refreshment and some form of explanation." She smiled a little grimly. "That poor Scorvan. We seem to be making a habit of unexpected crises—he must think us quite mad."

With the rain dripping from the edge of her hood Moragh watched Ryen and his party ride toward the gates, through them, and away over the grass beyond. Then she gave a small, weary sigh, turned on her heel, and walked back inside the citadel.

* * *

It wasn't until she was more than a mile from Carn Caille that the senselessness of what she had done came home to Indigo. Abruptly she pulled on the reins, slowing the gelding from its headlong gallop to a canter, a trot, finally to a thankful, blowing walk. Twisting round in the saddle Indigo looked back at the citadel, now no more than an indistinct blur in the rain, gray stones against gray sky. Calm reasoning was reestablishing itself after the turbulent flare-up, and she felt foolish and shamed. What could have possessed her to react as she had to the talking wolf? It was understandable that she should be shocked—who would not be?—but the overwhelming emotion surging in her had been far more intense. She'd felt a sense of sheer *panic*, and with it an inexplicable but terrible wrench of grief and loss. Only one thing had mattered to her at that moment: to flee from the enclosing walls around her and put as much distance between Carn Caille and herself as she could.

Why has she been so terrified? The hand holding the reins had fallen slack on the saddle pommel and, sensing no control, the gelding halted altogether and started to snatch mouthfuls of the spring grass. Indigo still sat motionless, hardly aware of the rain soaking her clothes and streaming from her hair as she stared back toward the citadel. The whole affair seemed nonsensical now, and a further embarrassment was the memory of the temerity—almost arrogance—with which she had burst into the stables and demanded a horse. Not just any horse, either, but the iron-gray. Why this animal and no other? For a moment, she recalled, her tangled mind had convinced her that the horse was her own property, an old and familiar friend. But that was impossible. She didn't own a horse—indeed, it came as a further shock now to realize that she knew how to ride. She was a seafarer and by rights she should never have sat a horse before in her life, but when she sprang up into the gelding's saddle a sure instinct had come to the surface and she'd ridden away as though born to it.

Born to it. . . . Perhaps, she thought a little wildly, what Vinar had half jokingly suggested was true. Perhaps she did have some forgotten connection with Carn Caille. In the moment when the wolf had spoken to her it had seemed to her that there *was* a link, and something had stirred in the depths of her subconscious. That had been the cause of her fear, she realized now; not the wolf itself but something that the wolf had seemed, for a fleeting moment, to represent or recall.

But if she had once had kinsmen here, or even if her name had simply been known, why had no one come forward to acknowledge her? That puzzle hinted at some unpleasant secret, something hidden or deliberately kept from her. But why? *Why?*

Her eyes focused again on the distant shape of the citadel. Chances were that someone would come after her before long. Vinar would be frantic, would want a search . . . but Indigo didn't want to go back yet. She needed a little more time before facing the inevitable ordeal of questions and explanations and apologies. Time to be alone. Time to *think*.

She faced forward once more and pulled the gelding's head up, touching her heels to its flanks to urge it into a trot. She had a good start on any pursuers; she'd ride on for a while at a more leisurely pace, give herself the chance to settle her jangled nerves and bring a little reason to bear on the situation. With the sun invisible behind the rain clouds it was hard to judge the direction she had taken from Carn Caille, but the land ahead looked easy enough, if barren. She spurred the gelding to a ground-eating canter, heading for the crest of a shallow ridge ahead. From the crest she could turn right to where a belt of trees, a thin peninsula stretching out from the forest that lay beyond Carn Caille, offered both shelter and a hiding place. She would be back at the citadel before sunset, and if Vinar and her hosts were angry she would simply have to apologize as best she could and hope to be forgiven.

The gelding slowed as it reached the ridge crest, snorting with the effort of the last short but steep climb, and stopped at the top of an escarpment, a drop of some fifty feet to sere scrubland below. This must be the edge of the great southern tundra; beyond that, Indigo knew, lay the vast and empty polar ice plains where no human ever ventured. . . .

Except for—

The thought flickered suddenly and shockingly through her mind, and her skin crawled. *Except for what?* She couldn't answer the question, but in that instant the fear had come clamoring back. Something out there, something on the tundra . . . *A long shadow, and a door, and she must not, must not, MUST NOT—*

She was jolted out of frozen terror as the gelding abruptly whinnied long and loudly, its sides shaking under her. The animal was looking away to the right; it pawed, setting a shower of loose stones rattling away down the escarpment, and Indigo saw what had attracted its attention. Another horse was approaching, picking its way along the ridge. It was a pure white creature, and on its back was a young woman, small and slender, crowned with vivid red-gold hair.

Indigo had seen Queen Brythere only once—and that briefly—in the great hall, but the bright hair was unmistakable. Brythere was watching Indigo intently and there was a distinct air of aggression in her posture as she urged her mount forward. As soon as she was within hailing distance, she called out.

"What are you doing here? What do you want?" Her

voice sounded shrill, angry. Indigo was still on edge after the sudden stab of terror, and mentally she bristled.

"What do you mean?" She shortened rein, her fingers fumbling, and the gelding tossed its head nervously. "I want nothing!"

Brythere jerked her horse to a halt and her resentful gaze raked the stranger who had dared to address her with such a lack of deference. "Have you been sent from Carn Caille to spy on me?" she demanded.

"No, I have not!" Indigo retorted. "I'm not concerned with you. Why should I be?"

Brythere was clearly startled. Then she uttered a brittle, faintly hysterical laugh.

"I find your manner very impertinent, madam! Do you know who I am?"

"Yes." Indigo was calmer now and her voice level. "You are the king's wife." She wondered suddenly why she had said that. *The king's wife* and not *the queen*. Strange . . .

Brythere's small, pretty mouth pursed. "Yes, I am Queen Brythere. And you are—?"

"They tell me my name is Indigo."

"Oh . . ." Brythere's expression and demeanor changed immediately. "Oh . . . The woman named after the color of mourning. The one who has lost her memory." She paused, looked hard at the gelding, and then harder at Indigo's face. "You were at the public court yesterday, weren't you? With that fair man, the Scorvan sailor. I saw you, just before—" Then she thought better of finishing the sentence. A funny little smile, almost a grimace, pulled at the sides of her lips, and abruptly she seemed to relax. "No, they wouldn't have sent *you* to follow me. Very well, then; you may accompany me. We shall ride back to Carn Caille together."

The rapid shift of mood was confusing Indigo, and she

shook her head. "I don't want to go back," she said. "Not yet."

"What? You prefer to ride in the drenching rain, and risk catching a rheum or worse?" Ignoring the fact that she herself had done precisely the same thing, Brythere laughed again. The laugh sounded artificial. "What nonsense! Besides, the gelding you're riding is one of my own, and I won't have him made to suffer the weather unnecessarily. We shall return together."

The matter of the horse forced Indigo's hand; unless she was prepared to walk back to the citadel she was in no position to argue. Reluctantly she acquiesced, and the two animals turned for home. For a few minutes neither woman spoke; then suddenly Brythere said, "What are you doing on the ridge?"

Indigo glanced sidelong at her. "Nothing of any importance."

She had the impression that Brythere didn't believe her. "You seemed to me to be looking at something," the queen said.

"Only at the landscape—what little I could see of it."

"The tundra?"

"Yes."

"Why?"

A sharp edge now to the question. Indigo frowned. "Should I have an especial reason?"

"No. But it seems a strange choice. It's hardly a prepossessing vista, after all." Then the queen made an odd little gesture that seemed to be midway between a shrug and a shiver. "But then even the bleakest of landscapes can be kinder than the other choice."

Cold fingers inexplicably touched Indigo's spine. "The *other* choice?" she repeated cautiously.

"To suffer the dreams that haunt the walls of Carn Caille. . . ." For a moment Brythere's tone was grim—then suddenly, mercurially, her manner shifted again and the bright, unconvincing smile reappeared on her face. "After all," she said with studied carelessness, "there are times, are there not, when anywhere can become wearying? Even one's own home."

Indigo stared. In the space between one speech and the next the queen had wiped out the impact of her first remark, twisting it into a harmless observation. It was as though she had dismissed—or even forgotten—the fact that she had, for a moment, starkly exposed her private thoughts. But in doing so, she had given Indigo an unnerving jolt.

It had been clear to Indigo from their first, brief encounter that there was something very amiss with the young queen. Quite what yesterday's fracas in the great hall had been about she didn't know, for when the fighting men burst in Vinar had pushed her behind him for safety and his bulk had blocked her view, while in all the furor she hadn't been able to make sense of the intruder's shouts. But she had seen Brythere being carried from the hall, apparently in a faint, and then in the night had come the distant screams that shocked her from the aftermath of her nightmare, and which, so she had discovered, came from the queen's apartments. At that time Indigo had been too dazed to take in much detail; she had ventured out into the corridor, but a servant hurrying by had assured her that no one had been hurt and there was nothing to worry about.

This morning, though, she had learned the rest of the story. These disturbances were, it seemed, a regular occurrence, for the queen was plagued by frequent and recurring nightmares. The talkative servant who volunteered this hinted at some form of hysterical condition, and Indigo had wondered at first if perhaps Brythere was mad. But that notion vanished when the servant casually let slip the nature of the queen's terrors—for, night after night, Brythere dreamed that someone was trying to murder her.

Choosing her words with care, and still watching the queen sidelong, Indigo said, "You spoke of suffering dreams, lady. I also had a nightmare last night. I understand that it was ... similar to yours."

Brythere's head came round sharply. "Similar?"

"An assassin. With a knife."

The queen's mouth worked for a moment, as though she might have been about to cry. Then she tossed her head, sending raindrops flying from the wet mass of her hair.

"Your revelation doesn't surprise me, Indigo." Her lips gave another little twist. "I would defy anyone to live for long inside those walls without dreaming of such things." A long pause, while the horses jogged on. "But you shouldn't trouble yourself about it. *You* have nothing to fear. That, I think, is my privilege."

The bitter note had crept back into her voice. Perplexed, and a little disconcerted, Indigo wanted to ask what Brythere had meant by that cryptic remark, but before she could formulate a question the queen spoke again.

"I would prefer not to discuss the subject of dreams any further," she said firmly. "It is neither entertaining nor pleasant. Do I make myself clear?"

Indigo sighed. "Yes. Although—"

"*No.*" Brythere's tone was emphatic, almost fierce. "If you please. We will simply ride and say nothing more." She shook her mare's reins. "Oh, one more matter. It's likely that the king will have sent men out to look for me, and we may meet the search party before we reach the gates. If we do, I do not want you to repeat a word of this conversation to anyone."

"As you wish." There was no point in trying to argue with her, Indigo acknowledged. Whatever secret lay at the root of Brythere's dreams, she wouldn't be persuaded to reveal it. But the queen's words nagged at her. *I would defy anyone to live for long inside those walls without dreaming of such things.* Perhaps, Indigo thought, the secret had less to do with Brythere than with Carn Caille itself. . . .

She thrust that thought away and concentrated on the path ahead. The two horses had quickened their pace without urging, sensing that they were heading homeward and eager for the comfort and shelter of their stables. Through the rain Carn Caille loomed closer, solid and a little bleak, while away to their left the forest spread in a vast smudge of gray-green. Looking at it, Indigo felt a faint resonance that might have been lost memory—rolling sea stretching from horizon to horizon, and her mount's trotting gait like the sway of a ship's deck—and, as she had done so often before, she tried to catch hold of the tantalizing hint and force it into focus. But her mind resisted her efforts, as it always did, and the memory wouldn't come. She sighed again and was about to look away when she saw something moving out from the forest's edge, heading toward Carn Caille. For a moment, blurred by the weather, it looked as though a single tree had somehow detached itself from its fellows and was bowling across the sward toward the fortress. Then, narrowing her eyes to stare harder, she saw that it was a human figure, running. For a few moments the figure continued on its path toward the fortress—then, abruptly, it halted, and Indigo realized that whoever it was had seen them.

She pointed across the sward, drawing Brythere's attention. "If the king has sent searchers, lady, I think one of them at least has discovered us."

Brythere jerked on her mount's reins, bringing it to a slithering halt. "Where?" She peered into the murk. "I can see no one."

"There," Indigo said. "Midway between Carn Caille and

the forest's edge." The distant figure was that of a man, she saw now. He was swathed in a cloak and it was impossible yet to make out any detail of form or feature, but his build and gait were wrong for a woman. And he was on the move again. "He's seen us. He's coming in our direction."

Brythere's mare jinked suddenly, and the queen yanked savagely on the reins. "*Quiet*, you foolish brute!" Then she smiled vividly at Indigo. "I can hardly see him. You must have excellent eyes; I suppose it comes of spending your life at sea. Ah, well, we shall ride on. It can't be Ryen or he'd be on horseback, and I'm not about to be intimidated by servants. Come."

She spurred the mare forward again and they trotted on over the turf. The distant figure was still heading toward them, though now its course seemed to be a little uneven, as if the going had become rough. And though she couldn't be sure, Indigo thought she heard a faint sound carried on the wind and penetrating the rain's steady hiss. The sound of someone shouting . . .

"You ride very well for a seafarer, Indigo." Brythere's voice cut into Indigo's thoughts suddenly. "I suppose you can't recall, now, where you learned?"

Indigo didn't meet her gaze. "No."

"That's a pity. It might have—"

She didn't finish. She had pulled on the reins again, slowing the mare to an unwilling walk, and Indigo was several yards ahead before she realized and reined in her own horse, looking back in puzzlement.

"Lady . . . ?"

Brythere was staring at the approaching figure, now on a course that would intercept them before they reached Carn Caille. She was trembling.

"*Stop!*" she hissed. "*Quickly!*"

Indigo hauled the gelding to a standstill, checking it

firmly as it tried to fight her control. The queen was rigid in her saddle.

"Who is it?" Brythere demanded, her voice harsh with fear. *"Who is it?"*

"I don't know." Curious, and unnerved by her tone, Indigo looked sidelong at her. "A man, but I can see no detail from here."

"He's coming toward us!" Brythere began to shake. "He's putting himself between us and the citadel!"

Confounded, Indigo tried to reassure her. "But he's just one solitary man—as you said, probably one of your own servants."

"No!" Brythere cried. "No, it's *him*! I *know* it's him!" Then suddenly and savagely she kicked her mare's flanks, spurring the animal into a standing gallop. Too startled to react, Indigo saw the white mare, a blur in the rain, flying over the ground at a breakneck pace as the queen rode desperately for the gates of Carn Caille. She was trying to beat the lurching figure as it veered to intercept her; three hundred yards from the citadel their paths crossed, and Indigo saw the man's arms flail wildly as he tried to reach toward Brythere. He was too late; the queen galloped by a bare three paces from his clutch, and as his hands closed on nothing the man fell heavily to the ground.

Alarmed, Indigo urged her gelding toward the prone figure. Brythere pulled up some way ahead, wheeling her horse and looking back, and her voice carried across the distance between them though Indigo couldn't hear what she was shouting. Her only thought was that the stranger might have collided with the queen's horse and be injured, but as she drew nearer she saw him stir and stagger unsteadily to his feet. Then when she came close enough to see him clearly she realized what was amiss with him. He wasn't hurt—but he *was* drunk. Back on

his feet he swayed like a sapling in a gale, and from the
folds of his filthy cloak he was struggling to extract an
unstoppered wineskin, spilling its contents over himself
as he wrestled ineptly, all the while mumbling in a
bleary monotone. Despite his height—and he was taller
than average—he was an old man, Indigo saw. Tendrils
of greasy white hair were escaping from under the
cloak's hood, and the hands clawing at the wineskin
were wrinkled and gnarled. Indigo felt a surge of distaste
but couldn't bring herself simply to ride on and leave
him in such a parlous state. She turned the gelding's
head and began to move toward him.

"Indigo!" Brythere's voice screeched hysterically across
the distance between them. "Indigo, no, *don't!*"

As the queen cried out, Indigo saw that beyond her
the gates of Carn Caille had swung open and several
horsemen were emerging. Brythere screamed again and
a man shouted in answer; the voice sounded like
Ryen's, and glancing quickly toward the citadel Indigo
glimpsed the king in the vanguard of the approaching
horsemen. The old man had also seen the riders, and he
uttered an extraordinary cry, almost like an animal's
yelp of pain. His hands froze in midmovement and the
wineskin fell to the ground, its contents spraying over
the grass. Then, in what appeared to be a passion of terror or rage or both, a cracked, frenzied voice issued
from under the cloak hood, shrieking at the oncoming
horsemen.

"Go back! Leave me be! LEAVE ME BE!"

With astonishing speed and agility the old man turned
and ran. Indigo was behind him; he hadn't seen her, and
the gelding reared as he rushed, blindly, straight at them.
Uttering another yelp, the old man swerved aside just in
time to avoid a collision, but he lost his balance, stumbled, and almost fell. As he flailed wildly to right him-

self the cloak hood fell back and, in the instant before he regained his feet and bolted like a hare, Indigo saw his face.

And shock jolted her like a physical blow as she recognized the man who, last night in her dreams, had tried to murder her.

•CHAPTER•XII•

"He escaped us." King Ryen pulled off his coat, and the servant who had entered the room with him hastened forward to take the sodden garment. "The Earth Mother alone knows how a man of his age has the speed and stamina to elude mounted men, but he managed it." As the servant departed bearing the coat, the king flexed his shoulders, stretched his arms, and moved toward the fire to warm himself.

"Your shirt's wet, too, Ryen," the dowager said from where she sat on the far side of the hearth. "You should change it, or you'll take a chill."

"In good time, Mother." He flicked her a smile to show that he felt less irritable than he sounded, then his expression changed as he turned to survey the faces of the other two people in the room, who had risen to their feet at his entrance.

"Where are Brythere and Indigo?" Ryen asked.

"Drying themselves and changing their clothes," Moragh told him. "They'll join us shortly. But before they do, there's something you should hear—"

"What I want to hear," Ryen interrupted, "is an explanation." His gaze focused on Vinar, not entirely without rancor. "Doubtless your lady had some reason for rushing from the citadel, purloining a horse that doesn't belong to her, and—"

"Ryen," Moragh said sharply, and her tone silenced him. "If you please." He turned, frowning, and the dowager continued. "Indigo's reasons can wait until later; she's already been scolded by Vinar and by me, and I'm sure she'll also wish to apologize to you for her foolishness. But this is a little more important. It concerns Perd."

"Oh?" Ryen's frown deepened.

"Yes. It seems," Moragh glanced meaningfully at Vinar, "that Indigo has encountered Perd before." She paused. "In a dream."

Vinar looked back at the king, uncomfortable and more than a little confused, for he didn't understand the dowager's concern with this matter, which was quite new to him. Indigo and Brythere had received a turbulent reception on reentering Carn Caille. Hearing the horses clatter into the courtyard, Vinar had run outside with Niahrin at his heels; as the two women dismounted, the dowager arrived on the scene and there had been a torrent of arguments, scolding, and expressions of mingled relief and anger. Amid all the fuss Vinar had tried to ask Indigo whatever had possessed her to run away as she'd done, but Indigo had turned his questions aside. Her face flushed and her manner hectic, she had started talking urgently about a nightmare and a mad old man. Her Grace had overheard this and suddenly intervened, and to Vinar's helpless bafflement both Indigo and the queen had been hurried away before he could say another word. Now he found himself in a room with Her Grace and Niahrin, and the king had come in, and still no one had explained to him what was going on.

Ryen said: "Mother, I don't understand—what do you mean, Indigo met Perd in a dream?"

"It was last night," Moragh told him. "Apparently she had a nightmare in which she saw two figures approaching her bed. One of them had a knife, and she saw his face clearly. It was Perd."

"Good Goddess . . ." The king's face paled under its tan. "Are you *sure*?"

"Quite certain. I questioned Indigo myself. There's no doubt of it, Ryen, she has had the same dream that's been plaguing Brythere for so long—and it happened on her first night under our roof."

"Hey, wait," Vinar cut in. They both looked at him in surprise and hastily he made an apologetic bow. "Sir—Lady— With all the proper respect—if there's someone been threatening Indigo that I don't know about—"

"No, no, Vinar." Moragh reached out and patted his arm reassuringly. "No one's threatening her. It was a dream, as she tried to tell you in the courtyard. Last night—"

"Ya, ya, I heard that." Vinar wouldn't normally have had the temerity to interrupt her, but his concern for Indigo overrode all else. "I heard her say she had a bad dream. But now you say she saw someone in her dream who wanted to kill her, and he's real!"

"Well, yes. But it isn't Indigo he wants to kill, Vinar. How she came to—I don't know, to pick up that particular thread, perhaps, in her unconscious mind, I can't begin to fathom. But there can be no doubt that she dreamed about this man last night, and that she and Brythere encountered him on their way back to Carn Caille today." She smiled, a wintry little smile. "And I said, it isn't Indigo whom Perd Nordenson wants to kill. It's us."

* * *

"He must be one of the few people still living who can re-member the great pestilence," Ryen said. "Or rather, who *could* remember it; for it seems he has no clear recollec-tion of the past at all. There's no doubt, as Niahrin seems to agree," he nodded toward the witch, "that Perd is quite mad now."

Moragh uttered a strangled snort. *"Now?"*

"Mother . . ." The king looked at her wearily and she shrugged. Ryen continued.

"Perhaps I was too lenient, and it would have been bet-ter for all concerned if I'd had Perd done away with as my—as some people felt I should. But Perd served my family for many years and served King Kalig's family be-fore that. The good Earth Mother alone knows what he must have suffered during the plague, what kin and friends he lost, what grief he has been forced to endure. It must have been enough to sow the seeds of madness in any man, and he can't be held to blame for what he has be-come as a result."

Moragh looked unimpressed—this was an old argument—but Vinar stared down at his boots, frowning as he tried to reconcile the king's reasoning with the blind hatred he felt on principle for Perd Nordenson.

Niahrin eventually broke the silence. She cleared her throat diffidently. "My lord . . . Your Grace . . . if I might venture to say, I think that the king is right." She was aware of Vinar looking at her with uncertain hostility, but pressed on. "I make no claim to know Perd well, but in the years when he lived in the forest he was never a dan-ger to anyone. Mad, indeed, and incurable by any human skills; but not an *evil* man." A memory flicked through her mind; Grimya, hackles up and snarling, her husky voice saying, *Evil—evil!* and she felt a sudden unpleasant fris-son. But then Perd had always hated wolves. . . .

She pushed the doubt away. "Perd Nordenson's mind is sorely damaged," she said. "And I suspect that his obsession with the queen has warped him further, to the point where he believes it is you, my lord, and Her Grace, who stand between him and his unfulfilled yearnings."

Moragh's eyes lit with interest. "You're saying that is the reason why he has made attempts on our lives? Because we are the obstacles in the way of his desire for Brythere?"

Niahrin's good eye met the dowager's gaze candidly. "In truth I don't know, ma'am. But you said, I think, that Perd has never actually tried to *harm* the queen?"

"Only followed her and frightened her; and the rest has all been in her dreams," Ryen murmured thoughtfully. "Yes . . . yes, it begins to make sense. . . ."

"No," Moragh said suddenly. "You're wrong, Ryen." She was still looking intently at the witch. "Niahrin's theory is all well and good, but it overlooks one vital thing. I mean no slight to you, my dear"—this to Niahrin—"for you couldn't have known of it. But our troubles with Perd Nordenson go back farther than this. They began when my son was no more than a babe in arms. There were attempts on my husband's life—indeed, on all our lives—in those days, and they could have had no connection with Brythere, for she wasn't even born! No; Brythere may have added an extra dimension to Perd's hatred of us, given him a new goad and a new focus, but she is not the cause of it. The cause, I believe, is deeper and older." She frowned. "Much, much older."

Vinar spoke up. "Then how is it that Indigo gets involved? She got nothing to do with this mad Perd and nothing to do with the queen. Yet now she has the same dream, and it's like Perd wants to hurt her, too! I don't understand any of it."

"You're not alone in that, Vinar," Ryen told him wryly. He glanced at Niahrin. "Do you have any answers?"

The witch shook her head. "None that I can be sure of, sir."

The king sighed. "And all this still begs the question of what's to be done about Perd himself now. We were so sure that this trouble was over and that we'd never see him again. *Why* did he take it into his deformed mind to come back?"

Niahrin had been asking herself the same question, but she said nothing. At length Moragh stood up.

"Whatever his reasoning, we shall have to be vigilant from now on. And I think our first priority should be to ensure that Perd can't return to Carn Caille."

Ryen grunted assent. "It's a long time since we instituted a full guard on the gates, but I'll see that it's done. Though after the fright we gave him today I doubt if Perd will have the audacity to approach the citadel again."

"We can but hope so," the dowager said. "And in the meantime . . ." She smiled at Vinar and Niahrin with sudden sympathy. "We must see what we can do to make our guests' stay more pleasant than it has been until now. Vinar's mission is still far from resolved, and Niahrin has put herself to great trouble in bringing the pet wolf here to be reunited with its mistress."

Niahrin returned the smile piquantly. "Sadly, ma'am, it hasn't been a happy reunion thus far." She ignored the sharp look Vinar gave her.

"No," Moragh agreed. "No, it has not. I understand that wolves are as loyal as dogs; the poor creature must be greatly distressed by Indigo's rejection. Well, we shall see what a little time can do. Vinar and Indigo are to stay at Carn Caille while we make investigations into the matter of tracing Indigo's family. I should like you to stay, too, my dear. I gather the wolf has grown fond of you, so your presence will be of great help. No, no," as Niahrin, astonished, started to protest that she wasn't worthy of such an invitation, "you are a very welcome guest, and I insist that you should remain."

The significance of her last words escaped Vinar and perhaps escaped Ryen, too, for he was staring out of the window, his thoughts elsewhere. But it didn't escape Niahrin. The witch inclined her head meekly.

"Of course, ma'am. Whatever you wish. Thank you."

At the dowager's bidding the guests were all invited to dine in the great hall that night. Niahrin was appalled at the prospect to begin with, visualizing a grand formal banquet at which she, with her scarred face and rough clothes, would stand out shamefully among such exalted company. But Mitha, the pleasant-faced chatelaine of Carn Caille's domestic arrangements, assured the witch that she had nothing to fear. Everyone from the highest to the lowest attended the evening meal, Mitha said; it was a communal affair for masters and servants alike, and more often than not the king's family were not even present. If Niahrin wished, Mitha would lend her a more formal dress for the occasion—they were about of a size with each other—but the witch would more likely be out of place if she dressed up than if she simply wore her everyday clothes.

Niahrin was reassured and began to anticipate the occasion with eagerness, but as matters turned out she was to be disappointed. Grimya, who for the time being was sharing Niahrin's room, was still sunk in deep misery over Indigo and was also terrified that Vinar might forget his promise and reveal her secret to the king. She flatly refused to show her face in the hall, despite the fact that it would have been quite permissible to bring her, and Niahrin felt that in all conscience she couldn't leave her alone to pine. They argued; for a while there was an impasse, but in the end Niahrin prevailed. Either they both went or they both stayed, she said, and if Grimya couldn't bring herself to go, then the matter was settled. So it was arranged with Mitha that Niahrin might go to the kitchens and fetch them a tray apiece, and the witch quashed her regrets and settled to the prospect of an uneventful evening.

There had been no reconciliation—if that was the right word—between Grimya and Indigo. Indeed, they hadn't so much as set eyes on each other since that first brief and unfortunate encounter, and Grimya's misery was such that she was unwilling to make the first move. If Indigo no longer remembered her, she said, and no longer wanted her friendship, then she didn't have the heart to try to make her change her mind.

She had, however, unbent a little in her attitude toward Vinar. Earlier the Scorvan had asked Niahrin if he might be allowed a few minutes alone with the wolf, and, with Grimya's cautious consent, Niahrin had left them to talk. When she returned, Vinar was waiting outside the door of her room. He didn't tell her what he and Grimya had said to each other and Niahrin didn't ask, but clearly the two had reached some kind of truce, and if Vinar's deception wasn't entirely forgiven it was at least understood and, in part, excused.

"Poor Grimya," Vinar said, looking back at the closed door and lowering his voice so the wolf wouldn't overhear. "She taken this badly." He turned back and his worried blue eyes focused on Niahrin. "I don't know what I can do for her, but if there's anything, you tell me, ya?"

"I will; I promise it." Niahrin had taken an instinctive liking to Vinar and was beginning to feel sorry for him. In all the tangled skeins of the mystery surrounding Indigo, he, it seemed, was the most innocent victim of all.

She made to lift the door-latch and go in when he touched her arm. "Nee-rin." His pronunciation of her name brought a smile to her lips, which she quelled. "Grimya said why she never told me she can talk. She said she'd promised Indigo, long time ago, never to tell no one unless Indigo said it was all right. That's fine; I understand that. But why didn't Indigo trust me? I wouldn't harm Grimya, she known that for a long time. Grimya and me were best of friends. So why didn't she trust me?"

Niahrin shook her head helplessly. "You know Indigo far better than I do, Vinar. How can I say what her reasons could have been?"

"Ya. Ya." He wasn't satisfied but he saw the logic of her answer. "I just thought . . . well, you being a witch . . . maybe you know things I don't; *see* things I don't. Ah, well. It's not to be helped."

Niahrin said, "I'm sorry." Then, after a pause, she added: "When you and Grimya talked, did she . . . say anything more about your betrothal?" She saw Vinar's expression begin to close and went on quickly, "It's none of my business, I know, but—"

"No," Vinar interrupted. "Is all right, I don't mind." He sighed and the momentary wariness fled. "She didn't say nothing. I know she's angry with what I did—thinks I cheated—and so she still don't like the idea, but maybe in time she'll come round."

"And you?" Niahrin asked gently.

"Me?" Vinar's face colored slightly. "Well . . . oh, sweet Sea Mother, I would have told Indigo the truth! I wouldn't have gone ahead, married her, without her knowing that she hadn't said yes before. She wouldn't, you see. She wouldn't agree. But I reckon if the wreck hadn't happened she *would* have said yes to me, and all she needed was a bit more time. I thought that, I *felt* that, like in my bones, you understand? So I reckoned, this way—this way, at least there'd be time. And when I *did* get to tell her the truth, she'd forgive me and marry me anyway." He hung his head. "That's what I thought, Neerin. I wouldn't have cheated her. I'm not that kind of man."

"No," said Niahrin, "I don't believe for a moment that you are."

His color deepened and he shuffled his feet, "Well . . . I'm glad I talked to Grimya, anyway. I better go, or I'll be late in the hall." Then his expression brightened a little. "There's to be music. Maybe they'll let Indigo play."

"Play?" Niahrin was nonplussed, then remembered something Grimya had once told her. "Oh—yes, she's a musician, isn't she? She plays the harp."

"More than that," Vinar said with peculiar emphasis. "More than that. Or it was . . . I wish you good night. And my thanks."

He bowed in the odd, stilted manner of the Scorvans and left Niahrin wondering why the tips of her fingers were prickling.

So now the long evening and night lay before them. Grimya appeared to be asleep; Niahrin thought she was feigning it because she didn't want to talk, but the witch saw no point in coercing her against her will. She had unpacked the handcart, though she kept it in the room in case Grimya should have need of it, and the few belongings she'd brought with her were now ranged around the room: a change of clothes neatly folded on the oak chest, Cadic's cudgel incongruously propped beside the hearth, and the tapestry . . . well, that was another matter. The tapestry was inside the chest now, where no casual eye could see it. Niahrin had resisted the temptation to look at it again, aware that its cryptic secrets would not begin to be revealed until the time was right and also aware that that time was not yet. She had brought her pipe, and with the thought of whiling away an hour or two she put it to her lips and started quietly to play.

The light in the room was soft, the fire warm and relaxing, and the last few days had taken their toll of her energy; when she began to feel soporific she didn't fight the lure. It would be pleasant to doze in this comfortable chair with her feet toasting before the hearth. Maybe, half asleep, she'd remember that tune Grimya had taught her; the lullaby . . .

Her fingers moved slowly, experimentally, on the pipes and she played a new run of notes that weren't a part of the song she was trying to recall but that pleased her. She played them again, then a third time, modulating the melody a little.

Then she saw that the flames in the grate were beginning to sway in time with her playing.

Niahrin's good eye opened wide and she stared into the fire. Her playing hesitated, and the flames seemed to hesitate, too, as though waiting for her to continue. Softly, cautiously, she blew a trill, and the flames shivered again. And Niahrin realized what she had done.

She'd never had the talent, though she knew of it and had seen the magic worked by others. The Islers' word for it was *Aisling*—a bardic creation, in words or simply in melody, that could, briefly, lift aside the curtain between the daylight world and the elemental worlds of dream and vision. Now, unbidden, Niahrin's pipe had lifted that curtain. Pictures in the fire . . . she could see them forming, feel them reaching out to her. Faces glimpsed as though through a mist, strangers' faces; and the echoes of voices that her senses told her belonged to other times and other planes. And somewhere a woman was weeping, mourning. . . .

Her fingers trembled, but the music wouldn't be denied. Quivering notes, rising and falling; a sad tune she didn't know, had never heard before, yet which she played as though it was her own. Then, faint and distant as a sum-

mer breeze in the forest, Niahrin heard the strains of a
harp begin to blend and harmonize with her music. She
drew in a shocked breath, almost breaking the melody; the
spectral harp seemed to hesitate and quickly she continued, the same phrase over and again, rising and falling,
rising and falling. . . .

In the fire, the ghosts of hands took form. Old hands,
gnarled and arthritic, yet graceful and swift and sure. They
moved within the flames, they *were* flames, and between
the callused fingers the harp strings glittered like sparks.
No face, no identity; just the hands. And the music . . .

As Niahrin gazed, transfixed, at the vision in the flames,
a voice that had no substance, a vast but silent voice, overwhelming yet breathtakingly gentle, swept over her and
through her bones and through the room—through, she
felt, the whole world.

The voice whispered: *CHILD, MY CHILD. IT WAS
NEVER OF MY DOING.*

The pipe dropped from Niahrin's hands and fell with a
clatter to the floor, and the spell snapped.

"Great Goddess!" The oath broke involuntarily from the
witch's lips, and across the room Grimya stirred with a
bark of surprise.

"Wh-at? What is it?"

Niahrin fumbled on the floor for the pipe. She was
shaking like a leaf.

"It's all right," she said, her voice oddly high-pitched to
her own ears. "Nothing's wrong. I— I must have drifted
off to sleep, and the pipe fell. It startled me, that was all."

She didn't turn her head but she could sense the wolf's
gaze boring into her back. Then Grimya said, "I do not believe you. Ss . . . something has happened."

Niahrin looked uneasily at the fire. There was nothing
remarkable there; just flames, sparks, the outlines of the
burning logs. The vision had gone.

"Grimya," she said, "did you . . . hear anything just now?"

"You were playing your pipe. I like the pipe. I like music."

The witch's lips were dry; she licked them. "You didn't hear . . . a harp?"

"A *hh-harp*?" Grimya's tone changed. Niahrin turned to look at her and saw that she was on her feet, her injured leg held up and her posture tense.

"Yes," she said. "I heard it, Grimya. It played with me, a harmony to my tune. And when I looked into the fire—"

She broke off abruptly. Someone had knocked at the door.

The wolf's head jerked round and she bared her teeth. Niahrin said, "Wait," and held up a hand, gesturing to Grimya to stay back. Whoever was outside, she knew intuitively that their visit was no coincidence. Her heart was pounding as she moved to lift the latch; her fingers fumbled. At last the door swung open. The dowager Moragh stood outside, and with her was the bard Jes Ragnarson.

"Niahrin." In the low light of the corridor outside Moragh's face was a shadow. "May we come in?"

"Your Grace . . ." Niahrin was confounded. These were not the people she had expected to see. And yet . . .

Moragh stepped into the room, Jes at her heels. The bard looked quickly but candidly at Niahrin's face and she sensed that he saw more than she would have liked him to see. As the door closed Moragh stopped, and her head came up like an animal's catching an unfamiliar and possibly dangerous scent.

"Something's amiss," she said. It was a statement, not a question.

Ah, Niahrin thought, so that was it. Whether or not she knew it, the dowager had some psychic gift, and that was what had drawn her here at this particular moment. Yes, this was more than coincidence. She should put her trust in Moragh.

Niahrin sighed. "I'm not sure that 'amiss' is quite the proper word for it, ma'am. But certainly something has happened." She looked quickly at Jes. "You're a bard, Jes Ragnarson, you will know better than anyone. Who in Carn Caille is skilled at the harp?"

"The harp?" Jes looked shocked, and Moragh cut in quickly. "Why? Why do you ask that?"

"Because, ma'am," Niahrin told her, "I heard someone playing the harp not five minutes ago. In an aisling."

Jes said softly. *"Good Goddess . . ."*

"You can create aislings?" Moragh demanded. Her face had paled. Niahrin shook her head.

"No, ma'am, I cannot. I've never had the gift. But tonight, just now, it seems that I—and a harp—did."

"Ah." It was less a word than a soft exhalation, and the dowager's eyes seemed to cloud. For a moment she was silent, as though debating some private thought. Then, abruptly, she made her decision.

"Ryen and Brythere are in the great hall, and Indigo and Vinar are with them. That is why Jes and I are here. We thought to speak privately with you, Niahrin, without the risk of being overheard." She bit her lower lip. "It simply seemed convenient, but I am beginning to think that there is more than mere chance at work."

Niahrin stared at her. "You echo my own thoughts, ma'am."

"Yes. Yes, I thought that might be the case. . . . Very well. There is something I would like to show you." She met the witch's gaze and Niahrin saw that beneath the mask of her composure, the dowager was deeply uneasy. "Please," Moragh said. "We need your help. And so, I think, does Indigo."

•CHAPTER•XIII•

To Niahrin's private relief, Moragh raised no objections when Grimya silently followed them from the room and limped along the corridors in their wake. Though she had had no chance to speak to the wolf, Niahrin knew that there would be trouble if they tried to leave her behind; and for her own part, she wanted Grimya to accompany the party. She would say nothing, of course, and she trusted Niahrin not to betray her secret. But whatever revelation lay in store, it was vital, Niahrin felt, that Grimya should be witness to it.

The procession through Carn Caille made the witch uneasy. The corridors were poorly lit and there seemed to be no one else about, so that the citadel felt strangely empty and abandoned. Faint snatches of sound could be heard in the distance, doubtless from the direction of the great hall, but the far-off merriment seemed unreal. Reality was echoing footsteps and eerie shadows, and cold drafts that snaked through gaps in the ancient stonework to chill the blood as they walked on through gloom. It brought to mind the bleak atmosphere of a funeral cortege, and Niahrin wished she had thought to put on her shawl.

Jes Ragnarson, at the head of the little group, led them to the south wing, which Niahrin had not visited before. And at last they stopped before the door that led to a certain suite of rooms.

This was the place that once had been the private sanctuary of King Kalig and his family. For the first two years of his reign Ryen's grandfather, the first King Ryen, had taken them for his own, but after a while he had begun to feel like an interloper.

These rooms still seemed to echo with the voices of Kalig, Imogen, and their son and daughter, whose kin, but for the tragedy of the plague, would have lived here still. And so the new king had withdrawn from the chambers, decreeing instead that they should be maintained as they had been in Kalig's day as a gesture of respect to the dead monarch and his family. Since then the rooms had been kept tended and cleaned and in good order, but they were no longer occupied. Cathal, Ryen's father, had kept up the observance, and Ryen in his turn followed suit. But though the old royal apartments were empty they were by no means forbidden territory. The door was not locked; it opened to Jes's touch, and the bard stood deferentially back to allow Moragh and Niahrin—and Grimya—to precede him.

They went quietly inside. Just beyond the door a lantern stood always ready with flint and tinder beside it; groping in the gloom Moragh found it and lifted the glass chimney to light the wick. The lantern was a beautiful thing, not of Southern Isles workmanship but brought long ago from the east; one of the many personal trinkets that Kalig and his family had left behind. Amber light tinted here and there

with rose-red filtered through the glass and lifted the room
from darkness; Jes closed the door and the dowager said
softly: "This way."

They moved through the outer room, the lantern's rosy
light illuminating the sheen of polished paneling and gracious, pristine furnishings, and came to an inner door that
Jes stepped forward to open. The room beyond was nothing remarkable, simply a small sanctum where Kalig and
his wife had liked to sit and enjoy each other's company.
In the daytime, light streamed in at a long window, offering a far-reaching and spectacular view south toward the
forests and the tundra. Now, in darkness, the view was invisible and the chilly air that always blew from the southern quarter created drafts that nipped Niahrin's ankles. But
here were the two artifacts that Moragh had wanted her
guest to see.

In the center of the little room stood a harp. No hand
had played it for half a century but its strings were bright
and the wood glowed with the sheen of frequent and careful polishing, and Moragh and her son both liked to think
that, if time could roll back and call him from the grave,
its old master would be pleased by what he found.

Niahrin saw the instrument and stopped, her eye widening. Though the lantern light was uncertain, the dowager
noted her reaction and smiled a thin little smile.

"It's a beautiful thing, isn't it? It belonged to a man
named Cushmagar. He was bard to King Kalig, my father-
elect's predecessor."

Grimya, pressing close to Niahrin's legs, uttered a soft
whimper. The witch looked at Moragh. "That is the King
Kalig who . . ."

"Who died with all his family in the plague of fifty
years ago, and so brought our dynasty to the throne. Yes."
Moragh moved toward the harp but made no move to
touch it. "According to Carn Caille's roll of honor,

Cushmagar was the finest and most divinely inspired of his ilk to grace the Southern Isles in many generations."

"What became of him?" Niahrin asked.

"He was one of the few here who survived the plague. He lived to occupy a high place in my father-elect's household. In fact he died on the day that my husband, Cathal, was born." Moragh's eyes clouded momentarily. "But since the Great Mother finally called Cushmagar to rest, legend has it that the harp has steadfastly refused to sound a single true note for any other player. The story goes that anyone who tries to play it will produce only a terrible discord."

In her mind, Niahrin heard spectral harmonies and saw hands in the flames. She swallowed.

"Has the legend ever been put to the test, Your Grace?"

"To the best of my knowledge, no one has taken up the challenge." Moragh glanced obliquely at the bard. "Not even Jes."

Old hands, Niahrin thought. Gnarled and cramped with arthritis, yet bestowing the sure touch of a master. Cushmagar had been an old man when he died. And if he was as great as his legend attested, he would have known the ways of the aisling. . . .

Raising the lantern higher, so that the harp sank into shadow once more, Moragh walked toward the fireplace at the far side of the room. The hearth stood empty, the grate clean and neat, and there was no dust on the bare overmantel. But above the mantel, framed by a drapery of indigo velvet, hung a portrait. Jes had followed the dowager, and Niahrin moved to stand beside them.

Four people gazed down from the frame of the painting. A man with auburn hair, graying a little at the temples, dressed in the formal court attire of a bygone age. Beside him a patrician woman, her smiling face serene. And, seated on low stools before this gracious pair, a young man and woman with the distinctive look of their sire. Niahrin looked at the face of the girl, and her breath caught in her throat.

Moragh spoke very quietly. "As far as we know," she said, "this is the only portrait ever painted of King Kalig and his family. It must have been completed a bare few months at most before the plague struck."

Niahrin didn't reply but only continued to stare numbly at the picture. The dowager and Jes exchanged an uneasy glance. Then at last, forcing the words past the constriction in her throat, Niahrin whispered:

"Dear Goddess! The girl—she is Indigo!"

"The likeness is extraordinary, isn't it?" Moragh's voice was carefully composed. "But she is not Indigo. The girl in the painting is the princess Anghara Kaligsdaughter, and she has been dead for more than half a century." She lowered the lantern at last and turned to face the witch. "Now, I think, you understand why we are so anxious to learn the truth about this mystery."

Niahrin did. Images were crowding into her mind, pieces of a puzzle that as yet didn't fit together but that were slowly forming a pattern if not a clear picture. The aisling, the tapestry, Indigo and Brythere's dreams, her own scrying. And the obsessions of a mad old man . . .

She let her pent breath out in a slow, unsteady exhalation. "Ma'am," she said, "forgive me if I presume, but . . . are you saying that you believe Indigo is—is a descendant of King Kalig's line?"

Even by the flattering light of the lantern Moragh's face looked haggard and old. "Yes," she said. "That is what I believe."

There was no need for her to elaborate; Niahrin knew what she had left unsaid, and she asked hesitantly, "Does the king know?"

"He knows, yes." Moragh met the witch's gaze candidly. "In fact he suspects that is why you are here, Niahrin. Ryen believes that the wise-women may well have divined the possibility of a new claimant to the throne of Carn Caille, and that perhaps you are their emissary come to make judgment on their behalf."

Niahrin was appalled. "I assure you, ma'am, I'm nothing of the kind!" she protested. "This"—indicating the painting with a helpless wave of her hand—"is entirely new to me!"

"Yet you knew Indigo's name. You knew she was a mariner from the Amberland wreck, and that the tame wolf you rescued belonged to her. If your powers enabled you to discover that much—"

"They didn't! It was—" Niahrin bit the words back as she realized that, unthinkingly, she had been about to give Grimya's secret away. Chagrined, thinking the wolf was beside her, she glanced down.

Grimya wasn't there.

"Grimya?" Her immediate predicament forgotten, Niahrin looked worriedly about the room. "She's gone! But—"

"She slipped out of the room just a few moments ago," Jes Ragnarson said. "I saw her leave; I think she's waiting by the outer door." He smiled. "She probably doesn't like the cold in here. Shall I fetch her back?"

What had been said that had made Grimya slink away? Niahrin felt a strange, atavistic shudder deep within her, then, realizing that Jes was waiting for an answer, she forced the feeling down.

"Ah—no; thank you, but there's no need. Let her bide where she is." *Sweet Earth,* she thought, *this grows deeper. It grows deeper.*

"Your Grace." She turned again to the dowager and addressed her formally and respectfully. "I can't explain to you how I discovered Indigo's name and her connection with Grimya, for I am ... bidden not to reveal it. But I give you my solemn word that I knew—and still know—nothing more about her. *Nothing*."

The dowager gazed steadily back for some time. Then she nodded. "Very well. I know that it's not in the witches' nature to lie—I accept your word." She forced a painful smile. "In truth, my dear, I saw how shocked you were when you looked at the painting for the first time. I don't doubt you for one moment. But you understand that I had to ask the question."

"Of course, ma'am."

The dowager moved away from the mantel; Niahrin saw her shiver as though a breath of icy wind had blown through the room. At length Moragh spoke again.

"I think," she said. "that you must see now, Niahrin, why we need your help."

"You wish me to use my powers, ma'am. To find out ... ?" Niahrin let the query hang unfinished.

"The truth about Indigo. Nothing more and nothing less." In the lamplight Moragh's gray eyes glinted. "If you have the power of the aislings—"

"But I haven't, ma'am. That was what I tried to tell you when you came to my room. I don't possess that gift; I've never possessed it, and what happened to me tonight was not my doing. I didn't call it and I didn't create it. But I think I know who did."

The dowager's posture sharpened and she glanced quickly toward her bard. "Jes is a skilled harpist. But—"

"No, ma'am, it wasn't Jes. In fact I believe it wasn't anyone who ... still lives within these walls." Niahrin turned to where the old harp stood. Light glinted on the strings; the sheen of the wood was like the sheen of polished amber.

"Your Grace," she said, "you said that King Kalig's old

bard survived the plague and lived on. And that he was divinely inspired."

Moragh was silent. Jes shifted uneasily.

"I can't presume to understand what might have moved the mind of such a great man," Niahrin continued. "That is for the Earth Mother alone to know. But if one of King Kalig's own *did* survive the pestilence, who above all others might have known of it?"

The dowager stood very still. "Yes," she whispered. "Yes ... the bard, the king's most trusted servant ... if, perhaps, there had been a bastard child . . ." Her lip twitched suddenly and she gave an odd little laugh. "That's an unkind suspicion, but it would be unrealistic to deny the possibility." She looked up. "Yet can a dead man speak to us across the years?"

"I truly don't know, ma'am," Niahrin replied. "But tonight, something—or someone—spoke to me through a harp and an aisling." She moved closer to the harp, resisting an urge to reach out and lay her hand on its smooth, shining curves. *Not for you, Niahrin, not for you!*

"Your Grace." Suddenly her voice sounded strange in her own ears, disembodied and a long, long way off. But the words were coming as though at someone else's volition. "Your Grace, has Vinar told you that Indigo, too, is a harpist of great skill?"

"Indigo?" The dowager's indrawn breath was a harsh sound in the quiet room; Jes Ragnarson murmured an oath under his breath. "No. No, he's said nothing of that."

Niahrin felt the sensation begin in the tips of her fingers, as it had done when she and Vinar had spoken together outside her room. A tingling, a prickling; a sign she knew and trusted. Another part of Granmer's strange legacy . . .

"Vinar said that he hoped Indigo might be asked to play in the great hall tonight." Again the words were flowing

unconsciously, beyond her control. "He said he hoped it
would cheer her. But I believe it will not, for the instrument she plays will not be the right one. It will not be . . ."
Her hand stretched out; realizing what she had been about
to do she withdrew it, though it seemed to take a tremendous effort, as though she were dreaming. "It will not be
this harp." For a moment an image of the tapestry she had
woven seemed to impose itself over the scene before her,
and she saw Moragh and Jes as if through the pictures her
weaving-spell had created. *The great gates of Carn Caille
had taken the shape of a harp, and the harp strings were
drawing back to admit the procession within the enfolding
walls. . . .*

"Cushmagar's harp has been waiting," Niahrin said, and
her voice quavered with a tremendous emotion that she
didn't understand. "It has been waiting for Indigo."

Grimya sensed that Niahrin was asleep, but nonetheless
she waited for what she judged to be the better part of an
hour before cautiously rising from her bed by the hearth
and limping toward the door.

The wolf's mind was in turmoil. When the three humans finally left the suite of rooms, Niahrin had found her
huddling unhappily by the outer door, and when Moragh
and Jes were gone and they could speak privately again
Grimya had rebuffed all the witch's efforts to find out
what was wrong. It wasn't that she didn't trust Niahrin.
She did; after Indigo the witch was perhaps the closest
friend Grimya had ever had. But the secret that Grimya
had carried with her for fifty years was one she couldn't
reveal; not to Niahrin, not to anyone. Long ago—several
lifetimes ago, had she been a normal wolf—she had *promised*. And whatever Indigo had become, whatever had happened to her mind to estrange her, Grimya would not
break that promise.

So when Niahrin gently tried to probe, the wolf turned her mind and her face away and refused to answer her questions. The witch knew there was more to her silence than met the eye, but she also knew Grimya well enough to realize that, until and unless she should choose to confide of her own will, no amount of cajoling would persuade her.

The door-latch was low enough for Grimya to reach and she could easily push it up with her muzzle; it fell back with a soft click that didn't penetrate Niahrin's dreams and the door swung open a few inches; enough for the wolf to slip out.

Though she didn't know exactly where Indigo's room was, something she had overheard Vinar say to Niahrin had given her a clue to the general direction. Instinct and scent would do the rest, and Grimya set off along the unlit corridor. What she would do when she found Indigo, she didn't know; she had no specific plan. But after what had happened tonight, she *had* to go to her friend and—if Indigo would give her the chance—warn her of what was afoot.

She limped on through the darkness, the uneven click of her claws the only sound in the still night. Somewhere on the east side, Vinar had said, near the tower with its cluster of small turrets at the corner of the citadel. The rain had stopped and the clouds were clearing; moonlight flickered intermittently beyond the windows she passed, throwing her shadow starkly out beside her. Then Grimya's pulse quickened as her nostrils detected the first traces of a familiar scent. There was an archway just ahead of her, set into the wall on the left; peering into it she saw a short side passage that ended in a flight of stone steps. At the top of the steps was a door, and Grimya knew she had found what she was searching for.

She started eagerly forward—then abruptly stopped, her

spirits sinking as she realized that she didn't know what to do. Oh, she could scratch at the door, yelp and whine until Indigo was roused from sleep and came to investigate the noise, but what would that achieve? What could she say to Indigo that might hope to break down the barrier between them? All she'd get would be angry words, perhaps even a cuff, for making a nuisance of herself. Since the painful fiasco of what should have been their reunion Indigo had refused to come near her; why should her attitude change now, in the middle of the night? And even if Indigo did unbend, Grimya reasoned, what would she tell her? That she had seen a portrait painted half a century ago, and that one of the figures in the portrait was Indigo herself? It was madness. Indigo wouldn't believe her and she would succeed only in widening the gulf between them.

The wolf uttered a small, sad whimper as the hopelessness of her dilemma swept over her. Her leg was hurting; she had taxed it too much today and now it throbbed with a dull, relentless ache that made her want to turn and bite at the pain to make it go away. She shouldn't have come. She should have had the wisdom to wait, bide her time until a more auspicious moment came her way, and until she could begin to win Indigo's trust. This would only make matters worse. Moving awkwardly now, ears and tail drooping with weariness and disillusionment, she started to turn about, to return to Niahrin.

The door at the top of the stairs creaked.

Grimya lurched round in time to see the door swinging open. No light spilled out from the room beyond but a shadow moved in the doorway, discernibly darker against the background. Then, slowly, the figure of a woman emerged.

"*Indi*—" But the eager cry was strangled in the wolf's throat as in a sudden brief glimmer of moonlight from the corridor behind her she saw the figure's face. Not Indigo, but an old woman, almost a crone, her braided hair white, her skin seamed. She seemed to be wearing a dark robe or gown, and her face, unhealthily pale above its folds, was distorted into an expression of pure malignance.

Appalled by this vision Grimya backed hastily away from the arch, but though the crone should by rights have heard the scrabble of her claws on the stone floor, she seemed oblivious to the wolf's presence. Who was she? Grimya asked herself desperately. What was she doing in Indigo's room? Heart pounding, she watched in mesmerized fright as the shuffling figure drew nearer. And then, as the moon came out once more and its radiance lit the passageway, the figure's face changed and Grimya saw Indigo walking toward her.

The wolf's body froze with shock. *This wasn't possible!* Only moments ago the crone had been there, she had *seen* her, and now—

Indigo came on. She passed by the spot where Grimya crouched motionless but she utterly ignored the wolf, staring ahead with eyes that seemed unnaturally wide and bright. There was a peculiar smile on her face, and Grimya realized suddenly that she was ... she sought frantically in her mind for the word ... sleepwalking. Unconscious, unaware, yet moving and acting as though with some purpose.

The hem of Indigo's night robe—how could she have mistaken white linen for a dark gown? Grimya wondered—brushed the floor only inches from the wolf's nose. Grimya made a tiny, anguished sound as confusion raged. What should she do? What *could* she do? Was it dangerous to wake a sleepwalker? Was it even possible? Her shock at the vision of the crone was swept away by this new fear and she struggled to her feet. If she barked, if she called out, what would happen? Would Indigo wake and perhaps stumble and fall, or would she simply continue on her unheeding way?

Then, before she could even begin to search for an answer to that question, Grimya saw what Indigo was holding in her left hand, and her heart almost stopped beating.

What did this mean? From rigid immobility the wolf's body began to tremble from muzzle to tail. She didn't understand—but dawning in her mind was a sense of terrible peril, of . . . yes, she would use the word, for it was right: of *evil*. Something was at work here, something that Grimya feared to name but that she sensed in her marrow as surely as though she could see and hear and touch it. And at its heart, at its core, was . . .

The train of thought collapsed as in the distance, beyond Carn Caille's walls, a solitary wolf howled.

As the lonely, melancholy sound died away the hair of Grimya's ruff bristled and an electric, prickling sensation shot through her. The wild wolves—they knew, and they were giving warning!

Terror swamped Grimya like a wave. She couldn't articulate it, didn't truly comprehend it, but it was an imperative and she couldn't fight it. Indigo was walking away, her gait strange and stiff but purposeful, and as she passed the next window a shaft of moonlight turned the knife in her hand to glinting silver.

Grimya lurched about. She couldn't run, couldn't move at anything more than an uneven, careening stumble, but she strained every muscle she possessed, railing silently but violently against her handicap as she struggled to reach and wake Niahrin.

•CHAPTER•XIV•

Indigo could hear laughter. She knew that it came from the rooms ahead of her and it brought a smile to her face as she quickened her pace. How well she remembered these corridors—time had changed nothing, it seemed, and even after her long absence she knew and recognized every turn, every door, every worn stone. The knowledge buoyed her. And the knowledge of what awaited her at her destination gladdened her heart.

She thought that a number of people passed her as she moved through the maze of Carn Caille. Familiar faces all, skimming by with a nod or a smile or a small gesture of obeisance. It didn't matter that their bodies seemed as insubstantial as shadows; tonight they were real to her, and that was all that counted.

Someone had been playing the harp a little earlier, but now the distant music had ceased. Cushmagar had doubtless gone to his bed; an early riser, he liked to retire before the rest of the court. In the morning she would ask him to teach her the melody that had so enchanted her in the great hall tonight. By then her mind would be clear and what she must do would be completed, so she would be able to give her whole attention to the music.

Walking swiftly, lightly—so lightly, in fact, that from time to time it seemed her feet didn't touch the cold stone floor at all—she made her confident way through the passages until at last the door she sought was before her. No need to knock; there had never been any need to knock. This was her sanctuary. This was *their* sanctuary. The latch lifted and she entered the apartments. For a moment only an odd smell assailed her, mustiness combined with a hint of something corrupted, like old meat left out to rot in the summer sun. But it vanished, and in the light of the candles that blazed in their wall sconces she went through to the inner room.

Her mother was sitting by the window. She looked up, and as her lovely, short-sighted eyes peered at the visitor a smile spread across her face.

"Indigo!" Queen Imogen was wearing a blood-red gown; strange, Indigo thought, for the color had never suited her. She came toward her daughter with arms outstretched for an embrace, and if for an instant she suddenly looked like the dowager Moragh Indigo pretended not to notice. That was, after all, part of the game.

They kissed, separated. Imogen's skin had a scent of sweetbriar, and of overripe fruit. "Come," she said, "come and sit with me and tell me your dreams."

Dreams? Indigo laughed. "I don't dream, Mother. I was listening to Cushmagar in the hall. He played a new air tonight. An aisling. I saw—"

She stopped.

"Saw . . . ?" Imogen's voice was gentle and strangely sad. "What did you see, Indigo? Was it that—your name, the color of death?" She sighed and walked a few paces away, so that Indigo could not touch her; so that even the knife wasn't in range.

But it didn't matter. Imogen wasn't the one.

"We should have chosen another name for you," the queen said, and now her tone was tinged with irritation. "We nearly did. We nearly named you Anghara. But then, when we knew ..." She shrugged, laughed. "Come and see Master Breym's portrait. It's completed at last. He brought it to us earlier today."

Indigo wanted to say, "Master Breym is dead," but that seemed to make no sense. She moved to stand beside her mother and looked up at the picture, draped in indigo velvet, hanging over the mantel as it had hung for fifty years.

"None of us has changed." She glanced at Imogen, saw confirmation, smiled. "None of us, Mother. Not even me."

"Now, how would I know that, with my eyes as they are?" Imogen stepped closer to the hearth, peering. "Mind, we'll have to have another one before long. When you wed Fenran. A painting of us all at your marriage feast would be fine; and perhaps a miniature, too, to send to my family in Khimiz."

"They are all dead, Mother," Indigo said calmly. "Long dead."

"Are they? Well, no matter. Then when Kirra takes a wife we shall have—"

"No!" Indigo's hand closed on the knife hilt. Imogen turned and regarded her with mild curiosity, and the words Indigo had rehearsed over and over again in preparation for this moment came in a sharp rush.

"No, Mother, Kirra will not marry. I won't allow it. *We* won't allow it. It isn't to be— It mustn't be, or—" Again she broke off.

The queen blinked. "What a strange child you are. You

must speak to your father about it. He will make the decision."

Indigo turned. "Father—"

King Kalig regarded her indulgently. A part of her mind, half buried, knew that moments ago he had not been in the room, but the rest of her, dreaming, hallucinating, accepted his presence without surprise. He, too, was dressed in blood red, and again she wondered why. There was no need for *him* to hide the stains.

"Father." She went to kiss him and it was as though she kissed old, polished bone, despite the fact that he stood warm and vigorous and alive before her.

King Kalig looked at his wife; a private look, not for their daughter's eyes. Indigo resented that. "Play for me, Anghara," he said, using the wrong name, the name they had decided not to give her. "Play Cushmagar's harp. He has left it ready for you."

She hadn't seen the harp as she entered the room, but now it was there, standing alone in the middle of the floor. How much time had passed since anyone dared to touch it? Who would have dared, since Cushmagar died?

"Play Cushmagar's aisling," her father commanded.

She did not disobey her father. She moved to the harp; no stool was set ready but nonetheless the instrument was at the perfect height. She needed only to stand before it. Her fingers flexed; she placed her hands over the strings, remembering the tune despite the fact that Cushmagar hadn't yet had the time to teach it to her. Tomorrow he might scold her for her presumption, but for now that was unimportant.

She plucked the first chord. Outside the walls of Carn Caille a wolf howled dismally, and the harp strings snapped beneath her fingers.

"No!" Indigo recoiled and the harp began to crumble, wood and metal collapsing in her hands, turning to corruption. Wildly she looked round, but Kalig and Imogen were gone.

From behind, someone's hands came to rest on her shoulders.

With a squeak of surprise Indigo spun round. Gray eyes looked into hers; laughing eyes, loving, mischievous, and pleased to have startled her. Black hair framing a wind-tanned face, and he was still wearing the old clothes in which they'd gone riding together earlier in the day. He should have changed them before the evening revels in the great hall; her brother, Kirra, had noticed and had made some untoward remark. It had sounded like a jest but Indigo knew better.

"My love." She forgot the ruined harp—which in any case had melted away now—and gave herself up to his embrace. "Fenran. My dearest. My husband."

For he was. The ring was on her finger, and even if he was ten years older now while she had not changed, it didn't matter. He started to kiss her and she said, turning her face aside, "No, love, no. My father and mother are watching."

"Your father and mother have gone," he told her, and looking over his shoulder she saw he was right. They were alone in the room. It was time, then.

"Carn Caille is asleep." Fenran, her lover, her husband, her coconspirator, pressed his lips against her ear and his voice was a whisper, harsh, strangely guttural. "All asleep."

"All asleep." She repeated it in a tone that matched his, her smile old and clever and bitter. "*They* are asleep, while we remain awake." She drew the knife then and showed it to him. His right hand closed over it and he ran his fingertips along the length of the blade. It did not cut him; there was no blood when he opened his fist again. Well and good. No blood, no stain.

*Only the stain in her mind. Surely, when they were both
younger, it hadn't been like this. Hadn't they been happier
then?*

Though she didn't voice her thoughts aloud, Fenran
knew them. "Yes," he said, "we were happier. But we'll
be happy again. When it's done, when it's over. We promised each other that, love, and we know it's true."

She looked at his face, his graying hair, and uttered a
soft laugh. It was an old woman's laugh but that didn't
disconcert her. Time couldn't be denied or avoided, and
much time had passed while they waited for this night.

There was a time, a time and a time. . . .

The voice, speaking apparently from the air above her
head, caused her to glance briefly upward but nothing
more. Cushmagar was no longer here to tell the old tales
with their hidden warnings. His time was gone. Kalig and
Imogen's time was gone. And soon the one obstacle that
still stood between them and what was rightfully their own
would be gone, too.

Strange and gratifying that, even though his hair was
white and his body growing frail, Fenran still stood tall
and unstooped. He pulled the hood of his cloak up over his
head, casting face and hair into shadow; she did the same,
and they became silhouettes in darkness. He took her
hand; in her other hand the knife hilt settled like an old
friend.

They left the room together.

"Niahrin! *Niahrin!*"

The witch surfaced through the shallows of vague
dreams and woke to find something big and dark and
heavy pressing down on her. For a moment, unprepared,
she almost panicked, but then Grimya's husky voice came
out of the darkness again and she felt the wolf's warm
breath against her face.

"Niahrin, you must wake up! Quickly, quickly! I need your hh-elp!"

Niahrin struggled out of the tangle she'd made of her blankets and sat up. "My dear, what is it, whatever's wrong?"

"It is Indigo!" Grimya sounded breathless and there was an undercurrent of pain in her tone. "Please, Niahrin, *hurry*!"

"Indigo?" The witch's fingers began to prickle unpleasantly. "What's happened, Grimya? What has Indigo done?"

As soon as she asked the question she felt a stab of shock. Not, *What has happened to Indigo?* but *What has Indigo done?* It was sheer, unthinking instinct but Niahrin had known immediately that if some danger threatened, Indigo was its cause and not its quarry. Grimya, however, was too agitated to notice what Niahrin had said. She had slithered down to the floor and was pulling at the hem of the witch's night robe, uttering muffled whimpers through a mouthful of linen.

"All right, all right, I'm coming! But I must have light; I can't see in the dark as you can!" Niahrin hastily lit a candle, then, remembering the last chilly sojourn in Carn Caille's corridors, wrapped her shawl about her before following the frantic Grimya across the room.

"My dear, you can barely walk!" she exclaimed as they neared the door. "What have you been *doing*?"

Grimya turned distraught eyes up to her. "I c-can walk! I must! I must show you!"

"Now, wait." Niahrin stopped and put a hand down to restrain the wolf as she made to reach up to the latch. "Before we go rushing anywhere, wouldn't it be more sensible to tell me what's afoot? If you go whimpering through Carn Caille in such a state and me running after you, we'll have every soul in the place awake and coming to see the to-do before we know where we are! Do you want that?"

"N ... no. But—"

"Well, then." Seeing that she had got through to the wolf Niahrin released her hold. "Before we take a step, tell me what has happened."

Grimya did. As she explained she realized miserably that what she had seen outside Indigo's door sounded a petty thing and not enough to have put her into such a state. But she had underestimated Niahrin. The witch knew instantly that there was far more to this matter than any bard, let alone Grimya, could have expressed in words, and when the wolf told her of the knife Indigo had held in her hand Niahrin's disquiet flowered suddenly from bud into blossom.

"What kind of knife?" she demanded. "From the kitchens?"

"No, not like that. Very long, very sharp. A *dagger*. And the hilt was d ... *ecorated*."

To the best of Niahrin's knowledge neither Indigo nor Vinar possessed any weapon at all.... "Grimya," the witch said, suddenly deadly serious, "where was Indigo going? Do you know?"

The wolf's head swung from side to side. "No. I ... do not know Carn Caille. But she was walking toward the south wing."

South ... No, that didn't fit with the premonition that was biting at Niahrin's mind. Somewhere else; somewhere else ...

Then, unbidden, an image formed before her inner eye, and she knew the answer.

"Grimya, wait here." Her voice was suddenly stern. "I think I know where to find Indigo, but I must move swiftly." Already her hand was reaching to the door. "Wait for me—I pray I'll not be long!"

She knew that Grimya wouldn't obey her, and as she began to run along the corridor she heard the scuffle of the wolf following at the best pace she could manage. The Mother alone knew what this night's exertions would do to her injured leg, but Niahrin had no time to stop and argue. If her suspicion was right—*if*, she reminded herself, clinging to that hope—then she had to move fast, or her intervention would come too late.

She took three wrong turnings on the way to her destination and each time was forced to retrace her steps, silently cursing Carn Caille's maze and her own ignorance. Grimya still followed stubbornly despite the fact that she could barely hobble by this time; the wolf longed to call out to Niahrin and ask where she was going, but she was too afraid to use her voice lest someone in the rooms they passed should awake and overhear.

But at last Niahrin found the tower she was looking for, at the apex of two corridors. There was an archway opening into the tower, she saw as she approached, and beyond the arch a flight of stairs spiraled upward.

Limping and slithering on the stone floor, Grimya caught up with her as she stood indecisively before the arch.

"Niahrin." The wolf mustered the courage to speak; there was nobody to overhear. She was breathless. "What is this place? It isn't where Indigo sleeps—her room is in an-*nother* part of —"

"Shh!" Niahrin held up a warning finger, peering into the darkness of the stairwell and wishing she could see what lay at the top. "I know that. But I think this is where she will come."

Grimya sniffed the air—and tensed. "Not *will*," she said.

The witch turned sharply. "What?"

"Not *will*. *Has*." Grimya raised her muzzle. "I scent her,

I scent Indigo! She has come here before us. The scent is very fresh."

Niahrin swore softly. "Where did she go?"

"I . . . cannot be sure. But . . ." Then suddenly Grimya raised her head and looked at the witch with dawning horror. "Niahrin, I think Indigo is still h-here! And if she is, then ss-omething terrible is going to happen!"

She had wanted the north tower. *They* had wanted it, for it was a pleasant retreat away from the main bustle of Carn Caille, and away, too, from the huge southerly vistas of the tundra and the disquieting summer light of the polar regions beyond. Once Indigo had loved those lands with their vast, bleak beauty, but that had been long ago and the old magic they once held for her had turned to something less pleasant, so she had not wanted to look at them again. But the tower had been denied them. Like so much else the tower had been claimed by another, and when words and arguments had failed to bring redress, bitterness had followed. Now the bitterness was all that remained and it ate at her from within like a wasting disease. She had loved her brother once, but that was past and forgotten, overshadowed by the resentments, the jealousies, the frustrations that had found their newest focus in the dissension over the tower.

But though the tower was a petty matter, the other grievances were not. She knew that; Fenran knew that; and now, together, they would resolve the injustice done to them once and for all. *Injustice.* The word reverberated in Indigo's mind like a litany. All their lives they had suffered injustice. That would end. No more disappointments. No more rivalries. Tonight they would lay claim to what should have been granted to them years ago.

Fenran was waiting in the main corridor. He had wanted to take her place here and carry out the deed with his own hand, but Indigo had said no. She had begun this task; she would complete it. That was only fair. So Fenran waited and watched, and she . . . She smiled, not letting the words formulate but aware of them in her mind, comforting and warm.

The tower room was not quite dark and not quite silent. Moonlight glimmered in at the tall, narrow window and played on the foot of the great canopied bed—which should have been *her* bed, *their* bed—and in the gloom beyond she could hear the faint, rhythmic sound of two sleepers breathing peacefully. Kirra and his wife had drunk the wine with its careful dose of a sleeping narcotic, and they would not wake. Light-footed and sly as mist Indigo moved toward the bed, and the knife in her hand gleamed as she held it poised.

Then from outside the gates of Carn Caille, shocking Niahrin as she stood indecisive by the tower stairs, shocking Grimya as she stared fearfully into the darkness, and breaking through the thrall of Indigo's dream, a wolf pack raised their massed voices to the night in a baying chorus of alarm.

In the tower room the violent jolt of waking knocked the breath from Indigo's lungs and sent her staggering backward. She swayed, regained her balance by a pure physical reflex—then her eyes opened and she stood blinking, stunned, in the middle of the floor.

Where was she? This wasn't the room they had given her—the furnishings were different, the chamber itself larger, and the window was in the wrong place. And in her hand . . . what . . . ?

She raised her hand, saw what she was holding, and her jaw dropped open in disbelief. Then, very slowly, she turned her head, looking in the direction of the bed. The curtains were drawn back; moonlight lit the head-posts and between them a tumble of pillows and the sheen of fair hair. The sleeper's face was turned away, but one pale-skinned arm showed above the blankets, hand spread, fingers slightly clenched, and on one finger a marriage-ring glinted. Indigo had seen the marriage-ring before. It was Queen Brythere's.

Realization came crawling up from the depths and into her conscious mind. Her hands started to shake; the knife dropped, hitting the floor with a small but emphatic sound, and Brythere stirred and muttered. Mind reeling with panic and heart thundering under her ribs as though it would burst, Indigo dropped to a crouch, groping desperately for the blade. She mustn't leave it here, mustn't leave it to be found, and as her fingers fumbled she prayed silently, frantically: *Don't let her wake; oh, sweet Earth, Great Mother, please don't let her wake—*

Suddenly a flicker of movement on the edge of vision arrested her. Indigo's head jerked up, and what she saw almost stopped her heart altogether—for a figure had risen against the bed's canopy and was gazing straight at her.

For one appalling moment Indigo lost all hope. The queen had woken; she was sitting up, she had seen her, and one scream for help would bring half the armed men in Carn Caille running. But the figure didn't scream, didn't even move ... and then Indigo realized that her first assumption had been wrong. This was not Brythere. Brythere still slept—but standing beyond her recumbent form, on the far side of the bed, was an old woman. Braided white hair hung to her waist. Her face was seamed, almost raddled, mouth sunken and with a bitter twist to it. And in the face with its all too familiar features and glinting, angry, blue-violet eyes, Indigo recognized the harbinger of her own self in years to come.

The crone smiled; not a pleasant smile but cruel, knowing and conspiratorial. Then she raised a hand and beckoned.

The self-control that Indigo had been struggling to maintain was no match for this apparition. Unable to stem her reaction she uttered a moan of sheer terror and, forgetting the lost knife, turned and fled. Behind her she was dimly aware of a sudden flurry and a high-pitched woman's voice calling out in query and alarm, but she didn't pause; as Brythere sat up and the phantom crone vanished, she was out of the chamber. She took the shallow stairs three and four at a time, twice missing her footing, once cannoning against the wall and grazing her hand against rough stone as she righted herself. She reached the bottom of the flight, flung herself through the arch, turned—and ran headlong into Niahrin.

"Indigo!" The witch caught hold of her arm, slewing her to a halt. For an instant the two women's eyes met and locked, Niahrin bewildered, Indigo terrified. Then with a violent strength that took Niahrin unawares Indigo wrenched her arm free and before the witch could react she was racing away down the corridor.

"*Indigo!*" Grimya cried in distress. "*Indigo!*" She tried to struggle after the fleeing figure, but Niahrin pounced on her and dragged her back. "No, Grimya, no, you'll never catch her! Hush, or we'll have half Carn Caille running here!"

But it was too late to consider that; whether it was Brythere's cry or the wolf's that had roused them, someone was already alerted. A door slammed, the sound muffled, then hasty footsteps approached from the direction opposite the one Indigo had taken. A woman's voice shouted a sharp order and more footfalls joined the first. They neared rapidly; Niahrin had had the presence of mind to hang on to Grimya's ruff, and she hauled the wolf bodily across the floor to where a small side passage opened onto the main corridor. If there was trouble and she was found here, she would be under suspicion and would have no answer to explain her presence.

"Hush, Grimya! Don't make a sound!" She whispered the order as they shrank back out of sight, praying that the wolf would obey. Then candlelight flickered, and three people came into view. Ketrin—the queen's sallow maid—with two men-at-arms at her back. Holding her breath, and with a hand ready to clamp Grimya's muzzle shut if she should seem about to make the least sound, Niahrin peered cautiously round the corner in time to see the maid and one of the men go through the arch toward the tower stairs. The second man remained, and Niahrin waited, counting the seconds, dreading that at any moment she might hear the uproar of a horrific discovery. But no uproar came; instead, after a few minutes that seemed like an hour, the two reappeared.

"The queen has had another bad dream." Ketrin's voice was clipped. "There's no cause for alarm. Inform Her Grace and ask her if she would attend, then you may both seek your beds."

The men bowed and left, and, risking a peep from her hiding place as they disappeared, Niahrin saw to her dismay that Ketrin was not about to return to Queen Brythere's chamber and allow her time to slip away with Grimya, but instead was waiting by the arch. Her face wore a peculiar expression that Niahrin couldn't begin to interpret.

The dowager Moragh arrived within minutes. She was in her night robes and was clearly not pleased to be roused from her bed; Niahrin heard the mutter of sharp words, but abruptly Ketrin's reply caused her to freeze where she stood, ears straining, as she caught the gist of what the maid was saying.

". . . under normal circumstances, Your Grace. But when I found this on the floor . . ."

A moment's silence. Then Moragh said: "Good Goddess . . ."

Holding her breath, knowing she was taking a dire risk but also that she must see what it was Ketrin had found, Niahrin peered round the edge of the wall.

Displayed on Ketrin's palm was a long-bladed knife.

"Whose is it?" Moragh's voice was low-pitched and savage. "Where did it come from?"

"I don't know, Your Grace. But it's not the kind used by our men. The hilt . . ." Her voice faded into a mumble as she turned her back to Niahrin, and the witch couldn't hear the rest of what she said. Then Moragh straightened.

"We'd best go to the queen. Say nothing to her, Ketrin. I don't want her to know about this. I will make investigations of my own."

The two women vanished into the archway and their footsteps diminished up the stairs.

Niahrin pressed her back against the wall, shutting her eyes. She was desperately relieved that she had escaped detection, but mingled with the relief was horror, for the blade's discovery had confirmed her worst suspicion. Driven by a sleepwalking trance, Indigo had intended to murder Queen Brythere. But *why*? What grudge could possibly lie buried in Indigo's lost memory that could make her wish to do such a thing? The queen was a virtual stranger to her; she had done Indigo no harm. . . .

Sweat broke out in cold prickles on the witch's skin as she realized how nearly tonight's events had ended in tragedy. The wolves' howling must have snapped Indigo out of her dream. But for them, Queen Brythere might now be lying dead among her blood-stained pillows.

Niahrin shook her head violently, pushing back the shuddering sensation that seemed to be trying to wrench at her spine. She wouldn't go after Indigo or make any attempt to speak with her; Grimya, too, must be firmly dis-

couraged from making any attempt to confront her
one-time friend—though when Niahrin glanced down at
the wolf she saw from her hunched, miserable posture that
she was too dispirited to try. That was as well, for Niahrin
would have enough to do now without the distraction of
constant worry over the wolf's whereabouts or attempts to
meddle. Tonight she had glimpsed another part of the tapestry's pattern, and though she still couldn't understand it,
it had at least shown her a direction in which to search.

She reached down, touched the top of Grimya's head
lightly. "Come, my dear." Her voice was soft and filled
with sympathy. "We'd best go back. There's nothing more
we can do for now."

Grimya returned the witch's gaze briefly to show she
understood, but she said nothing. As they emerged from
their hiding place into the main corridor a faint, cold
breath stole past them. Niahrin glanced back to the queen's
tower . . . and paused. Just for an instant a shadowy figure
seemed to move by the archway, and the witch thought she
glimpsed an odd, silvery glitter, as though two eyes had
caught and reflected the uncertain moonlight. Then suddenly her skin crawled as the chill little wind blew again
and seemed to whisper her name with a voice she knew
well.

"Perd . . . ?" But Niahrin's soft question died on her
tongue. The shadowy form was gone and with it the cold,
whispering breath. A mirage of moonlight, tricking an
imagination already made hectic. Perd wasn't there, hadn't
been there. *Couldn't* have been there.

Grimya seemed to have noticed nothing; she waited,
listless and silent, to make the weary trek back to their
room. Wrapping her shawl more closely about her shoulders, Niahrin turned away along the corridor.

•CHAPTER•XV•

Breakfast at Carn Caille was laid in the great hall and was a cheerfully haphazard affair. The serving of food began an hour after dawn but there were no set times for eating; people simply came in and took their meals as schedules and duties allowed, and the comings and goings lasted well into the morning.

Niahrin was late in arriving but hungry enough to hope fervently that there would be plenty of dishes left. She had slept like the dead on returning to her room after the night's excursion and to her great relief hadn't been plagued by dreams as she had feared. Her mind and body, it seemed, knew when enough was enough, and sheer exhaustion had granted her a few hours of much-needed oblivion. Now, feeling refreshed and only a little the worse for wear, she would be able to face the prospect of tackling the work ahead of her. But she refused to think about that until she had enjoyed a good breakfast.

There were some two dozen people in the hall when she entered, though none of the king's family was present. The diners were mostly men dressed in outdoor clothes, who Niahrin surmised had probably put in a good few hours' work before their morning meal. The rain had cleared, and from the angle of the sun slanting in at the windows she judged that it must be well past the tenth hour. She smiled a little guiltily at her own tardiness and moved toward the long tables to investigate the food. Cold meats, kidneys, porridge . . . ah, fish, and fresh at that. This was a rare delicacy, for although she lived near enough to the sea, her part of the forest was too sparsely populated for fresh fish to be worth carrying there for sale, and she didn't often make the journey to the coastal villages or the market at Ingan. But at Carn Caille fish was delivered almost daily, and she helped herself to a very generous portion that she topped with three slices of newly baked bread. Preferring ale to hot brew, she filled a mug and then carried her spoils to an unoccupied table. She received a few nods and smiles as she went and was gratified that no one seemed to be troubled by her disfigurement. She was simply accepted as one of their own, and it was a pleasant feeling.

She was eating hungrily and thinking about what she would take back for Grimya, who was still asleep, when two newcomers arrived. Casually glancing up from her plate, Niahrin was in time to see Vinar and Indigo enter the hall. Indigo's face was haggard; even from this distance the dark rings under her eyes were clearly visible, and she was holding on to Vinar's arm as though she might fall down without his support. Vinar, though, was a very different matter, and Niahrin frowned in surprise as she gave him a second, longer look. Everything about him exuded—well, *excitement* was the first word that came to the witch's mind. Excitement, eagerness, and a towering delight that he seemed to be having great difficulty in containing. Ludicrous though the idea was, Niahrin had the distinct impression that at the slightest excuse he would burst into song.

Then Vinar saw her. A broad grin spread across his face and he hailed her down the length of the hall, his big voice turning heads.

"Neerin! Hey, Neerin!" He started toward her, towing Indigo with him. For a moment Niahrin thought he was going to sweep her off her feet and give her a bone-crushing hug, but he restrained himself and instead grasped hold of her hand, squeezing it and pumping her arm.

"Neerin, we got news, great news!" Releasing her at last he pulled Indigo closer to his side. "And you can be first to know. Indigo and me, we're going to get married, right now!"

Niahrin stared at him in astonishment. Her mouth opened but she couldn't make a sound.

"Isn't that the best thing you heard in days?" Oblivious to her chagrin the big Scorvan plunked cheerfully down on the adjacent bench and pulled Indigo onto his knee. "Last night, my Indigo said yes to me. She said *yes*!" His roar of elated laughter turned heads a second time, and a few diners who were on their feet started to drift toward the table, curious to know what was afoot. "I said all along I'd wait till we find her kinsmen and do it proper, but now Indigo says yes and she don't care about waiting. She don't *want* to wait anymore—do you, my love?"

"No," Indigo said emphatically. "I don't want to wait. I don't want to wait any longer."

Vinar hugged her, and Niahrin, watching them, felt as though a fist had slammed into her stomach. As she spoke Indigo had smiled at the witch, but in her eyes was a glare of outright challenge and hostility.

Utterly confounded, Niahrin floundered. "But—" she

managed at last, "but what about—about—" Then she remembered that Indigo didn't know about Vinar's deception. She shot the Scorvan a horrified look, trying to convey what she meant without the need for words.

"Is all right." Vinar beamed at her. "I told Indigo what I done, and she's forgiven me." His shoulders shook with further laughter, suppressed this time. "I tell you, Neerin, it wasn't so easy to say the words and confess it all, but I did. So everything's right and proper and as it should be now, and I reckon I'm the happiest man in the Southern Isles!"

Some of the curious onlookers had reached them by this time and gathered the gist of the announcement; eagerly they offered congratulations, slapping Vinar's back, making jests, wanting to know when the wedding would be. Niahrin, her mind in turmoil, thought: *Sweet Earth, why has she done this? She knows what happened last night; she must know what she nearly did! Has she told Vinar? By all that's sacred, what if he doesn't know?*

Then she looked at Vinar again and realized the truth. He didn't know: it was impossible. He was no actor, and even if he had been, such an honest and decent man would never have behaved so joyfully in the wake of a revelation like that. Indigo had been willing enough to tell him about her first dream, but this, it seemed, was something she intended to keep to herself.

Indigo turned her head suddenly and her gaze met Niahrin's. The hostility in her eyes was, if anything, intensified, but underlying it Niahrin saw something else, which she recognized instantly as fear. No, not fear; that was too inadequate a word. Indigo was *terrified* that her secret might be in jeopardy, and her stare was both a warning to Niahrin to say nothing and a threat of what might befall her if the warning wasn't heeded.

The witch looked sharply away. She wasn't ready to answer Indigo's challenge, for she didn't know what to do. To blurt the truth to Vinar, now or later, was out of the question, for Indigo would need only to deny it. Vinar would take her word against that of the entire world if need be. But if she didn't warn him—

The thought broke off abruptly as from the direction of the doors someone exclaimed loudly and in amused surprise, "Look who has come to join us!"

Those at the tables and among the group surrounding Vinar and Indigo peered and craned. A tall, dark man laughed delightedly. "It's the tame wolf—she's come to get her breakfast!"

Niahrin scrambled hastily to her feet and saw Grimya. The wolf had entered the hall but now hesitated, taken aback by all the strange faces and unsure of her welcome. But as she looked uneasily about, a woman moved toward her from the serving table.

"Come, little forest friend, come in!" She bent, holding out a hand and making encouraging gestures. Grimya's ears pricked and her tail wagged tentatively, which brought further kindly laughter.

"She likes you, Alinnie!"

"She can scent the food, I expect. Fetch her a plate of the cold meats, someone."

"She's limping, look. Her hind leg has suffered some injury."

"One of the forest witches brought her. Is she here, is she in the hall?"

Snatching her wits back under control Niahrin opened her mouth to call out, "Yes, I'm here!" She had a frantic, half-formed notion to hurry Grimya out of the hall before the inevitable confrontation happened, but even as she started to climb over the bench she realized she was too late. Grimya had seen Indigo. For a moment the wolf was utterly still—then Vinar turned and saw her.

"Grimya!" He set Indigo down, sprang upright, and turned to face the wolf, his arms outspread. "Grimya, come and greet us!" Niahrin, horrified, knew what would happen and that she could do nothing to avert it; Vinar's joy was so all-encompassing that it would never for one moment occur to him not to share it with any living being who came within his sphere. With a sense of dreadful, helpless inevitability the witch saw the wolf's posture relax a little—whatever their differences Grimya was greatly fond of the Scorvan—and saw her come toward the table, her tail wagging more eagerly now but her gaze on Indigo. As soon as she was within reach Vinar dropped to his knees and hugged her exuberantly.

"Is good to see you, Grimya!" he exclaimed. "And now everything's going to be right again for all of us." He took the wolf's muzzle between his hands and gazed happily into her eyes. "Indigo said yes to me! We're going to be married, just so soon as we can!"

Grimya froze. Then swiftly, wildly, she looked to Niahrin, her eyes appealing desperately for a denial. Niahrin couldn't answer her aloud, but her expression betrayed the truth.

"Hey, now, Grimya!" Vinar started as with a violently convulsive wriggle the wolf broke free from his embrace and backed away. Her eyes glinted red. "Everything's all right! I told Indigo all the truth, and she don't mind! We can be friends again—"

He got no further. Grimya was oblivious to his words, even to his presence. Her haunches tensed—then, to the astonishment of all present, she sprang, snarling, at Indigo.

Taken completely by surprise, Indigo went down under the onslaught of the wolf's weight. But Grimya's handicap made her clumsy; as the two of them fell to the floor together she lost her balance and landed awkwardly, and with a fast hunter's reflex Indigo rolled out of range of her snapping teeth.

"Grimya!" Niahrin shrieked. Pushing Vinar aside she ran to grab the wolf by the scruff, dragging her away as she tried to launch another assault. "No, no, *stop it!*" Grimya made a terrible, strangled noise and squirmed, but she hung on. "No, Grimya, *no!* Let her alone!" And to Vinar as, belatedly, he tried either to help her or to attack the wolf in his turn—she didn't know which and didn't care at this moment—"Rot you, you fool, leave her to me!" He fell back, and Niahrin started to pull the struggling, growling Grimya toward the doors. She heard her own voice, though it seemed to belong to someone else; she was babbling excuses, explanations—*so many strangers—she's over excited—her leg makes her ill-tempered*—and dimly her senses registered the gauntlet she must run, sobered faces, muted whisperings, shock and embarrassment and indignation, as she struggled toward the doors. From the threshold she had one last glimpse of Indigo climbing unsteadily to her feet, of Vinar solicitous and bewildered at her side, before she hauled the wolf out of the hall and retreated away with her toward the sanctuary of their room.

"I just don't understand what got into her." Vinar's arm tightened around Indigo's shoulders and he squeezed her protectively, possessively against him. "I never known Grimya to behave that way before, nor anything like it." He sighed. "You know what? I think she's jealous. I reckon that's what it must be."

Indigo broke a piece of bread and chewed it. To his relief she seemed to have recovered quickly from the shock of Grimya's unexpected attack, and now that the well-wishers had tactfully withdrawn to other tables and left them to private conversation she was calm and composed again. She said: "Jealous or not, whatever her reasons might be, it makes no difference to me." Her head turned and her silver-flecked eyes gazed intently into his. "It doesn't change anything, Vinar—and if Grimya dislikes it, then she can find a home with someone else."

"Ya. Ya, you're right." Vinar felt a pang of sorrow, for he loved Grimya and it grieved him to have upset her so greatly. But if, as seemed inevitable, the wolf was determined to force Indigo to choose between the older and the newer love, he could only be glad that his betrothed's choice was so steadfast and unequivocal. However great Grimya's misery might be, he thought guiltily, it couldn't mar his own happiness. If this rift between them really couldn't be healed, she might find a new home with Niahrin. The witch seemed to be a kindly woman, warm-hearted and obviously very attached to the wolf. She, perhaps, might be able to offer Grimya new happiness and contentment if he and Indigo could not.

He removed his arm from his beloved's shoulders at last and turned his attention to his own breakfast. As yet he had had little time to assimilate the extraordinary and wonderful thing that had happened to him—and, being honest, he acknowledged that he wasn't overly anxious to ponder too deeply the reasons behind Indigo's sudden and unexpected change of heart. To Vinar, the whys and wherefores were unimportant; all that mattered was that Indigo wanted to become his wife, and for that he would be eternally grateful.

She had come to him in the early hours of the morning, entering his room and startling him from sleep, and clasping hold of his hands she had told him immediately and directly that she wanted them to be wed. Astounded, and still hazy from his sudden awakening, Vinar had at first been half convinced that he was dreaming. But Indigo's fervor and resolve had been such that, at last, he dared to believe that this was no dream, but reality—dizzying, joyful reality. Even the confession of his deception, which he made haltingly and in dread of her wrath, meant nothing to her. He loved her, she said; that was why he had acted as he had. She understood, and there was nothing to forgive. He loved her. That was all that counted. He *loved* her. Forget her family, she had said; forget Carn Caille and the search that had brought them here. She would marry him just as soon as the ceremony could be arranged, and they would go away together, back to sea, back to his home in Scorva.

Vinar knew nothing of what had taken place earlier that night. He knew nothing of the sleepwalking dream, of Indigo's visit to the queen's tower or of the torment she had undergone in the hours that followed. Back in her unlit room, sitting cross-legged on the floor, Indigo had rocked feverishly back and forth, hugging herself in a desperate but fruitless effort to keep her misery and fear at bay. Reaction came in shuddering waves, like an ague; horrific images of the crime she had so nearly committed flared in her inner vision, and with them terror of her own helplessness. What monstrous power had taken control of her sleeping mind? What horrors lay shut away in her lost memory that compelled her to thoughts of murder? And what would she do—what *could* she do—if the dream-compulsion attacked her again?

And at the root of it all was Carn Caille. Indigo was certain now that her coming here—or her return here, for she was haunted by a dark, dreadful sense of familiarity within these walls—had triggered something in her mind. *Dreams that haunt the walls,* Queen Brythere had said. Indigo shivered anew. She had believed that Carn Caille might hold the key to the lost legacy of her past and now she feared she had been proved right. But the legacy that beckoned her was a thing out of nightmare. The talking wolf, the madman Perd, the troubled royal household, they were all a part of it, she was sure. And Brythere's recurring dream, which she had shared and which now had almost turned into tragic reality. Indigo didn't want any more of it. Whatever lay hidden here, she didn't want to delve deeper; she wanted only to cast it away from her as she might cast out a demon.

Rocking and shivering alone in the darkness, she came to a decision. Her one desire was to escape from Carn Caille and the malevolent spell that it was casting over her, and her one hope, her one anchor and salvation, was Vinar. He had no part in this; he was as innocent as a new day, steadfast and sure, a clean and cleansing wind with the power to disperse the poisoned fog gathering around her. A *good* man—and he loved her. Indigo knew that her own feelings didn't match his and that perhaps they never would. But there were many degrees of love. And she cared for Vinar, she liked him, she respected him. Surely that was enough, and perhaps with time she could learn to love him in the way she knew he yearned for. He would help her. He would teach her. Above all, he would take her away from Carn Caille and protect her from the hideous specters of the memories she feared to regain.

So she had gone to him, and she had let him take her in his arms, and she had told him that she wanted to be his wife. Now, at the breakfast table in Carn Caille's hall and with her man, her betrothed, sitting tall and strong and gently possessive at her side, it was as though a dire burden had been lifted from Indigo's shoulders. Even the mutant wolf's violent and unforeseen reaction hadn't upset her; she was indifferent to the animal, for she knew that she need have nothing more to do with it. She had Vinar now. Vinar would take care of her. Vinar would keep her safe.

Why, then, *why* did she feel as though a part of her soul had died?

The decision that Grimya made within the next hour was one of the hardest of her life. At first she had been resolutely defiant; she said nothing as she was dragged unceremoniously back to the guest room, said nothing as Niahrin roundly berated her for her behavior, and said nothing when the witch, reduced at last to helpless exasperation, went to fetch her something to eat. When she had gone Grimya crouched on the floor, staring at the locked door but seeing only the images that paraded across her mind's eye—images that spanned fifty years of wandering; of friends and enemies, triumphs and failures, happiness and despair, and above all of the bond that she and Indigo had shared through all their trials. Now, the past was ashes. Indigo had forgotten her, forgotten the dream she had struggled for so long to fulfill, and in a little while the last blow would fall when she severed the links, and with them her unrealized hopes, forever.

And still one demon remained.

Grimya couldn't let Indigo do it. That had been the goad, she knew, behind the attack she had launched in the great hall, though she realized now that her action had been rash and foolish and had done only harm instead of the good she had intended. If only she had paused to think, instead of acting on a reckless impulse. But it was too late for regret, and there was no hope now of persuading Indigo to listen to her, let alone understand. If she was to avert the catastrophe that loomed, Grimya told herself, she must find another way. And for that, she would need human help.

By the time Niahrin returned, Grimya was resolved and ready. The witch came into the room and closed the door, then paused as she saw the wolf sitting rigidly upright in the middle of the floor. A cautious, questioning look came into her eyes and she said, "What is it, Grimya? Are you unwell?"

"No." The words didn't come easily, but Grimya had rehearsed them and was determined to say them. "I w-want to talk to you, Niahrin. There is something I must tell you."

For a moment Niahrin thought that she was simply going to apologize, but then a subtler intuition told her this was something else. She moved toward the fireside chair and sat down, still watching Grimya.

"Yes," she said gently. "I'm listening."

"It is . . ." Grimya hesitated, whimpered, mustered her courage again. "It is about Indigo. S . . . something you do not know. Nobody knows, except for me. She . . ." Again she faltered. Niahrin didn't press her but waited patiently. At last Grimya gulped, licked her muzzle, and continued.

"Do you rrr . . . emember the rooms we saw, where the king's family used to live? There was a picture there, and everyone says that the girl in the picture looks just like Indigo."

"Yes," Niahrin said again.

"There is a rr-reason. A reason why they are so alike."

"You mean that you know the truth?" Niahrin leaned forward. "Indigo *is* descended from King Kalig's line?"

"Not descended." Grimya looked up at her. Suddenly her eyes held a mute plea, and something—a feeling, she couldn't give it a name—squirmed in the pit of Niahrin's stomach. "Not *descended*," Grimya repeated desperately, "but the same. Indigo and the p . . . rincess. They are the same person."

The story took a long time to tell, and when it was done Niahrin did not speak for some while. She sat in the chair, still leaning forward to the hearth, and though the fire was unlit at this time of day she held her hands out as though to warm them at invisible flames. In her mind she saw an old man's fingers moving in the fire and heard the distant strains of a harp. . . .

At last she was able to break the silence; indeed she had to break it, or it would have suffocated her.

"Sweet Earth," she said softly. "Oh, sweet *Earth*."

Grimya moved slowly, hesitantly, toward her and pushed her muzzle against one of the witch's outstretched hands. "Niahrin . . . do you not . . . believe me?"

Niahrin's fingers clenched and she withdrew her hands, pressing them to her face. Her skin felt as though it were burning. "Yes," she said. "Yes, my dear, I believe you." *How could I not? The threads are beginning to weave together. Her name. The link with Carn Caille. The old bard Cushmagar, who knew Anghara and knew what she did; who died with his secret untold, leaving a harp that will no longer play true. And the reasons why she cannot marry Vinar—because she is old, so old in years; and because there is another who has a greater claim. King Ryen's fear, and Her Grace's fear, is well founded. Indigo is the rightful queen of the Southern Isles, returned to her home after fifty years.*

Grimya had told her everything. She had told her of the Tower of Regrets out on the southern tundra, and the taboo that in her frustration the young, reckless Indigo had broken. She had told of the demons that Indigo's folly had released, and of the night of terror and destruction and death when those ancient, evil forces had descended upon Carn Caille and wrought havoc. She had told of the curse that had fallen on Indigo's shoulders; the curse of immortality, that Indigo might never age and never die until those seven dark horrors had been faced once more, each in its turn, and destroyed. And she had told of her own and Indigo's long years together, years of trial and wandering, until at last six demons were gone from the world and only one remained. One demon, which Grimya believed awaited them here in the Southern Isles—and which, if Indigo should turn her back on it to marry Vinar, would bring her to ruin.

Niahrin's mind roiled. Seven demons, imprisoned in an ancient tower whose door must never be breached . . . the dim memory of a story told to her by her grandmother was echoing in her mind; but that had been an ancient legend, a fable and not a true tale. *Surely* not a true tale? And if, as Grimya had told her, those seven demons had come screaming down on Carn Caille with slaughter and bloodshed, why was it believed—no, not believed, *known*—that King Kalig and his family had died of the plague that swept through the Isles in that ill-fated year? Then, perhaps eeriest of all, there was Fenran, who was held prisoner in some nether hell and for whose sake Indigo had returned to her homeland. Fenran, sleeping—in spirit or in body—in a place called the Tower of Regrets, waiting to be awoken to life once more.

Where, and what, was this Tower of Regrets? Did it truly exist out there on the tundra, or was it an allegory for something else? Grimya couldn't answer the question, for she knew only what Indigo had told her and had never seen the tower with her own eyes. All she could say was that the tower had contained seven demons. But what was the nature of demons? Granmer had taught Niahrin something of their ways, but Granmer had also been cryptic. Demons, she had said, were not what they seemed, and any practitioner of the magic arts who presumed to understand their essence was either a liar or a fool. "Look into anything that reflects truth," Granmer had told her. "Into a raindrop, or the glass of a window, or the polished blade of a knife in your own tidy kitchen, and you may see demons that are as real as you are. Indeed, they may *be* as you are." She had refused to explain further, telling her granddaughter that her path lay elsewhere than among demonkind, but now her ambiguous words came back to the witch, and with them something else; something that struck a sour chord. Seven demons. And until they were all vanquished, Indigo's life must remain in limbo, for the curse had been laid on her by a power greater than her own.

Or had it? Niahrin wondered. *Or had it?*

Into her mind crept the memory of a voice, a sighing, the sense of a huge, gentle yet remote consciousness, speaking to her amid the spectral echoes of a harp. *CHILD, MY CHILD. IT WAS NEVER OF MY DOING. . . .*

Oh, yes. Oh, *yes.* There was more to this, so much more than even Grimya knew, and Niahrin felt a vast psychic shudder rack her mind and body together. Now she began to understand the images in the tapestry that the magic had caused her to weave. The twin suns, one angry, the other blind. The moon, mistress of destiny, hanging between them over Carn Caille, whose gate was a great harp through which a procession of tiny figures walked. Indigo and Grimya, herself and Vinar . . .

Yet there were still mysteries to be unraveled from those threads. The tapestry had not revealed all it had to tell, for in that procession had been Ryen and Brythere, and poor, mad Perd Nordenson.

Perd, who loved Queen Brythere, had come to Indigo in a nightmare and had tried to kill her. And Indigo had gone, sleeping, to Queen Brythere's chamber, with a knife in her hand. . . .

"Grimya." Niahrin moved suddenly, quickly from her chair and in a single stride was beside the wolf, cupping her muzzle in both hands and gazing hard into her eyes. "Grimya, there is so much I don't know! So much more I need to learn!"

Grimya wriggled uneasily. "I have told you everything I can, Niahrin!"

"Yes, yes, I understand, my dear, I mean no slight to you!" Niahrin was breathless with excitement, a suffocating excitement, frightening, almost uncontrollable. Intuition was flowing like a fast-moving river in her veins; she was certain now of what she must do. "But there is another dimension to this, one that we've yet to discover—perhaps one that even Indigo doesn't know. The king is involved in it, and the queen, and Perd Nordenson—" She saw Grimya's hackles bristle as she uttered that name and swiftly reached out to soothe and reassure. "I realize you mistrust him and think him evil, but he is a part of this, I'm sure of it. Grimya, listen. I think there is a way for us to discover what we need to know."

Grimya was suddenly very still, and when she spoke her voice was a guttural, breathless bark, *"How?"*

"By calling on the same power that touched me—touched us—last night. Before Jes and Her Grace came, do you remember?"

"I remember. You called it by a name. . . ."

"Aisling."

"Yess. And then, when we saw the harp—"

"Cushmagar's harp. The bard who was Indigo's teacher and mentor." Niahrin smiled with sad sympathy. "I understand now why you couldn't bring yourself to stay in that little shrine of a room, with the painting and the harp. But Cushmagar *knew*. He lived on after the plague, after the attack of the demons; he knew what really happened and he has left his memories behind. And perhaps more than memories."

Grimya growled softly. "You mean that he—the bard—was the one who—"

"Who spoke to me through the aisling. Yes. And if I can

touch that power again, if I can awaken it again, then maybe we shall have the answers we need."

For a moment Grimya remained motionless. Then suddenly, unexpectedly, she reared up and licked Niahrin's face. It was as near to a kiss as she could bestow, and the witch felt her heart lurch with pleasure at the impulsive gesture.

"Yess!" Grimya said eagerly. "*Yess!* For Indigo! To help Indigo! What must we do?"

Niahrin had a ready answer and she smiled again, this time with more than a hint of conspiracy.

"Tonight," she said, "when Carn Caille is asleep, we shall go back to the room where Cushmagar's harp is kept." She pushed down a strange, eerie sensation that clutched at her spine, telling herself that it was nothing more than anticipation. "If the aisling came once, it may come again. And this time, we shall be ready to hear and understand what it has to tell us."

•CHAPTER•XVI•

Niahrin dined in the great hall that evening. Her motive for joining the revels was threefold: firstly she wanted to create an innocent impression to ensure that no suspicions would be aroused and no one would come looking for her later; secondly she intended to watch and listen for any small clues that might help her in her search for the deeper truth behind Indigo's story; and thirdly she was firmly of the opinion that tonight's planned vigil would be best faced after the fortification of a good meal.

Grimya chose not to accompany her—the wolf was unwilling to face Indigo again after the morning's fracas—so Niahrin went alone to the hall. To her surprise, embarrassment, and private delight she was given a place at the king's table on its raised dais. All the royal family were present tonight: Ryen handsome and elegant in forest green, Brythere beside him in a russet gown that lent color to her pale cheeks, Moragh in plum-colored velvet at his

other hand. Jes Ragnarson sat by the young queen and
Niahrin was placed beside him, while at the far end were
Indigo and Vinar. At first Vinar seemed a little disconcerted by Niahrin's presence, but when she caught his eye
and raised her cup in a wry salute that conveyed both
apology and abashment his unease faded and he relaxed.
Indigo pretended not to be aware of the witch and sat silent, picking at her food. She did not look happy.

The meal was a splendid one, punctuated by a great deal
of cheerful noise from the tables below the dais, where the
rest of the household sat. There was noise in plenty at the
king's table, too; Ryen was jovial, Moragh hardly less so,
and Vinar in such high spirits that he could barely contain
them. Every few minutes his big, booming laugh rang out
across the hall, until Jes, who was keeping Niahrin entertained with lively and droll conversation, remarked in a
whisper that if the Scorvan stayed on land after his marriage he could do worse than settle by the coast and get
employment as a fog-sentry, without any need for a horn.

Vinar was in fact the one sour note in Niahrin's private
speculations. In all her life she couldn't remember having
seen a man so happy with his lot, and the thought that she
was setting out to wreck that happiness tore savagely at
her conscience. She liked Vinar and didn't want to hurt
him. But then, from what Grimya had told her, to do nothing would be an even greater unkindness and would bring
him still more pain in the long run. . . .

The meal was coming to an end when King Ryen rose
to his feet and shouted for silence. From the broad grin
that spread across Vinar's face Niahrin guessed what was
coming, and when Ryen bullied both Vinar and Indigo to
their feet and announced the news of their impending marriage, the cheer that went up in the hall, accompanied by
a stamping of feet and drumming of fists, nearly raised the
roof from its rafters. Half the company, Niahrin surmised,

hadn't the least idea who the happy couple were, but a wedding was a wedding and they roared their approval accordingly. Vinar beamed round at everyone, hugging Indigo to his side, while she, though her face was happily flushed and her eyes sparkled, seemed at the same time a little distracted, as though she felt that she had inadvertently wandered into a world that was not her own. Niahrin watched her covertly as the cheering died down, then her interest quickened as, at a signal from the king, Jes Ragnarson left his place and moved to where a stool had been set just below the dais. Two servants brought a harp—not, Niahrin noted instantly, Cushmagar's harp as she had illogically feared, but a much smaller instrument—and Jes began to play. He was good; *very* good. Niahrin began to suspect his protestations of modesty as he played first the traditional Islers' celebration reel, "Fill the Cup of Cheer," and then, in honor of the betrothed pair's trade, launched into a medley of sea songs. Within the space of one chorus the entire company was joining in, Niahrin included, and when the medley ended the shouts and stamping were deafening. Jes grinned then waved his hands for quiet, and as the furor died down his fingers plucked an eerie arpeggio from the harp strings.

"Friends." His tenor voice carried clearly through the hall and the last laughter and mutterings faded away into absolute silence. "Tonight we celebrate a joyous event. But even as we celebrate, it behooves us all, as Southern Islers, to remember that we are children of the sea and servants of the sea, and that through the Earth Mother's bounty we draw from the sea our life and our living." A strange, sad smile lit his face as though from within; as though, Niahrin thought, old memories were tugging at him. "From the sea we are come; to the sea we must return, for that is the way of the Isles. But the sea is a strong and enigmatic mistress; She calls some home before their time, and it is only right that we who are left behind should remember their passing and do them homage. So for Vinar and Indigo, for their friends and companions of the *Good Hope*, and for our Mother the Sea who grants peace and sanctuary to lost souls, I play now."

A shimmering cascade of notes rippled from the harp, and Niahrin felt her heart lurch as Jes's fingers plucked the first poignant strains of the "Amberland Wife's Lament."

The music was beautiful. She knew the sad old air, had heard it more times than she cared to count; but here in the silent hall of Carn Caille, under the hands of a man who, despite his youth, had the unmistakable touch and gift of a master of his calling, the lament took on a new dimension. Tonight, Jes Ragnarson was inspired. And when Niahrin raised her wet eyes and looked along the high table, she saw Vinar rapt, lost in the music, while at his side Indigo sat motionless, her face a still mask but her eyes alive with a pain and a longing that tore at the witch's soul and made her feel like an intruder looking upon a desperate, bewildered, and very private grief.

In a moment of wry amusement Niahrin reflected that her late-night forays about the corridors of Carn Caille were threatening to become a habit. But the thought was a sharp contrast to her mood and the smile faded quickly from her face as, with Grimya padding at her heels, she headed toward the old royal apartments. In one hand she carried an unlit candle, in the other her wooden pipe.

She had seen on her previous visit that King Kalig's rooms were not kept locked. Easing the door open, and invoking a silent prayer of gratitude that the hinges didn't creak, she slipped into the room with Grimya and felt for the flint and tinder that she had seen Moragh use. She didn't like to touch the ornate lantern, so she lit only her candle, and with the small flame flickering unsteadily but providing enough illumination to stop her from blundering into anything, she went through to the inner room.

Niahrin didn't want to look at the portrait; now that she had heard Grimya's story, the thought of gazing on the still, painted face of Princess Anghara gave her a peculiar and none too pleasant frisson. Setting her back toward the mantel she turned instead to Cushmagar's harp. She wouldn't touch it, of course—that would be wrong—but she moved close to it and sat down cross-legged on the floor, setting her candle beside her. The room was cold and the shadows made her uneasy; they seemed unnaturally deep, almost solid, as though something more than mere darkness lurked here among the preserved memories. She felt a rush of gratitude when Grimya lay down close beside her and reached out a hand to stroke the wolf's thickly furred back.

"Well." She flexed her fingers around the pipe, a little disconcerted by the sound of her own voice in the gloom and silence. "Best begin, eh? The Mother alone knows what we'll learn, if anything, but if we don't venture we shan't find out." She raised the pipe to her lips.

And an icy shock went through her as she heard a soft footfall in the outer room.

Niahrin dropped her pipe and sat petrified, staring toward the door. Grimya had half risen; her hackles were up and a low growl started in her throat, but even her eyesight wasn't enough to penetrate the darkness. The footfalls ceased . . . then came the sound of the door latch being lifted. . . .

Lamplight spilled into the room as the door swung open, and Niahrin gaped in consternation at Moragh and Jes Ragnarson framed on the threshold.

The silence was awful, and Niahrin thought it would never end. Then, very quietly, Moragh said, "Good evening, Niahrin. You seem a little more surprised to see us than we are to see you."

All the excuses, explanations, and dissemblings that the witch had been struggling to muster from her frozen brain collapsed, and she put a hand to her face in mortification, unable to utter a word.

The dowager said, "Come in, Jes, and close the door." Holding the lantern, she crossed the room to where Niahrin sat. Her shrewd gaze took in the harp, the pipe, Grimya's half-guilty, half-defensive posture, and eventually came to rest on Niahrin's scarlet face.

"Your Grace," Niahrin began desperately, "I didn't mean—"

Moragh held up a hand, silencing her. "There's no need to explain. I think Jes and I already know why you are here." She glanced, briefly, into the deep shadows where the portrait hung. "And I confess that we are also guilty of a little deception, for we expected this development, or something like it, and have been keeping a careful watch on you." To Niahrin's surprise, she smiled. "I'm not angry with you, my dear. Far from it. If you can solve the mystery, then you have my blessing to do whatever you feel is needed. But from now on, you will do it with us."

Niahrin swallowed something that was sticking in her throat. "With . . . you, ma'am?"

"Yes." The dowager turned to the young bard. "Go and fetch your own harp, Jes. In the light of what we've already learned, it might not be wise to attempt to use Cushmagar's instrument tonight."

Jes bowed and departed, leaving Niahrin blinking in confusion. The dowager moved closer, then, a little stiffly, sat down on the floor at the witch's side. She was still smiling but there was a hint of steel in her eyes.

"I take it, Niahrin," she said, "that you are hoping Cushmagar will speak to you again tonight?" Niahrin, still flushing, nodded, and Moragh sighed. "Then why such secrecy? Why come here alone, without a word to me?"

The witch hung her head. "I thought ... forgive me, ma'am, but I thought you'd deny me permission. This room"—she made a helpless gesture—"is a shrine, a—"

"It's no such thing, and you know it isn't. No: I think you can't quite bring yourself to trust me. I think that you—or someone—fear that to confide in me might bring harm to Indigo." Here the dowager gave Grimya such a hard, assessing look that Niahrin knew without doubt she suspected the wolf was no ordinary animal. Grimya whimpered slightly, and Moragh's smile grew a shade harder.

"It's clear to me now that there must be a connection between Indigo and Carn Caille, and that the matter of her resemblance to Princess Anghara is no coincidence. Until last night I wasn't certain, but now ..." The smile vanished altogether. "Well, you'd best see for yourself."

Moragh was wearing a heavy woolen gown with a short cloak over it; she reached into the cloak's folds and drew out something that glinted dully in the lamplight and said levelly, "Tell me, Niahrin, have you seen this before?"

Lying in her palm was a long-bladed knife. Grimya uttered a yelp and started to her feet; reacting swiftly, Niahrin gripped a handful of her ruff and pushed her down.

"Hush, Grimya, hush!" She raised her gaze reluctantly to Moragh's face and realized that she couldn't lie to her. "I can't be certain, Your Grace. But I think I have."

"Then you will probably know where it was found."

In a small voice the witch said, "I ... believe I do."

"Mmm. So it *was* your face I glimpsed peeping round the corner of the wall. I thought so." Moragh steepled her fingers together. "I may as well tell you that Brythere saw and recognized her intruder, so we know that it was Indigo in her room. You had, I presume, been following her?"

"She was sleepwalking, ma'am. Grimya saw her and alerted me, and—"

"There's no need to go into the fine details, not now. I don't want to know them yet. What I *do* want—and will have, Niahrin, so we'll save time and effort if you don't protest—is your trust, and your cooperation. Wasn't it only yesterday that you pledged to help me and to work with me in the solving of this mystery? This unhappy matter concerns us all, not only Indigo."

Niahrin felt shamed to the depths of her heart. Last night her instinct had urged her to trust Moragh. But then Indigo had embarked on her near-calamitous night foray, and the knife had been discovered, and in the morning Grimya had made her terrible confession of the truth—and Niahrin had lost her nerve. Logic had swamped instinct; she was afraid to confide in Moragh, afraid of what the dowager might do, and so she had retreated into secrecy. She should have known better. Above all, she should have known that Moragh could not be deceived or evaded so easily.

Niahrin looked at Grimya. She couldn't tell what the wolf was thinking, though she sensed a wave of unhappiness and fear in her mind. But whatever Grimya wanted, there was no choice now.

"Your Grace, I was wrong." She summoned the courage to look at Moragh and tried not to flinch from her disquietingly steady gaze. "I shouldn't have tried to keep this from you. But I was so afraid that—"

"Afraid that I would draw hasty conclusions and act upon them." Moragh's smile returned, and it was a gentle smile now. "Yes, my dear, I believe you, and I don't hold you to blame. In your place I think I'd have done as you did." Suddenly she reached out and laid a wrinkled but strong hand on the witch's arm. "But now there must be no more misgivings on either side. You must take us into your confidence, so that we might all work together."

Disquiet crept into Niahrin's eyes. ". . . *We*, Your Grace?"

"Jes and I. No one else. I've not told the king or queen anything of this and I don't intend to. Ryen is a good man and a good ruler but he would not see matters quite as we do; while Brythere . . . well, Brythere has enough fears already without adding more to her burden. She didn't see the knife—Ketrin is quick-witted—and she thinks only that Indigo was sleepwalking and somehow found her way to the tower. Maybe she and Ryen will eventually have to be told, but until and unless that time comes this shall remain a secret between the three . . . or the four . . . of us." Again she glanced cryptically at Grimya, who wouldn't meet her eyes. "Jes can be trusted implicitly," the dowager continued. "And he may prove to be of great value. He's a fine harpist, as you heard for yourself in the hall tonight. If you are to conjure the aisling again, you may have cause to be grateful for his music."

Niahrin nodded. "Yes. Yes, Your Grace." An odd little shiver of excitement ran through her, and at last she, too, managed the ghost of a smile. "Thank you."

Moragh made a dismissive gesture, bringing the mood sharply back to earth. She started to get to her feet; Niahrin scrambled hastily to help her and the dowager brushed down her robe.

"No matter how thorough the servants are, there's always dust . . . I presume you know how to light a fire and get it blazing quickly?" Baffled, Niahrin nodded. "Good. Then while we wait for Jes to return with his harp, perhaps between us we should kindle the wood that's ready in the hearth."

Niahrin's good eye widened, and the dowager laughed softly.

"Rowan, sweetbriar, and willow. Aren't they the right ingredients for a dream-fire? And apple, for the blessing that I think we all need."

Moragh must have known her intentions all along, Niahrin realized, and had done what she herself could not do. A fire set ready for the aisling. . . .

The witch shook her head, and a sound like suppressed laughter caught in her throat.

"Yes, Your Grace," she said meekly. "Whatever you command."

It was beginning. Niahrin sensed the first subtle shift in the atmosphere; the scent—she had no other word for it—of magic, mingling with the sweet, heady scents of the dream-fire. The flames burned steadily, warming the room and casting friendly shadows, and their light made a shining nimbus of Jes's brown hair as he sat with his small harp cradled in his lap. His head was bowed and his fingers moved swiftly, fluidly, over the harp strings as he played a rippling melody. Beyond him, in deeper shadow, Moragh gazed steadily at the fire, her eyes hooded, her face sharp in the firelight, while Niahrin herself wove a counterpoint to the harp, her pipe lilting and singing. The pattern their music made was hypnotic; the witch's body swayed gently to the rhythm and a trancelike sensation was creeping over her, as if a long-forgotten door had opened in her mind and she was drifting through its portal into another, more mystical world. There was a dreamlike edge to her vision now, a sparkling and a flickering wherever her eyes focused. Etched by that shimmering aura Jes and the dowager looked strange and marvelous and not quite human, and even her own hands seemed to belong to someone beautiful and eldritch, far removed from the ugly, earthy, and homely Niahrin that she knew.

Then the flames of the dream-fire began to swell and

sway with the music. Niahrin saw their dance begin, heard the dowager's soft intake of breath, and glimpsed the quick, eager light in Jes's eyes as he began to change the timber of his melody, following where the fire led. His expression was rapt with a joy almost akin to pain; he shook his head and the firelight sparked in his hair. Niahrin stopped playing and let the pipe fall into her lap; this was the young bard's moment, and the magic, the aisling, was coming in response to his call. The harp shimmered on . . . and slowly, gradually, the sound of a second harp, greater and richer and deeper, swelled from the air about them to blend with Jes's melody.

And in the fire the flames took on the shape of old, gnarled hands, and a face, seamed, wrinkled, eyes blinded by cataracts, appeared behind the hands like a specter.

Jes stifled a cry, and his playing stopped on a harsh discord. In the fire the old man's face—Cushmagar's face—smiled. He was gray, as though time had drained even his ghost of color, but his flame-hands moved with an old, sure expertise. And Niahrin felt the vibration like a breath on the nape of her neck as, behind her, the great harp that had lain untouched for fifty years gave voice to a soft, plaintive chord.

Jes caught his breath chokingly, and a voice dry as fallen leaves, soft as new grass, whispered,

"There was a time, a time and a time, before we who live now under the sun and the sky came to count time. That is how the legend began, and that is how it was told to Anghara when she began to hunger for something more than her future seemed to hold. But for each of us time has a different meaning, and for each of us there is a different legend. Anghara sought her legend at the Tower of Regrets. Anghara had the power to dream, and in dreaming to reach and hold to a part of her soul where dreams become reality, and so the door was opened and the choice

*was laid before her. That is another legend and I cannot
recount it, for my time is past and I am gone, and the end
of her story is yet to be told. The tower is fallen and its
door is closed, but the bolt may still be drawn and the bar
may still be lifted. And though these old eyes are blind,
there are other eyes that may open and see the threads of
what has befallen, and what might have been, and what
might come to be. The tale is not yet done; time has still
to run; and the call of the aisling shall receive an answer.
For there was a time, a time and a time, before we who
live now under the sun and the sky came to count
time. . . ."*

Like a dream slowly fading as the dreamer stirred and
woke, the gentle, lilting voice diminished away until with
a final sigh it was gone. The flames in the hearth swayed
quietly, as though to the rhythm of steady breathing, but
the ghost of Cushmagar had evaporated into a flickering
memory of light and smoke. For a moment the fire's fra-
grance surged powerfully in Niahrin's nostrils and she fancied she heard a rippling cadence of music, though Jes's
hands lay limp and powerless in his lap. Then the scent diminished and only the quiet crackling of wood broke the
silence.

Niahrin knew what she must do. Obliquely, Cushmagar
had told her how the aisling might bring them the answers
they needed, and, not daring to look at Jes again or beyond
him to where Moragh sat stunned and stricken, she raised
a hand to the patch over her left eye. For an instant her
mind jerked back to earth and she felt a sharp pang of
shame at the thought of revealing the whole ugly truth to
her companions, for in all the years since she had accepted
deformity as the price for her seer's gift, she had never exposed that to any outsider. To leaven her fear she wanted
to say something wry, jesting, but that would be inappro-
priate and grotesque. Pride had no place in this, and

quickly, before the little worm of sadness within her could make her change her mind, she lifted the eye patch.

Moragh and Jes saw what the patch concealed, but neither uttered the slightest sound—and even had they done so, Niahrin wouldn't have known it. In the instant that the patch was pulled away, two worlds meshed and became one before her. The walls seemed to swell, fade, swell again, and the dreamlike auras of odd, shifting color she had seen earlier suddenly intensified, as though a new dimension had been added to the room to bring it into sharper, deeper focus. The scene in Niahrin's vision shimmered briefly.

And a figure stood before the hearth.

It had the stature of a child. It was dressed only in a simple gray tabard, and its face was framed by a nimbus of soft silver hair. Its eyes, too, were silver, flecked with blue-violet, and as its lips parted Niahrin saw that it had tiny, sharp, white teeth, like the teeth of a little cat.

The child said: "I am Anghara." And Niahrin recognized the being that Grimya had described to her and that she had named *Nemesis*.

Nemesis smiled, a sad, wistful smile. Again the room seemed to shimmer, and abruptly two figures stood where before there had been one. Niahrin knew this being, too, for Grimya had described the creature that she believed to be the Earth Mother's emissary and instigator of Indigo's burden. Looking into the being's milky golden eyes Niahrin was certain now that she knew the truth better than Grimya, and when the entity said, quietly and sadly, "I, too, am Anghara," it was final confirmation.

Then suddenly vision warped once more, and a third figure appeared. Niahrin's mouth opened in astonishment and she was about to cry out, "Grimya!" when she realized her mistake. Grimya was still crouching at her side, and this wolf's coat was paler, less brindled, and its eyes not the amber of Grimya's eyes but a strange shade of blue. Or indigo ...

The wolf said, softly and in a disturbingly natural human voice, "I, too, am Anghara. We are all her sisters. We are all a part of what she has been."

Quickly, wildly, Niahrin looked sidelong at her companions. Jes was leaning forward, eyes intensely wide but with wonder more than fear. Moragh, though, was rigid, and her face looked gray and drawn with shock.

"I see them," she whispered hoarsely; then a shuddering tremor ran through her and her gaze snapped from Niahrin to the three phantasms. "But I don't *understand*! Princess Anghara is dead; she has been dead for fifty years! And she was human, while you—"

"Anghara did not die," Nemesis interrupted her, its voice soft yet stifling Moragh's words as effectively as if the being had roared her to silence. "She is here, in Carn Caille. We are her; she is us. And there is one other."

Moragh's lip began to tremble. "I don't understand ..." Yet her tone suggested that she did and was terrified by the knowledge. "Where is Anghara? *Who is she?*"

"She is Indigo. And she is us. We are all a part of the one soul."

The dowager made a dreadful choking sound, and Jes turned to her in alarm.

"Your Grace—"

"No—" She forestalled him, pushing his solicitous hand away. "No, Jes, I'm all right." She paused. "You—see them? You heard what they ... what it ... said?"

The bard's face was stark. "Yes, Your Grace. I heard."

She swallowed, striving to regain her composure. "My son was ... was more right than ever he knew. ..." Her lip trembled again; she bit it, hard, and looked at Nemesis again. "But how can a living soul be haunted by ghosts?"

Niahrin cut in hastily, whispering. "Your Grace, they are

not ghosts. They are—" She sought for a word and, apparently from nowhere, it came. "They are *aspects*."

Nemesis smiled wistfully again. Then, as though the witch had blinked momentarily, the three figures were suddenly one creature, a bizarre blend of human and animal, silver-haired, milky-eyed, lithe and furred.

A composite voice spoke. "We are all a part of the whole, you see. But we are not complete and cannot be complete unless our sister is healed. We need you. We need your help, or Anghara will be lost forever and our long quest will have been in vain."

"Your quest?" Niahrin asked.

"A quest. A search. A journey." The creature spread its graceful, claw-tipped hands in a gesture that seemed to imply a plea. "We have traveled a long way, and for a long time, and the journey was almost over. But now our sister has forgotten us, and the threads that bound us together have been broken. Indigo must remember us; she must remember us and accept us and be whole again, be Anghara again, so that the last threads of the tapestry may be woven."

"And if they are not woven?" the witch asked softly, deeply disturbed by the metaphor the being had chosen. "If Anghara is not healed . . . what then?" She didn't dare look at Moragh.

The being sighed. "If she is not healed, there can be no true life for us. Only shadows. Only shadows."

Niahrin's skin crawled as she sensed, on a level far deeper than her consciousness could interpret, that by *us* the being did not mean merely itself and Indigo. She thought of Queen Brythere and the nightmares that were drawing so perilously close to reality. She thought of the king and his clear estrangement from his wife. She thought of the dowager, afraid for what the future might hold . . . *Only shadows.* And she thought of someone else. . . .

She found herself speaking. The words came to her suddenly and involuntarily, forming in her mind from a part of herself where another, older wisdom lay dormant and from whence it had risen only rarely in her life. Granmer's gift had many facets. . . .

"We would help you." Her voice took on a singsong quality, as though she had slipped into a trance. "But if we are to help we must also understand. We must know Anghara's story—*your* story—and we must know how the threads of other lives are woven into her tapestry." She paused as an intuitive impulse pricked her mind, then, yielding to it, added, "And one life in particular."

"Yes." The being's eyes focused briefly but intently on her alone, and she saw cognition, respect, and a hint of complicity mingling in the look. "Yes, we understand. You mean the man you know as Perd Nordenson."

The crawling sensation came back and Niahrin felt as though spiders were prowling over her arms and torso. One phrase; one phrase gave her the clue. . . . "The man we *know* as Perd?" she repeated very quietly.

The apparition turned its head and looked at the wolf, who crouched close to Niahrin, trembling, staring in mute unhappiness. "Grimya senses the truth, even though she does not consciously know it," the being said with sympathy and affection in its voice. "She has sensed an aura of evil about Perd Nordenson, and her judgment is sound." The strange eyes, silver and indigo now stirring in their milky depths, regarded the witch again. "Anghara knows that Fenran did not die fifty years ago. She believes that he has been imprisoned by the very demons she set loose, in an agonizing limbo from which he has no respite, waiting until she can conquer the last of those seven terrors and set him free. In one sense Anghara is right in her belief; Fenran *is* alive, he *is* a prisoner of demons, trapped in limbo, and only she has the power to release him. But the demons are demons of his own creation, and his prison is the prison of his own mind. He has been waiting for Anghara not in the Tower of Regrets, nor in some astral netherland, but here, in Carn Caille. He is an old man now, he has changed his name and forgotten the old one, and he is no longer sane. But Fenran—or, as you know him, Perd Nordenson—is still waiting for Anghara."

Away to her right, beyond Jes, Niahrin heard the dowager utter a faint, strange wail. The composite figure that was Indigo and yet not Indigo wavered, and quickly praying that Moragh would control her emotions, the witch said, "Then the queen Perd loves is not Queen Brythere but—"

"He loves Anghara. Anghara was not destined to be queen. Yet if others were to die . . ."

Then Niahrin understood. Indigo's sleepwalking trance, the deadly knife . . . and the glimpse, one glimpse that she had dismissed as illusion, of Perd Nordenson waiting in the shadows at the foot of Brythere's tower. Mad Perd, nursing an ancient love and an ancient grudge that now were so tangled and fused together that he could no longer tell one from the other. Perd, in the ruins of whose mind lay the knowledge that he loved the queen, and who saw behind the masks of other faces the shadow of his real love, whose place he believed they had usurped. Anghara . . . not destined to be queen. *But if others were to die . . .*

Suddenly Niahrin began to feel queasy, and the queasiness grew until the room seemed to lurch around her like the pitching deck of a ship in a storm. She knew the signs; the magic was draining her, as it always did, and the energy that flowed from within her and gave strength to her seer's eye was rapidly diminishing. For the second time the figure of the entity wavered and threatened to fade. It seemed to be speaking but she could no longer hear the words; if she weakened much more she would lose the power and the fragile thread of contact would be broken. But there was so much more she needed to *know*.

Someone gripped her arm and through blurring vision she saw Jes beside her. He had sensed what was happening and was trying to lend her his own strength. Niahrin made a tremendous effort, clinging to the power, forcing her lips to form words.

"Please!" Her voice sounded hoarse and ugly in her ears. "There's little time—my strength is failing—please, tell us what we must do!"

The being's answer came in faint, echoing waves. "There is one more demon. One more, and the most dangerous of all, for it lies within them. Follow the threads that lead to what would have been or what could have been—that is your talent and the surest path for you."

"But how?" Niahrin asked desperately. "How can I find the thread?"

"Fenran holds the key. Unlock the door in his mind. That is our only hope. Please, Niahrin. Please. Pl—"

The voice cut off sharply, vanishing into acute silence, and at the same moment the image of the composite being winked out. The fire in the hearth flared—and with a sharp, smothered gasp Niahrin keeled over and slumped senseless to the floor.

•CHAPTER•XVII•

"Then it's settled!" A wide, benevolent smile spread across Moragh's face as she looked at the couple before her. "You shall be married here at Carn Caille, and the king will officiate at the ceremony! I am *so* pleased!"

Vinar's cheeks flushed and, greatly daring, he caught the dowager's hand in both of his and squeezed her fingers. "Thank you, Your Grace, ma'am! This is—well, it's better and more splendid than anything we could have hoped. That's right, Indigo, huh?"

"Yes," Indigo said faintly. "Yes, indeed . . . Your Grace is very kind to us. *Too* kind. There's no reason why you should—"

"Why I should take such trouble? Nonsense, my dear! You and Vinar are our good friends. Besides, it's a while since we've had the excuse for a grand celebration here. You wouldn't deny me my own pleasure, would you?"

There was, of course, no answer to that, and at last Indigo managed to return the dowager's smile. "No, Your Grace. Of course not. Thank you."

Moragh was well aware that Ryen, still at the dais table, was looking at her with intense curiosity, but she had taken care to steer Indigo and Vinar out of earshot so that their conversation shouldn't be overheard. Ryen would not be pleased when he learned what she'd done, for he was still far from happy about Indigo's continuing presence at his court. Doubtless there would be a storm when she told him, Moragh thought, but she would explain—or explain as much as she considered judicious—and bully, cajole, or blackmail him into complying with her wishes. It was the only way to ensure that Indigo stayed at Carn Caille until she and Jes and Niahrin could carry out the next stage of their plan.

"Now," she said, taking Indigo's arm, "we must think about our preparations. Firstly, my dear, there's the question of your gown. My own senior tiring-woman is a very talented seamstress; you shall go to her this afternoon to have your measurements taken, and we'll all put our heads together to choose a fabric. Blue, I think; a light blue, like the summer sky, will suit you to perfection and bring out the full color of your lovely eyes. And a train in cream, or perhaps even silver if we have suitable material. Then, of course, there are Vinar's clothes to consider; and the choice of attendants and pledge-friends—"

Vinar, listening avidly, interrupted. "I'd like Neerin to be one of the pledge-friends. She done a lot to help us." Then a little sadly he amended, "Or at least she tried, even if it didn't work out the way she hoped."

Indigo looked as though she were about to object, but Moragh didn't give her the chance. "That's a good thought, and I'm sure Niahrin will be delighted," she said.

Vinar looked around the hall. "We could ask her now, only she don't seem to be here."

"Ah . . . ah, so she doesn't. I believe someone told me she's unwell this morning."

"Neerin, not well? Maybe we should go and see her—"

"No." Thinking quickly, and hoping her tone hadn't aroused his suspicion, Moragh dissembled with the skill of long practice. "Strictly between us, Vinar, I think it's an unfortunate aftereffect of last night's revels. She was drinking wine at dinner, and I don't think she's used to it."

"Oh. Ya. Well, we can see her later." His smile returned. "You were saying, ma'am. About the preparations . . ."

Later, when they were alone, Indigo said, "I wish we didn't have to do this, Vinar. I don't want to stay here, not after the . . . that nightmare. And knowing that mad old man may still be in the vicinity."

Vinar's arms went warmly and protectively around her. "He can't hurt you," he said decisively. "Her Grace told me all about him, remember? It isn't you he wants—and even if it was, you think he'd get anywhere near you with me here?"

Indigo bit her lower lip. "But if he's nothing to do with me, why did I dream about him before I'd even set eyes on him?" Her face turned up to his and he saw real fear in her eyes. "*Why* did I do that, Vinar?"

"I don't know, and that's truth. But I reckon you must have . . . well, *caught* that dream, you understand me?"

Despite herself Indigo couldn't suppress a brief laugh. "You make it sound as simple as catching a cold!"

"Well, so it could be. I mean, we know about the dream the queen keeps having, just like the one you got that first night here. Her Grace said to me, she said you must have 'picked up the thread' was how she put it." He hugged her tightly, suddenly grinning. "Maybe you're a witch like Neerin, huh?"

"I'm nothing of the kind." But Vinar's abounding good

humor was starting to work its magic as it so often did, and the laughter in Indigo's voice was unmistakable now. "I'm just me, just Indigo Nonesdaughter. But soon it'll be different. I'll be Indigo Vinarswife, and then nothing else will matter."

"That's not how we say it in Scorva," Vinar told her with mock admonishment. "You'll be Indigo Shillan. Take my pa's family name, same as me."

She pressed her face against his chest. "But I still wish we didn't have to stay here. I wish we could leave Carn Caille now and be married in the next town, then sail for Scorva and your family home."

"And miss the grand wedding Her Grace got planned for us? We can't say no to her, not when she been so kind. And think how proud we'll be, to have the king himself to see over the ceremony!" Then, realizing she still wasn't convinced, he added consolingly, "Likely it'll only be a few days, love. It don't take that long to get a celebration ready. Then as soon as it's done we can go."

She looked up again. "Promise me that?"

"Promise!"

Indigo nodded. "You see, it's just that . . . just that the longer we stay, the more afraid I am that . . . it will happen again."

She meant far more than just a simple nightmare. In her mind was the memory of a bright-bladed knife, and the shocked face of Queen Brythere; and, presiding over all, the bitter, raddled crone who bore the mark of her own aged self. But Vinar could not guess that and must never, ever be told.

Moragh and Jes were the only two people in Carn Caille who knew the real cause of Niahrin's malady and, determined that it should stay that way, Moragh had put word about that the witch was suffering from overindulgence and did not wish to be disturbed. By midmorning Niahrin still hadn't roused from her deep, almost comatose sleep, and Jes elected to sit with her for an hour or two. Shortly before noon Moragh made her covert way to the room, bearing a small, cloth-covered try; the bard rose as she entered, and to her relief the dowager saw that Niahrin was at last awake, though her face looked drawn in the frame of pillows with which Jes had propped her.

"I've brought you some hot soup, my dear," she said, setting the tray down on the bedside table. "Drink it all if you can; there are restorative herbs in it."

Niahrin smiled a pallid apology. "I'm sorry to be such a nuisance, ma'am, putting you to trouble—"

"You're doing nothing of the kind. But for you we'd still be floundering in the dark." Moragh smiled. "You were very courageous."

Niahrin shook her head, though it seemed to take a toll of what little energy she had. "No, ma'am, it wasn't a matter of courage. I just let it go on too long—it always happens if I do that; it's a failing." She couldn't say any more because Moragh had sat down on the bed and was starting to spoon-feed her.

Feeling utterly foolish Niahrin obediently opened her mouth and swallowed the broth, which was rich and warming and had the taste of venison in it. After a few spoonfuls, though, she snatched the chance to ask, "Please, ma'am, do you know where Grimya is? I looked for her when I woke, but she'd gone."

"Ah. Grimya." Moragh and Jes exchanged a glance that Niahrin couldn't fathom, then Moragh said briskly, "Well, we might as well tell you now. Niahrin, my dear, we know all about Grimya. She told us the entire story herself, last night."

"She told. . . ." Then Niahrin realized what the dowager meant. "Oh," she said. "Oh."

Moragh continued, "When Jes and I brought you back to your room—and I assure you that was no simple task even with two of us to carry you—Grimya was obviously in very great distress. I suspected the truth about her, so I challenged her directly—" She raised her eyebrows. "Or perhaps I should be strictly honest and admit that I bullied her. She, poor innocent creature, finally realized that dumb silence would no longer do, and she gave in. She told us everything that wasn't revealed during last night's . . . adventure." She laughed huskily. "Under other circumstances it would have been a shock to discover that she could talk. But less than an hour before, I had heard the voice of Cushmagar the bard, I had learned that Princess Anghara has lived unchanging and unaging for fifty years, and I had seen three phantoms who are a part of her materialize before my eyes. After that, how could I be surprised by such a trivial thing as an animal that speaks?" She shook her head as though momentarily casting doubt on what she had just said, then shrugged the feeling off. "Grimya is very brave and very intelligent. I know she was afraid we might turn against Indigo—against Anghara—and I could quite see why. But she also understood that we could not help her unless we knew the full story. She judged that we could be trusted." A faint smile touched the edges of her mouth. "I took that as a very great compliment."

Niahrin was astonished but also, she realized, deeply relieved. The burden of keeping Grimya's secret, with all its attendant difficulties, had been weighing her down to a far greater degree than she'd admitted to herself until this moment. "I'm glad she told you, Your Grace," she said at last. "I wanted to. But I couldn't break my promise to her."

"She knows you would not have done. She's very fond of you, Niahrin. Rightly so, I think." Then, seeing that the witch was embarrassed by the compliment, Moragh patted her hand and changed briskly back to her original topic. "So, Grimya and Jes and I discussed what should be done. One thing was made clear to us last night: If we are to help Anghara, we must seek the missing thread of which the . . . the being spoke. And it seems there is only one way to do that."

"Through Perd."

"Or Fenran, as maybe we should now call him. However, we can't hope to have his willing cooperation. I doubt if he's capable of giving it, even if he should want to. So that leaves us with one option. He must be coerced. We must find a way of reaching into his damaged mind and drawing out the truth. And that, I'm afraid my dear, is a task for you."

Niahrin nodded. She had anticipated something like this. "Yes," she said soberly, then met the dowager's eyes with candor. "If I have the ability."

"That's something we shan't know until we put it to the test. But before we can do that we have to find our quarry, and that brings us back to Grimya. Perd—Fenran—obviously has no intention of leaving the district, so he must have found himself a hideaway nearby. The forest is the likeliest place, so Grimya has gone there to try to track him down."

The witch frowned into her soup bowl. She was suddenly ravenously hungry, a sure sign that her exhaustion was wearing off at last, and she reached for the spoon.

"He won't be easy to find, ma'am, even for Grimya. He may be mad but he's cunning, and skilled in woodcraft. And her leg still isn't fully healed. She doesn't have speed or stamina."

"She knows that. But she means to ask the wild wolves for their help."

Niahrin was so startled that she dropped the spoon, splashing soup over the bedcover. "The wild wolves?

Ma'am, Grimya's *terrified* of the wild wolves! She fears—"

"That if they discover her mutation they'll turn on her as her own pack did when she was a cub." Moragh nodded. "She told us that sad tale. But she also feels that if Indigo is to be helped, she must overcome her fear. As I said a little earlier, she is very brave."

"Yes," Niahrin agreed softly. "Yes. Very brave indeed . . ."

"There's little Jes and I can do until she returns, except to pray that she is successful," the dowager added. "Our task, for the present, is to ensure that no suspicions are roused within Carn Caille. But you, Niahrin, should eat, rest, and recuperate." She picked up the fallen spoon and pushed it back into the witch's hand. Her eyes bore an odd expression, a mixture of guilt and compassion. "You, more than any of us, are likely to need all the strength you possess before this is over."

Despite her courageous words to Moragh, Grimya was frightened. There was no milder word for it and no means of avoiding the truth; the fear was lodged deep within her, immovable, like a physical pain. For a short while after entering the forest she had been able to push it away as the delights of the woodland itself assailed her senses. Forestborn, she loved the dappling sunlight and shade, the moist undergrowth, the sounds and scents and byways all crying out to be explored; this was her natural habitat and it was a long time since she had been able to enjoy it to the full. But the fear never entirely left her, and now, as she stopped and stared at the trunk of a fallen tree that lay across the narrow track ahead of her, it came surging back. For her nostrils had caught the clear scent of another wolf, and though she couldn't yet see it, she knew that it was only a matter of yards away from her.

Her head swung from side to side, testing the air, and her heart began to pound hard and erratically. Where was the wolf? She was downwind of it so it was unlikely to have scented her, but had it seen her? And if so, what would it do? She couldn't run; she had kept up a jog-trot from Carn Caille and that was easy and comfortable enough, but her weakened leg couldn't yet cope with a faster gait. If the strange wolf should sense her *difference* and attack her, what would she do? What *could* she do?

There was a sudden rustle in the undergrowth on the far side of the fallen tree and a bird voiced a shrill alarm call and flew away, wings clattering. Grimya dropped to a defensive crouch, ears pricked, belly flat to the ground, staring hard at the bushes, which were quivering slightly as though something had disturbed them. Suddenly she glimpsed a blur of brownish gray—and then a small shape sprang out of hiding, jumped up onto the felled trunk, and stood staring at her with its mouth open and its stumpy tail waving.

It was a cub; not even half grown, and bristling with the wide-eyed, eager curiosity of the very young. It yelped, once, then went into a mock crouch, stern in the air and tongue lolling in a clear invitation to play. Grimya began to rise, a little of the tension draining from her as she saw that the cub's intent was entirely friendly—but an instant later the fear came back, and with it a feeling close to panic as she reasoned that its mother must surely be nearby, and that she must be the matriarch of the pack, for it was a rule among wolves that only the leader and his mate were permitted to produce children of their own.

The cub yelped again, baffled by the lack of response from this new playmate. From its mind Grimya felt a tumble of quick, keen thoughts, and was startled to find that she could understand them. The language of wolves was something less than telepathy—which had been her own undoing—yet more than simple sound, though sound played a vital part. It was more like a shared understanding, instinct and concepts and images blending in a form of communication impossible to explain to any human. For more than half a century Grimya had had neither the need nor the desire to use the "tongue" of her own cubhood. Could she remember it now? Could she get through to this eager little creature who wanted to be her friend and make herself understood?

She uttered a sound from the back of her throat, not quite a chirrup, not quite a whine, but with echoes of both, and in the old wolf-way, the way her mother had taught her, she projected the concept of *friend.*

"Friend!" The affirmation was instant, and with it came a flurry of questions. *"Who? Where from? Play?"*

"New," Grimya told the cub. *"Stranger, but kind. No harm."*

"No harm," the cub agreed and bounced down from the tree trunk, pattering toward her with muzzle raised for the sniffing, licking greeting that was proper between members of the same pack, or of a pack accepting a new member. The gesture gave Grimya heart and she stood still while the cub jumped and snuffled and then, being young, rolled to show submission to an elder.

"Play?" it cajoled. *"Chase and bite and hunt?"*

Grimya made the warning sound that conveyed refusal to comply, then whined to show that she implied no threat or unkindness. She wanted to make her companion understand that there were serious matters afoot and she needed help, but the cub was too preoccupied with the idea of fun and games, and with its own curiosity and pride at having discovered the stranger. Then suddenly it stiffened, eyes focusing beyond and behind her. Alarm filled Grimya; she turned—

Five more wolves were watching her from the track.

She hadn't scented them, for the wind was wrong, but she knew immediately that their leader—a large, rangy, near-black creature with a magnificent ruff of fur—was the pack king. The female at the leader's side voiced a sharp command, and the cub, abashed, slunk toward her, head and tail lowered. As it dived between its mother's forelegs the leader lowered his own head and his lips drew back, showing his teeth.

Instinct came to Grimya's rescue. At the moment the leader made the threat-gesture she dropped to the ground and groveled, paws outspread, her head pressed sideways against the damp softness of last year's leaves. Opening her mouth she let her tongue show, licking the air, and she whined, at the same time projecting, *"Friend. Friend. Stranger, but friend. Reverence and respect. No harm."*

The king wolf paced slowly toward her and stood over her. For what seemed a very long time he stared down, while Grimya lay submissive, uttering small, obeisant sounds. Then, to her astonishment, the king wolf communicated clearly,

"We know who you are. Western friends are here. They told us. Waiting for you; they and we."

The great black head came down, and a tremor ran through Grimya's body as the king wolf first sniffed her muzzle, then licked her face, then nipped her right ear—a simple assertion of authority, this, and with no hostile intent—and at last gave his companions permission to come forward and investigate the newcomer for themselves. There were three females among his followers and one younger male; he and one of the females, Grimya learned, were not of the king wolf's own pack but were the "western friends." They had come from Niahrin's district and were, she realized, members of the same pack that had followed her and the witch on the road to Carn Caille. Grimya's excitement grew, but she knew that the formalities of greeting and acquaintanceship must be completed before she dared speak to them about Perd Nordenson, and so she submitted obediently and patiently to her new friends' scrutiny. The females showed great concern over her injured leg, licking and pawing at it, but she assured them that it was healing correctly and that she was able to hunt and feed herself. At last it seemed they were satisfied, and the king wolf called them together. They would not confer here but in another location, within his territory still and not far. Grimya was allowed to her feet then and, after she had shaken herself thoroughly, the wolves led her away. The matriarch veered off after a short while and left them, the cub bounding at her side and darting fascinated glances back over its shoulder, and she was taken deeper into the forest, to a place where dense growths of birch and young oak hung over the bank of a shallow stream. Here the wolves sat in a semicircle, with Grimya in the center where all could see her, and the king allowed them all to address her.

What they had to say was astonishing to Grimya. The wolves had divined the secret of her *difference*— indeed, the western pack had known it since she was first brought to Niahrin's cottage—but, far from feeling hatred or hostility toward her, their attitude was solicitous and sympathetic. The westerners had sensed, too, that there was a link between Grimya and the mad old man who had come to live in their territory several summers ago, and who had long been a focus of great interest to them. There was something strange about that man, they said, something dark and hidden and *wrong*. Could Grimya tell them more?

Grimya did, though she soon found that the wolf-tongue, and the wolves' interpretation of what they heard, had limitations. There was a wide gulf between the pack's way of understanding and the human reasoning that she had learned over the years, and Grimya began to realize just how greatly her long life with Indigo had changed her. It was not an overly pleasant thought. But she was able to explain enough, and the wolves' response was adamant. Loyalty to friends was an unwavering principle among their kind: they had accepted Grimya as their friend, and if she in turn had a friend who needed help, help would be freely given. They knew where the mad human was living, for in their curiosity they had tracked him to his den, though they did not approach him and had warned their young ones to stay well away. However, they didn't think he would be taken easily. He was likely to fight, and men would be needed to overpower him. But the king wolf promised that he and his pack would help. They knew and respected the hunters from Carn Caille; they would lead them to the mad human and lend their numbers and skills in trapping him. All Grimya needed to do was bring her men to this place and call out.

Grimya was deeply grateful to the wild pack. She thanked them profusely, rolling and groveling to show her appreciation, and when the king wolf sealed their agreement he allowed her the privilege of licking his muzzle and head in return. The three lesser wolves also licked her, then when at last she was preparing to take her leave Grimya abruptly remembered something.

"I would ask"— she turned to the king wolf and dipped her head meekly—*"I would ask."*

"Ask. Yes."

"Two moon-times ago, you sang. I heard. Why was the singing?"

For a moment the king wolf gazed steadily into her eyes. Then he replied, *"There was trouble. We had the scent. We gave a warning for you, because you are one of our own."*

So they *had* sensed the evil afoot in Carn Caille that

night, and the eerie clamor outside the citadel had not been chance. . . . Grimya lowered her muzzle to the ground.

"I give you my gratitude," she said. *"And the humans in the stone den give you gratitude, also. You gave warning, and you saved the life of the mate of the king human."*

One of the females yipped, and the king wolf blinked in some surprise. *"A good thing,"* he said. *"A good thing to do. Yes. We will celebrate the good thing together. We will sing together. Sing with us."*

As one the four wolves raised their heads and began to howl on a long, eldritch note. For a few moments Grimya held back; then suddenly an old and half-forgotten instinct filled her and she joined in their song as it rose and fell, rose and fell. There was joy in the song, and pride, and satisfaction, and when finally it ended with a last descending echo there were no farewells, no acknowledgments, but simply a movement and a rustling in the undergrowth, and the wolves melted away and were gone.

Grimya stared at the bushes, where only a slight swaying among the low branches betrayed the direction her new friends had taken, and suddenly felt desolate and lonely, torn between two worlds yet fully at home in neither. She couldn't be a true wolf again, no matter how great the yearnings evoked by the singing and the friendship of the pack; yet she was still wolf enough to regret the breaking of those old ties and wish that, perhaps, her life could have been different.

But then she thought of Indigo. Indigo had been her friend—her dearest and often her only friend—since long before the black wolf's grandsire had been born. Even if Indigo had now forgotten and abandoned her, *she* was what mattered most of all. Loyalty was the wolves' supreme creed, and Grimya's loyalty was to Indigo. She had come here for Indigo's sake, and for Indigo's sake she must put aside her own sadness and longing and return to her other friends—her *human* friends—to report success.

A bird started to sing from a tree on the far side of the stream, a bright, piping song of four notes repeated over and over again. There was no trace of the wild wolves now and even their scent was fading. Grimya rose to her feet, and after a last wistful glance around, turned in the direction of Carn Caille.

•CHAPTER•XVIII•

Five men, led by the dowager Moragh, rode out from Carn Caille that afternoon. They wore hunting colors but their weapons were not those of huntsmen; their dogs were left behind and in their place went Grimya, pacing beside Moragh's horse. Clearly this was no ordinary expedition—but the five men were all foresters of Moragh's personal acquaintance, and the dowager knew she could rely on their silence.

Niahrin was resting. Until the dowager and her party returned she could do nothing, and she was still weakened from her experience of the previous night. The servants had been instructed not to disturb her and so she stayed in her bed, hoping to sleep and hoping more fervently that she wouldn't dream.

She did sleep, and was surprised, when she woke, to discover that she'd slept right through the afternoon and into early evening. Grimya hadn't yet returned, but as she sat up and rubbed her eyes Niahrin saw a message-slate propped up on the table beside her bed. Written on the slate were just two words.

"Success. Jes."

The witch's heart gave a small, queasy lurch.

Over the next few days King Ryen became more and more certain that his mother was hatching some plot of which he knew nothing. She seemed to be constantly busy, and on the few occasions when he was able to command her attention she skillfully evaded his attempts to probe into her activities. Once Ryen tried to confront her, asking point-blank what was afoot, but Moragh only smiled in the way she normally reserved for distant acquaintances and replied that she was, of course, concerned with the planning of Indigo and Vinar's wedding and nothing more sinister than that. Ryen didn't believe her, but had to be content with her answer.

The wedding was another bone of contention. Ryen had been baffled and, at first, annoyed by Moragh's insistence that Carn Caille should play host to the event, but by making her offer to the betrothed couple the dowager had effectively forced his hand and he had no option but to put a cheerful face on the whole matter. But after a while the king's attitude softened; though he was discomfited by the mystery of Indigo's heritage and, in truth, would have preferred her to leave Carn Caille without any delay, he couldn't in fairness hold her personally responsible for this uncomfortable situation. So he gave in with good enough grace, and the preparations began in earnest.

Carn Caille was hurled into a ferment of activity as Moragh set about organizing and directing everyone in his or her appointed role. The dowager took care that the couple themselves, and Indigo in particular, were kept fully occupied; and by a mixture of cajolement and bullying she inveigled Ryen into her schemes to such a degree that the king had no time for any unwanted investigations in other areas. Here she found an unexpected ally in Brythere. The queen was delighted with the marriage announcement and threw herself into the fray with surprising enthusiasm and energy; almost, Moragh thought, to the point of obsession, as though this concrete distraction from her own troubles was something to be clung to as a shipwrecked mariner might cling to a floating spar. The dowager gave her daughter-elect free rein and offered a prayer of thanks for her unwitting but invaluable contribution. And meanwhile, unnoticed amid the general fervor, the deeper strategy was taking form—and a prisoner in a long-disused and all but forgotten cellar beneath the foundations of Carn Caille was being prepared for an encounter with the past.

Perd's capture had been accomplished with remarkable ease. The forest wolves had sensed the hunters' approach early, and the king wolf and five of the fleetest members of his pack were waiting when Moragh and her party arrived at the meeting place by the stream. The men were astonished to find that these wild creatures not only seemed to understand the nature of their mission but were eager to help them, but Moragh offered no explanations and they didn't presume to question her.

They found the old man in the lair he'd made for himself, an old storage hut in a clearing, once used by the foresters but long abandoned and fallen into disrepair. Three female wolves who had been watching the hut from the cover of nearby undergrowth melted away as the king led the humans into the clearing, and Moragh herself rode forward and issued a clear challenge. There was no answer, and at a command from the dowager three of the men went into the hut. The interior reeked of alcohol among other more noisome smells, and they found Perd insensible and snoring, clutching two empty wineskins to his chest as though they were his dearest possessions. He came to when they hauled him outside, and as soon as his bleary eyes focused on the dowager he began to struggle and shout and swear. But in his condition he was no match for even one of the huntsmen, and he was carried back to Carn Caille like a choice deer, slung helplessly over the pommel of a horse's saddle. With well-practiced ingenuity Moragh had arranged for him to be smuggled into the fortress and secured in the already prepared cellar; then with her own hand she mixed a strong narcotic draught and forced it down his throat, to send him back to his dreams.

Four days after the capture Moragh and Niahrin were still busy at their secret assignment. Perd had been made as comfortable as circumstances permitted: the cellar was warm and he had bed and blankets and lamps to light the darkness. Niahrin had even taken it upon herself to wash him from head to foot and dress the assortment of cuts and bruises that she found on his body. He was still drugged, only roused from his stupor twice a day for the sake of food and other necessities, but the nature of the drugs was changing as the two women experimented, studied, experimented further and noted the results of their efforts. Their first intent was to give the old man rest, long periods of dreamless sleep during which the hopelessly entangled skeins of his mind might have the chance to unravel. Then they administered concoctions of other, rarer herbs, whose purpose was to reach into the locked-away realms of memory while he slept. And lastly came the most vital yet most perilous experiment: the drug that, if it was successful, would give Niahrin control of his waking consciousness through hypnotic magic.

After six days they were ready—or, as Niahrin admitted privately, as ready as they could hope to be. Whether or not they would succeed in what they were to attempt was a question she didn't dare try to answer, but there was no time now for second thoughts. While she concentrated on Perd, the wedding preparations at Carn Caille had been gathering pace and momentum, and now the die was cast beyond recall. In three more days Indigo and Vinar were to be joined in marriage. The thing must be done now, or it would be too late.

As she made her way toward the cellar stairs for the appointed rendezvous with Moragh and Jes, Niahrin was torn between dread at what lay ahead and relief that, for better or worse, the tension of waiting would soon be ended. Over the last few days she had grown more and more fearful that their secret would be uncovered; she knew that the king already suspected something in the wind, and even Vinar, she thought, was starting to look askance at her. Only yesterday he had commented wistfully that she seemed always to be so busy that she was missing the fun of the wedding arrangements. The remark had caught Niahrin completely unawares, and she had felt herself blush to the roots of her hair as she dissembled. Whether or not Vinar had been convinced she didn't know, but she doubted it; for all his bluff manner the Scorvan was nobody's fool. Thankfully he had let it go at that, but the witch would be heartily thankful when the need for subterfuge was over.

Grimya was not to be with them tonight. Her presence might have caused trouble with Perd, and the wolf herself felt very ambivalent about the whole affair. She had offered instead to stand sentry for them and divert anyone who might stray too near, and so she was now patrolling the entrance to the long, narrow passage that led to the cellar stairs. Her last words as she and Niahrin parted were a hoarsely whispered *"Good luck!"*

As Moragh unlocked the cellar door and they filed inside, Niahrin reflected that they would need all the luck Grimya could wish them tonight, and a good deal more.

Perd, she saw immediately, was asleep on his pallet bed. In the soft light of two lanterns set in the wall-brackets, his face looked younger, the ravages of time and insanity smoothed almost into kindness. He must have been handsome in his youth, the witch thought; a little wild and raffish, perhaps, but more than capable of turning heads and winning hearts. The unexpected insight gave her a peculiar frisson and she looked quickly away, feeling like a voyeur.

Moragh motioned to Jes to set down the flask and two cups he was carrying and took two small silver vials from her reticule.

"Firstly the stimulant to waken him, and then the hypnotic." She glanced at Niahrin. "Shall I prepare the first dose?"

The witch nodded and put a hand into her own pocket. Her fingers closed on the bundle of fine flax, wound about its distaff and ready for spinning. As she drew it out, the dowager smiled and gestured toward a corner of the room, where something stood covered by a shawl.

"The wheel is ready," she said and flexed her fingers. "I only hope that I can say the same for my skills with it, after so many years."

Niahrin returned the smile a little uncomfortably and moved to lift the shawl away. The spinning wheel was an old and small one but beautifully kept—it had once belonged to her own mother, so Moragh had said—and as she set the distaff in place Niahrin stroked the burnished wood appreciatively and tried not to think of her own wheel, lest she should be reminded of her last experience in the spinning-room at her home.

Jes filled one of the cups from his flask and handed it to the dowager, who crossed the room to Perd's bedside. Holding the cup to his lips she spoke quietly but firmly.

"Perd Nordenson. Wake up, Perd. Wake up and drink."

The old man muttered. He seemed unwilling to stir, but

there was wine in the cup and Perd could never resist the lure of wine; as his nostrils caught the scent of it his hands reached out, making grasping motions.

"Ah-ah!" Moragh spoke as though admonishing a small child and withdrew the cup. "Sit up, Perd, and open your eyes properly. We must not neglect our manners!"

Jes's lips twitched with amusement, but the old man was reflexively obeying. Moragh allowed him two mouthfuls before taking the cup away again, and slowly, blearily, his eyes opened.

"Niahrin?" He had seen the witch and tried to focus on her face. ". . . you doing here?" He shook his head as though to clear it and his slurred voice veered toward petulance. "S'isn't your forest . . . shouldn't be here."

"He's by no means fully conscious yet," Moragh said in an undertone. "But the herbs are working. Jes, take the cup; it wouldn't do to let him have any more or he'll be properly awake before we're ready. Then fill the other cup, and add five drops from the second vial."

Perd gave an outraged shout as he saw the cup vanishing. "Wine! Give me the wine, I want the wine—"

"You shall have wine! Finer wine, with more power—but only if you control your impatience! There now, that's better." As the old man subsided Moragh nodded to Niahrin. "We're ready. I think I should begin."

The two women exchanged places, Niahrin at the bedside while the dowager seated herself on the stool before the spinning wheel. For a few moments the room seemed peculiarly still, the only sound that of wine splashing into the second cup as Jes poured. Perd was sitting up now but frowning, bewildered and more than a little wary. Abruptly his voice broke the hiatus.

"What is it? What are you doing? Niahrin, you're staring at me—I don't like to be stared at, you know I don't like—"

"Hush." Niahrin spoke so sharply that he was silenced in midcomplaint. He blinked, the frown deepening.

"You never speak to me like that, Niahrin. I've never heard you speak to me like that."

Niahrin held his half-puzzled, half-angry gaze. She didn't answer him, but with one hand she gave a small, prearranged signal to Moragh, and the spinning wheel began to turn. Perd started, hissing like a cornered cat, and his head whipped round.

"What's she doing?"

"Spinning, Perd. Only spinning." The wheel was beginning to move faster, its spokes almost a blur now, and as the rhythmic clack and whirr reverberated in the room, a thin, shining thread of flax began to take form under Moragh's hands.

Niahrin glanced at Jes and said, "Give him the wine now."

"Wine . . ." Perd reached eagerly for the cup, snatching it from the bard and tilting it to his lips. Jes, alarmed, made to grab it back before he could drain it, but Niahrin said, "No, it's all right. Let him drink it all. Better that he does."

The old man's throat convulsed as he swallowed; he finished the cup's contents almost without a pause then held it out. "More! Give me more!"

"No, Perd." Niahrin was aware of Jes moving soft-footed behind her, to stand between her and Moragh at the spinning wheel. The skein of flax was coiling into the dowager's lap; swiftly Jes reached to grasp the end of the skein and held it toward Niahrin. She took it, flexed it between her fingers, her gaze never leaving Perd's face. Then she spoke.

"Perd. Perd Nordenson." With a smooth, practiced movement she tied a knot in the flax, pulled it tight. "Perd Nordenson, look at me. Look at me, Perd."

He turned slowly, cautiously, and their eyes met. Niahrin tied a second knot in the flax. "Listen, Perd. Listen. Listen to my voice. Watch, Perd. Watch. Watch my hands." A third knot, and in her mind she rehearsed the words of the old chant that Granmer had taught her long ago. . . .

"Perd. Perd. Listen and watch. Listen and watch." She spoke in time to the steady rhythm of Moragh's wheel, her voice low, compelling, and despite his reluctance Perd couldn't resist the lure. His gaze was drawn to the witch's fingers; for a few moments his mouth worked spasmodically, as if he was trying to formulate a protest, but the drug was already beginning to take effect and he couldn't summon the will to look away.

"Listen and watch, Perd. Listen and watch." Niahrin cast a rapid glance in Jes's direction and the bard understood; he crossed to the lanterns in their wall brackets and turned down the wicks. It seemed to Niahrin that darkness flowed out like a living substance from the cellar walls as the lights dimmed, and Perd, Jes, Moragh, and the spinning wheel became no more than silhouettes, like puppets in a shadow play. Only the faint halo of Perd's white hair was visible to the witch; that, and a glimmer of reflection from his eyes.

Niahrin felt the touch of the old magic, the stirring in the marrow of her bones, and she raised her left hand to her left eye. Just audible amid the sounds of the spinning wheel was someone breathing harshly. Niahrin's fingers touched the eye patch and she lifted it away.

Perd's face sprang into stark relief as though lit up from within, and it was no longer the face of the old man she knew. As ordinary perception gave way to another and more powerful form of vision, Niahrin saw the years fall from him and the vitality of the young man he had once been flood back. But the young man's eyes were hard and angry, and the curve of his mouth had a bitter, thwarted edge, and though she wished it might have been otherwise, Niahrin saw the taint of insanity dormant and waiting behind the handsome mask.

This, then, was Fenran, as he truly had been. . . .

She grasped the skein of flax once more, and her fingers began to work and twist anew as she spoke the words of the ancient chant, each phrase a new knot in the cord she was making.

"Three for sowing, and three for the mowing, and three for the birds of the night. Three for the calling, and three for the falling, and three by the lantern light. . . ." As the first syllables were uttered the image of youth fled from the face before her, and Perd's familiar features gazed back. He was utterly hypnotized now, staring at each knot she made in a blend of fascination and dread. A tiny whimper formed and died in his throat; unmoved by his distress, Niahrin continued to chant, and as she did so Jes moved to take the length of cord she had knotted. Then he stepped toward the bed, pushed the cord's end into Perd's unresisting hands, and as Niahrin tied more knots, and more, and more, the bard began to wind the length she paid out slowly and lightly around the old man's shoulders.

"Three for the burning, and three for the turning, and three for the lost ones who roam. Three for the ember, and three to remember, and three for guiding them home." Niahrin had begun to sing rather than speak the rhyme, and her husky contralto had a soothing, almost entrancing quality that despite his alertness made Jes feel as though he were slipping away into dreams. Still the spinning wheel turned; still the witch tied the knots, and the cord was paid out, and Jes wrapped it gently around the submissive figure in the bed, binding Perd to the spell.

"Three for the binding, and three for the finding, and

three to ransom the cost. Three for the past, and three make it fast, and three to recall what is lost." The witch's left eye seemed to light with a peculiar inner glow, and a muscle in her face twitched. Her fingers stopped twisting and she pulled the last length of cord—the last three knots—tight in her clenched fists. Then, startlingly, the timber of her voice changed, dropping to a deep, menacing pitch.

"Speak." The sheer compulsion in the word sent a violent tremor through Jes's nerves. *"I am the moon's daughter and the sun's child, and the power in whose name I command you must be obeyed. Speak, Son of the North. Say, Son of the North. Tell me the name your fathers gave you."*

Perd began to quiver. An extraordinary sound rose from deep in his lungs and he tried to give shape to it, but his tongue wouldn't obey him. His shoulders convulsed as he suddenly became aware of the cord wound around him; he tried to throw it off but the spell of the knots was too strong and he could only writhe impotently.

"Speak," Niahrin said again, more gently but still with implacable sternness. "Speak of the old days, Son of the North. Speak of the days when you were young and the world was untainted for you. Go back, old man. Go back to youth. Go back. Go back."

For the second time Perd's face began to change. Whether Jes or Moragh saw it Niahrin didn't know and couldn't speculate; her mind was split between two levels of consciousness, one mundane, the other dizzying, disembodied, threatening at every moment to pitch her off a precipice.

"Go back." Power was flowing from her, into the knots, through the cord. Her will and Perd's were locked in a struggle for dominance—he had more resilience than she had expected and it was draining her, she could feel her resources beginning to deplete. *He must yield . . . Goddess help me, he must. . . .*

Suddenly the old man—but he wasn't an old man anymore; he was young again, he was Fenran again—jerked stiffly upright. His eyes rolled upward in their sockets and he uttered a thin whine.

"I love her. . . ." Tears started to leak from his eyes. "I told them that, I *told* them, but they wouldn't let me see her! And there are so many, so *many* of them, all in the way, standing in *our* way! Dead. But she isn't. She didn't die. *We* didn't die. And all this time, all these years, I've been *waiting*, and they won't let me *see* her, and they won't let us have what we want!" Perd was babbling, words spilling and tumbling, and Niahrin couldn't make sense of the disjointed flood. She strove to muster her fractured wits, trying to hold herself to earth without breaking the spell—and then abruptly, shockingly, Perd's voice changed. The familiar, time-worn cadences vanished, and in a sharp, spirited, and youthful tone he said, "It's rightfully hers, and so it's rightfully mine! Damn it, I'm her *husband*—I presume that counts for something, even in this benighted kingdom?"

Taken aback, Niahrin stared at him. The facial transformation was complete. Black hair, tanned skin, the glow of vigorous health . . . but Fenran's gray eyes were narrowed and flinty, and his mouth had set in a hard, angry line.

"Don't pretend you don't *know*," he said contemptuously. "You all *know*, whatever you might claim to the contrary. You know the truth, and you know how long it's been going on. It was just the small things to begin with, wasn't it? Small insults. The tower room; that was a perfect example. You knew we wanted it, we *said* so often enough, but oh, no, Kirra had to have first choice. Kirra and his wife. Because Kirra is to be king, and that means

he comes first in *everything*. It's always Kirra, damned
Kirra!"

Niahrin had heard Moragh's harsh indrawing of breath
when Fenran first spoke the name but she could spare no
attention for the dowager. Holding the bitter gray gaze she
tried to keep her voice steady as she said, quietly, "Kirra
is dead, Fenran."

"Dead?" He laughed, a brief, savage bark. "Oh, no.
Kirra is alive." With his tongue he touched his lower lip,
reminding the witch unpleasantly of a snake contemplating
a meal. "As yet, he is very *much* alive; he and his wife,
who calls herself queen now old Kalig has gone." Then, so
fast that it was as if his mind had suddenly been invaded
by an entirely different person, his expression changed and
became reflective, almost amiable.

"She used to be quite a beauty, you know. When Kirra
first married her. We even liked her then; the four of us
used to ride together, hunt together; all manner of pastimes
and interests we shared. Of course it didn't last. How
could it? We found out the truth soon enough after Kalig
died; we found out just what kind of friends they were.
Greedy. So *greedy*. Everything for them, and nothing for
us. Damn it, hadn't we done enough? Didn't we have our
rightful *place*, as something more than the king's relatives,
depending on His Patronizing Majesty's grace and favor?"
The fury was coming back. There was spittle on his lips
and his voice rose petulantly. "We should have ruled
jointly! All four of us. Why not? Anghara agreed. Not at
first, but later, when she began to see what they were
doing to us, pushing us out, leaving us with nothing. I
won't have that. Scraps from the king's table; grace and
favor; *condescension*. I won't *tolerate* it. It isn't *enough*.
And she's lost her looks now, Kirra's wife. Middle-aged
and complacent; it happens to a lot of women. No looks
and no children. She's barren, and even the witches can't

do anything about that, for all their skills." Another harsh laugh. "What an irony! No children. Who'll be Kirra's heir, then? Well, we know who *is* the heir. Everyone knows. But Kirra has no intention of dying, and we're growing old along with him. Nothing for us to do but wait, only the waiting won't bring us any comfort because we're likely as not to die before he does. Growing older, waiting to inherit or die, while Kirra enjoys it all. Unless something changes. Unless it's *made* to change. You understand that; of course you do. Well, then. Let Kirra enjoy his tenure while he can. It won't last much longer. The poison, or the knife. Or a hunting accident. Such things happen, don't they? And then there'll be no more insults, no more patronage, no more *waiting*."

From the deep shadows where the spinning wheel stood, Niahrin heard Moragh whisper, "Oh, great Mother . . . what is he saying? *What is he saying?*"

The witch believed she knew, but it was vital that nothing should break into the enchantment. Her hold on Perd's mind was precarious, and any diversion might snap the link with the deep-buried psyche of Fenran. Even now she knew that she had little time left; her power was flagging, and the strain was taking a far greater toll on her than the aisling magic and the summoning of Nemesis had done. But a vital question remained unanswered—she *had* to resolve it and confirm or disprove her suspicions.

"Fenran." The singsong quality returned to her voice as she brought him back under the control of the hypnotic spell. "Fenran, hear me and answer. Hear me and answer." To her relief his eyes immediately lost their focus and his lips curved in a vague smile.

"I hear you. I'll answer. I'll tell you all about her. Why should I not? After all, she is the queen now."

Moragh made an inarticulate sound; Niahrin ignored it. "Who is the queen, Fenran?" Yes, she was right; in the past minute since he had launched on his tirade against Kirra his face had been altering again. He was aging: it was gradual but the signs were unmistakable now. Lines on his face, a salting of white in the black hair . . . and the bitterness and resentment had set into his mouth, making it thin and cruel. "Who is the queen?" she repeated.

"Anghara is the queen. My wife. The rightful queen."

"How old is the queen now? How old is your wife?"

He gave the odd, unpleasant laugh once more. "Old enough to know her own mind. As we both do. Thirty years, we waited. Thirty years before our patience ran out. Some people know, of course. It was inevitable. Kirra's bard, Helder Berisson; he knew. But Helder met with an accident. He put out to sea, fishing—very unwise in such weather and in a small, unseaworthy boat. Poor Helder. We all mourned him."

Jes flashed a bewildered glance at Niahrin. *"But I knew Helder Berisson!"* he protested in a hissing whisper. *"He didn't drown at sea; he lived to be an old man, and he was—"*

"Hush!" Niahrin made a frantic gesture. Fenran, apparently oblivious to the exchange, began to speak again.

"Helder knew, and there are others. But they don't speak of it now. They have learned better than to speak of it, for we have many eyes and many ears within these walls. We are above the law, for we *are* the law. We rule. *We* rule."

"And are you happy in your rulership?" Niahrin asked softly. "You and Anghara, you and the queen. Are you happy?"

"Happy?" Fenran's mouth twisted and his aging face grew ugly. "What is *that* worth?"

"To some it is worth everything. Do you love each other, you and your wife the queen?"

"Love is for children. I have something better and more powerful and more desirable than love."

Ah, yes, the witch thought, ah, *yes*. He had given it away, the core of the thing, the central thread around which this warp and weft of *might-have-been* was woven. She had caught the undercurrent in his voice, the hint of untold misery of which he had no conscious awareness, and she had begun to understand the significance of the twin suns, one bitter and the other occluded, in her own tapestry.

"Fenran. Fenran. Fenran." She sang his name. "You have spun a fine thread and told a fine tale. But that is not how it was for you."

"No!" His eyes snapped wide, blazing. "It is—"

"Be still." The command echoed stridently in the cellar's confined space, and Fenran rocked back as though she had physically struck him. Forcing back the ague-like shivering fit that was trying to grip her Niahrin drew a deep breath.

"Listen and answer, Fenran. Listen and answer. Tell me where Perd has gone."

He jerked his head aside. "There is no such man!"

"There is, Fenran. There is. Tell me where Perd is hiding. Show me where Perd is hiding. Tell me Perd's story; the story that was and not the story that might have been."

"There is . . . no such story."

"I know that there is. I am Niahrin, and Niahrin knows Perd and she knows what became of Perd's dreams. For Anghara dared to cross the threshold of the tower, and Anghara released the demons, and so there was no marriage for her and for Fenran, but only death and separation."

Fenran's voice rose to a hoarse yell. *"She did not die!"*

"No. But Kalig died, and Kirra died, and Anghara was gone and so there were no others save for you. But they would not make you king, Fenran. They pitied you, but they would not make you king." Niahrin was hardly aware of what she was saying; her mind was probing deep into Fenran's consciousness and she drew out what she saw there, grasping it and dragging it out of the dark where it had lain for so long and up, writhing, squalling, into the light. A hideous, misshapen thing, better strangled at birth. But it was the *truth*.

"They denied you the throne, Fenran. They denied you the power you craved and instead came new masters: Ryen, then Cathal, then a second Ryen. Did you serve your new masters well? Did they know your true name and your true story? Perhaps you did not tell them. Perhaps, instead, you *waited*."

"N . . . no . . ."

She cut implacably through his protest. "What did you wait for, Fenran? Did you wait for Anghara to return? Did the thought of her return fill your dreams and obscss your days? Did you wait for her to come and to claim her birthright, so that you might at last share in it and take the throne at her side?"

"She is the queen! The rightful queen!"

"But she left you. She left you behind, when the demons came. Why did she go away, Fenran? Why did she flee from her home and her heritage?"

"She had no choice!"

"She had a choice. She could have stayed at your side, to walk with you into the world of *might-have-been*. Your world, Fenran, of jealousy and intrigue and violence and death. But Anghara chose a different path. The path to the Tower of Regrets, to the demons of her own mind and not of yours." The witch paused, struggling to pull air into her lungs. "Have you ever forgiven her for that, Fenran? Or is that, too, a part of Perd's madness—the knowledge that Anghara was stronger than you, that she had the courage to seek her own way and face her own demons? She could have hidden in the cloak of shadows that you wrapped about her and sought to find her heart's desire by wielding the power of death, as you did. But you have not found your heart's desire, Fenran. Your demons still walk behind you, stepping in the footprints you have left, and when you sleep you still hear them laughing, for you do not have the courage to face them. Anghara had the courage. You chose the power of death, but she chose the power of life. Her demons are all but vanquished now, and only one remains. Do you know its name, Fenran? Do you have the courage to speak that name aloud?"

Fenran was staring at her, transfixed. A muscle in his jaw worked frenziedly, out of control, and he seemed to be trying to speak but couldn't. Niahrin's head spun. What had she said? What had she done? The words had come, they had poured from her, but she couldn't *remember.* . . .

With no forewarning the figure on the bed before her dissolved, seeming to crack apart like a clay statue. She had one dreadful glimpse of a man so old that he was all but a hairless, fleshless, living skeleton, then suddenly the young Fenran was back—but a Fenran she had never seen before, mouth gentle, eyes warm; a handsome youth untainted by greed or cruelty or scheming. The son of the North, friend and lover, to whom Princess Anghara had given her heart.

He said, in a voice so filled with grief and bewilderment that it brought tears to the witch's eyes, "Please . . . I don't understand. . . ."

And the mask shattered again. The old, mad Perd was back, and spittle flecked his lips as he lurched forward, struggling in his bonds and screaming into Niahrin's face.

"But she understands! She understands! Ask her—make her tell! Make her play the aisling, and then she will remember and take back what is rightfully hers!"

* * *

Someone had placed the patch back over Niahrin's left eye and was now trying to make her drink a mouthful of wine, but she didn't want it and at last gained enough control over her muscles to push the proffered cup gently away. Impressions and images were tumbling around in her memory like balls of yarn tangled by a litter of excited kittens; she dimly recalled seeing Jes sitting on the flailing, struggling figure of Perd and holding him down while Moragh forced something into his mouth, but the commotion had stopped now and the cellar was quiet. The witch looked hazily about her, blinking, then to her surprise heard her own voice say clearly, "Fenran?"

"He's gone." A hand, Jes's, she thought, touched her forehead and the bard said, "I think she's feverish, Your Grace. Little wonder, after—"

"No, no." Niahrin tried to climb to her feet—how had she come to be sitting on the floor with her back propped against the wall?—but the effort was beyond her and she slumped back. "I'm all right," she insisted. "Not feverish. It was just a—an echo. In my mind." Her vision was clearing now and she saw that the lamps had been turned up and the cellar put back in order. Had it been disordered? She couldn't remember. . . . Someone had covered the spinning wheel, and there was no sign of the flaxen knot-cord.

"Perd—" she said.

"—is sleeping." It was Moragh's voice. "He's unharmed, I think. Exhausted, but nothing more. When he wakes I doubt if he'll even remember what happened."

Jes was still looking at the witch. "I think we should take her to her room, Your Grace," he said in an aside that Niahrin overheard. "Whatever she says, this has taken its toll. Her face is gray."

Niahrin tried to make a sharp, jesting retort to that, but

she was suddenly seized by a terrible stomach cramp. She doubled over, gasping and cursing with shock and pain, and quickly Moragh was at her side, helping Jes to lift her to her feet.

"Sweet Earth . . ." Niahrin muttered through clamped teeth. "I feel . . ."

"Sh! No need to speak." Jes slipped a supporting arm about her ribs. "Can you stand; will your legs bear you? Good, that's good. Won't be long now; we'll soon have you comfortable in bed."

"I feel . . ." Niahrin mumbled again, and then her stomach heaved and she was violently sick. Appalled, her only thought was that she had disgraced herself and Jes and Moragh would surely despise her, before the cellar seemed to turn upside down and, for the second time in a bare few days, she fainted.

•CHAPTER•XIX•

Niahrin was still unwell by midmorning, and on Moragh's orders she was confined to bed. The dowager wanted to call in a physician to attend to her, but the witch refused. This was only to be expected, she said, after such a prolonged and difficult magical operation; there was always a price to be paid for any major power-raising and the effects would wear off before long. Besides, physicians had outlandish ideas and methods and she didn't want to be a prey for their experiments. A day's fasting and some herbal simples would soon put her right.

So Moragh left her to recover in her own good time, having extracted Grimya's promise to alert her if the witch should take any turn for the worse. However, though she was careful not to let Niahrin know it, the dowager was worried. Tomorrow was the wedding eve; time was snapping at their heels and they had less than two full days to formulate the final step of their plan. Moragh could only pray fervently that they would be ready.

The atmosphere in Carn Caille was becoming ebulliently hectic as the great day drew nearer. The fact that the bride and groom had no known kin or old friends in the Southern Isles to invite as guests made not the slightest difference; everyone in the citadel would attend and celebrate with them, and the festivity would be one to remember. So now activity was at fever pitch as last-minute particulars were attended to, small oversights remedied, and those who had an active part to play rehearsed their roles. Indigo was the center of attention, surrounded from dawn to dusk by a covey of excited women determined to ensure that she would look as magnificent as any royal bride. She surrendered to their ministrations with a faintly bewildered air, but the increasingly lively bustle around her gave her no time for reflection and certainly none for second thoughts. Not that she had any such thoughts, she told herself emphatically, nor any doubts. She *wanted* to be wed to Vinar, wanted it more than anything in the world. And when it was done and the revelry over they would leave, and she could at last forget Carn Caille and the dreadful memories of her sojourn here.

And forget the dreams. . . .

Her one relief, small though it was, was that there had been no repercussions from the horrifying sleepwalking episode. To begin with she had lived in terror that the witch, Niahrin, would give her away; there was no doubt that Niahrin had recognized her in the corridor, and one word from her would bring disaster. But clearly the witch had chosen to keep silent, and nor had she tackled Indigo in private; indeed, they had hardly exchanged a single word since that night. Indigo didn't understand. Niahrin owed her no favors—why had she not spoken out?

And the knife was another mystery; it must surely have

been found in Brythere's bedchamber, so why had there been no outcry, not so much as a whisper, about an assassination attempt? And the most arcane and frightening question, the one that haunted her every waking hour: *Why had it happened at all? What monstrous power had come out of the darkness of her lost memory and made her try to kill Brythere?*

She had not walked in her sleep again. Each night she took a sedative draught—one of the servants had procured it for her and it had been easy to invent an excuse for needing it—and that seemed to be sufficient to keep her safely in her bed. But the draught didn't stop the dreams, and they were growing worse. Violent dreams, intense and ominous, in which she floated like a wraith through the corridors of Carn Caille, searching for someone or something that she could never locate. Or sometimes riding across a bleak landscape that she knew instinctively was the southern tundra, striving frantically to outrun an invisible and unnameable horror. Twice she had seen the two sinister figures again, standing at the foot of her bed, and thinking herself awake she had screamed only to see the figures vanish back into the realm of nightmare. And the dreams were always followed by a voice in her mind, husky, intimate, whispering over and again, *"Now, my love. Now, my love. Now, my love."*

She had, fleetingly, contemplated speaking with the wolf, but the idea had been short-lived. According to Vinar, Grimya knew very little of Indigo's history and nothing of her kin; she said that they had been together only for a few years and that Indigo was simply a working mariner. There was no reason why she should lie ... and even if she did know more than she was willing to reveal, Indigo didn't want to hear it. When she and Vinar had set out from Amberland she had been determined that, no matter how long the search might take, she would find her family and discover her lost history. That had changed. She didn't *want* to regain her memory now; better that it should stay buried in the past and not rise again to haunt her. Two more days and Grimya, Niahrin, Carn Caille, and the dreams could be left behind and forgotten. A new life, a new beginning. Nothing, Indigo prayed fervently, *nothing* could stand in its way now.

By evening Niahrin was much recovered and strong enough to eat the hearty meal that Jes brought to her on a tray. Jes also carried a message from Moragh: Perd had vanished from the cellar. How he had contrived it the bard didn't know, but at some time between their departure and the breakfast hour he had revived from the sleeping draught and escaped; doubtless, Moragh said, back to the forest. Niahrin was alarmed, but Jes seemed to feel there was no cause for concern. As he pointed out, it was as well to be rid of the old man, for his presence in the citadel couldn't have been kept secret for much longer. Perd had served his purpose, and any further part he might have to play was in the hands of other powers now.

Grimya especially was glad to see the bard. All day she had been fretting to learn the details of the night's work, but Niahrin had been in no state to answer her questions. Jes told her the whole tale and in addition relayed the gist of a further brief conference he had had with the dowager that morning. Perd—they still couldn't think of him as Fenran—had provided them with the vital clue when, in the last moments before he started to rave again and had to be forcibly sedated, he had said, *"Make her play the aisling, and then she will remember."* It was clear, Jes said, what they should do. Aisling magic was the key to Indigo's memory, and the aisling they must use was imbued in Cushmagar's harp. A dream of the past, a dream of Carn Caille as it had been fifty years ago, and of what might have taken place within its walls, had Anghara chosen a different path. The harp had been waiting, as Cushmagar had hinted in the firelit vision. And when Indigo's hands touched the strings, the aisling would wake.

Niahrin frowned thoughtfully, one hand stroking Grimya's ruff. "But can she be persuaded to play? If all depends on her cooperation . . ."

Jes smiled dryly. "Her Grace shares your doubts, and she has found a way." From the tray he had brought he took a small scroll of fine-quality parchment. "This is for you. The others have already been delivered."

Niahrin unrolled the parchment. In an elegant hand, with the dowager's own signature and seal at the foot, it read:

In accordance with the traditions of the Southern Isles, Her Grace the Dowager Queen Moragh bids Vinar Shillan, his bride, Indigo, and their pledge-friends to join her in solemn observance of Nuptial Benediction on the eve of the marriage celebrations. Please present yourself at the Lesser Hall one hour after sunset on the appointed day.

By command of
Moragh

"Oh," Niahrin said, and her mouth twitched.

Jes grinned. "It shames me to say it, but I'd completely forgotten that old custom. It's largely fallen into disuse, hasn't it? But it was commonplace in the old days, and Her Grace remembers all the details of the ceremony. So here we have the perfect means of ensuring that Indigo is where we want her, and that you and I, as pledge-friends, can also have a reason to be present."

The witch nodded slowly; then abruptly her expression changed. "But Jes, Vinar will be there." She looked up anxiously. "And not only Vinar! You and I are his pledge-friends, but who has Indigo chosen for hers?"

"Ah. There's the complication, I'm afraid. Her Grace is one—but the other is the queen."

"The queen . . . ?" Niahrin's eyes widened. "Great Goddess, Jes, what are you *thinking* of? If Queen Brythere is to be present tomorrow night—"

"Wait, wait!" Jes held up both hands to silence her. "Her Grace and I have racked our minds, but there's no help for it! Commanding Indigo to a Benediction is the *only* way of ensuring that she doesn't find some means to avoid us. She's already wary of you—little wonder, when she knows you saw her at the queen's tower that night—and I don't think she trusts me, either. If Her Grace were simply to invite her to her chambers on some informal pretext, then the moment she set eyes on us she'd find some excuse, a feigned illness perhaps, to leave. We can't take that risk. There must be *no* room for suspicion, and this is the only way. Niahrin, listen." He sat down on the bed and took both her hands in his. "Her Grace reasons that the king and queen are sure to find out what's afoot before too long. The king has already begun to ask awkward questions. They'll have to be told the truth eventually, and . . . well, if they find out this way, then perhaps it will be just as well." He grimaced wryly. "Certainly it'll save me from the travail of some very complicated and lengthy explanations at a later date."

Niahrin considered this for some while. There was a certain logic in it, she had to admit, and she took Jes's point about the problem of gaining Indigo's compliance. But the idea of Brythere, with all her hauntings and horrors, being a witness to what might happen . . .

"Her Grace has also invited the king," Jes said quietly. "In one sense that makes matters worse, I know, but at least he'll be there to care for the queen if the need should arise."

First the queen, now the king ... next it would be half the servants in the citadel, Niahrin thought. She pushed the flash of anger away—it was unworthy, and unfair to Moragh—and said, "Well, it seems, as you say, that there's no help for it. But I don't like the idea at all. And ... Oh, Jes!" Suddenly her expression grew stricken. "What about poor Vinar? If the aisling should work—what will it do to him? What will it *do*?"

Jes sighed heavily. "I don't know, Niahrin. None of us can know, or even predict."

"But if her memory comes back—that poor, innocent man; he loves her so *much*! Oh, Jes, it's too cruel!"

Jes shook his head, struggling to find an answer for the unanswerable; but Grimya spoke up softly.

"Niahrin, I know how you are f-feeling. But wouldn't it be crueler still to let Vinar marry Indigo? Isn't that what we have said from the beginning, and isn't it trrue?" She whined. "It s-seems to me that if this is the only way to stop that from happening, we must take it."

Niahrin wiped her eye with her sleeve, thinking what a fool she was to let sentiment get the better of her at her age.

"You're right, of course, Grimya," she said, abashed. "And it *is* what we said from the beginning. I'm just being absurd, I suppose, now that the time has come to put theory into practice. Don't pay any heed to me." She smiled wanly, first at the wolf and then at Jes. "And don't fear that I'll let you down. I won't." A pause, and then she added, so quietly that Jes didn't quite catch her words, *"But oh, that poor, poor man ..."*

Moragh, meanwhile, had had another tussle with Ryen.

"A Nuptial Benediction?" The king ran both hands

through his hair as though his scalp was irritating him. "Don't be ridiculous, Mother! That custom had been consigned to history when I was a child, and to revive it now is nonsensical!"

"I want it to be observed," Moragh said stubbornly. "And I want both you and Brythere to be there."

"Damn it, we've already done enough for Vinar and Indigo—far more than enough, in my opinion—without reviving obsolete rituals into the bargain! *No*, Mother. Firstly there simply isn't time for this charade, and secondly I am *not* obliged to agree to anything you want simply because you want it. You may do whatever you please, but don't expect Brythere or me to put ourselves out any further!"

Moragh realized that she had chosen an inopportune moment to broach the subject, but it was too late to retract now. So she said firmly, "I'm sorry, Ryen, but you and Brythere will have to be present, for I've already issued the invitations to the others involved."

"You've done what?" Ryen's eyes lit hotly. "Without even *consulting* me?" A muscle in his jaw worked violently. "Mother, this has gone far enough! I don't know what frivolous humors have got into you since Vinar and Indigo came to Carn Caille, but I'm growing heartily sick of the whole affair! Those two have disrupted our lives since they first set foot here, and the sooner they're married and away, the better off we shall all be!"

Moragh's anger flared. She had resolved not to drop any hint of her real purpose, but the words were out before she could consider them. "I wish," she snapped, "that I could agree with you. But I'm afraid, Ryen, that you are wrong!"

The king stared at her. "What do you mean?"

Dear Goddess, Moragh thought, *I've said too much. . . .*

"Mother." Ryen crossed the distance between them in two strides and gripped her arm. "Mother, there's more to this than meets the eye, isn't there? You know something that you've not told me. Something about Indigo." Hardly realizing that he did so, he shook her. "Tell me!"

She pulled herself free with a sharp movement. "Don't treat me as though I were some minion!"

"I'm sorry, I'm sorry. . . ." He wrestled his anger under control, then sighed. "I'm *sorry*, Mother. I didn't mean . . ." The sentence trailed off in a helpless gesture. "But I've suspected for a while that there's something afoot that you've been hiding from me. For the Goddess's sake, isn't it time to be honest?"

Perhaps it was, the dowager thought. Or at least, as honest as she dared be without jeopardizing everything. . . .

She drew a deep breath. "Very well, I suppose there's no help for it. You're quite right, Ryen. There is something afoot, and I have been keeping it from you."

"Then in the name of—"

"Please. Hear me out." She couldn't bring herself to look him directly in the eye. "There is a good reason why it would not be advisable to tell you the whole story now. To begin with there's not enough time left for a full explanation—and believe me, it would need to be *very* full indeed. I'm not even . . . not even sure if you would believe it, not yet. . . . But tomorrow night, if all goes according to plan, you will learn the truth. You and Brythere. And Vinar."

"Vinar? You mean he, too, knows nothing about this?"

"That's right. Under no circumstances could I tell him; it would be . . . too brutal. But the truth will have to come out, and it must be done before the wedding. That is why I have arranged the Benediction, Ryen. To ensure that all those involved are brought together, in private, before it's too late."

For a long, long moment Ryen watched his mother, and in the mask of her face he saw something of the turmoil that beset her mind at this moment. He was not, he knew, the most sensitive of men, but . . .

"Mother." He stepped forward again, but this time his touch was gentle. "You're asking me to trust you for a little while longer, is that it?"

Moragh nodded. Her eyelashes were wet. "Yes. That's what I'm asking."

"Very well." He kissed her lightly on the brow. "I'll do what you want, and so will Brythere."

Another nod. "Thank you."

He withdrew his hand. "But I still don't understand why you couldn't have told me this before and asked me to cooperate. Do you think I would have refused? Do you really think I'm that stubborn and foolish?"

"No," Moragh said. "I don't think that, and I meant no insult to you. But I couldn't be completely sure; and even if there was a chance, the smallest *chance*, that you might have refused, I—I couldn't take that risk, Ryen. This is too important."

"Important to whom? To Indigo?"

"Not only to her. I think it may be of the most vital importance to us all." Moragh sniffed, then suddenly flexed her shoulders with a brisk movement, as though shaking off some unseen pressure. "Thank you, Ryen. I see now that I should have confided in you from the beginning." She managed a wan smile. "Thank you for giving me the benefit of the doubt now."

She started to move toward the door, but his voice halted her.

"Mother. Just one question. Will you answer it, if you can?"

Moragh turned. "Of course, my son."

"Is Indigo what we first thought her to be? Do you believe that she *is* related to King Kalig and his family?"

For a moment the dowager gazed down at the floor.

Then she said, "Yes. Indigo is related to Kalig. But as to your other question . . . I shall say this, Ryen, but I must beg you not to ask me to reveal any more before tomorrow night." She seemed to steel herself. "She is not what either of us had thought her to be. She is most certainly not that at all."

The door tapped quietly shut behind her as she went out.

The wedding eve dawned cloudless and hot, and at breakfast it was generally and cheerfully agreed that this was the first day of true summer. From early morning Niahrin was as nervous as a newborn kitten and was thankful when an energetic seamstress came to give her a final fitting of the dress Moragh had decreed she should wear. Parading in front of a looking glass, with Grimya getting under her feet and the seamstress chiding through a mouthful of pins, brought the witch firmly down to earth and did much to alleviate the flutterings in her stomach, and by sunset she was ready to face the coming ordeal, if not with composure then at least without too many terrors.

The lesser hall was in Carn Caille's west wing. It served as both a public hall for smaller formal events and a place where the royal family could entertain personal guests or friends when numbers were too great to be accommodated in their private apartments. Niahrin and Grimya arrived early and found Moragh and Jes already present. Moragh was looking over the table that had been set ready with food and wine, while Jes sat at a full-sized harp, head bent and eyes closed in concentration as he rehearsed a piece of music. Niahrin's heart skipped a beat when she saw the harp, but the bard gave her a reassuring smile.

"This is my own instrument, not Cushmagar's. His"—he nodded significantly toward the window—"is there."

The harp's shape, Niahrin saw, had been disguised under the dust sheet that covered it; anyone glancing casually at it would be unlikely to recognize it for what it was.

"You've brought your pipe?" Moragh looked up from where she was repositioning an arrangement that wasn't entirely to her satisfaction. She looked elegant and calm, but her voice was tense.

"Yes, ma'am." Niahrin displayed the instrument, then looked in more detail at her surroundings. This chamber was laid out like the great hall in miniature: there was a raised dais at one end and a capacious hearth at the other, and tall, many-paned windows were set into the west wall to catch the evening light. Tonight, though, it seemed that every available inch of space was filled with greenery. Swaths of plaited summer leaves decked the walls, flower garlands covered the windows, and over the mantel evergreen branches made a lush frame for the blazing fire. The table itself, on the dais, was a sea of vivid, springing color amid which the dishes and flagons were barely visible. Niahrin looked at it all in wonder, and seeing the surprise and delight in her eyes Moragh smiled thinly.

"Simply tradition, my dear. It has meant a great deal of hard work, but it seemed safer to follow the proper form." Then her mouth turned down at the corners. "The others should be here soon. Take your place; here, beside the chair set for Vinar." She glanced at Jes. "Best leave the harp and sit down."

Niahrin slid into her seat, Jes beside her. The witch's heart was hammering, and as she looked at the displayed food her stomach protested at the thought of trying to eat anything. She would have to try, for the formalities must be got through, and Indigo lulled into unwariness, before the real purpose of the evening could begin. And whatever happened, Niahrin reminded herself vehemently, she mustn't get drunk.

"Grimya," Moragh smiled down at the wolf. "Come and sit here, by me." The wolf complied, jumping up onto the stool that had been set ready. The dowager swept a last, assessing glance across the table. "Well, then. If we're not ready now, we never shall be. So . . . may the Goddess send us good fortune and success."

The early part of the celebration came close to disaster. The culprits were Ryen, Indigo, Grimya, and—as she was all too painfully aware—Niahrin herself. However hard the witch tried to banish it, a specter of Vinar was haunting her. Not Vinar as he was now, merry and exuberant with one arm about Indigo's shoulders and the other hand raising his cup in toasts to everyone and everything, but Vinar as he might be—*would* be—when tonight was over. The thought tore at her conscience and her heart, and she couldn't bear to meet the Scorvan's eyes or respond to his good humor. Ryen, too, was ill at ease; no actor, he veered awkwardly between reticent silence and exaggerated jollity, and he was also drinking too much despite frequent warning looks from Moragh. And Indigo and Grimya were both behaving as if the other didn't exist.

It was thanks to Jes that, finally, the atmosphere took a turn for the better. Niahrin sensed the level of desperate effort that went into the bard's manipulations, but at last, like a skillful captain steering his ship through stormy waters to safety, he brought the mood round and everyone began to relax. With a deeply approving look in her eyes Moragh poured more wine for everyone, then, as the most senior woman present, rose to speak the traditional Benediction, wishing the bounty of earth, sun, and rain upon the betrothed couple and asking for the Earth Mother's blessing upon their union. There were tears in her eyes as she spoke the ritual words, and Niahrin and Jes, knowing the true reason for them, looked uneasily down at their own clasped hands. Then everyone stood to make the Pledge Toast, which involved draining a full cup in one raising—the wine, Niahrin realized thankfully, was weak—and after that Jes, as Vinar's pledge-friend, delivered a brief and witty speech thanking the king, queen, and dowager for their kindness and hospitality and announcing that the ceremonies were over and it was time for the entertainments to begin.

Vinar had been casting speculative glances at Jes's harp for some while, and when he leaned to whisper something into Indigo's ear Moragh noticed and nodded meaningfully at Niahrin. Indigo looked doubtful but then smiled and shrugged, and as Jes moved to sit at the instrument Vinar sat back with a grin of satisfaction. Chairs were turned to face the harp, and the bard began with a lively medley of dance tunes, which soon had even Ryen tapping his foot in time. This was followed by two sea songs, with everyone joining in the choruses, and then Jes held out a hand toward the witch.

"Niahrin has a fine voice, and she is also an accomplished player of the reed pipe. I ask her to join me now."

Niahrin made a show of protesting modesty—as had been agreed, to set an example for Indigo to follow—and Moragh, taking her cue, insisted to the point of personally leading her out to stand at Jes's side. They performed a foresters' song, then the witch took up her pipe for two round-dances and a hornpipe. While they were playing, she noticed, Indigo drank two more cups of wine, as though for courage, and when the hornpipe ended Moragh clapped her hands and beamed.

"That was lovely, Niahrin! Now, Indigo." She leaned toward the couple. "I understand that you, too, are a musician. Can we persuade you to play for us?"

"I . . . ah . . ."

Vinar interrupted. "Come on, Indigo! What did I say to

you, only just now? I said, You shouldn't be so timid; you should play, like you did that time we stayed at Rogan and Jansa's tavern!"

"That was different," Indigo said, but without real conviction. "In company like this, and with a bard as gifted as Jes—I couldn't!"

"Of course you could, my dear!" Moragh asserted. "We are all friends, and there's no more formality here than in any village! Don't disappoint us—after all, this is the last chance we shall have to hear you before you leave us!"

Indigo smiled tentatively, first at Vinar and then at the dowager. "Well . . . perhaps if someone else will play with me . . ."

"That's my Indigo!" Vinar kissed her soundly. "Play that tune they did at the village revel—you know, the one with the piper, so Neerin can join in too. You know that one, I hear you humming it."

"It's for three instruments, not two. . . ." Indigo said.

Jes, hardly able to credit such luck, sprang up. "Then three instruments it shall be!" he said and gave Indigo such an ingenuous grin that she suspected nothing amiss. "To tell the truth, I'd hoped we might play together, so I asked for another harp to be brought. Here." Crossing to the window he took hold of the dust sheet covering Cushmagar's harp and pulled it away.

The sudden silence was broken by a sharp gasp from Ryen. Moragh frantically kicked her son's ankle under the table, and her hand clamped down on his as he seemed about to scramble to his feet. The king turned a wild, bewildered glance on her; beside him Brythere had paled and her mouth was opening as though to voice a protest. The dowager shook her head emphatically, her eyes pleading for silence; belatedly understanding, Ryen made a pretense of coughing and said loudly, "Well, well! That old relic—I didn't think to see that in use again!"

Indigo turned her head. She was frowning, but with puzzlement rather than doubt. Moragh smiled at her.

"My husband's grandfather kept this old harp—though I will say it was wasted on him; he was no musician, by all accounts, and so he never played it." Cleverly worded, Niahrin thought; Moragh had not actually told a lie. Brythere, recovering her wits, started to say, "But surely—" and the dowager smoothly interrupted.

"But surely it must have been quite an undertaking to bring it back into tune after all these years; yes, I quite agree," she said, giving Brythere no chance to say more. "That was generous of you to go to such trouble, Jes."

Jes bowed. "A pleasure, Your Grace. As the only harpist in Carn Caille, it isn't often that I get a chance to play with a fellow exponent." He drew up a stool. "Indigo, sit here. Now, can you hum the first few notes of the tune for us?"

Indigo did—though she was still frowning at the harp, and her frown had deepened, as though something was tugging at the back of her mind—and Jes nodded. "I know it well. Shall I play first harp, and you second?"

"Yes. Yes, thank you." Indigo sat down, but didn't touch the harp strings. Something was definitely troubling her now, Niahrin saw. But it hadn't yet taken a strong enough hold; she was still willing to go along with them. *Only a few moments more,* the witch prayed silently; *please, only a few moments . . .*

Jes coaxed a rippling arpeggio from his own instrument, and Niahrin took up her pipe. She, too, knew this tune well, but as the solo harp began and she waited to come in on the second verse, she watched the bard sidelong, alert for the prearranged cue. Harp and pipe began to weave together, and despite her apprehension, which was nagging quite intensely now, Indigo found herself beguiled by the music. Instinctively her hands flexed; she counted the beat in her mind, reached out, and her fingers touched the strings.

For the first time in fifty years, the rich tones of Cushmagar's harp sounded in Carn Caille. Niahrin felt as though a huge, cold hand had taken hold of her spine; the pipe faltered and squeaked before she could regain her self-control. At the table Ryen was rigid, Brythere open-mouthed with one hand clutching at her husband's sleeve; Grimya was crouching, eyes red with fear, and Moragh leaned forward, knuckles white as she gripped the table's edge and her eyes filled with an avid, almost fanatical light. Vinar, suspecting nothing, only smiled at Indigo with fond pride; and Indigo herself . . .

Something was wrong. She knew it, *felt* it. Something was wrong with the harp. It felt strange under her fingers, almost as if it was a figment of a dream and not real at all. But the sound it created was beautiful, enthralling; she had never heard an instrument so rich and fine. . . .

Or had she?

Her vision dimmed suddenly—what had happened to the lamps?—and, startled, she raised her head. Why were they all watching her in that way? Their expressions were strange, fixed; there were shadows on their faces, and Vinar—*but he wasn't Vinar anymore! Someone else, some-one else—and the king, he looked older, his beard and hair different, and the woman beside him wasn't Queen Brythere—*

"Nnn—" The sound, inarticulate, came from her own throat but she couldn't turn it into words, for her tongue wouldn't obey.

"Nn— aah—" *No*, she wanted to say, *No, stop, stop it, before—*

Jes knew, and he gave Niahrin the signal. Instantly the music changed, and the familiar Southern Isles song metamorphosized into the slow, haunting melody of the aisling. Niahrin saw Indigo's eyes widen in horror; summoning her own power the witch caught her shocked gaze, held it, locked it, turned fully to face her. Indigo's mouth was working but she could make no sound, and her hands on the harp were taking up the melody now, moving of their own volition as she followed helplessly where the others led. The notes rose and fell, rose and fell, hypnotic and compelling as they repeated over and over again—

Indigo cried out; a cry of pain and fear and misery that rose shrilly to the rafters. Instantly Vinar was on his feet, but Ryen sprang after him, dragging him back.

"No!" the king shouted. "Leave her, man! Let her be!"

At that moment, with no warning, an ice-cold wind blasted through the hall. Every lamp and candle went out, plunging them into gloom—and the music changed again. Jes and Niahrin heard the change and they stopped playing as though they'd been stung. Niahrin's pipe dropped, clattering, to the floor, and Jes grabbed at his own harp as it rocked wildly. But Indigo played on. Her head was flung back, her spine bending as though in terrible pain, and her fingers flew over the strings of the great harp as out of the past, out of the darkness, out of the world of *might-have-been*, the other and greater aisling, Cushmagar's legacy and his warning, surged into her and through her with an awesome and dreadful power.

•CHAPTER•XX•

From the far end of the hall a composite voice spoke softly yet with overwhelming and dramatic clarity.

"ANGHARA."

Indigo's hands were flung from the strings and she fell backward, crashing off the stool to the floor. For several seconds there was a foreboding silence. Dazed, Indigo slowly started to climb to her feet—

"ANGHARA. DO YOU REMEMBER US, ANGHARA?"

The fire flared up, thrusting back the shadows, and from the hearth, materializing out of the flames and stepping into the room, three forms appeared. Nemesis led them; behind the silver-haired child came the figure with the milky eyes and the pale-furred wolf. Nemesis smiled sorrowfully and held out one hand as though in conciliation.

"Won't you remember us, Sister? Won't you remember and come back?"

"No . . ." Indigo's mind was rioting. "No . . . I don't know you. . . ."

"But you do, Sister. You know us all." Nemesis took a pace forward, then another, and another, and the other two phantoms followed. "Come, Anghara. Come. Let us all be one again."

Indigo backed away and collided with Cushmagar's harp. The strings vibrated, giving off an eerie moan.

"What do you want from me? I don't know you; don't you understand? Keep away from me—keep back!" And she whirled round, her voice rising desperately. "Vinar! Vinar, please, *help me*!"

With a bellow of fear and rage Vinar thrust the king's restraining hand away and dived forward; Ryen tried to grab him but missed, and he ran toward Indigo.

"Stop him!" Moragh cried desperately. "Someone stop him—Grimya!"

What took place in the next few seconds happened so quickly that it left Niahrin reeling. A gray blur streaked from behind the table, and Grimya launched herself at Vinar in a powerful leap. Her full weight cannoned into him and he went down with a bellow, arms and legs flailing. Ryen, too, was shouting, Brythere calling out in a mixture of astonishment and fear—and with a swift, fluid movement the three phantoms streaked toward Indigo. Raw brilliance flared suddenly through the hall, as though lightning had momentarily illuminated the windows, and the shock of it stopped them all in their tracks. Vinar lay on the floor, bemused; Ryen and Brythere were stunned into silence; Jes and Moragh stood like figures in a tableau; while Niahrin found that she had dropped to a crouch and was instinctively trying to cover her head with her hands. And the three phantoms had vanished. . . .

Indigo, standing alone amid the aftermath of the brief mayhem, swayed suddenly, and a small sound bubbled between her lips. Calling her name, Vinar scrambled to his feet and started toward her ... then stopped as she turned and looked at him. Her face wore a puzzled expression, but her manner had a new uncharacteristic confidence. In a voice that sounded quite unlike the Indigo they all knew, she said calmly, "Who are you?"

Vinar's eyes bulged with shock. "Who ... Indigo, what are you saying? What do you mean? It's me, Vinar— *Vinar!*" He tried to make a move toward her, but Grimya snarled again and he thought better of it. His tone became bewildered, piteous. *"Indigo—"*

"Vinar." Moragh was at his side, taking his arm. "I think you'd best sit down."

"But—"

"Look at her, Vinar. Look closely."

He did and saw what she and Niahrin and Jes had already seen. Indigo's physical appearance, as well as her demeanor, had changed. Her eyes had lost their familiar color and taken on a milky cast. Streaks of silver glinted in her hair. And when she tilted her head and gave him an odd little smile, there was something of the wolf in her look. . . .

"I'm sorry," she said, pleasantly but without any emotion. "I don't believe we have been introduced."

"But ..." Vinar whispered again. He was trying, struggling, but he couldn't find words to form the questions. Like a child he let Moragh shepherd him back to his place while Indigo stared after him; reaching his chair he sank down and buried his face in his hands.

Moragh straightened. She darted a quick glance at Niahrin, then spoke. "Indigo. Do you know who I am?"

Indigo's milky eyes turned silver. "Are you addressing me, madam?" she asked. "Forgive me, but I think you've made a mistake. My name is not Indigo."

Moragh held her gaze steadily. "Then what is your name?"

"I am Anghara."

Brythere made a shocked, strangled noise, and Ryen's chair scraped back "*Anghara?* That isn't—"

"Ryen, be silent!" Moragh snapped urgently. "Don't question her; don't argue." She flung another look at Niahrin, this time in appeal. "Niahrin, what must we do?"

Before the witch could think, let alone answer, Indigo turned to regard her curiously. The movement was slow, as if she wasn't sure of herself. Then the peculiar little smile came back.

"I recall seeing you somewhere before. Weren't you . . ." The smile was replaced by a frown. "No. Not that. That couldn't have happened. . . ."

As she spoke her eyes were constantly changing their color; now silver, now milky, now amber. Finally they became blue-violet again. Grimya whimpered and pressed close to Niahrin's leg; the sound and movement caught Indigo's attention and she looked down.

"I like wolves," she said. "But I've never before seen one in Carn Caille. Is she your pet?"

"No," Niahrin replied. "She is my friend—and your friend, too. Don't you remember her? Don't you remember Grimya?"

"Grimya . . . no, I think not. There was a— But no. That was a dream. Only a dream."

Jes had moved up to Niahrin's side; softly the witch murmured so that only he could hear: "*She's beginning to recall something, Jes. Warn Her Grace; tell her to say nothing. I'm going to try to turn the key.*"

The bard nodded and withdrew, moving toward the table. Indigo's gaze followed him. "Is that young man a bard?" she asked.

"He is a bard."

"Ah. I thought so. He has the look. . . . We had a bard, but he was older. His name was . . . was . . ."

She was still watching Jes, and carefully, while her attention was distracted, Niahrin raised a hand and slipped the patch from her left eye. She knew that her timing must be perfect, and, soft-footed, took two cautious steps that brought her closer to Indigo's side. Then she said, quietly but clearly: "His name was Cushmagar."

"What?" Indigo turned—and Niahrin's witch-gaze snared her.

"No . . ." Indigo whispered. "No, don't . . . I don't want . . ."

"Hush." Niahrin's voice slid smoothly into the hypnotic lilt with which she had cast her spell over Perd. But she needed no knot-cord tonight to conjure the magic into being. The dormant power of this enchantment was already waking; not within herself, but within Indigo. In unveiling her eye, Niahrin had merely opened the door—what the door revealed was for Indigo alone to see.

"Anghara. Anghara. Anghara." Slowly Niahrin brought her right hand up as she repeated Indigo's true name three times. She stretched her arm toward Indigo's stricken face and her first and middle fingers extended in an old enchanters' sign. "Look to me, Anghara, for I have the gift of sight, and past and future are in my eye. Look, Anghara. Look."

The hall was utterly still, utterly silent. Indigo stared, mesmerized, into the witch's face. She couldn't turn away; Niahrin had caught her like a bird in a trap, and suddenly it seemed to her that the witch altered and became someone else, someone she knew well. . . .

"Imyssa . . . ?" Unknowing, Indigo spoke the name of her old nurse. The image of Imyssa's seamed face wavered, and for a moment a scarred cheek and a hideous eye showed in its place; but then that faded and the nurse beamed fondly at her.

"There now, poppet, all done; and who can say you're not the prettiest thing ever to grace a king's own table?" The voice came not from the physical world but from somewhere within her, spectral, echoing, a distant memory. *"What song will you play for your dear father and mother tonight, my princess?"*

What song will you play . . . "Oh, no . . ." Indigo said aloud, her voice shaking. "No, no. Not that . . ."

But other voices were joining in. "What song, Anghara? What song will it be tonight? Play for us, Anghara. Play for us, as you have done so often before." Indigo tried to shut them out, but they swelled like a tide, beating against her ears, against the walls of her mind—*What song tonight? What song tonight?*

And one voice among them all, an old voice but warm and strong and kindly, said: "My harp is here, Princess, and it is waiting. Come, Anghara. Come."

As though in a dream, she turned. The harp was there, his harp, Cushmagar's, standing where it always stood by the king's dais. The firelight reflected on the polished wood, burnishing it to an amber glow. And they were all here, all with her; her family, her friends, and all the dear and cherished souls who shared her life. . . .

The seven silent watchers in the hall hardly dared to breathe for fear of intruding on the hush as Indigo walked slowly, blindly but surely to Cushmagar's harp. Even Vinar had lifted his head and was staring, though his face was racked with bewildered misery. A faint rustle of silk broke the silence as Indigo sat down. She smiled at the company, but her eyes were closed and what she saw in her inner vision was a scene from another time and another place. Then she laid her cheek against the harp's smooth, carved wood and began to play.

Much later, Niahrin knew that the music Indigo conjured from Cushmagar's harp that night had never been
heard in the mortal world before and would never be heard
again. It was, indeed, an aisling; but an aisling so strange
and beautiful and melancholy that it reached into her very
soul, opening it like a flower and yet tearing her apart with
a depth of emotion that was almost too great for her mind
and body to bear. Faintly, as the exquisite, heartbreaking
melody soared and rippled and filled the hall with its light
and shadow, she heard the sound of a woman weeping, but
whether it was Moragh or Brythere or even herself who
sobbed so helplessly she could not say and did not know.
Indigo played on and on, her hands wild, her face, framed
by the mass of her hair, rapt and stark. Her eyes were open
now, though she gazed like one possessed into a world the
others could never reach, and her slim figure was wreathed
in a silver aura that blew about her like smoke.

Then, at the far end of the hall, the fire began to change.
The flames were dancing, swaying as the rhythm of the
music became more turbulent, but suddenly Niahrin realized that the color was draining from them. They began to
merge and blend, turning paler, paler, and their brightness
increased until the hearth seemed to be filled with a daz-
zling circle of white light.

And from the heart of the light, with the solemnity of a
strange, unearthly pageant, came a procession of human
figures.

Kalig was at their head, a tall, imposing bear of a man
with the crown of the Southern Isles glittering on his red-
brown hair. On his arm walked Imogen, his patrician and
beautiful queen from Khimiz on the Eastern Continent;
they looked about them, and they inclined their heads re-
gally and smiled as though acknowledging the adulation of
a great, invisible crowd.

The pageant paused. For a moment the phantom figures

were still, then Kalig and Imogen came on alone. At the table, Ryen and Brythere were on their feet. The young queen clung to her husband in terror, but though she wanted to look away she couldn't turn her head, couldn't tear her gaze from the silent, graceful ghosts parading slowly toward her. Ryen's face was a torment of battling emotions, awe and fear and sorrow all vying for precedence; as Kalig and Imogen drew nearer he began to move out from the table, as though to greet them—or, fearing them, to make way for an older and greater claim. . . .

But the spectral king and queen did not reach the dais. Instead they turned aside, to where Indigo, oblivious in her bewitchment, played on. As they approached the harp their figures began to shrink until they were barely more than dolls; then they passed under the arch of the great wooden frame, seemed to merge for a moment with the quivering strings, and, like will-o'-the-wisps, were gone.

And Niahrin remembered her tapestry. . . .

By the hearth, framed in the glowing circle of light, the procession began to move again. Now at their head was Prince Kirra, son of Kalig and brother of Anghara; a young man in his prime with the look of vibrant life, laughing, or so it seemed, with an invisible companion. Behind him walked an old woman, small and kindly and vigorous as a wrinkled little wren, who wagged her finger and smiled silently, fondly, chiding. Then others: servants, huntsmen, foresters, arm in arm, smiling, jesting, waving to distant friends whom their eyes alone could see. One by one and two by two they paraded the length of the hall, turned, shrank, and merged into the singing, lamenting harp.

And then the nature of the procession began to change. First came a sea captain, with a powerful, fearsome-looking woman by his side. Then an older man and woman, he pinch-faced and fussing, she adorned with a headdress of clinking copper discs, and with them a youth who had the swagger of arrogance. In their wake came a girl who clutched a pewter brooch in the shape of a bird, and who wept for shame at her own diseased face, and with her was a tall, gaunt man, his wild gray hair in a cluster of braids and his eyes filled with raging grief. Then a dark-skinned, sensually handsome man, and a woman of the same race whose expression was wistfully sad; between them they shepherded a fair-haired boy and a tiny, beautiful, golden-haired girl, while at their heels strutted a little woman with cropped hair and the jewel-studded cheeks that marked her as a Davakotian mariner. All these passed through the arch of the harp in their turn, and still Indigo, oblivious, played her melancholy music.

Then came a flurry of wilder movement amid the circle of light. Suddenly the harp's song changed and grew quicker, livelier, and from the hearth came a tumble of laughing people, from a small girl to a middle-aged man. They all had vivid red hair; one tossed jugglers' clubs, another performed a dizzying whirl of backsprings, while others joined hands and spun into a merry dance. Though their antics were soundless, Niahrin could almost hear the thump of tambourine and eerie ring of hurdy-gurdy blending with the harp; almost hear the shouts of a crowd applauding and calling for more. But the troupers did not stay; like the rest they became one with the harp, one with Indigo's memories, and abruptly the music changed again, to a slow, strange modulation as the next vision appeared.

This phantom was not human. Solitary, aloof, a huge, pale-furred tiger paced silently from the bright circle. It looked to neither right nor left but walked with the grace and confidence of unchallenged power, and on its head and along the length of his back a sprinkling of snow glinted. Behind it, at a respectful distance, walked a woman whose face was shrouded by a fur hood; then three young men, one oddly familiar to Niahrin, and two young women, and lastly an older man helped by another woman who seemed to be trying to comfort him. These in their turn vanished, and more women appeared, mahogany-skinned and scantily clad, sweat gleaming on their arms and faces. Two of them, one tall and harsh-faced, the other shorter, almost squat, seemed to be arguing. Following them—Niahrin blinked in surprise at this—was a crocodile of skipping children that seemed to go on and on and on, until finally their custodian appeared, chivvying the last stragglers along. He was an imposing figure, with a rose-bud mouth that looked out of place on such a somber face, but as he passed through the hall he smiled a smile so gentle that it could have melted stone.

The children and their benefactor shrank and vanished into the harp, and still Indigo played. But now her unseeing eyes were filled with tears, and the aisling was changing again, to a surging melody that yearned and cried and seemed to bring hope and despair at one and the same time. And one more vision entered the hall.

He appeared within the circle of light like a man emerging from the depths of a dream. Silver sparks glinted in his black hair as he stepped from the hearth, and he paused, looking around him, frowning slightly. Unlike the specters that had come before, he seemed to be aware of the hall and the frozen watchers. Then he saw Indigo. . . .

"Anghara?" The voice sent a sharp thrill through Niahrin, for in it she recognized the familiar ring of Perd Nordenson's tones. The harp fell suddenly, shockingly silent, and Indigo's head jerked up. Her eyes focused, and her intake of breath was loud in the hall as the last echoes of the aisling died away.

"Fenran . . ." The harp crashed over with a clattering, echoing din, and Indigo sprang to her feet. "FENRAN!"

She ran toward him, her arms outstretched. Niahrin

heard Vinar give an anguished cry as Indigo and the apparition of her lover embraced. There was a scuffle on the dais, raised voices, a heavy thump; but Indigo and Fenran were aware only of each other. At last they drew apart.

"Fenran . . . Oh, my love . . ." Indigo's face was alight with joy. But Fenran smiled, and it was the same scornful, cruel, and cunning smile that Niahrin had seen on Perd's face in the cellar.

"No," he said. "Not yet. Not yet. Don't you understand, Anghara? It isn't over yet!"

He turned. His gray eyes raked the dais and its stunned occupants, and he laughed.

"We are not done with you," he said, and then his gaze fixed on the witch. "Only one demon remains, Niahrin. Isn't that what you told me? Well, my dear, you were right. We both know its name now—but do *you* have the courage to speak that name aloud?"

And Fenran vanished.

"No!" Indigo reeled back, her hands clawing and clasping at empty air. "No, NO! *FENRAN!*"

She flung herself toward the door of the hall. Jes, recovering his wits more quickly than the others, shouted, "No, don't let her go!" He started after her, Niahrin on his heels, but Grimya was faster. She streaked past Indigo and skidded to a halt, spinning round to block her way to the door.

"Indigo, wait!" she panted, hoarse with exertion and emotion. "Wait, *p . . . please!*"

The others were hastening after Niahrin and Jes; hearing the wolf, Brythere snatched at her husband's arm. "Ryen, it spoke! The animal *spoke!*"

Indigo stared down at her old friend. "Grimya . . ." Her voice shook; she seemed confused. Then suddenly the mental barrier that had locked their minds apart since the shipwreck collapsed, and in a great rush Grimya heard her agonized thoughts.

Oh, Grimya, oh love—what's happened to me? What have I done? And she covered her face with her hands, tears streaming down her face.

"Indigo!" It was Vinar's voice. He pushed past Niahrin and Jes, ran to Indigo's side. "Indigo, what's happened?" He caught hold of her, tried to put his arms around her. "Indigo, I don't understand! *Please*—"

She looked up at him, and his hands fell away as he saw the truth in her eyes.

"It's come back," she said softly, and there was stark tragedy in her voice. "My memory—it's come back. I remember everything. *Everything*. And ... And ..." But there were no words to explain to him, nothing that would enable him to understand.

The others were gathering round them now. Strangers' faces, anxious, concerned, afraid. Indigo couldn't bear to look at them. The pain within her was too terrible; she wanted only to run, to flee.

To flee ...

Fenran! Grimya felt the huge surge of emotion that flooded her friend's mind and knew what she meant to do.

Indigo, no, you can't—

Yes, Grimya! Yes, I must! Don't you see, don't you remember? He's waiting for me! He's waiting at the Tower of Regrets! Indigo swung round, facing the watchers, facing Vinar.

"Please," she said, her voice low-pitched and shaking. "I know now why I came here, and I know what I have to do. Please, don't try to prevent me. I can't make you understand, and there isn't time to try. I have to go."

"No, Indigo!" Vinar cried. "No, you can't, you—"

"Vinar." Her tone was so gentle and so sorrowful that it silenced him in midsentence. She looked into his blue eyes, saw the hurt she had brought on him, and it almost broke her heart. But she could offer him nothing now. She had to tell him the truth, however bitter.

"Vinar, I can't marry you. It would have been wrong, so *wrong*; and it would have brought ruin on us both. I'm only sorry that I've brought ... that I've brought you such ..." She drew in an ugly, wracking breath. "Great Goddess, I'm sorry, I'm so *sorry*."

"Indigo—" Moragh started forward, her hands held out. "My dear, if only we can—"

"No." Indigo moved quickly back out of her reach. "No, Your Grace. There's nothing to be said; nothing could make any difference. I must go—he's waiting for me, Fenran is waiting for me. *I must find him!*"

Evading Grimya, she had reached the door and her hand was on the latch before anyone could stop her. The door jerked open; white-faced, eyes brimming, Indigo looked back one last time at Vinar.

"I'm sorry. . . ." she said again. And she was gone, the sound of her running footsteps diminishing along the corridor.

For several seconds everyone in the hall was too stunned to speak or move. Then suddenly the king said explosively, "Damn her, what does she think she's—"

"Ryen, don't." Moragh's voice rang out as he started toward the door in Indigo's wake. Ryen paused and looked at her angrily, and she said, "Let her go."

"Let her *go*?"

"Yes." The dowager's face was pale and very set. "This is out of our hands now."

"But she's—" Then Ryen's argument collapsed as he realized that he didn't know what Indigo had done, or what she intended to do, or even what she truly was. He gestured with a kind of wild helplessness toward Vinar, who was standing immobile as a corpse, staring blankly at the

door. "What about *him*? For his sake, if for no other reason, we must fetch her back!"

"My lord." Jes spoke up. "Her Grace is right." He
stepped away from Niahrin's side and faced the king.
"What Indigo—or perhaps I should now say Anghara—
means to do is a matter for her and her alone. We can't
help her, and we can't help Vinar, not now." He paused. "I
think, with respect, that what we have all witnessed here
tonight is proof enough of that."

Ryen's eyes narrowed. "You knew. You knew all along,
and you didn't tell me. . . ."

"Yes, my lord. I knew." Jes hung his head. "I can only
ask your forgiveness."

For a long moment Ryen stared at him. Then abruptly
he turned on his heel and looked hard at Niahrin.

"You're the wise-woman—and it's clear from what happened tonight that you were also a main conspirator in this
mad affair. Well, so be it. What do *you* say we should do?"

Niahrin was looking uneasily at Grimya. "I agree with
Her Grace, sire," she said quietly. "We must let Indigo go.
We have no other choice. Besides . . ." She hesitated, then
met his gaze. "I think she will return to Carn Caille before
too long."

The dowager stepped forward and touched her son's
hand lightly. "Ryen, there's nothing to be gained from
standing here arguing amongst ourselves. There is still a
great deal about this affair that you and Brythere don't
know"—she glanced at her daughter-elect,—who was
frowning, seemingly lost in thought—"and we must also
try to do something for poor Vinar, who has suffered a
greater shock than any of us. Let's go to my rooms, and
Jes and Niahrin and I will explain as much as we are
able."

"But Indigo . . ." Ryen still wasn't entirely willing to

give up the idea of searching for her. "Do you *know* where she's gone?"

Moragh and Niahrin exchanged a brief look that spoke volumes, and the dowager said, "I believe so. But I also believe that it would not be wise to follow her." Deftly and firmly she linked arms with her son and with the other hand drew Brythere toward her. "Come, my dears. It will be best, and there's nothing else for us to do as yet."

A smaller door, behind the dais, connected directly with the private royal apartments, and she led Ryen and Brythere toward it. Jes gently coaxed the stunned Vinar after them, and all five left the hall. But Grimya did not follow, and Niahrin hung back, dropping to a crouch beside the wolf.

"What is it, my dear?" she asked softly.

Grimya whimpered and looked at her with troubled eyes. "I c-cannot stay," she said huskily. "Niahrin, I must go after Indigo. I know what you said, but . . . I cannot let her go alone. I am afraid for her, and . . . and she is my ff . . . *friend*."

The witch understood. And she was aware of the rest, the thing that Grimya did not and would not say. The wolf knew that there was a far greater threat in the wind tonight than simply the danger to Indigo. The witch knew it, too . . . but, for the present at least, they would keep that secret between them.

She didn't speak, but she reached out and put her arms about the wolf, hugging her close for a few moments. Grimya licked her face, then Niahrin stood up again and she moved toward the main door, slipping through it like a shadow, and was gone. Niahrin closed her good eye and her fingers moved in a charm-sign.

"The Mother send you good fortune, dear one," she whispered.

A light footfall sounded behind her, and Niahrin whirled.

Jes was standing by the dais table. Seeing the witch's chagrin he smiled and walked slowly toward her.

"Don't fear; I'll say nothing to anyone." He nodded toward the door. "She's gone after Indigo?"

"Yes. I . . . don't think I could have stopped her." Niahrin hesitated, then added, "Even if I had wanted to."

The bard nodded again. "It's probably as well." There was a long pause. Then: "Niahrin . . . this isn't over yet, is it?"

It was the question that Niahrin had been trying not to dwell on. She shivered, knew Jes saw the shiver, and turned her head away.

"No," she said quietly. "I don't know what will happen, what form it will take. But I know where Indigo has gone, and I believe I understand now what that place is and what it has the power to do." She looked at him at last. "This is not over yet, Jes. Not for Indigo, and not for us."

•CHAPTER•XXI•

The full moon rode high in a sky streaked with thin, racing clouds, and the beams of her light swept across the landscape in shifting, ever-changing patterns of black and silver. Silver etched the mane and the pricked ears of the iron-gray gelding as it galloped, and the sound of its hooves was dim thunder echoing in the night's silence.

Indigo crouched over the gelding's neck, her hair, unbound, flying like a banner. She felt the snap of the wind in her face, the rhythmic, flowing power of the horse's muscles beneath her, and the memories of another time, another age, another such ride, burned like fire in her blood. She had been young then, young and rash and reckless; and the rendezvous she had kept on that terrible day had brought catastrophe. But now it was to be different. Now the time for remorse and for grief was over, for tonight that ancient tragedy would at last be expunged and its consequences set to rights. Tonight, she would meet her destiny again—and it would be a very different destiny from the one that had haunted her for fifty years.

Tears were still falling as she rode, urging the gelding on even faster. Tears for the old memories of her family, her friends, and all that had been lost; tears for herself and the burden she had carried through half a century of wandering. Tears, too, for Vinar, whom she had unjustly deceived without ever wishing to hurt. But beneath the tears, and eclipsing their power over her, was the joy of knowing that the long, long time of hoping and waiting and yearning was almost at an end. Her journey was over. Fenran was waiting, and she was coming home.

Far ahead of her, far to the south, a pale, cold glow shone on the horizon. Indigo's heart surged, for she knew that this spectral phantasm was the light of the moon reflecting from the huge polar lands, the lands where the snow never melted and the world was made of ice. High above the ice unearthly mirages flickered and played across the sky; the eerie beacon lights of a dream country, a world in which nightmares might take corporeal form . . . but there would be no more nightmares, for her destination was near.

And she believed that she had conquered her final demon.

At last she saw it. A smudge of darkness in the moonlight ahead, a shadow that was more than a shadow, angular and anomalous among the softer contours of rock and scrub and scree. The gelding tossed its head suddenly, snorting and jinking, but she shortened rein and drove her heels hard into its flanks, her mind goading the animal as though by will alone she could give it wings. The shadow drew closer, closer; then a cloud drifted briefly across the moon and suddenly the shadow was gone and she was riding blind. Terrified by the sudden darkness the gelding whinnied shrilly, and the rhythm of its hoofbeats changed to a clattering, chaotic slither as it slewed and reared high, almost unseating her. Clinging to the flying mane Indigo screamed her fury and frustration at the horse, struggling to bring it under control. Then the cloud was swept away, the moon glared down once more—and the Tower of Regrets loomed grim and forbidding before her.

The gelding reared again, its iron shoes striking sparks from the stony ground as its forehooves flailed and came down with jarring impact. Indigo hunched her knees and sprang from its back, gathering the reins as she landed and pulling hard on the bit. For a moment she thought she might be trampled, but at last the gelding quieted and stood snorting and shuddering, its withers flecked with sweat. There was a bush nearby, a poor stunted thing but strongly and deeply rooted, and she led the horse to it and tied the reins securely around a branch. Her heart was pounding and her stomach roiling; her fingers fumbled with the knot but finally it was fastened. And the gelding was already forgotten as she turned at last to face the culmination of her dreams.

Fifty years ago, the Tower of Regrets had stood untouched and unimpaired in its lonely isolation upon the tundra. Now, it was in ruins. The roof was gone and the walls crumbled to ragged, broken pinnacles, etched sharply against the sky. Rubble was scattered widely around the tower's foot, and Indigo began to pick her way slowly among the debris, knowing how and why it had come to be there. There were even traces of scorching on some of the smashed stones. . . .

She saw the door when she was only twelve or fifteen paces from the ruin, and she stopped as yet more memories crowded back into her mind. The door was just a simple rectangle of wood, so ancient that it was all but petrified. There was no keyhole—she knew that and did not look for one—but traces of rust showed where before there had been a metal latch, rotted away to nothing now. Indigo stood very still for a few moments. She could hear the faint sound of the gelding grazing the bush, then there was a scrape and ring of iron as it shifted restlessly, but she did not turn.

She had only to open the door. Only to open it, and he would be there. . . .

She stepped forward, and her hand reached out—

"Indigo!"

The cry was so sudden and unexpected that Indigo's heart crashed against her ribs with shock. She spun round, nearly losing her balance as her foot turned on a stone, and her eyes widened.

Grimya stood five paces away, head down, eyes glowing as the moonlight caught them.

"Grimya . . ." A tide of conflicting emotions assailed Indigo. "What are you doing? What do you want?"

The wolf gazed back, and now her eyes pleaded. "I c-could not let you go alone."

Indigo's fists clenched at her sides. "You shouldn't be here! There's no place for you here—this is something I must do—*need* to do—alone!"

"Per-haps it is, But I thhink that here there is a choice waiting for you, and I know which choice you will make. I do not want you to make that choice!"

"A *choice*? No, Grimya—there is no choice. *None*."

"There is. I *know*. I have s . . . seen, Indigo. I have seen what would have become of you if you had not opened this door such a long time ago. And I know that what I saw will truly happen, if you open it again now."

Indigo's pulse was thick in her veins. She was suddenly confused, and the confusion bred anger.

"How can you *know*?" she demanded. "You don't—you can't! What have you 'seen' that has been hidden from me?"

"All that Niahrin showed me. All that Fenran has become."

"Fen . . . ?" Then Indigo's anger caught fire. "Damn your insolence, what do you know of Fenran? Nothing, you know *nothing* of him, and neither does that damned witch!"

"But we *do*!" Grimya argued piteously. "There is more than you know, more than you under-stand! Indigo, please, listen to me! Give me the chance to ex . . . explain, and then you will—"

"No!" She shook her head wildly, denying it, denying even the possibility that something could be wrong, and she flared at the wolf. "Grimya, why are you doing this? All our years together, all the searching, all the waiting, and now at the last you turn against me! You have no *right* to say what you're saying! You have no right to follow me or to interfere! I thought you were my *friend* and now—"

"It is because I am your friend that I have done it!" Grimya pleaded desperately. "Because you are my friend and I love you! Indigo, we've been wrong! Wrong about Fenran, wrong about the tower, wrong about *everything*! Niahrin has shown me—"

From the darkness behind them a new voice spoke.

"Niahrin has shown you a great deal, she-wolf. But it can make no difference now."

"Fenran!" Indigo spun around—and froze.

He had opened the door silently and emerged from the tower without either of them being aware of his presence. But his hair was white and his figure emaciated and his face seamed with age. The man whom Carn Caille had known as Perd Nordenson smiled, and in the moonlight his face was hard as stone.

"Don't you recognize me, love? After all these years, don't you know me anymore?"

Grimya whimpered, and Indigo took a step back. "You . . . you're not . . . you can't be Fenran. . . ."

The wind lifted the thin tendrils of his hair. "Half a century as the prisoner of demons wreaks changes. But my imprisonment wasn't as you'd envisaged it, Anghara. It was another kind of limbo; a limbo lived in this world, growing older and madder without you, and always waiting, while hope became harder to cling to as time passed. The demons that held me were the demons of insanity. I *was* insane; I know it now, and I think I even knew it then, in my few lucid moments. But all this time I've been waiting for you to come back, so that we can make the choice again . . . and this time make it together."

Indigo had begun to shake as though with a palsy, and she couldn't make it stop. And she couldn't believe that this man was her lost love: though in a deep, dark part of her psyche something was stirring. . . .

She said, her voice barely audible, "I don't understand. . . ."

"No. But you shall. We have a chance, Anghara. We have a chance to put right all the old wrongs and be as we were in the old days. Before the demons came." He held out one hand, beckoning to her. "Come, love. Walk into the tower again. The demons are gone. You vanquished them. Now you and I shall put the last of their number to rest."

Grimya cried, "Indigo, don't!" and Fenran turned a malevolent stare on her.

"Ah; the voice of your conscience. I have hated wolves for a long time, and now I understand why. Go away, she-wolf. Go back to your forest and hide there. We want nothing more to do with you."

Indigo had turned in response to Grimya's plea, and now she looked back toward Fenran in sudden doubt. "Grimya means no harm! She simply doesn't—" The words snapped off. The old man had vanished, and in his place stood Fenran as she had known and loved him: young, unchanged, *alive*.

"Oh, Great Goddess . . ." She put a clenched fist to her mouth. *"Oh, sweet Earth . . ."*

"Anghara." He held out his arms, and his voice was warm. "Must I wait any longer for you to return?"

A shattering wave of emotion exploded through Indigo and she ran to him, forgetting his harsh words, forgetting Grimya, forgetting everything but the dizzying exultation of their reunion. She felt his arms enfold her, and the warmth and strength of his body as he crushed her to him; smelled the achingly familiar scents of his hair, his skin, his clothes. Her mouth sought his with frantic hunger and her mind and heart drowned in his kiss.

"Come back, Anghara, my love!" His voice was an urgent, passionate whisper, thrilling through her. "Come back—help me turn back time and be young again! The tower—the tower holds the key and the power, don't you see, don't you understand? Enter the tower with me, and it will shape our dreams and our destinies as it did before—only this time there will be no demons and no partings!"

Grimya heard his words and knew that her hope was gone. Indigo was snared, for the memory of a love more than half a century old was too strong for any other power to challenge. No matter what might become of her, what surely *would* become of her, Indigo would turn to Fenran and follow where he led. Back to the Tower of Regrets, to face her destiny and choose her path once more. Fenran offered her the chance to fold back time, wipe out the past and begin again; and for him it would mean a renewal of life, a return to youth and to the place he had once held both in her heart and at her side. For fifty years Indigo had clung to her memories of him, his image a precious jewel to be regained, the single goal that had given her strength and hope through all the darkest days. But time and distance had distorted those memories, and the man whom Indigo had come home to find was not the real man, not the true Fenran. Grimya had seen the true Fenran, with all his flaws and failings; hungry for dominance, greedy for power, jealous and resentful of any who stood between him and his desires. Fenran had the ambitions of a king, and the youthful Anghara, as a king's daughter, had been the first stepping stone on the road to those ambitions.

But Indigo was blind. She could not see and would not see the truth that Perd had shown to Grimya and her friends at Carn Caille. She knew only that her long exile was over, the old promise fulfilled, and her lover had come back to her again.

They had turned their backs on Grimya now and were moving toward the tower door, arms entwined about each other as though they would at any moment merge and become one. Grimya's heart lurched agonizingly within her. She couldn't let Indigo go like this. However futile it might be, she had to try one last time—

She cried out distraughtly: "Indigo!"

Indigo paused and turned her head. The wolf was on her feet, shaking from head to tail. "Indigo," she begged, "P . . . *lease* hear me!" Fenran looked back angrily; his grip on Indigo tightened and he tried to lead her on once more. Desperately Grimya drew breath, and cried, "Do this for me, *please*; if you will do nothing else, do this, for the s-sake of our frriendship! Ask him—ask Fenran—ask him what will become of you! Ask him what you will both be, in fifty more years from now!"

For a moment Indigo stood motionless. A tiny frown appeared on her face, and hope leaped in Grimya. But then Indigo's expression cleared. She smiled, but the smile was one of pity and had no true meaning.

"I'm sorry that it must end like this for you, Grimya," she said. "You've been a good friend to me, and I won't forget you. But this is the end of my journey. Good-bye, dear Grimya. And bless you."

She turned away and walked with Fenran into the Tower of Regrets.

Grimya made no sound. She only stared at the ruined tower, and at the gaping black rectangle of the doorway, standing open like the mouth of a deep and terrible pit. The figures of Indigo and Fenran stepped into that mouth, became one with the darkness, vanished, and the sound of the door closing seemed to echo across the tundra with hollow and terrible finality.

For perhaps a minute the night was silent. Then the silence was broken by a mournful, echoing sound as the wolf raised her muzzle and uttered a lonely howl of misery and desolation, a lament for the truth that Indigo did not understand and refused to hear.

Fenran was Indigo's seventh demon . . . and by far the most powerful of all.

"He's sleeping?" Jes came quietly into the room and looked down at Vinar's blond head on the pillow.

"Yes. At last." Niahrin's face was compassionate as she remembered the sobbing, the heartbreak, the bewilderment as she had sat beside the bed and held Vinar's hands and tried to bring some tiny spark of comfort to a soul who could not be comforted. She had told Vinar all she could—he had wanted that, he had pleaded to know, and she couldn't deny him what he asked—but even though he had struggled to understand, as yet he was too deluged by grief. In time, perhaps, the grief would fade and understanding come, but not yet. Not for a long time yet.

"Will he ever be able to forgive her, I wonder?" Jes mused softly.

The witch looked up. "Oh, yes. Vinar isn't that kind of man; it isn't in him to hold a grudge, or even, I think, to be bitter. I think he *has* forgiven her. He simply can't bear her loss."

"Then he puts all of us to shame." The bard moved quietly to the window and lifted back the curtain. "Well, they all know now. Her Grace and I told Ryen and Brythere the whole story." Wearily he pinched the bridge of his nose. "That was not easy. But they're prepared, now, for whatever may come. And as to that . . ."

"As to that . . . ?"

He let the curtain fall. "Niahrin, will you come with me? There is something I have to do, in the hall." His brown eyes glinted oddly in the candlelight. "Please?"

She understood that there was more behind the request and nodded. "Of course." She glanced back at Vinar. "He won't wake for a while. Grief has exhausted him. . . ."

They left the room together and padded through the deserted corridors. Carn Caille was shrouded in silence; the servants were long abed and the only light in the citadel was a dim glow from behind the closed curtains of Moragh's private apartments on the far side of the courtyard. The lantern Jes carried cast a comforting pool of brightness, but even so Niahrin felt a primal shudder run through her as he opened the door of the lesser hall and they stepped inside. The hall was as they had left it: dishes and cups uncleared, the fire still alive, though only embers remained now. In the flickering shadows the swaths of flowers and leaves looked incongruous; almost, Niahrin thought, obscene. . . .

"It's the harp," Jes said quietly as they crossed the floor. "Cushmagar's harp. It doesn't seem . . . decent, somehow, to leave it lying where it fell, and the thought of that has been troubling me this past hour and more." He turned to the witch and smiled abashedly. "Does that sound fool-ish?"

She smiled, but uneasily. "No. No, it doesn't."

They moved toward the window. Cushmagar's harp lay in a patch of moonlight that filtered through the garlands. As they drew near Niahrin saw a gleam of something smaller on the floor. Her pipe . . . she bent to pick it up, fingering the smooth wood, then joined the bard where he stood by the toppled harp.

"It's not as heavy as it looks," Jes said. "If we both—"

He froze. They had both heard it; a faint echo of sound, like a soft moan.

Jes's face blanched. *"It came from the harp. . . ."*

Niahrin didn't answer. She had sensed, she realized, from the moment Jes had asked her to accompany him here that something like this would happen. And Cushmagar's harp . . . yes, it was the obvious medium! From across the years, across the gulf of death, the old bard was again sending them a warning. . . .

"Jes!" she said. "Take the harp—quickly, help me lift it up!" Suddenly she knew exactly what must be done. As though her seeing-eye had opened again of its own accord, the past and the future and the worlds of *might-have-been* were awakening and blending once more. She seized the instrument, pulling with all her strength; Jes, impelled by her certainty, grasped it from the other side. The harp came up, rocked, settled—and the strings quivered vio-lently as a dreadful, clashing discord rang though the hall. Niahrin sprang back in shock, but Jes's hands were still clamped to the instrument.

"Niahrin!" There was panic in his voice. "Niahrin, I can't let go of it! *I can't let go!*"

He was struggling, his feet slithering on the stone floor, but it was as though other, invisible hands had taken hold of his fingers and were gripping them with supernatural strength. The harp rocked again, wildly, and gave voice to another appalling cacophony—and abruptly Niahrin understood.

"Jes, let it play!" she cried. "Let it play through you—that's what it wants, that's what it's trying to tell us! *Play*, Jes!"

The young bard's face was beaded with sweat. Swinging round, Niahrin snatched up the stool set beside his own harp a few paces away and thrust it toward him. *"Play!"* she urged him again.

He had no choice but to obey. Even as his legs gave way under him and he collapsed onto the stool, his fingers were already moving, and the harp's ugly din modulated suddenly into music. Fast, angry, almost desperate music, as the aisling-power surged anew and flooded into his hands. Niahrin's own hands went up, tearing at her eye patch—there was no time for reasoning, no room for logic, she just *knew* what had to be done, and with all the strength of her will she summoned the seeing-power to rise within her. Twisted shadows flickered through the hall as her earthly and unearthly vision clashed; there were faces in the shadows, faces and people, but she couldn't see them clearly, the power wasn't enough. . . .

"Granmer!" Niahrin's voice shrilled out. "Granmer, if you ever loved your grandchild, help me! Lend me your strength and your skill, and help me now!"

She felt a rushing sensation, as of a chill south wind—then suddenly, violently, the scene before her changed and she was looking on mayhem. *A great courtyard filled with men and women, a seething mass of humanity all fighting for their lives—and bearing down on them, wave upon endless wave, a legion out of nightmare: winged monsters, slavering horrors, the denizens of a hell beyond imagining. Black smoke billowed over the high walls, and there were flames in the smoke, and beyond the hideous, tumbling pall the sun and the moon were clashing together in the sky, and the sun was black and the moon was bronze, and the howling din of battle shook stone and air together as besieged and besiegers alike fought and screamed and died. And high on the wall she saw them: two human figures, laughing as they urged the demons on to greater destruction. The crone and the madman, the queen and her consort—Indigo and Fenran—*

Niahrin shrieked like a banshee and flung both hands up to cover her face. *She couldn't look, couldn't bear witness; this was too great a horror to endure—*

"Niahrin!" The world of the battle swelled, shattered, and calm crashed down about her as the vision vanished. She was prone on the floor and Jes was crouching over her, trying to pull her upright. The harp had released him and was silent, though the last echoes of the savage music still rang in the witch's ears. But as she rolled painfully over and sat up, Niahrin looked into the bard's eyes and knew that he, too, had seen—and understood—what the aisling had revealed.

"Niahrin." Jes's face was dead white and his breathing shallow and harsh. "Niahrin, was it true? Is that what will happen, if . . ."

"If Indigo returns to Fenran. If she enters the tower and turns back time. Yes." Niahrin tried to sit straighter and coughed. Saliva filled her mouth but she couldn't swallow it. "The demons will come back, Jes. Before—fifty years ago—they were Indigo's own demons; the desires and emotions and flaws within herself, which she had to face and reconcile if she was ever to be fulfilled. But this time . . ." She coughed again, rackingly. "This time they are Fenran's, and they have terrible power, for Fenran has not conquered his demons in the way that Indigo conquered hers. Instead, he has . . . he has nurtured them, fed them, *courted* them, and they have taken control of him.

Perhaps it never could have been otherwise. Perhaps Fenran simply does not possess the—the courage that Indigo had, the courage to make the journey that would have reconciled the darkness and the light within him. I don't know, Jes. I don't know. But if Indigo chooses his way, his path, then the demons will return, and the vision will be true."

The bard scrambled to his feet. "Niahrin, we have to stop it! Somehow, we have to—"

"We can't! We haven't the power—we can't force Indigo to make the right choice! Don't you understand? She has reached the darkest night, but it is *her* darkness. She *has* to choose freely!"

"No!" Jes insisted. "No, you're wrong! How can Indigo be free to choose when she doesn't even understand what she is choosing? She doesn't *know*, Niahrin—she doesn't know the truth about Fenran; no one has told her, no one has shown her!"

With a shock that was like a sword-thrust to the pit of her stomach Niahrin realized that he was right. Indigo could not choose freely, for her knowledge was warped by the old, false memories. She could not realize where her path would lead. There was no one to show her the nature of her final demon. . . .

Jes saw the understanding and horror that dawned in the witch's face, and he gripped her shoulders hard. "Niahrin, there must be a way! There *has* to be! If we were to take the fastest horses, ride after her—"

"We'd be too late. Maybe it's already too late—Jes, there's nothing we can do to stop Indigo, nothing that—" The words broke off.

"What?" Jes demanded urgently. "What is it, what have you thought?"

"Grimya . . ." Pushing his hands away Niahrin scrambled to her feet. "Grimya went after her to the tower."

"But we can't reach Grimya."

"She's telepathic." The witch glanced quickly at him. "Didn't you know? Of course; how could you? But she told me of it."

Jes's eyes lit. "Can you reach her mind?"

"No. I—I've never had that talent." *Yet she and the wolf had become so close. . . . Was it possible? Could she break through the barrier?*

"Try." Jes took hold of her again. "Please, Niahrin, *try*. There's nothing to lose!"

The power of the aisling had been so great. Surely, there was a chance. . . . Suddenly Niahrin's fingers began to prickle. It was the old sign, the signal that the scent of magic was stirring. . . .

Rapidly the witch made a decision. She stepped away from Jes, moved quickly down the hall toward the hearth. *South* . . . yes, this was south. And the fire, still glowing faintly, could give her the impetus she would need.

She dropped to a crouch on the hearthstone, and her voice hissed from her throat.

"Grimya! Grimya, hear me! Grimya, hear me!"

The dying fire sizzled and seemed to emit a faint whine. Like the whine of a wolf . . . Niahrin latched on to that, held it fiercely in her mind.

"Grimya. Grimya. Hear me, Grimya."

A little scatter of sparks flew upward. Sparks, like a wolf's eyes . . .

"Grimya. See, Grimya. See. See what I show." With all her will she conjured back the vision of the aisling, the slaughter, the smoke and flames, the howling demons, the two figures on the wall, and around the images she bound the deeper understanding, the knowledge of what would come to pass.

"Grimya. Grimya. See, Grimya. See."

Far away, so faint, a sound in her mind. A word, a voice she knew. . . .

"*Niahrin . . . Niahrin. I sense you, but I cannot hear. I cannot hear, I cannot see. . . .*"

Niahrin shut her right eye tightly, blotting out her physical surroundings, concentrating desperately on that tiny spark of a voice.

"*Grimya! Hear me, Grimya! Try! Help me!*"

"*It is not enough . . . not enough. . . .*"

Then Niahrin knew that there was only one way in which to focus the power and give it the strength she needed. One surge, one moment, would be enough. One act, to propel her across the gulf and link her with the wolf. . . .

She gathered the vision with all the intensity she was capable of summoning; gathered her courage—

"*Grimya! See, Grimya! SEE!*" And she plunged her hands into the fire.

Pain flared through her fingers as they thrust deep into the embers' searing heat. Sparks exploded upward; some caught in her hair, smoldering; and with a shock that almost eclipsed the physical agony she felt the power rush from her and out into the night in a single, overwhelming wave.

"Niahrin!" Jes was running to her, pulling her hands from the fire, dragging her back across the hearthstone to safety. She slumped against him, teeth clamping down on her lower lip as suddenly the full force of the pain hit her. Her hands, blistered and scarlet, clawed helplessly as she tried in vain to push the agony away, and her face was haggard with shock. But even in the midst of her distress she turned to him.

"It worked. . . ." Her voice was a thin croak. "I reached her; I made it happen." She sucked air into her lungs with an ugly, seething sound. "But, oh, Jes . . . it hurts . . . how it *hurts!*"

•CHAPTER•XXII•

The moon's light could not reach them here. Darkness crowded close, like soft, suffocating folds of velvet, but they needed no illumination. *"So many long years,"* he had whispered to her, and the safe, surrounding walls of the Tower of Regrets took up his gentle voice and sent it shimmering back in a wash of echoes. *"Oh, my love, my precious Anghara, it has been so many, many long years. . . ."*

And now the words they said, the murmurings and the sweetnesses between the kisses, no longer mattered, no longer had any meaning or purpose. Simply to hear the sound of his voice, to feel the touch of his hands as he stroked away her tears, to *be* with him, to be *with* him. . . . This was the ecstasy, the rapture, the ultimate and final fulfillment of her dreams. *If I should die now, if that were to be, then I would die contented that my life had been complete. . . .*

"Anghara, Anghara . . ." On his lips her name took on a special timbre, an exquisite intimacy that they alone shared and understood. "It's time, love. It's time. Help me, my darling. Make me complete again, and let us take back what we have lost. . . ."

As he spoke he was drawing her toward the wall . . . and suddenly there was a light within the Tower of Regrets. Faint and pale, like the tiny lamp of a glowworm, it shone low in a dusty corner, and Indigo gazed down at it in wonder.

"What is it?" she asked softly.

Fenran kissed her hair. "Don't you know, love? Don't you remember? Look." He sank to a crouch, drawing her with him, and his hand stretched out toward the little pinpoint of light. "Look, Anghara."

The pinpoint swelled suddenly to a diffused glow, and Indigo's mind reeled back half a century into the past.

On the floor of the tower stood a chest. It was made of metal—or something that looked like metal—and its color was not quite silver, not quite bronze, not quite a steely blue-gray. The light shone not on the chest but *from* it, and by its dim radiance she saw that the chest bore no decoration; not even a line to show where casket and lid might join.

Fenran's hand reached for hers and held her fingers tightly. "Now do you remember, my love?"

She did, and the emotion that rose in her was one of terror and awe combined. *Fifty years ago, here in this very tower, she had come upon an unadorned casket and she had raised the lid and . . .*

"Oh, no . . ." She began to back away. "Oh, no, *no* . . ."

"Hush!" Fenran caught hold of her and drew her protectively against him. "It's all right, Anghara, it's all right! There are no demons, not now. Don't you see? This time it is the means of choosing your destiny again, of turning time back and giving us our second chance. Our chance *together*. Lift the lid, my sweet one. Lift it again, and see."

She stared at the chest, unable to speak.

"Our second chance, my love," Fenran repeated. His voice was gentle, coaxing, filled with excitement and with hope. "Do you understand what this casket is? It is a well-spring, and what it holds is the future. Your future, my future; everyone's and anyone's, if they only have the courage to open it and look within."

Indigo was trembling. "But . . . but I have looked within it once before. And—"

"There is always a choice to be made. Before, you chose wrongly—you chose out of fear and not out of love. This time, it will be different."

His hand was moving, guiding hers toward the chest's shining surface. But she was still afraid. . . .

"Fenran . . ." Her voice quavered. "Fenran . . . what will our future hold? What will happen to us, if we . . . ?"

"Let me show you." The pressure on her fingers increased, urgent now. "Please, Anghara. *Please*, love. Don't deny me my hopes—don't deny our chance of happiness!"

She turned to meet his eyes, and when she saw the look in them the last of her resistance collapsed. *Hadn't this been her sole ambition through fifty years of wandering and striving? Wasn't this what she had yearned for, waited for, prayed for? She had failed Fenran once—she would not fail him again!*

She heard her own voice say: *"Yes . . ."*

They touched the casket together. There was a sense of movement, of stirring, at their touch; Indigo heard a quick *hiss*, like air escaping, and for an instant her nostrils flared as they caught a smell—almost a stench—that flicked past her face. Then the cold metal seemed to vibrate under their fingers, and the lid rose.

Indigo didn't know what she had expected to see inside

the chest. There had been no time to think or speculate . . . but as she gazed down, the memories of her last, forbidden sojourn focused sharply in her mind. For, as before, the chest was empty. *Not one relic or clue; not even a trace of dust to show where something had rotted away . . . and she felt again the sick, breathless feeling of having been cheated, having broken every law and every taboo to come to the Tower of Regrets, only for the tower to deceive her. . . .*

"Fenran . . ." She released her hold on the lid and clutched at his arm, whispering in dismay that mingled with sudden apprehension. "There's nothing there! I thought that this time there would be—"

And her voice broke off as, behind her, something uttered a soft, satisfied sigh.

Indigo sprang to her feet and spun round so fast that she kicked the chest aside, slamming it against the wall. Two shadowy figures had materialized in the tower at her back, and as she saw them her eyes widened with horror.

"Fenran—" She reached for him, her hand groping in the gloom. But he wasn't there. And the two figures, the old madman with her lover's face and the embittered crone with blue-violet eyes, were smiling at her, and holding out, between them, a knife with a long, glinting blade.

Indigo screamed Fenran's name, whirling again. He was gone, he had vanished—and the two phantoms were advancing on her, slowly but resolutely, the knife poised now and pointing at her heart.

Indigo's fear flashed into panic. She flung herself to the door and wrenched at it so hard that the ancient hinges snapped and the door fell outward, crashing to the ground and hurling up a cloud of dust.

"Fenran!" She raced over the fallen door as though it were a drawbridge and stumbled out onto the tundra. *"Fenran! Where are you?"*

A blur of movement to one side, something racing toward her, and she swung round—but it wasn't Fenran; it was Grimya, a gray streak in the moonlight, frantic, yelping.

"Indigo, what has happened?" Intensified by a frenzied mental surge, Grimya's voice battered through the whirlwind that her mind had become.

"Where is he?" Their earlier conflict forgotten, Indigo threw herself to her knees beside the wolf, grabbing hold of her ruff as she screamed. *"Where is Fenran?"*

"He rr-ran out—I tried to stop him, tried to catch him, but—"

"Where did he go? *Where?* You've got to tell me!"

"North!" Grimya panted. "North, toward—"

A sudden ominous rumbling drowned out the rest of her words. Jerking as though from a physical blow, Indigo spun to face the Tower of Regrets and uttered a choking gasp that became a moan of horror.

The tower was shaking. Cracks were appearing in the walls; high up, at the broken summit, slabs of masonry rocked and teetered and began to fall. And from inside, streamers of thick smoke were rising.

Only it wasn't smoke; it was darkness. Foul, oily, suffocating darkness; the darkness of a living hell released onto the Earth, the darkness of demons. It was happening again. Just as it had happened fifty years ago—it was happening again!

"Grimya, help me!" She scrabbled round, lost her balance, fell, was up again, one hand reaching out to the wolf. "Help me, please—in the Mother's name, I must find Fenran!"

But Grimya didn't answer. She had frozen rigid, and though her eyes stared at the tower they were unfocused, blind. A rasping sound came from her throat; a shudder went through her—

"It's Niahrin! She is trying to reach us!"

Indigo's panic flared afresh. The darkness was rising above the tower now, blacker, denser—"Damn Niahrin!" she yelled. "Grimya, don't you understand, don't you see what's happening? We have to—"

Grimya snarled, and the second shudder that racked her almost hurled her off her feet. She staggered sideways, and the force of her mental cry shook Indigo rigid. *It is not enough, Niahrin! It is not enough!*

From the tower came another deep roar, and the whole ruin groaned like a monstrous soul in torment. The air turned foul and reeking, and the darkness was taking form. Indigo screamed at Grimya again, trying to make her listen, but the wolf was oblivious. Then suddenly, shockingly, she flung her brindled head up and gave vent to a howl that rang across the night.

YES! YES! I HEAR! I SEE!

She swung about, her amber eyes locked with Indigo's—and the message that Niahrin had projected smashed into Indigo's consciousness. She saw the entire scene—the courtyard, the battle, the demons—and with the images came the knowledge with which Niahrin had imbued her desperate call. She saw herself and Fenran, as they would become if this thing, this madness, came to pass. She saw all the hatred, the jealousy, the frustration of the new life ahead of her. Life with her lover, her husband; but a life tainted by Fenran's—and her own—hunger to be something more than simply subordinates of a king.

Yet they would be together. . . .

She saw her father, growing old, going in his time to the Goddess. She saw her brother—*but he was dead, Kirra was dead*—ascending the throne of the Southern Isles, while her life and Fenran's became devoid of meaning and of purpose; a ceaseless round of pleasures and indulgences, forever in the shadow of others, power denied them, their existence pointless and empty. And she felt the sting of that growing resentment and heard her lover's voice soft in her ear: *Surely there should be more for us? Surely we are worth more than this?* She felt her own mind and heart turning, tangling in the web of petty spites and imagined grievances. A life unfulfilled, always second best, a queen in waiting . . .

But they would be together. . . .

In Carn Caille, as Jes snatched Niahrin's hands from the fire, the last image hit Indigo like a thunderbolt. *Old—they were old, and they were bitter, and there was nothing left for them but the blind solace of wine and the savagery of their ever-increasing quarrels and the bitter rancor that, when it could find no other outlet, they turned upon themselves and each other. And, finally, the act of murder. Murder, to give them what they had craved, what they had never had the courage to seek in other ways: a life that was more than shadows. The life that, in fifty years of wandering, Indigo had found, but Fenran had not. . . .*

From the Tower of Regrets an agonized, insensate howling went up, and the earth beneath her feet shook with a monstrous tremor. A block of stone half again her own height crashed to the earth only yards from where Indigo stood, and the howling rose to a shriek, like the voice of a hurricane.

"Grimya!" Indigo's hair streamed in the gale that blasted suddenly and violently from the crumbling tower; she leaned into the wind as a vast wing of dark blotted out the moon. *"Carn Caille—we must get back to Carn Caille!"*

She started to run, stumbling, careening. There had been a horse, an iron-gray horse; not Sleeth, her own mare from half a century past, but another. Tied to a bush, she had left it—the gale's vast concussion sent her reeling, and somewhere in the murk ahead there was a shape, rearing and screaming in terror. Indigo's hands clawed out, but even as she reached for the bush and the knot, the branch broke and the gelding was away like a leaf in a blizzard, hurtling past her, gone into the raging night. Indigo shrieked, sprawling in dust that stormed around and over her. *It had gone, her only chance had gone; without the horse she couldn't outrun what was coming! The demons were erupting from the tower again, and time was roaring back on itself, and she couldn't stop it, hadn't the speed, hadn't the power—*

Something crashed against her, and she caught the scent of a warm, living presence, dense fur, familiar and loved—

"Indigo!" Grimya howled in her ear, reinforcing her cry with a massive mental impulse. "Remember the old days! Remember the things we did! Wolf, Indigo—*wolf!* Remember!"

Wolf—it was like a snarling, a yelping in her mind, the word, the concept, the memory—long ago; long ago when there had been the need, when there had been a demon to defeat—

"Change, Indigo! Change! Wolf! Be wolf!"

Her mind and body stretched. The pain was shattering; the pain of changing, of shifting her shape and her consciousness to the *other. Wolf! Wolf! Speed and sleekness and litheness, running, chasing, hunting—*

A new howl echoed skyward, and it was the howl of two voices in stirring harmony. The pain was gone and there was only the thrill of a form newborn, of eyes that pierced the dark, of muscles that powered her forward with an alien yet so-familiar strength, as two shapes, lithe as water, gray against the black darkness boiling from the Tower of Regrets, streaked away into the north, racing the demons home.

* * *

Moragh's head came up sharply and she hissed, "*Listen!*
What was that sound?"

She dropped the bandage with which she had been binding Niahrin's salved hands and moved quickly toward the
window of Niahrin's room. Jes and the witch stared after
her and she began to say, "I heard nothing, Your Grace—"
but she silenced him with a sharp gesture.

"There's something out there. Beyond the citadel . . ."

Suddenly Niahrin gasped, and the dowager swung
round. "What is it?"

"My hands—not the pain, not the burning. They're
prickling."

They all knew the meaning of that sign, and Moragh
said, "Jes, fetch the king. *Now.* And then rouse the guard-
captain; tell him to arm his men and set lookouts on the
wall—the king's order, and to be carried out *immediately*!"

Jes heard the stark fear underlying her brisk tones. He
ran from the room, and Moragh turned to the witch.

"It's beginning, Niahrin. Whatever it is—I feel it."

Niahrin was already on her feet. "What can I do,
ma'am?"

"As yet, nothing. Though the Mother alone knows what
will be needed of you before tonight's over."

Moments later Ryen appeared, Brythere behind him.
The queen was still dressed, Moragh saw with relief; she
had been about to retire when Niahrin was hurt but had
providentially changed her mind. The dowager rounded on
them.

"Ryen, there isn't time to explain my reasoning now,
but Carn Caille must be put at battle readiness."

"What?" Ryen was astounded. "Mother—"

"There's no *time*!" she repeated furiously. "Something
happened in the hall—another aisling, a warning—for all
our sakes, don't stand arguing but do as I ask!"

Ryen had heard too much tonight—and seen too

much—to be skeptical, and relief filled Moragh as she saw
him nod. "Very well. But—what in the name of all that's
holy are we fighting?"

"Demons, Ryen. That's all I can tell you. *Demons.*"

Brythere uttered a frightened whimper, and the dowager
hastened forward.

"Brythere, you'll stay here with us, at least for the time
being." She glanced at her son. "*Go,* Ryen!"

He went, his footfalls drumming away down the corridor. Already there were other noises in the citadel; movement, muffled voices; then a clatter of metal against metal
and the sound of men running in the courtyard.

"I think, ma'am," Niahrin said quietly, "that it would be
wise to alert everyone in Carn Caille." Sharply, the memory of her last vision focused in her mind. "And tell them
to arm themselves with whatever weapons they can."

She was already crossing to the corner where the stave
that Cadic Haymanson had given her stood propped.
Fighting had never been her way, and with her hands as
they were she couldn't even hold it properly, but any de-
fense was better than none at all. . . . Moragh saw what she
was doing and nodded curtly. "Yes. Yes, you're right." She
headed for the door. "I'll see to it. Look after the queen."

As the dowager departed, a shout rang from outside.
"Fetch the king! Fetch the king!"

Niahrin and Brythere reached the window together. Lanterns and torches were being lit in parts of the citadel, but
their light wasn't yet enough to illuminate the courtyard
and all they could see was a confusion of hurrying shadows. Suddenly Brythere's mouth set in a determined line.

"I must find out what's afoot," she said.

Niahrin, taken aback, protested, "Ma'am, Her Grace
said—"

Brythere turned on her. "Whatever Her Grace did or did
not say, if we are in danger—if my *husband* is in danger—

then I shall not sit here and do nothing! Come or not, as you please, but I am going!"

Niahrin was stunned by the outburst, and more stunned still by the sudden rush of courage in such a timid mouse of a woman, but before she could say a word Brythere was gone. Tucking the wooden club under her arm Niahrin followed and found the corridors alive with activity as a stream of people, from armsmen to scribes, stewards to the lowest menials, came bleary-eyed from their beds at the urgent summons. As she battled through the milling confusion a voice shouted Niahrin's name.

It was Vinar, haggard and hollow-eyed. He grabbed her arm, grateful to find a familiar face amid the melee. "Neerin, what's happening? What's this about?"

She turned to face him. "Can you fight?"

"Ya—course I can! Why, what—"

"Get a weapon, anything you know how to use. Carn Caille is under attack!"

"Attack?" His eyes widened—then widened still further. "Where's Indigo? Is she—"

"She's gone, Vinar." He knew the whole story; she had to be blunt with him, even brutal. "She went to the Tower of Regrets, and what's happening now is the result of what she's done there."

Vinar put a hand over his face. "Oh, no . . . that can't be so!"

"It is so. You can't help her, Vinar. None of us can, not now. All we can do is join battle against what she's conjured from the tower."

With a tremendous effort the Scorvan took a grip on his emotions. His hand dropped to his side and he nodded. "All right. All right, I understand you." Then his face hardened. "She went to him, didn't she? To that Fen . . . Fenran."

"Yes."

"Then all this is his doing. Ya, I see that." Pure venom lit Vinar's eyes. "That one, I will kill. I will *kill*!"

The witch put her bandaged hands briefly over his, a parting gesture that implied more than a good-luck wish. "Pray you don't have to!"

The courtyard was in an uproar. Men were mustering but they were bewildered and many still half asleep; armed warriors tangled with servants hefting everything from meat cleavers to iron pots, and over all was heard the bellow of sergeants and captains trying to make order out of the chaos. Several figures were on the battlements, silhouetted against the moonlit sky; they were pointing and gesticulating urgently, and Niahrin intercepted a running man whose jerkin bore a military device.

"What have they seen?" she yelled, waving a hand in the direction of the lookouts.

The man knew who she was. "Something coming up from the south!" he shouted back. "Like a black cloud, or smoke!" He made a superstitious sign. "We'll need your magic, lady, before the night's out!"

Suddenly from the wall a new wave of shouting went up, audible even above the general din below. Niahrin heard the word *gates* and she forged her way toward the stone arch and keep. Near the foot of the keep her path crossed with that of a tall, well-built man, and she recognized Ryen.

"Sir! Sir, what is it?"

He stopped, startled, then recognized her. "Niahrin— thank the Mother; we need your advice! There's some foul darkness boiling up from the south, heading toward us. And the lookout's just seen two animals trying to outrun it."

"Animals—?" Niahrin's heart turned over under her ribs.

"Wolves, we think, but we can't be sure."

Suddenly in Niahrin's mind there was a faint stab of sound, as though a voice was calling to her across a colossal distance. No words—it was too faint for that—but a flicker of communication. A desperate cry for help.

"Sir!" Niahrin almost screamed in her agitation. "It's Grimya! I know it is, I can hear her in my mind, calling! Please—please, let her in!"

Ryen stared in astonishment. Then he swung on his heel, and his voice went up like a bull-roarer.

"OPEN THE GATES!"

The men at the keep were stunned by the order but ran nonetheless to obey. The gates shuddered as the huge bars were lifted, then with a groan they began to swing back. The press of soldiers parted to let Ryen through, and Niahrin darted behind him, jostling as she tried to see.

The gates opened, and through them with a yelping, howling cry two sleek shapes came hurtling, ears flat to their heads, tails streaming behind them. They careered to a halt and collapsed at the king's feet, foam dripping from their jaws as they panted agonizingly for breath. One, Niahrin knew from her brindled coat, was Grimya, but the other—

Suddenly the second wolf's body twisted, contorted. It whimpered—and the whimper turned into a human groan as, before the shocked crowd of watchers, the animal's form changed and in its place Indigo hunched on all fours, fighting to drag air into her lungs.

Ryen swore in shock and the men around him backed away as though from a snake. Indigo began to cough wrackingly; she couldn't speak and her hair and clothes were soaked with sweat. But Grimya was struggling to her feet.

"Niahrin!" She saw the witch through eyes blurred with pain and exhaustion and staggered toward her.

"Niahrin, they are coming! The demons are coming! It is hh-happening again—"

Even as she choked out her warning, the moonlight vanished and a vast shadow swept over Carn Caille. Faces turned skyward and for an instant the courtyard was utterly silent. Then shattering the hiatus, a huge, hot blast of wind came roaring out of the dark, and carried on the wind, like a nightmare come to life, they heard a distant sound, a wailing, gibbering, shrieking. . . .

Indigo jerked her head up, and Niahrin saw the sheer terror in her eyes. "No . . ." Indigo whispered, but even as the desperate denial came she knew that it was hopeless, useless. It was too late. Far too late . . .

And from the battlements, a lone cry against the rising tumult, a man's frenzied voice went up:

"It's upon us! Fight! For Carn Caille, for our lives— FIGHT!"

A massive mental shock wave smashed Indigo's mind back though time. Those words—*they were the very same words with which Fenran had rallied her to battle fifty years ago!*

And suddenly past and present exploded into one hideous reality as the howling cacophony swelled to a deafening crescendo, and the wing of darkness boiled over the fortress wall—

—erupting into a thousand howling, phantasmic forms that bore down like a tide. Human screams mingled with their insensate and demonic shrieking, and doll-like figures fell flailing and cartwheeling from the walls as the phantom legions unleashed from the Tower of Regrets poured over the wall. Winged monstrosities, flapping, aborted horrors, things with heads and tails of serpents, great gaping mouths filled with fangs like knives, talons and claws and mutated hands, scales, hair, white and lep-

rous skin—every nightmare ever conjured, every demon ever dreamed, falling on the defenders of Carn Caille—

"Rally!" King Ryen roared. "Carn Caille! Rally to your captains!"

But he wasn't Ryen—he was Kalig, her father, bellowing the order he had bellowed half a century before, and the men surging across the courtyard at his command weren't Ryen's men but the men of the past; shouting, screaming, flailing about them with swords and axes and knives as the demonic attackers exploded from the black cloud. Metal clashed with an echoing clamor and she heard the twang of longbows and the heavier *thwack* of crossbows as arrows and bolts hurtled in every direction. Voices shrieked in terror or agony or rage; there was a sword in her own hand and she was hacking to right and left, hewing at a monster that was half horse and half toad, stabbing at a white-winged, taloned abortion that dived at her from above. To her left was her brother, Kirra; to her right a witch with a scarred face and a patch over one eye swung a blackthorn club, and above the din a wolf was howling, howling—

Someone shrieked, *"To your right!"* and Creagin, her father's guard captain, rushed past her, his face smeared with his own blood but fighting like a madman as a flock of jumping, laughing ghouls pursued him across the courtyard.

And somewhere, somewhere, the wolf was still howling, and the howl was a word, a word she didn't know—
"INDIGO! INDIGO!"

The king—*Ryen? Kalig? She couldn't tell*—was gone into the mayhem, and his captains were striving to obey his order and form their men into some semblance of fighting ranks. Others were spilling from Carn Caille's interior now—*courtiers, councillors, stewards, grooms, artisans, every man and not a few women capable of wielding a weapon*—her old friends, good companions, kind servants, all who had been part of her life so long ago. She tried to fight toward them, but they turned aside, streaming away from her, and she couldn't reach, couldn't touch—

Then in her head she heard the wolf howling again and heard its mental scream.

Indigo! You must stop it! Only you can—only you!

Indigo—she didn't know Indigo, she wasn't Indigo—she was Anghara, only Anghara! And she had no power to stop this or to defeat the demons! She had called the demons, she alone, and the crime of this horror must be laid at her feet—

"NO!" The wolf's denial dinned in her mind. *"IT ISN'T TRUE! NOT THIS TIME! THIS TIME YOU HAVE THE POWER, INDIGO—STOP IT, STOP IT BEFORE IT'S TOO LATE! FIND FENRAN AND STOP IT!"*

"Fenran . . ." She hissed his name aloud in her shock. And then she remembered. . . . Her lover. Her husband. Her coconspirator . . .

They will all be gone, my love, and then you and I shall have what we have always desired. . . .

She whirled round.

He was standing at Carn Caille's main door, from which the last of the rushing, tumbling defenders had now streamed out into the courtyard. His black hair blew wildly in the gale, and the sword in his hands was slick with blood from tip to hilt. Blood stained his hands, too, but he was smiling.

And behind the mask was the face of an old and bitter man, who held out a knife and urged her to *Use it, my love, my sweet Anghara, use it, use it, and give us our desire. . . .*

The uproar and chaos of battle seemed to fall away around Indigo, and suddenly she and Fenran stood alone amid stillness, two solitary figures at the eye of the storm.

Across the gulf that divided them—three bare steps, but it was greater, so much greater than any physical distance— Fenran smiled, tossed the sword aside, and held out his arms to her.

"Anghara! I have waited so long for this moment!"

Behind him, livid orange light blazed suddenly to life inside Carn Caille. Indigo saw flames leaping, heard their roar—and Fenran was suddenly a black silhouette against a wall of fire.

And from within the citadel, a woman's voice started to scream.

Indigo screeched, *"MOTHER!!" Queen Imogen's gown was on fire, and her ladies were beating ineffectually at the flames, their cries ringing across the courtyard. She wouldn't reach her mother in time; at any moment the fireball would erupt and she would be blasted back, and Imogen and her ladies were dying, and dying with them in the conflagration were Moragh and Brythere—*

"Stop it!" she howled at Fenran like an animal. "Stop it, Fenran! It's wrong, it's evil—don't you see, don't you realize what you're doing? *IT WAS NEVER MEANT TO BE LIKE THIS!!"*

Against the backdrop of Carn Caille's blazing halls Fenran's face was suddenly eerily lit, and he was smiling.

"Oh, but it was, my love. One way or another, this is how we always meant it to be."

"No! I did not—*I did not!"*

"But you made the choice, my darling. And because of your love for me, you chose *this*."

Across the gulf, across the divide, Indigo stared at her lover. The man for whose sake she had suffered fifty years of wandering, fifty years of exile. For half a century she had clung to the dear and precious memories of him, memories of the love and the bond they shared that neither time nor distance could sully.

And for half a century she had been deluded.

A shuddering, savage breath rattled into her throat and she drew it down, deep down, in her lungs.

"Then," she said, and in her voice was understanding and grief—and bitter contempt, "I choose again!"

With a crisp movement her head turned to the right— and Nemesis stood at her side. She turned to the left—and the milky-eyed figure that for so long she had wrongly believed was an emissary of another power appeared. A glance down—and a pale-furred wolf stood braced before her. Four creatures and one creature together, they faced Fenran, and as one they spoke.

"I am Anghara. And I choose my own path—the path of *life*!"

Nemesis's hand snapped up, and the silver-eyed child held a crossbow. The milky-eyed being held out a single bolt. Indigo took them. She loaded; and she looked again at Fenran.

"No," he said softly. "You can't do it. I love you, Anghara."

Three words. Just three words, yet they tore at her heart as no other words he'd uttered had done. *Until this moment he hadn't said it. Sweet caresses, soft promises, the kisses and the intimacies and all the other whisperings that lovers exchanged ... but not that. Not the simple words "I love you." Until now ... and she knew it was true. ...*

"Oh, Fenran ..." In terrible distress she began to shake. "I—I can't—" A sob wracked her. "I made my choice. I made it fifty years ago. And I've been wrong; so wrong. ..."

"Yes. You've been wrong. But now, we can put it right."

Indigo looked back at him through eyes that streamed with tears and said, "You don't understand. Perhaps you never could."

She raised the crossbow, and fired.

•CHAPTER•XXIII•

"**I** don't think I want to see her." Vinar stared down at his own clasped hands, then looked up and, with an effort, gave Niahrin a tenuous smile. "Better if not, eh? Better for all."

The sunlight slanting through the window made a halo of his blond hair, but could do nothing to lighten the look in his eyes. He returned to gazing at the fireplace of his room, and Niahrin sensed that what he looked at in his inner vision was as empty as the newly swept grate.

"I understand, my dear," she said gently. "But I must say my good-byes. Will you wait here for me?"

"Ya. Ya, I wait." She moved toward the door and suddenly he added, "Tell her that—" He hesitated. "No. Doesn't matter. Whether she knows or not, it don't make no difference now."

Niahrin's expression was full of sympathy. "Is there no message at all you want me to carry?"

There was a long pause, then he smiled again. "Just tell her Vinar says good luck."

As she walked toward the dowager's apartments where they were all to gather this one last time, Niahrin pondered, as she had done so often over the past two days, on the people whose lives would never be the same again—*could* never be the same—as a result of Indigo's return to Carn Caille. King Ryen and his family. Jes Ragnarson. Herself. Vinar. Grimya. And above all, the one person whose deeds had brought them all to this hour of parting and this day of new beginnings.

That the demon attack had taken place was not in doubt in the witch's mind. She remembered, as they all did, the boiling darkness, the howling cacophony, the din and blood and tumult of battle against the demonic legions that came shrieking over the fortress wall. But now it was as though that horror had been lived only in a dream and not on the physical plane. How and when the change had come she would never know, but at one instant she had been fighting for her life, and the next there was an explosion—she had no better word for it—of light and noise, and she was snatched off her feet and flung up, up, turning over and over like a doll in a tide-race, blinded and deafened and helpless. Then she had felt herself plummeting down; she had tried to scream but there was no air in her lungs, and as it seemed she must surely hit the ground again and be dashed to pieces there came a sound vaster than any that had gone before, as though the whole Earth had drawn in its breath. The blinding light was sucked away from her in a spinning vortex, and Niahrin sprawled on the courtyard flagstones in a choking cloud of dust as the past was swept aside, time crashed back into the present, and the echoes of a titanic concussion hurtled away from Carn Caille.

For what had seemed like an hour but was in reality

mere seconds she had lain prone, not daring to move. All around her was darkness, silence. Then near to her something slithered. . . .

She shot upright, terror lancing through her. But there were no demons, and there was no battle. The sound she had heard was that of a foot sliding on stone; two paces from her a man with a sergeant's insignia was turning slowly, his mouth open and his eyes bulging as he stared around him. In his hand a drawn sword hung slackly, its blade shining and untainted. And by the cool moonlight that showered down from a clear night sky Niahrin saw that the courtyard was filled with a throng of silent, bewildered people. They held swords, bows, staves, kitchen implements . . . every man and woman clutched a weapon of some kind, but there was no enemy to be seen. No demons. No gibbering ghouls. Nothing to fight. It was as if the entire population of Carn Caille had suffered a single, common nightmare and in their sleep had answered its call and come running to join battle with an enemy that did not exist.

Then, breaking the stunned hush, a voice spoke from the semidarkness.

"Go back to your beds." It was King Ryen's voice, calm, quiet, authoritative. "I cannot explain what has happened to us all, for I do not yet fully understand it. But Carn Caille is not in peril. This has been a nightmare, just a nightmare, and no one has suffered harm. Go back. Be at peace."

They accepted his order with the gratitude of small children looking to their elders for guidance and example, and the small tide of humanity began to flow slowly toward the main doors. Faces drifted past Niahrin, some bemused, others simply blank; the crowd thinned out until the courtyard was almost empty. Niahrin heard the jingle of a soldier's metal accouterments and saw a small detachment of armed men talking to Ryen. Then the soldiers, too, made their way a little reluctantly from the courtyard; and at last only one small group was left.

They were all there. Ryen and Brythere, Moragh, Jes. Even Vinar, though he stood apart from the others. His eyes were tightly shut and he had covered his face with his hands. Niahrin climbed unsteadily to her feet and walked toward them. Then at the corner of her vision she saw someone else. . . .

Indigo and Grimya were approaching from the far side of the courtyard. Indigo's hair hung in ragged, sweat-soaked strands over her face; under its shadow Niahrin could not see her expression, but her head was bowed and her feet dragged across the flagstones as though with un-utterable weariness. Grimya pressed close against her, gaz-ing up, and the love and pity in the wolf's amber eyes brought a catch of emotion to Niahrin's throat. Five paces from the small group they stopped, and Indigo raised her head. She didn't speak. She only looked at them, one by one, and the tears that flowed down her cheeks fell onto her right hand; the hand that held a 'crossbow. Her gaze rested longest of all on Vinar, but the Scorvan made no move, though his mouth worked soundlessly as if he, too, was about to cry. Then Indigo turned and, with Grimya still close behind her, walked away into the citadel.

They found Fenran not far from the door. He lay where the moonlight couldn't reach him, and at first it seemed that his corpse was only a shadow among shadows. But the limp, lifeless body was real enough, and when Ryen and Jes turned him over they saw the crossbow bolt that had pierced his heart.

Niahrin stared down at the tangled white hair, the lined and seamed face, the familiar features, contorted with the madness that had eaten at his mind like a cancer for so many years.

"Poor Fenran," she said softly. "Poor Perd . . ."

Moragh, who had also been gazing down at the corpse, glanced at her keenly. "You're a kindly soul, Niahrin. There are few others, I think, who feel any pity for him now."

Niahrin looked sadly back at the dowager. "I can't condemn him for one mistake, Your Grace, no matter how great that mistake was. Fenran's only true crime was that he did not have the courage to find his own destiny but instead sought to live his life through others."

Moragh smiled, but it was a hard smile. "The coward's way."

"Perhaps. But then I think of Indigo's story, and I ask myself if, faced with a choice between the coward's way and what she has undergone, I would have been any braver than Fenran was."

So now it was finally over. And today, this hour, Indigo was leaving Carn Caille.

They had told her she should stay. Ryen, Moragh, even Brythere. She was the rightful queen, they said, Kalig's daughter of Kalig's line, and if she wished to claim her throne they would not stand in her way. But Indigo had seen the fear in their eyes even as they offered the gift; fear of her, of what she was, of what she might become. She did not wish harm to them—how could she? They had done her no hurt. And they had been haunted long enough by the ghosts that she had conjured.

Now, as they all met for the last time in Moragh's chambers, she gave them her final refusal. "I will not stay," she said, smiling gently. "I gave up my claims here fifty years ago. It would not be right for me to resurrect them . . . and I have no desire to do so."

Ryen stared down at his feet, and it was Moragh who finally asked the question that was in all their minds.

"What will become of you, Indigo?"

"I don't know. I can't say." Indigo turned and looked at Niahrin. "Perhaps you can answer that question better than I can."

Niahrin shook her head. "I cannot answer it. What you are, and what you will become, stem from a power whose wellspring is within you, and I would not presume to understand such a power."

Indigo continued to look at her. "But if I asked you to give that power a name . . . ?"

The witch gazed steadily back, and with an old wisdom said, "I would give it two. I would name it *life* and *freedom*. For they are what you chose, in the beginning. Your own life, and the freedom to live it."

There was silence for a few moments, then Indigo smiled again. "Yes," she said quietly. "Yes, Niahrin, I think you're right. It took me a very long time to learn that lesson, to learn that I *was* free; that my demons were of my own making and that I must face and conquer them in my own way. But now, I am beginning to understand."

Niahrin returned the smile. "Of the Earth Mother's many gifts to us, I believe that understanding is the greatest of all."

The five of them went with her to the courtyard, where all her belongings were set ready. The iron-gray gelding— Brythere's personal gift to her—was saddled and waiting, sniffing the sunlight and the brisk, sweet-smelling wind and anxious to be away. Slung with the saddlebags across its haunches were two good hunting knives from Ryen's armory, and a small but beautifully inlaid lap-harp, chosen by Jes and stowed safe in a padded bag on which Moragh had embroidered, with her own hand, the royal seal of the Southern Isles. But Grimya was missing.

"She has gone, I think," Niahrin said gently, "to say her farewells to Vinar."

Indigo's face clouded and she looked across the courtyard. The window of Vinar's room was clearly visible, but no figure stood there, and the curtains were drawn across the glass.

"I . . . cannot offer him any comfort." Indigo spoke in a low voice. "But Grimya will say the things that . . . that I want him to know. He is a good man. He was far more than good to me."

Moments later the wolf appeared from the citadel. She approached them with her tail and ears drooping, but despite her sad demeanor Niahrin, at least, saw the look in her eyes and sensed the happiness that she tried for their sakes to conceal. As she neared Indigo her pace quickened—then she hesitated and turned to Niahrin.

"Grimya . . . my dear, my dear . . ." Niahrin could find no other words as she knelt down and hugged the wolf for the last time. A tear dripped onto Grimya's fur and the witch sniffed, hastily dabbing at her eye with her sleeve. "Oh, look at me; what a fool I am, crying at my age!"

Grimya licked the tears away. "I w-will not forget you, Niahrin. I will *never* forget."

"Nor I, my dear . . . Nor I." Afraid that she was about to make an utter exhibition of herself Niahrin released her and started to stand up. But she still heard Grimya's last whisper, which was for her ears alone.

"Look after poor Vinar."

Ryen kissed Indigo, and then, to the surprise of all, Brythere suddenly stepped forward and embraced her tightly and warmly.

"Thank you!" the young queen said fervently. Indigo gazed at her, puzzled, and she added, "You took away the nightmares, Indigo. There is nothing to fear in Carn Caille now."

Moragh heard, and as Brythere drew back she held out both her hands. "You have given us our freedom, as you now have yours," she said. "The Earth Mother bless you, my dear, as do I. Good fortune!"

The gray gelding stamped restlessly; the gates stood open and the long, hazy swath of the greensward stretched away before its eager gaze, with all the promise of summer. Indigo mounted and gathered up the reins.

"I seem to have said so many good-byes," she said with a catch in her voice. "But this . . ." For the last time she gazed around her at the familiar stones of her old home . . . but it was not her home now. The entire world was her home, hers and Grimya's. Carn Caille belonged to others, and that was how it should be.

She heard the gates closing, but they were now so far away that the sound was barely audible across the sward. They had watched, she knew, until the horse was nearly out of sight, and three times she had looked back and waved to the little group of figures diminishing into the distance. But with that far-off sound as the old citadel fell behind, the final cord was cut, the final link severed.

Westward, the great forest stretched away; eastward was farmland and pasture. Behind her, Carn Caille was no bigger than a child's toy, silent and peaceful on the edge of the tundra, while ahead the road stretched on and away. An urge filled Indigo to look back one last time, but she did not turn her head. Back there were the old days, and the darkness, and Fenran. They would honor him, they had said. For her sake—and for his—they would give him the rites due any man and lay him to rest with dignity. And perhaps, one day, the ache would heal and she would forget. . . .

You are thinking of him, Indigo. Don't be ashamed of that.

Grimya's gentle telepathic voice flowed into her mind, and Indigo realized that she was weeping again. Through her tears she smiled down at the wolf.

Yes, I was thinking of him. I loved him, Grimya. I love him still.

I know. How could you not? Grimya was gazing up at her, and her amber eyes were filled with understanding. Suddenly Indigo reined the gelding to a halt. She slid from the saddle and dropped to a crouch beside the wolf, her arms reaching out. Grimya ran to her, and her warm, thickly furred body pressed against Indigo's face and torso like a healing balm.

It will take a long time for the hurt to go. But for all that time we will be together. You and I. I know it, Indigo. I know it.

Indigo knew it, too. What power it was that had granted them their special gift, she could not say and would never truly comprehend. Perhaps it was, as Niahrin had hinted, the true gift of life; perhaps, even, the immortality that for so long she had believed to be the Earth Mother's curse on her. But it was not a curse, and if the Earth Mother had moved in this then She had moved only through the medium of their own unyielding wills. This was *their* life, *their* freedom. Theirs, to make of what they chose.

"I don't know what will become of us, Grimya," she said. "We may live forever. Who can say? But whatever befalls us—"

"We will be to ... *together*!" The wolf blinked, then with a gesture as artless and sincere as the first affectionate flounderings of a newborn cub, she licked Indigo's face and hair with her long red tongue. "I love you, Indigo," she said. "And I am your *frriend*!"

In the distance, then, they heard a sound. It seemed to come from the green sea of the western forest, and the summer wind gave it a shimmering, shivering quality that stirred Indigo's heart. Far away, from their home among the trees, the wild wolves were singing.

Grimya looked back. "They are singing for us!" she said, and her voice was filled with wonder. Then she, too, raised her head, and her answering howl rang out, sending back a message of gratitude and homage to the king wolf and his pack.

The sounds died slowly away. Somewhere high above them a lark's trill emerged from the final echoes, rising and falling, rising and falling. Grimya blinked and licked her own muzzle.

"I ll-ike to sing," she said.

Indigo smiled and stroked her head. "So do I, love. And in the future, we shall have many occasions for singing. For I think we have much to teach."

The wolf dipped her head, an old and achingly familiar gesture. *"Yess."* Her ears lifted eagerly, and she added with deep satisfaction, "And much to learn!"

The gelding turned its head as Indigo mounted again and nudged at her leg in a playful manner that made her laugh. She gathered up the reins and, shading her eyes against the day's brightness, stared ahead. In a world filled with summer and sunlight, the landscape of the Southern Isles stretched away to a far horizon; and over the horizon were towns and villages, forests and fields, and, farther still, the great highways of the oceans and all that lay beyond . . . the whole of the beautiful, bountiful Earth. Hers—*theirs*—to roam and to see and to experience. She had thought their journey was over, but she had been wrong. Their journey was only just beginning.

EPILOGUE:
•SEVEN YEARS' PASSING•

The ship was called *Witchboon*, and she was beautiful: a sleek, fast Lynx-class clipper, Ranna-built and crewed by men and women from five different seafaring nations. Her husband had said that the Lynxes were born with the wind in their heads, and who would know such a thing better than he, bred as he and all his forefathers were to a mariner's life? And what better-named vessel could they have chosen together than *Witchboon* to carry them home?

The leavetaking at Ranna had been emotional, for she had not expected so many friends to come and see them on their way. Self-effacing as she had always been, it simply hadn't occurred to her that they were held in such affection and regard. But they had all come: the foresters and the farmers, the fishermen of Amberland and their wives, even a contingent from the town of Ingan; people to whom she had given potions or salves or even simple advice and who did not forget the kindness of the modest little witch with the scarred face. Niahrin had cried quite unashamedly as the ship nosed out from her berth and her sails rattled up and filled with wind, ready for the open sea. But her husband had kissed her and reminded her that this was only good-bye and not farewell, and that next summer they would come back again; and their little son was bouncing eagerly at the ship's rail, already bombarding his Da with questions about the voyage and the sea and the welcome they would have when they docked in Scorva's finest harbor; the welcome from Granfer and Granmer and all the aunts and uncles and cousins whom he and Mama had never met. Sometimes, even now, the miracle of this vivid, laughing child—her son, and his father's living image—struck Niahrin anew, and when it did she gave thanks to the Earth Mother who had granted her the blessing, undreamed of for so long, of such fulfillment and happiness.

And when, as sometimes happened, she glimpsed in her husband's blue eyes the memory of another earlier love, she felt no rancor and no doubts. Neither of them would ever forget Indigo, and that was as it should be. But Vinar had found another contentment, and his wife and son were the joy of his life, his dears and darlings. Vinar wanted nothing more, and in pride he was taking them home.

And among the well-wishers on the dockside there had been a messenger from Carn Caille, splendid in the king's own livery and bearing a special and private pouch that he had pressed into Vinar's hand. There were letters in the pouch—one from Ryen and Brythere, and another from the dowager Moragh; and with the letters a child's brightly colored drawing, depicting the *Witchboon* sailing away from Ranna with good-fortune banners streaming from her masts and the sun smiling in a cloudless sky. The eldest of Ryen and Brythere's three children, at whose welcome-day Niahrin and Vinar had been honored guests, did not forget her name-friends, and beneath the picture the Princess Aisling had carefully written her own name, with many kiss signs.

The quays of Ranna were falling astern; in the distance the towering cliffs of Amberland rose like the humped back of a slumbering beast on the horizon. The smell of the sea was in Niahrin's nostrils, and she turned to the man at her side. He gazed back at her, and through the link that had developed between them, the private, intimate meeting of minds, he knew what she was thinking.

"They will love you, Neerin." He bent from his great height and kissed her. "There's nothing for you to fear at our new home in Scorva. My people will love you. Just as I do."

Niahrin closed her eyes, glad to feel the strength and warmth of his arm around her. Her scarred face softened as Vinar kissed her again, and in her mind two faces swam into focus. One, the face of a woman with indigo eyes and a cloud of auburn hair, seemed to smile at her. And the other, a brindled wolf, parted her jaws and showed teeth and tongue in an animal's equivalent of human laughter. And across time and distance, the witch heard Grimya's voice.

Be happy, Niahrin and Vinar. Be happy—as we are!

FANTASY BY
LOUISE COOPER

☐	53401-8 NEMESIS: INDIGO #1	$4.99
☐	53401-9 INFERNO: INDIGO #2	$3.95
☐	50667-7 INFANTA: INDIGO #3	$4.95
☐	50798-3 NOCTURNE: INDIGO #4	$4.95
☐	50799-1 TROIKA: INDIGO #5	$4.99
☐	50802-5 AVATAR: INDIGO #6	$4.99
☐	53392-5 THE INITIATE	$2.95
☐	53397-6 MIRAGE	$3.95